BLOOD MOON OVER BOHEMIA

SUSAN D. MUSTAFA
AND
DISTRICT ATTORNEY CHARLES J. BALLAY

authorHOUSE

AuthorHouse™
1663 Liberty Drive
Bloomington, IN 47403
www.authorhouse.com
Phone: 833-262-8899

This is a work of historical fiction inspired by real events. Apart from the well known historical figures and actual people, events, and locales in the narrative, all other characters and the plot have been created from interviews with people who have knowledge of the history and culture of the East Bank of Plaquemines Parish. Dialogue between actual historical figures and fictional characters has been created to provide a sense of authenticity for this work. The known historical characters are listed in the Historical Notes.

Published by AuthorHouse 12/06/2024

ISBN: 979-8-8230-3608-5 (sc)
ISBN: 979-8-8230-3609-2 (hc)
ISBN: 979-8-8230-3607-8 (e)

Library of Congress Control Number: 2024922100

Print information available on the last page.

Cover design by Cathy Bond

This book is printed on acid-free paper.

*For the men, women, and children
who once lived on the lower east bank of the
Mississippi River in Plaquemines Parish.*

*You are long gone, but what
happened to you has not been forgotten.*

This is your story.

CONTENTS

LOUISIANA PRONUNCIATIONS

Arnaud's (Ar-nos)
Baptiste (Baa-teest)
Batture (Baach-er)
Bay Lanaux (Luh-no)
Bayou Chicot (Chee-koh)
Bayou de Glaises (Glayz)
Bayou de la Cheniere (Sheh-near)
Bayou Lamoque (Luh-mohk)
Bertaut (Bur-toh)
Bonnet Carré (Bon-ee Cair-ee)
Caenarvon (Cuh-nar-vun)
Cousin (Coo-zan)
Couvillion (Coo-vee-on)
Cuselich (Cue-se-lich)
Eggs Sardou (Sar-doo)
Fucich Bayou (Few-sich)
Nairn (Nair-in)
Nicholls (Nik-uhl)
Pelitire (Pel-i-tair-ee)
Plaquemines Parish (Plak-eh-mens)
Pointe á la Hache (Point ah la hash)
Remoulade (Rem-uh-laud)
Sanon (Suh-non) Estillion (Es-till-ee-on) Duveillaume (Duh-voo-la-may)

CHAPTER 1

July 1984

The creaking of the rocking chairs, their old wooden boards bent and loosened over time, was comforting, familiar, to the old couple, who had sat on that same porch in those same chairs for more than fifty years. Slats had been replaced. Wobbly spindles had been wedged back into place. Chipped paint had been carefully sanded off and covered with white, then yellow, then green, and then white again. Nothing had ever stopped the creaking.

Every evening, as dusk settled over the Delta, Abraham Jackson and his wife, Hester, rocked in those chairs, holding hands while looking across the field at the levee that sometimes protected them from the rising waters of the mighty Mississippi River and obscured from view the site of their former lives.

Lives that had once held so much promise.

Today, he at eighty-eight, and she at eighty-six, simply reminisced over what should have been, what could have been, as they embarked on their journey toward the peaceful solace of their final sleep that, at their age, could come any time. They hoped they'd go together, as neither wished to remain in this world without the other. Holding hands, like they had always done. Smiling, blessed by a love that had lasted some seventy years. Their lives had always been about survival, and now they struggled more than ever to survive—to live to see one more sunrise, one more dusk, surrounded by their memories that were mounted in frames on the walls of their shotgun home.

"Look, Hester," Abraham said, pointing a shaking, bony finger toward the mast of a ship passing on the river. "There goes another one."

"I wonder where they're going," Hester mused.

Abraham grinned and reached for Hester's hand. "Remember when we used to play guessing games about where they were headed? You used to always think it was some exotic place. You and Anna-Marie. Me and Claude always said the same thing. They were headed either to the Gulf or New Orleans, depending on the direction they were taking."

"Yes." Hester said. "Anna-Marie used to get so frustrated with y'all."

"Claude loved to tease her just to watch her get mad."

Hester laughed softly. "She did have a temper. That's for sure. And no problem at all speaking her mind."

Abraham watched the ship until it was out of sight. "I sure miss going out on my boat. That's been the worst part of getting old—not being able to fish oysters."

Hester looked at her husband's hands, gnarled and covered with scars from the sharp shells of the oysters upon which they had depended for so many years.

"Yeah. You always loved being on the water. So did Claude. Remember he used to ask to tag along with you whenever he could?"

"We sure had some good times. We fished in every single bay and bayou across the river when we were young."

Hester sighed. "I know, but that was before all those politicians set their sights on Bohemia. Remember that Leonus Lozano?"

"I don't want to hear that name," Abraham grunted. "He was as bad as any of them, maybe worse."

"Everything could have been so different for us, for everyone." Hester squeezed Abraham's hand.

"That Leonus called us colored and worse," Abraham continued, his voice rising, "like we were from another planet instead of another country. We didn't ask to come here. We were brought here to be belittled and robbed of what was rightfully ours, but it's not over yet," Abraham reassured her. "One way or another, they're gonna pay. Somebody has to be held accountable."

"All the money in the world can't make up for what they took," Hester agreed. "Bohemia's never been the same, and now there's nothing left. Just a few overgrown levees with some useless land in between. Remember Couvillion's General Store in Union Settlement? You used to ride your horse there every afternoon to pick up the mail and visit with Claude and

Anna-Marie. What was that horse's name? Oh, yes. Lincoln. You named him after that president."

"Of course, I remember. I loved that horse," Abraham said. "Anna-Marie and Claude, they've always been different. Special. And that Austrian, the one who walked with the limp. What was his name? Niko something. Used to come across the river every morning to pick up the mail and bring it back every afternoon. He could barely walk, but he could get in and out of that boat. I swear, I watched him sometimes, and I don't know how he made it with that big sack of mail, but he never missed a lick."

"Nikolas," Hester said. "That was his name. Nice man. Friendly. Didn't care about what color folks were. Always had a kind word and always gave me an extra page of coupons from *The Gazette*. Sometimes he brought me pie."

"That's how folks were then. Some folks anyway, but I know he had a hankering for you," Abraham said.

"No, he didn't," Hester said, blushing, "but Anna-Marie and Claude thought that, too."

"Yeah. I don't know what we would have done without them. They've never once treated us like we were beneath them, even when others did. They've always been there for us, through thick and thin. They never listened to what other folks said and paid no never mind to how other folks treated black folks. Anna-Marie always had a mind of her own. Without her, we wouldn't know how to read or write. And just think about the education she gave Isaac. When he went off to college, he was way ahead of the rest."

"Well, there was that one time." Hester said.

"Don't you bring that up again. That's long gone."

"You did help them after that hurricane way back in 1915. Remember?"

"I remember," Abraham said. "That's when I met you. I couldn't forget that."

"And you looked out for Claude in that First World War. Claude never forgot that. I can't count the times he's told the story about how you saved his life. But most folks on the river were good-hearted like that back then," Hester continued. "Even at Bohemia Plantation. My grandmamma used to tell me stories. She was treated real well. It was those others, the big city folks. Those were the ones that had the devil in them."

"The devil and a lot of greed," Abraham agreed, staring at the wrinkled hand that held his. "I'm sorry, Hester, for everything I couldn't give you. You deserved so much more than this life we've shared." He leaned back and closed his eyes.

Hester yanked his arm, bolting him upright. "Abraham Jackson. You gave me love. You gave me Isaac. You gave me a home. And if it weren't for those politicians, we would have had plenty. Don't let me hear you say that again."

Abraham laughed, a loud, booming laugh that echoed through the night. "Watch yourself, woman. That arm might fall off."

Hester giggled. "I sure don't want that to happen. That's your cane arm."

"Well, maybe we still have a chance to beat them before we die," Abraham said. "We've got a little time left."

"There's always hope. The Good Lord sure gave us that."

"That's about all He gave us. The devil took everything else."

"That's enough of that, Abraham. Let's go to bed. Isaac is coming tomorrow. He said he has news about Bohemia, but I can't imagine what it is. I hope it's not bad. I can't take any more bad news."

"Probably something to do with one of those lawsuits. Another big city judge in a big city suit deciding what's ours and what's not. I swear I can't take another loss."

Hester reached for his cane and handed it to him. "Maybe, just maybe, you won't have to," she said. "Maybe one day we'll all get back everything they stole from us. Maybe we'll get to meet our Maker together. In Bohemia."

Anna-Marie peered into the mirror, twisting this way and that, making sure the lines of her dress flowed evenly around her thin body. Since she had been a young girl, Anna-Marie had always taken special pains with her appearance. Her *maman* had insisted upon that. "You always want to look pretty," she had said, speaking in her native French. "People take notice. You are a Bertaut. That name means something in these parts, and it's your job to represent that name."

Anna-Marie had taken those words to heart. Even now, at eighty-eight years old, she got up every morning, sipped on a cup of freshly brewed café au lait, and then commenced to looking as pretty as she could. Although she had been a Couvillion for the better part of six decades, she still had Bertaut blood running through her veins, and she had always paid this homage to her *maman* even though their relationship had suffered after Anna-Marie married "beneath her," as her *maman* had been fond of saying.

Anna-Marie flipped her long, wavy, silver hair to one side, a habit she had developed as a teenager, and raked her fingers through it to give it extra fluff. "Claude," she called, aware that he probably wouldn't hear her. "Claude, are you ready? We've got a lot to do today. After church, Hester and Abraham are coming over. Hester said Sanon is coming, too. It's all so mysterious. Isaac is flying in, and he wants to talk to all of us. I wonder what he wants to tell us. It must be important for him to come all the way from Atlanta."

She could hear Claude's wheelchair rolling down the hallway, and she slowly ambled to join him, her cane clicking on the wooden floors as it steadied her steps.

"Mornin', love," she said, her cheerful voice still lilting with a slight French accent.

Claude responded, "Mornin'," and then smiled when she walked in front of him. "Still my pretty girl," he murmured.

Anna-Marie beamed, just as she had all those years ago when she first saw Claude working behind the counter in the general store. "I wonder if Isaac has good news about Bohemia."

"Don't get your hopes up," Claude said. "In fifty or sixty years, there hasn't been any good news from Bohemia. What makes you think today will be any different? I don't want you to be disappointed. Besides, aside from those who are coming over today, most of the folks we knew in Bohemia are gone from this world. What good will it do us? We have everything we need."

"It's not just for us, and you know it," Anna-Marie reminded him. "It's for Claude Jr. and Charlie and Madeleine and Jeanne. And for our grandchildren. It's for Abraham and Hester and Isaac. Besides, it's the principle of the thing. It's just not right. Never has been."

Claude managed a smile that only stretched halfway across his face, courtesy of a stroke ten years before. "Always were full of righteous indignation, weren't you? But that's what I love about you. We had so many dreams back then, didn't we?"

"You and my papa made all of my dreams come true, but still, this needs to be set right," Anna-Marie said, turning to open the front door. "Look what it did to Abraham and Hester. Think about what their lives could have been like." She wheeled her husband across the wide porch and down a makeshift ramp that protruded off their Antebellum-style four-bedroom home that had grown too large for them after their children became adults and moved away.

"I wouldn't worry. I know you, and you won't let it be until everyone gets what they deserve," Claude said, slowly loading his wheelchair into the back of the pickup truck and holding on to the side as he made his way toward the passenger door.

Anna-Marie got behind the steering wheel and turned the key in the ignition while she waited patiently for her husband to maneuver his way inside. She didn't dare try to help him. That would be an insult. As long as he could breathe, Claude could maneuver himself wherever he needed to go. "And when I can't," he often said, "go ahead and put a bullet in me because I'm done."

Their children had recently suggested that perhaps they should consider a retirement home, but she and Claude had vehemently objected. They had lived in their home in the tiny settlement of Homeplace for almost sixty years, and they weren't about to leave it now.

Anna-Marie looked at the slim, gold and diamond watch on her arm, all that she had left of her *maman*, checking to make sure they had enough time. "We don't want to miss the ferry, or we'll have to wait thirty minutes and we'll be late getting back."

"Don't fret. I called Johnny. He said he'd hold it until we get there."

Anna-Marie laughed. "Of course, you did. I swear, Claude. You always act like everybody owes us a favor."

"Well, they might. I don't even remember how many folks we extended credit to back when we had the general store. I have the receipts in a lockbox somewhere. Half of them never paid."

"They couldn't, and you know it. And then when those politicians stole our land, everyone scattered like the wind. We were never going to collect.

Can you imagine what the lives of all those people we knew would have been like if things had worked out differently?"

"Yes, yes I can. Abraham and Hester surely could have used that money. Abraham used to work his fingers to the bone on that oyster boat and then he would return home and work the farm. That man always worked from morning to night. He sure had my back in World War I. No denying that."

"Well, maybe Isaac's news will change all that."

Claude smiled, but Anna-Marie knew that he wasn't hopeful. She was much more optimistic than he. She always had been. In the worst of times, her optimism, misplaced as it sometimes was, had carried them through.

They had driven about fifteen miles when Anna-Marie pulled into the ferry landing. "Look. Here it comes. Perfect timing. Remember when we used to get out and watch it cross?"

"I spent many a day jumping around on these rickety boards on my way to Pointe á la Hache," Claude said, nodding. "Roll your window down. Smell the river."

Anna-Marie rolled her window down and took a deep breath. "That's one thing that never changes, never gets old," she said. "Something about this river. No matter how many times it rises up to destroy us, we never want to leave it."

"True. I wish I could still get on a boat with Abraham. We'd be on the water every day."

"I know. You used to love it when Abraham took you out fishing oysters with him," Anna-Marie said, patting her husband's leg. "Maybe that will be our heaven. Forever in a boat on a river."

Claude laughed. "I do like that idea. Now steer carefully and watch the sides," he instructed when the ferry reached the dock and the ramp was lowered.

As they rode down the ramp, Anna-Marie noticed the way her husband clasped his hands tightly together. I'm making him nervous, she thought. Claude didn't like for her to drive alone anymore, but when he rode along, he became a nervous wreck. They crossed the river in silence—Anna-Marie imagining what Isaac wanted to talk to them about and Claude praying they'd get there in one piece.

When they arrived at St. Thomas Catholic Church in Pointe á la

Hache, where Claude had attended church all of his life, there were only a few cars in the parking lot. "Remember when we could hardly get a seat because the church was so packed?" Anna-Marie commented.

"I remember," Claude said. "That was a long time ago."

Anna-Marie felt a familiar sadness for a moment. "Yes, it was. That was before they stole our land and made us move."

"We managed to make a new life for ourselves despite them," Claude said.

"Yes, we did, but things were never the same, and you know that."

Claude nodded, reaching for the door handle. "Well, let's go in and give thanks for the blessings we do have."

Anna-Marie waited for him to get settled into his wheelchair, and then she pushed him carefully into the church. As she listened to the mass, her mind wandered to her conversation with Hester the day before.

"Isaac has news," Hester had said. "He wouldn't tell me what it is. He just said we should all hear it together."

Anna-Marie knew that could only mean one thing. Isaac had news about Bohemia. But was it good news or bad news? she wondered. She bowed her head and said a silent prayer. Lord, please let Isaac bring us good news. Please.

Suddenly, Anna-Marie felt her spirits lift. That feeling stayed with her all the way back across the river to Homeplace.

As soon as they arrived at their home, Anna-Marie began heating a big cast iron pot of gumbo loaded with crabs, oysters, shrimp, tomatoes, and okra that she had cooked the day before. She had just put a loaf of French bread in the oven and was draining the rice when she heard a knock at the door.

"That must be Isaac," she said, taking off her apron. "Get the door, will you, Claude?"

She listened to the sound of the wheels of his wheelchair squeaking as he made his way to the living room. Suddenly, she felt unsettled, yet excited at the same time.

"Please, Lord, let today be the day we've been waiting for," she whispered.

The East Bank of the River

CHAPTER 2

September 1915

Hester clung to the oak tree for dear life. Half-tucked inside a small hollow where a branch met its massive trunk, she had tied her skinny legs around the branch with her bright blue dress so she wouldn't fall into the water quickly rising beneath her. Sheets of rain whirled around her, flying sideways from one direction and then suddenly switching direction and pelting her from the other side. The tree, leaves stripped by the howling winds, afforded her little protection. That endless howling terrified the young girl. She had never heard anything like it, the sound swirling and swelling until it reached a horrifying crescendo that went on and on and on.

Her family had known the storm was coming. Boat captains had warned them days before about a huge hurricane kicking up the Gulf of Mexico. They had witnessed the arrival of the frigate birds, or storm birds as locals called them, their small black bodies and white or red underbellies almost invisible beneath their massive wings that spanned sometimes up to seven-and-a-half feet. Storm birds came into the Gulf only when a hurricane was brewing. Hurricane warnings came often in South Louisiana, and most of the time they meant nothing. Storms would veer off to Florida or Texas or Mississippi and simply skirt the Bayou State. This time had been different. They had known something big was afoot when the birds flew in and then started flying out of the marsh in droves a few days later.

"The birds are gone," Hester's father, Big Jake, had announced earlier that morning. "Saw them flying out with my own eyes. That's a bad sign. And that young kid that works at the general store got a telegram that said this one is coming straight for us."

"Hester, go get as many buckets as you can find and fill them with water," her mother, Bernice, had instructed. "Take your brother with you. And be quick. We've got to get to the boat before this storm moves in, child."

"Yes ma'am. Come on, Isaac," Hester said, reaching for her younger brother's hand. "We need to hurry."

Hester and Isaac ran to the barn and gathered as many buckets as they could find and then hurried to the cistern to fill them. While Isaac pumped the water, Hester looked at the darkening sky. The breeze, always flowing from the river, had turned to wind, and her simple dress swirled up and around her legs as she picked up two of the buckets. Balancing one in each hand, she gingerly stepped over crawfish holes and small branches that marred her path, trying to hurry while at the same time keeping an eye on Isaac, who followed her, splashing water carelessly over the sides of his buckets.

"Be careful," Hester warned. "We'll need every drop."

By the time they reached their house, Isaac's bucket was only half-full.

"How many buckets did you find?" Bernice asked.

"About ten," Hester replied.

"Then go on. You've got two more trips between you. And make sure Isaac doesn't lose his along the way."

Hester and Isaac made two more trips until ten buckets of water lined their weathered porch. Hester and her mother poured the water into glass bottles that had once contained milk.

"Now you see why I save everything," Bernice said as they filled each bottle. "Some of these we'll take to the boat, and some we'll leave here. Your father will put them up high. Now help me gather the food."

Hester grabbed a burlap sack and filled it with satsumas, picked from the trees in their yard. In another sack, she packed pecans and figs, and in another, small watermelons that had been harvested the week before.

"Get those watermelons out of there. They're too heavy," Bernice said. "We've got to carry all this to the boat, and we don't have much time."

Hester followed her mother's instructions and replaced the watermelons with rice cakes. Then she tied the sacks with long, blonde rope, slung them over both shoulders and struggled toward Fucich Bayou, where her father had anchored their oyster boat. Shrimp boats, oyster boats, fishing boats, and houseboats lined the bayou with bateaus and pirogues tied securely to their sides, obscuring the water from sight, each laden with food and water and families, each tied securely to the next boat in line. The folks in this area knew that the best way to ride out a hurricane was on the water, where you could rise with the incoming tidal surge that normally overwhelmed homes.

Here, on one of three narrow fingers that branched out into the Gulf, life was about survival, and that was all that mattered. Floods and hurricanes had a way of diminishing both racial and economic disparities. Whether black, white, Serbian, Italian, French, rich, poor, each family simply tied off to the next boat oblivious to any differences between them. In small towns up and down the Mississippi River, it was the same. Folks depended on each other for survival.

What was happening on this day was nothing out of the ordinary for these hardy folks. Just nine years before, in September 1906, a northeast wind, the likes of which few people had ever experienced, churned the marshland into a frenzy and flooded every town from Bohemia Plantation down to the Gulf of Mexico. Those who lived above Bohemia Plantation in towns like Pointe á la Hache were spared because the back levee, fortified only days before the wind came, had done its job and protected the land and homeowners. Union Settlement, Nestor, Daisy, Point Pleasant, Nicholls, and Dime, and further down to Fort St. Phillip, Ostrica, and Olga, had not been so fortunate. The seven feet of salt water that inundated the area had damaged homes, devastated farms that produced vegetables to sell at markets in New Orleans, killed citrus crops, and swept away the rice that had been carefully stacked on five-foot-high trestles for safekeeping.

After gathering what they could salvage of their possessions, the villagers did what they always did. They rebuilt. They replanted. And they prayed that God would spare them from the next storm on the horizon.

Now, nine years later, they glanced at the menacing clouds that were gathering and hurried to pack anything they could think of that would help them survive not only the hurricane but its aftermath. By the time they climbed into their boats, gathered their children close, and steeled themselves for what was to come, the wind was blowing harder and the water was already beginning to rise.

"Get back in here, son," Big Jake yelled, his booming voice rising above the fury a few hours later when the storm hit its height.

Isaac, only eleven years old, had slipped out of the cabin where the family was huddled, climbed onto the bow, and stretched his arms out as if embracing the wind. He turned to heed his father's command, grinning, as a huge gust of wind, followed by an even bigger wave, almost overturned the boat.

Then he was gone.

"Isaac!" Bernice screamed in chorus with her husband. Despite the vicious rocking of the boat, Hester's parents ran from the cabin, both struggling to hold onto the wooden rails while staring desperately into the water looking for some sign of their only son.

Paralyzed with fear, Hester stayed in the cabin for a minute trying to process what had just happened. Isaac was gone. No! This couldn't be! Finally, she inched her way toward the cabin door, and held onto a rope as she made her way toward her parents. She peered over the side of the boat, and through the din, she thought she saw the bright, yellow shirt Isaac had been wearing.

"He's there!" she screamed, pointing, but her parents couldn't hear her. Without thinking, she climbed onto the railing, let go of the rope, and jumped. She had always been a strong swimmer, much stronger than her brother, and she didn't think twice. She had to get to Isaac.

Hester could feel the current pulling her through the warm, frenzied water. She held her breath and prayed to the God they sang about in church, begging him to help her get to her brother. She could feel things scratching her face, hitting her body, but she kicked her feet as fast as she could, trying to keep up with the rhythm of the current. Then she slammed into something. For a moment, there in the midst of the torrent, she almost succumbed to the darkness, but Hester was made of sterner stuff. She surfaced and barely made out the outline of a small pirogue right in front of her. She grabbed it and pushed herself over the side, almost tipping it over. She landed in the bottom with a thud, and lay there, panting, coughing, feeling the air that filled her lungs.

Then nothing.

Hester was jarred to consciousness when the pirogue smashed into a tree, hurtling her back into the water. When she surfaced, she could see the tree a few feet away, and she kicked with all her might. Fortunately, a wave propelled her forward, and she grabbed a low-hanging branch and held on tight. When the wave receded, she swung her legs up, wrapping them around the branch, and then maneuvered herself on top of it. She inched her way toward the trunk, struggling to keep her balance on what was left of the bark, and felt rather than saw the hollow that would become her refuge. She wedged herself into the small space and tied her legs to the tree, praying that the water would not rise higher.

"Isaac," Hester whispered just before the howling wind, terrorizing in its intensity, ushered her back into unconsciousness.

CHAPTER 3

Abraham Jackson paddled his small pirogue carefully through the debris that floated on floodwaters the day after the hurricane hit. The water was slowly receding, but as far as the eye could see, there were fallen trees, wooden shacks half submerged, boats stuck on top of the levee, dead animals—the remnants of everything that had been destroyed during the storm. He paddled slowly, his eyes flicking this way and that, searching for signs of life. He had already rescued three people—an Italian man and his two sons, who were barely hanging on to what was left of the rafters that had once held their roof in place. After bringing them to the True Vine Baptist Church in Nestor, he went back out to paddle along the banks of the bayou, looking for survivors.

It was quiet, too quiet. The normal sounds of the wildlife that usually inhabited the bayou—the buzzing and chirping, the scurrying—had been silenced by the storm. The only sounds were the humming of the flies and the occasional squawking of a buzzard honing in on the dead flesh of animals. And the swooshing sound of Abraham's paddles hitting the water or moving debris out of the way.

Abraham had been paddling, or push-poling when necessary, in the hot sun for what seemed like hours when he saw a common sight—blue clothing hanging from a tree limb. He turned and paddled toward the tree just to be sure. When he got close enough, he saw a body lying precariously on a thick branch, partially wedged in a hollow. He retrieved his rope and tied off, and then began to climb. Abraham was young and strong and had spent his life climbing trees, so scrambling up this sturdy oak was easy. When he reached the hollow, he saw a half-naked girl. Her eyes were closed, her body lifeless. Her face was bloodied, and her arms purple with bruises. He put his head to her chest and listened.

He could hear a faint beating.

Hurriedly, he untied her legs from the tree, steadying her with his muscular frame, and heaved her over one shoulder. Carefully, he maneuvered his way down, afraid to hurt her, and when he reached the water, he laid her gently in the boat. After placing a wet piece of cloth, torn from his shirt, on her forehead, Abraham paddled as fast as he could toward his home a few miles away.

Although the water was receding, there were still several inches covering the floors when Abraham strode inside his parents' old shotgun house with the girl in his arms.

"What is this?" Florence, Abraham's mother, cried when he laid the girl on the wooden kitchen table.

"I found her in a tree. We've got to help her. She's barely breathing."

"Leave us," Florence said. "I'll take care of her. You go see if anyone else needs rescuing."

Abraham took one last look at the girl and headed back to the pirogue. Before darkness descended a few hours later, Abraham found a couple, Anna-Marie and Claude Couvillion, on top of the general store in Union Settlement, hanging onto the remaining roof and each other. Abraham looked around and spotted a ladder that had been hurtled a few yards away and helped them to safety.

"We were in the attic, but the water kept getting higher," Anna-Marie told Abraham. "We escaped through the side door and climbed onto the roof." Back then, many homes had exterior attic doors for that very purpose, and people kept an axe in the attic in case they had to hack through the roof to escape a flood.

Abraham glanced at Anna-Marie, struck by the look in her eyes, that same look that most Louisianans get when they survey the evisceration of their possessions after a hurricane.

Claude shook his head as he looked around the store, which he always kept neatly stocked. The aisles were now cluttered with broken jars that had been filled with fig, peach, and pear preserves and empty sacks that had once held flour and sugar and rice. Inedible fruit and vegetables from the farms along the river and empty cigar boxes were just strewn about. "I don't know how we're going to clean this mess up. We've lost most of our inventory."

"We're alive," Anna-Marie reminded him. "That's all that matters."

"I have to go," Abraham said. "It's getting dark, and I found a girl who was half dead. I want to check on her."

"Do you know who she is?" Anna-Marie asked.

"No ma'am, but I'm sure we'll find out soon enough. Someone's bound to be looking for her. My mama's nursing her, so I'm sure she'll be just fine. I'll come back tomorrow and check on y'all."

"Thank you," Claude said. "I won't forget what you did for us." Surprising Abraham, he reached out and shook his hand. While free people of color were treated relatively well by white folks who lived along the river, there were still boundaries, and Claude had just crossed one.

"It was nothing," Abraham said, before climbing back in his boat and heading home. By the time he arrived, it was almost dark, but he could see an oil lantern glowing in the kitchen.

"How is she?" he asked his mother, kicking off his wet boots and shimmying out of his shirt. He noticed that the water had been swept out and that a huge pot of chicken soup was boiling on the wood-burning cast-iron stove.

"She's going to be okay," Florence said. "I gave her a sponge bath, and cleaned her wounds. She has a nasty gash on her head, but she came to about an hour ago. Doesn't remember much, but her name is Hester. She can't remember her last name. I think she's Mulatto. Sure looks whiter than the rest of us. While she was sleeping, she kept saying 'Isaac' over and over, but when I asked her about it, she started crying, so I let it be. Your daddy put her in your room, so you'll have to sleep on the porch. He's out cleaning the barn, but he'll be back soon."

"Can I see her?"

"Yeah, go on in, but if she's sleeping, let her be. A body heals when it's resting. If she's awake, feed her this." Florence handed him a bowl of freshly made soup. That bowl was the only one that had survived the storm.

"Yes, Mama. I just want to see for myself that she's okay."

Abraham reached for a candle and made his way through the kitchen and living area, through his parents' room, to his bedroom. In a shotgun house, one room leads right into the next in a straight line. These houses, native to Louisiana, got their name because you can shoot a shotgun through the front door, and if all the doors to each room are open, the pellets will travel all the way to the back of the house. He placed the candle on a homemade dresser near the bed and sat down, staring at the girl. She can't be very comfortable, Abraham thought, noticing that someone had removed the wet mattress from the bed and laid some boards lengthwise across the slats. It had been covered with an old thick quilt that his grandmother had stitched for his mother decades before. Another lighter quilt covered the girl's thin body. Abraham realized his daddy must have pulled them from the attic, along with the lumpy pillow upon which she rested her head.

Long, black hair fanned out behind her head, and her caramel skin glowed in the candlelight. She's beautiful, like an angel, Abraham thought. He could see that the cuts on her face and arms had been slathered with his mama's herbal ointment. Impulsively, he leaned over and laid his head on her chest, listening for her heartbeat. It sounded stronger now. Relieved, he sat up and was startled to see big, brown eyes staring up at him.

"I'm sorry," he said. "I wanted to make sure your heart was pumping. You were barely breathing when I found you."

"You're Abraham?" Hester asked, her voice a whisper.

"Yes," Abraham said.

"Your mama said you saved me."

Abraham smiled and nodded. "Do you remember how you got in that tree?"

"No," Hester said. "I don't remember much. I've been trying, but it's all a blur."

"Well, don't fret yourself. Just rest and heal, and I'll try to get some answers for you. I'm going into town tomorrow. Surely someone is looking for you."

Hester smiled, and Abraham couldn't help but notice how that smile transformed her. He stared for a few seconds, and then caught himself. "You need to eat," he said gruffly, reaching for the bowl. He helped her sit up, fluffing the pillow behind her. Then he spoon-fed her the soup. When she had eaten every drop, he wiped her mouth and helped her lie back down. "You get some rest now," he said, tucking the quilt under her chin. "You should feel better tomorrow."

Abraham walked out of the room feeling a little differently than when he had walked in. There was something about the girl, something he couldn't quite put his finger on, but he knew that everything had changed for him. He didn't know how, but he knew.

"She's going to be okay, isn't she?" he asked Florence, picking up a sponge to help her clean mud from the icebox.

"Yes, child. She'll be okay. Might take a while for her to remember, but maybe she doesn't want to. Sometimes that happens."

"Tomorrow I'll go into town and see if anyone is looking for her."

"You should do that. Now tell me about what you saw out there today."

"It's bad, mama. Real bad, but people are already cleaning up. The East Bank will be back in no time."

"Yes, it will. We're survivors, pure and simple."

Abraham kissed her on the cheek and went outside to get a blanket off the clothesline that Florence had tied back into place. He sat down on the porch and stared at the stars. At nineteen years old, he didn't understand why things like this had to happen, but he said a silent prayer, thanking God that he and his family had survived.

And the girl. Hester.

Abraham said it aloud. "Hester."

He liked that name.

CHAPTER 4

Anna-Marie glanced at Claude, noticing the despair that seemed etched into his face, like he had been beaten. Together, they were cleaning the store, valiantly trying to remove the muck that stuck like glue to all of the merchandise and to the floors and walls. She walked over and put her arm around his waist.

"We'll get it done," she assured him.

Claude looked down at his young wife and tried to smile. "I know we will, but right now it seems an impossible task."

Two years before, at the age of twenty, Claude had taken over the family business when his father, Charles, had taken ill. Claude's mother had died in childbirth, a common occurrence back then. Charles and his sister, Collette, had raised Claude, who, when he wasn't working on his lessons, spent every day helping his father in the store. Claude could gauge the minute a vegetable started to turn, when it was time to discard milk that was souring, and if a piece of fabric was too thin to be of use to anyone. By the time he turned fifteen, he worked full-time at the store that doubled as the settlement's post office and sometimes at the saloon in the adjoining room, dedicating himself to learning his father's business.

He had met Anna-Marie when he was nineteen. He remembered that day well because absolutely nothing had gone right since he had opened the store that morning. His cousin, Spit, nicknamed that because he always had a wad of something in his mouth that caused him to drool, had come to work late, drunk as usual, and stumbling over everything in his path. Claude had told him to go home and sleep it off, but Spit insisted he could work even while knocking over a bin of red delicious apples. While chasing them down the aisle, Spit took out the bananas, oranges and a sack of flour, too. Claude rushed to steady his cousin and walked him outside. "Go on home," he said. "I'll take care of this."

In between weighing meat and waiting on customers, Claude swept up the flour and washed the fruit. He was still bent over an old galvanized washtub set back in a corner when Anna-Marie walked in. She was young, sixteen or so, and the most beautiful girl he had ever seen. He had heard about her, of course. Everyone had. She was a Bertaut, the daughter of Antoine Bertaut of Bertaut & Biggs, the largest rice-milling company in South Louisiana and the owner of a nice swath of land in Nestor. Half the town worked for Bertaut & Biggs, and all of the male employees loved to talk about the girl. "So beautiful," they said. "An errant girl. Definitely got a mind of her own. Don't listen to anyone. Drives her mama mad. A real handful, that one, but she sure is pretty."

Claude watched her wander around the store for a moment before he stood up and walked over to the push-button cash register. When she placed a few items on the counter—milk, fresh hen eggs, and a bottle of Coca-Cola—he opened his mouth to speak, but nothing came out. For the first time in his life, he became tongue-tied. The velvety brown eyes staring at him made him nervous, a feeling to which he was unaccustomed. And when she laughed, he just stared.

"Well, a mighty fine day to you, too," she said, although he had not uttered a word.

Claude cleared his throat and finally managed, "*Bonjour, mademoiselle.* Can I get you anything else?"

"A pound of cured ham would be nice. And some cheese, the kind with the holes in it," Anna-Marie replied.

Claude hurried to do her bidding, almost tripping over his own feet, and then feverishly tried to regain his composure. As he wrapped her meat, he could hear her giggling. He wondered why.

When he placed her ham and cheese on the counter, she handed him a lacy handkerchief. "You might wet that and clean up a bit," she said, grinning. "It looks like you went face first into a bin of flour."

Mortified, Claude hurried to the washtub and splashed water on his face.

"I'm sorry," he sputtered. "It's been a morning."

Anna-Marie smiled. "I thought it was cute. And funny," she said. "What's your name?

"Claude. Claude Couvillion."

"I'm Anna-Marie. It's nice to meet you."

"Same to you, Miss."

"Are you going to Miss Penny's picnic on Sunday?" Anna-Maria asked.

"No, I have to work. We open after church on Sundays."

"Well, that simply won't do. You'll have to be late. She makes the best pot of smothered marsh hens you'll find on the river."

"Everyone knows that, but I really can't," Claude said, for the first time wishing he didn't have to work.

"Then I shall bring you some," Anna-Marie announced, gathering her groceries before walking out of the store with a wave.

Claude stood there staring at the door wondering what had just happened to him. He had never before been at such a loss for words. Normally, he was friendly, helpful, and could converse on any subject. His father had drilled that into him. The general store, aside from being the only store for five miles, thrived because customers came just to gab about who had another baby, or how many crops they had planted, or what had happened in Daisy a few miles down the river, or even just the weather. Claude could gab with the best of them. Except for today.

Claude shook his head and returned to the washtub. Subconsciously, he could hear his father saying, "That fruit isn't going to wash itself."

Still, he couldn't get the girl off his mind.

The following Sunday, Claude woke up early and dressed in his finest summer suit—gray with a black and white striped tie. He wanted to look his best, just in case the girl came back. After checking on his father, he climbed into the Model T roadster he had acquired in a swap a few months before and drove along the levee towards Pointe á la Hache, where he attended St. Thomas Catholic Church every Sunday. His father insisted. Since he had been a young boy, every week, Claude, Charles, and Collette dressed in their Sunday best and went to church. It wasn't that Charles was overly religious. It was because Charles knew that's what Claude's mother would have wanted, and it was his way of respecting her memory, of raising Claude like she would have raised him.

Claude thought about the girl as he drove. Her long, brown hair, pulled back into a wavy ponytail that trailed down her back to her waist. Her eyes, big and brown and so full of life. Her laughter, soft and lilting. He knew she was of marrying age. Everyone had been talking about it.

23

He'd heard that her papa had handpicked some rich businessman from New Orleans for her, but that she was rebelling against the idea. There were no secrets anywhere along the river. Folks' business was everybody's business. Claude laughed out loud at his fanciful thoughts because he knew there was no way the girl's papa would let someone like him court her. Yes, business was good, but Antoine Bertaut had made a fortune at the mill. Leastways, that's what folks said. Still, he couldn't help but hope she'd come back.

It was quarter after three in the afternoon when the bell on the door announced her arrival. Claude looked up when she walked in. He had been watching that door like a hawk. She was smiling and looking even prettier than she had the last time. This time, he was prepared.

"Happy Sunday, Anna-Marie," he said, liking the way her name sounded.

"Happy Sunday, sir," she said. "I've brought you some of Miss Penny's marsh hens like I promised and some collard greens."

"Thank you," Claude said, accepting the basket she handed him. "It smells delicious."

"Well, you know Miss Penny can make collards like nobody's business. Go ahead. Don't mind me," Anna-Marie said when she saw him eyeing the basket hungrily.

Claude pulled two chairs behind the counter. "Come sit with me," he said. "We can share."

"I was hoping you'd say that. I didn't eat anything. I thought we'd have our own picnic," Anna-Marie said, smiling brightly.

The girl had filled the basket with enough food to feed an army—the marsh hens smothered in onions and garlic, collard greens soaked in white vinegar, and browned blood sausage. She had even thought to bring plates, forks, and napkins.

"Thank you," Claude said, filling a plate for Anna-Marie and another for himself. "I'm honored that you did this for me, although it might set some tongues wagging." He had noticed the way Mildred, the settlement's most notorious gossip, had summed up the situation when she walked into the store. A not-so-subtle sniff and the turning-up of her chin signaled her disapproval.

Anna-Marie giggled. "Well, if she's talking about us, she's leaving someone else alone. Besides, I like stirring up trouble. Haven't you heard?"

Claude grinned. "I have heard a little, but I didn't believe a word of it."

Anna-Marie leaned forward and looked into his eyes. "Believe it. Believe every word," she said.

Claude burst out laughing.

"Especially the part about how my papa wants me to marry that horrid little man from New Orleans. That's not going to happen. I met him once, and that was enough. Horrid. Just horrid."

"You're going to defy your father?" Claude was taken aback, but impressed.

"Yes. Besides, I've already met the man I'm going to marry," Anna-Marie announced.

Claude's fork stopped in mid-air. "You have?"

"Yes, I have."

Claude tried to keep his disappointment from showing. "Does your papa know?"

"I haven't told him yet, but I will soon. As soon as the man agrees."

"This man doesn't know you're going to marry him?"

"No," said Anna-Marie, like there was nothing unusual about this.

"Does he live around here?" Claude asked, although he didn't really want to know the answer.

"Why yes, he does. Right here in Union Settlement."

Claude took a bite of his food to keep from saying anything else, but the marsh hen had lost its flavor.

"He works at the general store," Anna-Marie continued.

Claude almost choked. "You want to marry Spit?" he sputtered between coughs.

Anna-Marie laughed out loud. "No, silly. It's you. I'm going to marry you. I knew it the first time I saw you all covered in flour."

Claude desperately tried to collect himself, aware that Mildred was standing only a few feet away, and she was listening intently.

"Shhh, Anna-Marie. You shouldn't say things like that."

"It's true. On my grandmére's grave, it's true."

Claude felt like his head was spinning. He put his plate on a box of lard and stood up to wait on Mildred, doing his best to hurry her out of the store.

"Congratulations," Mildred said, before turning to go.

Claude turned red. "She's just playing," he said.

"No, I'm not," Anna-Marie piped in. She stood up and smiled at Mildred. "Don't tell anyone, though, because I haven't told my papa."

"You can count on me," Mildred said, her face glowing with excitement. She couldn't wait to spread the word. On the river, something like this was big news. "I won't say a word."

When she was gone, Claude turned to Anna-Marie. "You know she's going to tell everyone."

"Of course." Anna-Marie was positively beaming.

"And do I have any say in this?" Claude asked.

Anna-Marie looked up at him. "You're very tall," she said.

"That doesn't answer my question. Do I have a say in this?"

"You don't want to marry me?" Anna-Marie asked.

Claude began stuttering again. "Well, I didn't say that."

"So you do want to marry me?"

"I didn't say that either."

"Well, which is it? You do or you don't?" Anna-Marie stood on her tiptoes and kissed him on the cheek.

"Any man would want to marry you," he muttered.

"So, it's settled then. I'll go tell my papa."

Claude just stood there, befuddled, as she gathered her basket and said good-bye.

"I'll see you tomorrow," she said, and with a wave of her white-gloved hand she was gone.

Claude sat down with a thud, mulling over what had just happened. And then a big smile spread across his handsome face. That beautiful, crazy girl who seemed adept at placing him in a state of utter confusion wanted to marry him. He was getting married. Claude jumped up and ran outside. "I'm getting married," he yelled loud enough to startle the old hound dog sleeping on the porch.

Three months later, Anna-Marie Bertaut and Claude Couvillion were wed. Anna-Marie's parents had thrown a fit, to be sure. They had threatened boarding school, a convent, banishment. Nothing had worked.

Anna-Marie had made her choice, for better or worse, and she would not be deterred.

And as Claude watched his bride walk up the aisle of the St. Louis Cathedral in New Orleans on September 16, 1913, dressed in all of her wedding finery, he knew without a doubt she had made the right choice. He would spend the rest of his life loving her above all else.

CHAPTER 5

Abraham ran into his bedroom to see what the ruckus was about. It was late, midnight, about a week after the hurricane, and he had awakened when he heard the scream. Hester was asleep, but she was thrashing about in the bed, crying. He sat down beside her and pulled her into his arms, resting his chin on her head. "Shush," he said. "It's okay. I'm here. You're going to be all right."

Hester buried her face in his chest, relishing the feeling of safety she felt with his arms wrapped around her. After a moment, she wiped her eyes with the back of her hand. "I think I had a bad dream," she said.

"You did. You were screaming." Abraham reached for her hand. "Do you remember what it was about?"

"There was a boy in the water. I was trying to reach him." Hester started crying again. "I swam as hard as I could, but I couldn't reach him. I got swept away."

"Did you know this boy?"

"I think so. I don't know," Suddenly her eyes widened. "Isaac. His name was Isaac. I remember screaming that name in my head over and over as I was swimming."

"Do you know who he is?"

Hester struggled to remember, and then she shook her head. "No, I don't know."

"It's okay," Abraham said. "It'll come to you in its own time. Now lie down and try to sleep. You'll feel better in the morning."

Hester lay down, and Abraham covered her with the quilt. "Sleep now."

"Will you stay with me for a while?" Hester asked.

"Yes. I'll be right here," Abraham said.

Abraham sat in the chair all night keeping watch over the girl. She seemed so fragile, but he knew it had taken an incredible strength to survive the hurricane in a tree. She must have been terrified, he thought. He wanted to protect her, to make sure she never again suffered the kind of anguish he had heard in her scream.

The next morning, he fed her a biscuit covered in milk gravy and then walked to the general store, as he had every morning since the storm to see if anyone had mentioned a missing girl.

"Mornin', Claude," Abraham said when he walked in before tipping his hat to Anna-Marie.

"Mornin'," Claude said.

"Y'all need some help around here?" Abraham asked, noticing that Anna-Marie was still cleaning muddied wooden shelves.

"We don't turn down help," Claude said. "Anna-Marie will show you what needs to be done."

"This way," Anna-Marie said. "We're trying to salvage whatever we can. Of course, we're going to discount all of it. Perhaps you could help me make some signs." She pointed to a bin filled with jars of honey and molasses that had survived the hurricane. "I'm glad we stocked up on molasses before the storm. The sugar cane crop is bound to suffer this year. Would you mind wiping those down, and then we can price them?"

"Yes ma'am. Happy to," Abraham said, taking the wet cloth Anna-Marie handed him. "Have y'all heard any news?"

"The news isn't good," Claude said, reaching for a jar. "I heard tell that churches in New Orleans were destroyed. Folks are saying that the river rose twelve feet, but I don't know about all that. I heard some houses further downriver were blown clean across the river. One man said the general store in Daisy is gone. Just destroyed. A lot of folks lost everything."

Abraham shook his head. "Has anyone mentioned a missing girl?"

"Not missing, no, but Captain Henry Peterson came in this morning talking about a family that drowned in Fucich Bayou. They were on their boat, tied up with the others, when the storm hit. The son, a young boy called Isaac, fell overboard."

Abraham stopped him. "Isaac, you say?"

"That's what the captain said—Isaac. Seems the sister jumped in the bayou to save him. Then the father. They never came back. They found the father and son not far from each other in the marsh. The mother was still on the boat. The captain seemed to think she died of fright and fear, like her heart couldn't bear what was happening. Damnedest thing."

"What about the girl? Did he call her by her name? Did they find her?"

"He didn't say they found her. Sounded like he knew them, but the captain knows everyone. People are always hopping on his packet boat to get downriver or to New Orleans."

"I know. I've done that myself. Did he say where he was going?"

"Probably to Nestor to check on his boat," Claude guessed. "He said it had sustained some damage, but I'm not sure which side of the river it's on."

"I'm sorry. I have to go." Abraham reached for his hat and straightened it on his head.

"Do you think the girl you found could be this girl?"

"I don't know, but I have to find out. The girl had a nightmare, said she was swimming and screaming for Isaac, but she couldn't remember who Isaac was."

"Oh my," Anna-Marie piped in. "Claude, you drive him wherever he needs to go. We have to get to the bottom of this. I'll watch the store." She straightened her apron and walked behind the counter.

"Thank you, ma'am," Abraham said.

"Enough with all that ma'am stuff," Anna-Marie said. "My name's Anna-Marie, and that's what you'll call me."

Abraham tipped his hat and then walked outside with Claude. He was about to get into the back of the roadster when Claude stopped him. "No," Claude said. "You'll ride right up here with me."

Abraham seemed uneasy as they drove down the road riddled with potholes that had been filled in with oyster shells toward Nestor. It was a short drive, about five miles to the dock where the captain's boat, *Neptune*, was usually anchored.

"I'm not sure he'll be at the dock," Claude told Abraham as they drove south.

"I hope he's there. I'm praying that the girl hasn't lost her whole family," Abraham responded.

When they arrived, they saw a few people gathered near the river. "He's there," Claude said, pointing.

Abraham hurried from the car and walked over to the group. He waited until they finished their conversation and then said, "Excuse me, sir," to the captain. "Claude here was telling me you knew a family that passed in the storm."

Captain Henry nodded and spit some tobacco juice into the water, his weathered face clouded. "Yes. What's your interest?" he asked.

"I found a Mulatto girl in a tree between Union Settlement and Nestor. She don't remember much, but she had a dream about a boy named Isaac, and she was trying to save him."

Captain Henry's eyes widened. "What's the girl's name?"

"Hester."

"*Quel Soulagement*," the captain exclaimed. "We thought she was dead like the others, but we couldn't find her. How old is she?"

"About seventeen," Abraham said.

"It must be her then. She's from Nestor. Her parents—Bernice and Big Jake and her brother Isaac—they're gone. God rest their souls."

"Did she have other brothers or sisters?" Claude asked.

"No, sir. The girl's all alone now. Bless her heart. She might have some extended family down there in that Mulatto camp outside of Ostrica, but I don't know for sure. At least she's not dead, so that's something."

"Do you know her surname?" Abraham asked.

The captain thought for a moment. "She's a Baptiste. Her papa has some land and an old house on the other side of Nestor. Grew oranges and had a patch of rice on the river side of the levee. The folks in Nestor will know where. Everyone over there knew Big Jake. He was also a handyman. Could fix anything."

"Thank you, Captain," Abraham said, and he and Claude climbed back into the roadster.

Abraham was quiet on the way back to Union Settlement. He worried about how to tell Hester who she was and that her family was gone. In her condition, he knew that would not be good. "I think I'm going to wait until she's healed before I tell her," he finally said.

"That's wise," Claude agreed. "She survived, and she's come this far. Probably best not to stir up that hornet's nest just yet."

When they arrived at the general store, they told Anna-Maria what they had learned. "That's horrible," she said. "I will go visit the poor child as soon as I can."

Abraham looked at her, perplexed. "Do you think that's wise, ma'am?"

"Of course," Anna-Marie said. "Why wouldn't it be?"

Abraham shuffled his feet. "Well, most white folks wouldn't visit us in our home."

Anna-Marie smiled. "Well now, Abraham. You will soon find that I'm not most white folks, and besides I couldn't give a care what other white folks do or don't do."

Abraham looked at Claude, who shrugged his shoulders and grinned. "My wife doesn't seem to follow many of normal society's rules," he said, "and far be it from me to try to change her."

Anna-Marie tore some wet cloth from a spool and began cleaning mud from a jar of honey. "It wouldn't do him any good to try," she told Abraham. "My parents never should have sent me to that school in Paris. I came home with a lot of different ideas about things. By the way, a lady was in earlier saying that more than two hundred people perished in the storm between Ostrica and New Orleans."

"That's not surprising," Claude said. "When we finish fixing this place, we'll see how we can help other folks."

Anna-Marie smiled her approval at him before turning to Abraham. "I finished cleaning the jars. Let's make some signs."

Abraham hung his head for a minute then looked at her. "I'm sorry, ma'am, but I don't know how to read or write. Always worked on the boats. Never had no lessons."

Anna-Marie smiled brightly. "Well, then I'll teach you. Come with me. I have some boxes we can use to make signs. They're wet, but they'll do. They'll dry soon enough."

Abraham helped her tear the boxes apart and then watched as Anna-Marie wrote on them.

"This is an A," she said. "The first letter of the alphabet. Apple starts with A." She wrote the word on the box and then asked Abraham to write it on his piece of the box. She explained each letter and its sound, then practiced spelling the word aloud with Abraham. A few minutes later, he could spell apple.

"See, already you can read," she said.

Abraham managed a bashful grin. "Yes ma'am. Thank you, ma'am."

"When things get back to normal, I'll teach you a new word every time you come in."

"Much appreciated," Abraham said. "I must go now because I want to check on the girl, and then I'm going to help pull logs out of the river. They're saying the packet boats can't get through because of the logs, and I might want to keep some of them. I may build my own house soon."

Claude shook his hand. "Thank you for the help," he said. "Let us know if there's anything we can do for the girl."

"Will do," Abraham said.

As he walked home, he thought about Hester. He worried about how the loss of her family would affect her. When he got back to his parents' home, he went into the kitchen, wrapped his arms around his mother, hugged her tight, and then he told her what he had learned.

CHAPTER 6

It had been three weeks since the storm when Abraham walked into his mother's kitchen and found Florence filling a basket with containers of shrimp stew and rice she had made the day before with river shrimp that Abraham and his father, Emmanuel, had retrieved from their shrimp boxes. The water had receded, but folks along the river were still dealing with the aftermath. The news from around Plaquemines Parish was dismal—levees breached, communities closer to the Gulf on the West Bank completely demolished, more than two hundred people dead and thousands left without homes. Oyster boats had also been hard hit, and Abraham was grateful that his had survived with only minor damage that had been easily fixed. That boat meant everything to his family. It ensured their survival. The word coming out of New Orleans was equally bleak—sunken boats, overtopped levees, and damage to famous architectural landmarks, but the loss of life had been significantly lower in the city. The hurricane had produced the highest winds on record to date and had flooded areas all along the Gulf Coast.

"I'm going to take the boat and head down toward Ostrica to see how bad it is down the river," Abraham said.

"Not today," Florence said. "Today, you are taking Hester on a picnic. She needs some exercise and sunshine. And it's time you told her about her family."

Abraham had been putting that off for as long as he could, but he knew it was time. Hester was healing and able to move around now. She had asked him several times if anyone had asked about her, and he had just shaken his head.

"Yes ma'am. I'll tell her," he said, reaching for the picnic basket before joining Hester on the porch.

"Mama made us a picnic," he said. "Would you like to go for a walk?"

Hester smiled and stood up, still a little unsteady on her feet. Abraham reached for her hand and led her down a pathway on the right side of the house. They walked for a while and then came upon an old cemetery filled with small monuments and tombstones, the older ones made of slate and the newer ones of brownstone. There were no flowers to honor the dead, as those had been washed away with everything else, but the stones that covered the lost souls still lined up like soldiers, standing tall, both beautiful and lonely at the same time. Abraham cleared a spot and sat the basket down on a flowered, cotton tablecloth. "Please," he said, indicating that Hester should sit. "Let's eat."

Abraham began to peel the shrimp, one for Hester, one for him, one for Hester, one for him.

"I can peel them, too," Hester said. "You don't have to peel all of them."

Abraham managed a smile and handed her a few. "I'm used to peeling them. Every time we boil shrimp, I peel all of them because my mama cooked them. Just seems like the right thing to do."

"That's nice. You shuck a lot of oysters, too, don't you?"

Abraham looked down at his scarred hands and grinned. "How could you tell?"

Hester reached for one of his hands and looked it over. "It's quite obvious."

"I've been fishing oysters for as long as I can remember," Abraham explained. "And before me, my father. He built our boat with his own hands, but since he caught the fever, he's not as strong as he used to be. Doesn't have the stamina for fishing oysters anymore. He spent a while at Hotel Dieu in 1905. They call it God's Hotel."

"Yellow fever? I've heard about that."

"Yes ma'am. Lots of folks spent time there. Too many never came back."

"I'm glad your daddy made it."

"Me, too," Abraham said, turning his head so she wouldn't see the tear that had formed. He wrapped up the heads and shells of the shrimp and placed them in the basket. "I need to talk to you, Hester. I found out who you are."

Hester's face brightened. "You did?"

"Yes. You're Hester Baptiste. You live on a small citrus farm a few miles down river, close to Nestor."

Hester jumped up. "Can you take me there?" she said, her voice filled with excitement.

"I will. Soon. But there's something you should know."

Hester noticed the sadness in Abraham's eyes and sat back down, bracing herself.

Abraham took a deep breath. "It's your parents. And your brother. They passed in the storm."

"My parents? My brother?" Hester looked at him earnestly. "Do you know anything about them?"

"Yes. Your mother's name is Bernice. They call your father Big Jake. And your brother's name is…" Abraham reached for Hester's hands and folded them into his. "Isaac," he said.

"Isaac? From my dream? I was trying to save my brother?"

Abraham brushed away a tear from her face. "Yes, Hester," he said, softly. "A man by the name of Captain Henry told me that folks said your brother fell overboard, and you went after him. Your father went after both of you. Your mother was so overcome when no one came back that her heart plumb gave out."

The sound that escaped Hester wasn't a cry or a scream but a wail that came from deep inside. Abraham pulled her into his arms, rocking back and forth as fast as he could. "Go ahead, cry," he said, stroking her hair.

After a while, Hester looked up at him through swollen eyes.

"I remember," she said. "I remember everything. I tried to save him, but I couldn't get to him. I didn't know my daddy jumped in. And my poor mama." She began crying inconsolably.

Abraham held her for what seemed like hours, rocking her and letting her cry. Finally, as the sun was setting over the Delta, she stirred and said, "What am I going to do now?"

"You're going to stay with me," Abraham said. "I'm going to take care of you. When you're ready, I'll take you home to collect your things, but for right now, don't worry. I'm here. You'll get by okay."

It took almost a month before Hester could muster the courage to visit her home, but the day came in early November. Abraham walked the four miles with her. A cool breeze blowing from the river accompanied them.

"Things are looking better," Abraham said, as they walked, although they occasionally came upon a pile of someone's belongings strewn about that reminded them of what had been lost.

"I'm scared of what I'm going to find," Hester admitted.

"Prepare yourself," Abraham said. "There's no telling."

Hester's steps slowed the closer they got to her home. She couldn't bear any more heartbreak.

Abraham reached for her hand. "Come along, girl. We can do this."

"I can't." Hester sat down on the side of the road in a grassy area. "I thought I was ready, but I'm not."

Abraham gently pulled her to her feet. "We'll do this together. I'm here. I will always be here with you."

For the last mile, Hester, filled with dread about what she would find when they reached her home, allowed Abraham to pull her along until they reached the edge of an orange grove. Carefully weaving their way through a maze of downed branches and trees and twisted metal, they finally reached the house. Part of the roof was missing, but the house was still standing. When they walked onto the porch, they could already smell the mold that had settled inside.

"It'll need a good cleaning," Abraham said, opening the front door. Then he heard a noise coming from the back of the house. "Who's there?" he yelled.

"It's me. Poopdeck. I'm just cleaning up in here." A boy about fifteen years old walked toward them. He stopped dead in his tracks when he saw Hester. "Good Lawd Almighty, you're alive," he said, staring like he was seeing a ghost. "Folks said you was dead."

Abraham turned to look at Hester. "You know him?"

"Yes," Hester said. "He worked for my daddy, picking oranges when it was time to harvest."

"I couldn't just leave this house in a mess," Poopdeck said. "I've been cleaning when I can."

"Thank you," Hester said.

"I'm sorry about your kin. Where've you been?"

Hester's eyes filled with tears. "Abraham here found me in a tree. His family has been taking care of me since the storm. I just found out about Mama and Daddy and Isaac."

"Well, this place is all yours now. If you want, I'll get it shipshape in no time."

Hester nodded her head, and Abraham said, "Much obliged."

"I'm going to see if I can find any of my clothes." Hester carefully picked her way through the debris that cluttered the kitchen floor.

"We'll go out and look at those trees," Abraham said, understanding that she might need a few minutes alone.

After finding some saws hanging on pegs in the barn, Abraham and Poopdeck began cutting branches off the trees that lay on the ground. "How much did Big Jake pay you?" Abraham asked, observing how steadily the boy worked with the saw.

"Sometimes as much as a dollar a day, depending," Poopdeck said.

"Depending?" Abraham asked.

"Depending on how much I got done."

"How long do you think it would take you to get this place fixed up?"

"It's a fine mess," Poopdeck said. "About a month, excepting Sundays, I guess."

Abraham thought about that for a moment. "What's your given name?"

"I'm a Cousin, Albert Cousin, but everybody calls me Poopdeck, seeing as how I pooped on the deck of a boat once when I was a kid. I swear I did. In front of God and everybody. The name stuck, but I don't mind so much. It's funny."

"Well, then Albert. You're hired, but I want this place spic and span in one month. I'll come help you when I can."

"Thank you, sir. Thank you. I can always use the work. I won't let you down."

Poopdeck went back to sawing while Abraham went to check on Hester. He found her sitting on a bench on the porch holding a bucket, crying softly. Hester looked up when she heard Abraham's footsteps.

"Me and Isaac collected water in a bucket like this right before the storm. It's the last thing we did together," she said.

Abraham took a seat beside her. And together on the rickety bench, quietly they sat, absorbing the stillness of the home that had once been filled with the sounds of Isaac playing, the smells of Bernice cooking, and the heavy footsteps of Big Jake coming in after a hard day of work.

Finally, Abraham pulled Hester to her feet, and they walked back to Union Settlement hand in hand, the bucket swinging from Hester's other hand.

One month later, they returned.

Poopdeck, true to his word, had cleaned everything. The mud was gone, the wood-burning stove was sparkling and had fresh firewood inside, the trees had been cut—the branches burned and the logs stacked neatly on the side of the barn. Shiny new tin covered the roof. Everything that had broken had been removed. Everything that could be salvaged was in its proper place. The smell of mold was gone, thanks to gallons of Fresnol that had been poured onto the floors and scrubbed into walls.

"Who did all this?" Hester asked.

"Mostly Albert," Abraham replied. "I helped when I could get away."

"Who's Albert?"

Abraham started laughing. "Poopdeck is Albert. That's his real name."

"I never knew that," Hester said, laughing with him. Abraham stared at her. It was the first time he had heard her laugh.

"Let's sit down," he said. "I want to talk to you."

"What is it?" Hester said, vivid memories of the last time he had sounded so serious giving her pause.

"I've been thinking," Abraham began. "I've been saving for a while to build a house. I've been pulling logs from the river and building furniture. I've got a table and chairs, some benches, and two beds that I've finished already. I checked, and this house and the land around it are rightfully yours. Your daddy had it registered in his name after his father passed, and Louisiana allows women to inherit land now. I asked that everything be transferred to your name."

"You want me to leave your home?" Hester asked.

"No," Abraham said. "I want to move here. With you. I want us to be married. I can work the farm and plant the rice. And when I'm not doing that, I'll be on my boat. I can make a good living for us with oysters. You can come out with me if you want."

"You don't have to marry me because you feel sorry for me," Hester said. "I won't have that. I'm young and strong. I can work this farm myself. I used to help my daddy all the time."

"I don't want to marry you because I feel sorry for you. I want to marry you because you belong with me. We belong together. Don't you know it, too?"

Hester nodded. "I do, but…"

"No buts. I want you to be my wife. I've known it from the day I pulled you from that tree. You are mine, Hester Baptiste, but you have to want to be mine."

"I really do, but I'm Mulatto, and your family comes from Africa. My father would roll over in his grave. It's just not done. We have different customs, different beliefs."

"You can teach me yours, and I can teach you mine," Abraham said. "I think your father would be grateful that you are safe and cared for. As for what other folks think, I don't care. Do you?"

Hester thought about that for a moment, and then she looked at him and smiled. "No, I don't. Thank you, Abraham, for your very kind offer. I will gladly become your wife."

The following week, Abraham and Hester were married outside of the Plaquemines Parish Courthouse in Pointe á la Hache in front of Abraham's parents, Poopdeck, and Claude and Anna-Marie Couvillion. Anna-Marie had insisted upon an invitation when Abraham told her that he and Hester were to be married.

CHAPTER 7

March 1917

By 1917, New Orleans had evolved into a seafood mecca dependent on the men who worked long, hard hours to fish oysters, crabs, and shrimp, which were plentiful in the numerous waterways that surrounded the city. Ships laden with goods from the north sailed in and out of New Orleans daily, but the oyster luggers from Plaquemines Parish were forced to dock at English Turn, ten miles downriver. These boats, some up to forty feet long and weighing up to eight tons, were filled with Austrians (often referred to as Takos), French, and Italians, whose ancestors had landed in New Orleans and then spread down the river, establishing villages and towns along the way.

Blacks, whose families had lived and worked near the river for decades, had also learned this valuable trade. With metal tongs and handmade baskets, they worked for oystermen tonging and culling oysters from reefs in American Bay, Black Bay, Battledore Reef, and other bays and bayous spread throughout the area. One sack of oysters went for one- to-two dollars, and they were sold to luggermen or to canneries located up and down the river. A good living could be made from mid-September to May off the valuable oyster leases that were split three ways—one-third to the owner of the lease, one-third to the boat owner, and one-third to the workers who actually fished the oysters. Off-season, oystermen worked their farms, hunted muskrat and alligators, or shrimped and fished to survive.

Because of this port, the French Quarter thrived. People came from all over the country to shop at the French Market or to sample the tasty delicacies native to Louisiana that could be found in the numerous upscale restaurants housed between rowdy barrooms, filled with tourists, sailors, businessmen, and fishermen, and clandestine brothels that catered to any man's fancy. Horses and buggies traveled between automobiles that lined the narrow, busy streets. Dressed with lacy, wrought iron balconies, the Spanish and French-styled architecture of the French Quarter elicited admiration the world over. Art galleries, museums, and antique stores, filled with exquisite jewels and hand-carved armoires and trunks from centuries past, attracted a more elite clientele than the artisans who hung out in Pirates Alley next to Jackson Square, where the St. Louis Cathedral, the crown jewel of the Quarter, hosted Sunday masses, during which sinners repented for the sins of the previous evening. Thirteen blocks long and six blocks wide, with Canal Street, Esplanade Avenue, North Rampart Street, and the Mississippi River as its borders, the French Quarter offered both elegance and debauchery in equal measures.

The Orleans Levee District, which originated in 1890, was housed at Common Street, about a ten-minute walk from the Quarter. Major floods, more than thirty between 1735 and 1916, had necessitated the formation of the district as well as other levee districts throughout Louisiana. New Orleans had flooded nine times during those years. Because the city had become a valuable asset as one of the largest ports in the country, it had to be protected at all costs.

In 1816, New Orleans flooded when a breach of a levee in Kenner, located thirteen miles to the west, poured water into the city. In 1849, a crevasse in the Carrollton area flooded the whole city, and floodwaters did not recede for six weeks. In 1854, the Board of Swampland Commissioners was formed and charged with building levees and maintaining them in four levee districts that had been created. That board evolved into the Board of Public Works, which lasted some twenty years.

The Civil War put a halt to the construction for several years, but a crevasse at Bonnet Carré that flooded New Orleans in 1871 prompted Congress to create the Mississippi River Commission, which planned construction of levees in the lower Mississippi River Valley. The U.S. Army Corps of Engineers formed districts, including one in New Orleans, to complete the work on the levees. It wasn't long before Louisiana created its own levee boards, giving them extraordinary power to tax citizens for the building of levees and to expropriate land if necessary to use as easements for those levees.

In 1890, the Orleans Levee District was established by Act 93, along with its Board of Commissioners, whose members were commissioned to serve a six-year term.

In early March 1917, Jefferson Davenport, a member of the Board of Commissioners for the Orleans Levee District, sat at his desk and reviewed a United States Geological Survey prepared by the Department of the Interior, dated 1910, and titled "Oil and Gas in Louisiana." This survey, written by G. D. Harris, detailed the oilfields in Louisiana. Jefferson paid close attention to a paragraph at the bottom of page ten:

"As already remarked (p. 8), if the saline nucleus is many feet beneath the surface say 1,000 feet, as at Spindletop, or at an unknown greater depth, as at Jennings and if between these depths and the surface there are pervious layers overlain by extensive impervious layers, the conditions are favorable for the collection of oil and gas, particularly at or near the apex of the dome, where they are obtained easily and in immense quantities."

Jefferson had read the section of the survey that explained the relationship between oil and salt domes many times, and now he had a plan, one that had been simmering for some time and would place him in control of millions of dollars. He knew he would need help. This was not something he could accomplish alone, and it would take time.

Years, in fact.

Today, he planned to take the first step. He was meeting two friends and fellow commissioners at Antoine's Restaurant. On this unusually cool day, he decided to walk. As he quickly made his way down Common Street and then Carondelet and Bourbon Streets and finally onto St. Louis Street, he envisioned how his fellow commissioners would react to his plan, creating scenarios and his responses as he walked. A lone saxophone played a somber tune in the distance, but Jefferson didn't hear it, focused as he was on what he would say.

He looked at his watch when he reached Antoine's. He knew he was early, but he didn't care. At any given time, a line filled with tourists could form down St. Louis Street, especially on a Friday afternoon, with everyone trying to get a table. Established in 1840, Antoine's famous Oysters Rockefeller or Eggs Sardou lured locals and tourists alike. Jefferson had been caught in that line one too many times, so he had deliberately arrived before 5:00 p.m., hoping that he could beat the rush. He had timed it perfectly. Wilson, the maître d', spotted him and waved him in.

"My reservation isn't until five," Jefferson said.

"That's okay, Mr. Davenport. We always have a table for you. Two more will be joining you?"

"Yes, Mr. Bertaut and Mr. Ragliosi."

"I'll bring them over as soon as they arrive," Wilson said, shaking out a linen napkin and handing it to Jefferson.

"Thank you, Wilson," Jefferson said, placing the napkin on his lap. "I could use a drink."

"I'll send Jamison right over," Wilson said, with the slightest of bows.

A few minutes later, Jefferson impatiently tapped his fingers on the table while he sipped on an old-fashioned and perused the menu he knew by heart. He hated waiting, and he knew that his friends knew that. He was on his second cocktail by the time they finally arrived.

"Apologies," Pierre Bertaut said, pulling out a chair. "Had a meeting go long. Them engineers can talk your ear off when they get going."

"We tried to cut it short, but we're probably lucky we got out when we did. Everyone was asking where you were," Sal Ragliosi said, looking at Jefferson. "Those levees aren't going to rebuild themselves. As you know, the hurricane caused thirteen crevasses along the river. The engineers think this could take years."

Jefferson motioned for the waiter and waited while the two men ordered a cocktail. "They always think that. Make a mountain out of a molehill every time, like this hasn't happened before. Each time, we go a little higher and a little stronger, but that's not why I wanted to meet with you."

"What's on your mind?" Pierre asked.

"Let's order first." Jefferson handed his menu to Pierre and snapped his fingers to get Jamison's attention before ordering Oysters Rockefeller and a filet mignon topped with white lump crabmeat and hollandaise sauce. When Pierre and Sal had finished ordering, Jefferson cleared his throat. "I don't know if you've been paying attention, but oil companies are going into Texas and drilling near salt domes. Have you heard about that?"

Pierre and Sal shook their heads.

"No," Sal said, "but what does that have to do with us?"

"Doesn't your cousin own that milling company down there in Nestor—Bertaut & Biggs?" Jefferson asked Pierre.

"Yes," Pierre answered him with a perplexed look on his face.

"And doesn't he own a lot of land down there?"

"Yes, he does." Pierre wondered where this was going.

"Did you know there's a huge salt dome down there right in the middle of the river? It spreads from the river into Nestor."

"So?" Pierre said.

"So we've got to figure out a way to get our hands on all of that land down there," Jefferson announced.

"My cousin will never sell," Pierre said. "He makes too much money on rice. And then there's the sugarcane. Not the business it once was, but it still brings in a pretty penny."

"I'm not talking about selling, leastways not to us personally." Jefferson pulled the survey out of his briefcase and opened it to page ten. "I've been studying this, and I'm telling you, there has to be oil around that Potash Salt Dome down there. It won't be long before Humble and Standard Oil come calling, and we need to be ready."

"You do realize that's in Plaquemines Parish?" Sal reminded him.

"I do. But we are the commissioners of the board of the Orleans Levee District," Jefferson said. "Let me remind you that we've been granted virtually unlimited authority through the Louisiana Legislature to protect New Orleans above all else through whatever means are necessary. We also have the power to generate our own income and to operate in surrounding parishes, including Plaquemines, when necessary to protect the Crescent City."

"I still don't get it," Sal said. "What does oil have to do with protecting New Orleans?"

Jefferson leaned back in his chair and smiled. "Gentlemen, oil has everything to do with it. I've been thinking about it, and I think I know what we can do. Hurricanes and floods, boys, that's the business we're in." Jefferson was just beginning to expound on his idea when he looked up. Suddenly, he stopped talking. Sal and Pierre were wondering why when a young man approached their table.

"Why, Leonus Lozano, as I live and breathe. Look what the cat done drug in," Jefferson said, turning to Sal and Pierre. "You gentlemen know this feller, don't you?"

"I haven't had the pleasure," Sal said, standing up to shake Leonus' hand while Pierre remained seated and studied the young man.

He had an air about him, like he was somehow more important than everyone else. He was young, just twenty-five, and much too young to be filled with so much confidence. Bushy eyebrows, barely concealed by the brim of his tall hat, framed dark eyes that rarely blinked. Intentional intimidation practiced with a handheld mirror back when he was a teenager. A big, fat cigar protruded from his fingers, and occasionally he relit it, puffing noisily, oblivious to the cloud of pungent smoke billowing around him.

"I heard you just graduated from Tulane," Jefferson said.

"I did," Leonus said. "I have plans to start a practice here and one across the river. You can't have your hands in too many pots, you know. And who knows, before long I may be tossing my hat in for a judgeship."

"Mighty ambitious for such a young whippersnapper, aren't you?" Jefferson commented, disdainfully.

"Yes sir. I am." Leonus tipped his hat. "Gentlemen. I bid you good day."

"I do not like that young man," Jefferson said, when Leonus was gone. "I have a feeling about him. He's going to be trouble all the way around."

"Did you notice how he looked down his nose at us? I wanted to take him outside and show him what for," Sal said.

"I'm sure there will be plenty of time for that. That boy will be a burr in our backsides. Just you wait and see," Jefferson said.

"I ain't worried about him," Pierre said. "I'm more interested in this big plan of yours. Let's get back to that. What's this about oil and salt domes and floods?"

"Like I was saying, oil's coming to Louisiana sooner rather than later," Jefferson said. "The question is how do we cash in on it?"

"Obviously, you have a plan or we wouldn't still be sitting here." Sal looked at his watch. He knew his wife, Gladys, would be wondering why he wasn't home yet.

"She can wait," Pierre said, noticing that Sal was getting antsy. "Let's hear him out."

"Salt domes—they're the key. We've got one sitting in our backyard.

We just need to figure out a way to get our hands on it. Imagine what we could do for New Orleans with all that money. We could build that airport at the lakefront. We could build better levees, higher levees, around the lake," Jefferson said.

"How are we going to get folks to sell their land?" Sal asked. "I know Antoine Bertaut isn't going to sell, and he owns a lot of arpents down there." (In Louisiana, land is measured by arpents instead of acres. One square arpent is approximately eighty-four percent of an acre.)

"He'll sell if he's forced to," Jefferson said.

"And how are we going to do that? You do realize you're speaking about my kinfolk?" Pierre reminded him.

Jefferson downed his drink. "He'll be compensated," he assured Pierre.

"How're you going to do that? You been talking, but I don't hear nothing concrete." Pierre stood up and reached for his hat.

"Sit down," Jefferson said. "Hear me out."

Pierre sat down, still holding his hat.

"This hurricane gave me an idea. I've been percolating on this for a while, and I think I've got it figured out. You know how they have all those levees down there. Some were built by the Indians hundreds of years ago, but many are natural levees forged through years of the Mississippi rising and falling and leaving silt behind. Well, how do you feel about a spillway there, a spillway to protect New Orleans from flooding?"

"Pardon me for sounding like a fool," Sal jumped in, "but how is a spillway some fifty miles south of New Orleans going to protect the city from a river that runs north to south?"

"That's the beauty of it," Jefferson said. "Instead of building new levees, we'll tear down old ones. We'll create a natural spillway. Theoretically, it could help protect New Orleans from flooding during hurricanes because the water won't build up in the river. A natural spillway could give the water somewhere to go."

"That's going to be a hard sell," Pierre said.

"Well, now, that depends. I have a few engineers in my back pocket, and the governor is a friend who likes to make money," Jefferson countered. "I don't think it will be that difficult."

"How are we going to get those folks to sell? They've been living down there all their lives, and you know as well as I do, they cling to their roots."

"They won't be given a choice," Jefferson said. "They will sell, or we'll expropriate the land."

"I don't know," Pierre said. "This doesn't sound right."

Jefferson snorted. "Right, wrong, who cares? Oil is coming. The only question that matters is, who's going to profit from it? Those poor people down there wouldn't know what to do with it. They'll be happy to get what we give them for their land. They'll start a new life with more money than they ever had, and they'll be happy as clams. We'll bide our time and cash in on the mineral rights when oil comes calling. What's so wrong about that? It's foresight. That's what I call it. Foresight."

Sal thought about it for a minute, and then he smiled. "I'm in."

More reluctantly, Pierre nodded his agreement.

Jefferson leaned forward and held out his hand. "Gentlemen, we have a plan. Your word of honor, this stays between us until we've worked out the details." The men shook hands.

So intent were they on their conniving, none of them noticed that Leonus Lozano had sat down at the table behind them to eavesdrop on their conversation. His first step, he thought, would be to befriend the Grand Prairie Levee Board members. And the governor. That would be very important. The land they were talking about was in Plaquemines Parish. Those boys would play hell stealing it from him. And while Jefferson, Pierre, and Sal mapped out the plan at the next table, Leonus began to plot his own path to riches. Finally, he stood up.

"Gentlemen," he said, tipping his hat as he walked by their table.

CHAPTER 8

April 1917

Poopdeck paddled as fast as he could, his voice carrying over the water as he yelled, "Has anybody seen Abraham? Abraham Jackson? Anybody seen him?"

Someone shouted back, "Just up the bayou a-ways. Saw him near an oyster reef. Looked like he was making a good haul."

"Thanks," Poopdeck yelled, paddling even harder. He had to get to Abraham. Ten minutes later, he saw his friend's boat. "Abraham!"

Abraham turned and saw Poopdeck furiously paddling toward him, barely missing another boat anchored beside him.

Poopdeck stood up, nearly tipping his pirogue over. "Abraham, you've got to get home. Now. Miss Hester's having the baby! Hurry! Something's wrong. I'm on my way to get the remedy man."

"Hester told you to do that?" Abraham asked, pulling up his anchor as fast as he could.

"Yes sir. The midwife is there and Miss Anna-Marie. Miss Hester sent me to find you and told me to get the remedy man."

"Something must be very wrong if she told you that." Abraham knew Hester wouldn't ask for the remedy man unless she was in dire straits. She knew Abraham didn't believe in the voodoo that was such a big part of her culture. "Did she tell you where to find him?"

"He's in the Mulatto camp. It's too far to go by pirogue, so I'm going to borrow my cousin's boat. He docks it not too far from here. I'll be back as soon as I can."

"Go on," Abraham said. "Hurry. I can't get out of here until you move."

Abraham had already began inching forward, barely waiting for

Poopdeck to get out of his way. He made his way across Fucich Bayou as fast as he could, his hand clenched on the tiller. He knew he shouldn't have left that morning. He had known Hester wasn't herself. She had looked so uncomfortable, and every now and then he heard a grimace. He had told her he would stay with her, but she had insisted. "I don't need you fretting over me," she said. "I'm fine. The baby's just moving around a lot."

Reluctantly, he had walked to the landing where his boat was docked, a nagging feeling accompanying him. He knew it was too early. The baby wasn't supposed to come until the next month. An overcast sky didn't help his mood, and as he plucked oysters from the bed with his metal tongs, he worried. He knew how much this baby meant to Hester. He thought about how happy she had been when he had pulled the old crib from the attic in the barn. Isaac's crib. Tears had spilled down her cheeks, but they were happy tears. They were naming the baby Isaac if it was a boy, and Hester explained that her father had built that crib when her mother was pregnant with Isaac.

"I was only five, but I remember how proud Daddy was when he showed Mama," she told Abraham. "We put a little mattress in it, and I helped Mama make a small pillow for him. Mama sewed a net to put around it to keep the mosquitoes out."

For the next few months, Hester had stitched her own mosquito net. She had sewed a pillow and made curtains out of the blue material decorated with yellow ducks that Anna-Marie had given her. "What if the baby's a girl?" Abraham had asked her.

"Girls like ducks, too," Hester had tossed back at him. She wasn't worried. She knew she was carrying a boy. The baby had to be a boy so that she could name him after her brother.

Abraham had smiled, big and toothy, and had wrapped his arms around his wife. He loved the life they were building together. He loved picking oranges and dropping rice seeds into little holes by the river, then waiting for the river to rise and cover them. He loved cracking his whip at the ricebirds who tried to steal his crop. He loved taking Hester on his boat and teaching her how to spot mature oysters and showing her how to tell if one might yield a pearl. Abraham had spent hours stringing a necklace for Hester from the pearls he had spent years collecting. But mostly, he loved his wife. Every minute of their life together. And as he maneuvered his boat into the landing, he realized that he had never been more afraid. He couldn't bear the thought that he might lose her in childbirth. That sort of thing happened more often than he cared to think about. The thought propelled him into a run, and like lightening, he tore through the countryside until he reached the door to their home, where he stopped for a moment, panting, gasping, struggling to fill his lungs with air. Then he heard a scream.

He barreled through the door and ran to the bedroom. Anna-Marie met him at the door and pushed him back, closing the door behind her.

"You have to stay calm, Abraham," she warned. "Do not let her see one ounce of worry on your face."

"How is she?" Abraham asked.

"She's bleeding, and the baby is turned. The midwife can't get it out. Hester has pushed so much that she's exhausted," Anna-Marie explained. "I'm worried because she's losing her strength. Poopdeck went for the remedy man. I hope he hurries."

"Can I go in?" Abraham asked.

"Yes, if you do as I say. Don't let her see that you're scared. She needs your strength right now."

Abraham took a deep breath, nodded, and opened the door. He saw the blood on the sheets first and then he saw the terror in Hester's eyes mixed with sorrow. "I can't do it," she said, faintly. "I can't push no more."

Abraham reached deep down and managed a smile. "Of course you can. You're my girl." He placed a wet cloth on her forehead and reached for her hand, wrapping his around it. "Take my strength," he said, just as Hester doubled over in the bed, holding her belly. She let out a shrill scream.

The midwife checked her and then shook her head.

"It's okay," Abraham said soothingly, stroking Hester's cheek. "The baby will come when he's ready."

"Where's the remedy man?" Hester asked.

"Albert went to get him. They should be here soon."

"I hope they hurry," the midwife said when Hester screamed again. "Take a deep breath and push," she ordered.

Hester took a deep breath and pushed, screaming all the while and squeezing Abraham's hand.

Abraham looked at the midwife. She shook her head and gestured that he should leave the room.

"I'm going to go see if they are coming," Abraham said to Hester. "I'll be right back."

The midwife followed him out. "Have you ever delivered a litter of pups?" she asked.

"No, but I've delivered calves."

"Go put on some gloves. There's water boiling on the stove. Drop them in there first. You may have to pull this baby out."

Abraham stared at her. "I can't do that to her," he said.

"You don't have a choice. If you don't, one or both of them is going to die."

Abraham hurried into the kitchen and grabbed a pair of gloves from a shelf. He dropped them in the pot and then grabbed a wooden spoon to scoop them out. Just then, he heard footsteps on the porch. The door swung open, and a tall, slender man with small bones weaved through his long black braids rushed inside.

"Where is she?" the man asked, his voice thick as molasses.

Abraham turned to see cerulean blue eyes, startling in their intensity, contrasted by smooth caramel-colored skin, staring at him. He could not have been a day older than Abraham, but his eyes reflected wisdom beyond his years. Still, Abraham hesitated.

Then he heard another scream.

"This way," he said, running through the living room to the bedroom. "There."

Abraham watched as the man peered into Hester's eyes and felt her stomach. Then he pointed to the bloodied sheets. "May I?"

Abraham nodded, noticing that Hester's breathing had slowed and her eyes were rolling back in her head.

The remedy man examined Hester. When he was finished, he pulled a bowl out of his bag. He mixed some herbs and a liquid together, and then he held the bowl to Hester's lips. "Drink, child," he said.

"This will help with the bleeding and slow the contractions," he told Abraham.

Abraham wasn't comfortable with this strange man and his potion, and he was about to object when he felt Anna-Marie's hand firmly on his arm. He looked at her, and she shook her head.

"Leave us," the remedy man said to Abraham when Hester tensed up again. "Leave us now. You stay," he said to the midwife.

"I'm not going anywhere," Abraham said.

"Yes, you are," Anna-Marie said gently. "Come with me, Abraham. Hester trusted him enough to fetch him. You should trust him, too." She gently pushed him from the room.

A few minutes later, they heard Hester scream again.

"No," Anna-Marie said when Abraham bolted for the bedroom door. "She's screaming. That means she's still with us."

Abraham paced back and forth through the house, and then sat down and put his head in his hands. "Is she going to make it?" he asked, tears streaming down his face.

"I don't know. She's lost a lot of blood, and if they can't get the baby out, I don't know. Pray, Abraham. That's what you can do for her."

Abraham bowed his head and prayed like he had never prayed before. "Please," he begged. "Please don't take her from me. Please take away her suffering. Please don't take Isaac from her again. Please."

A few minutes later, Abraham and Anna-Marie heard a wail coming from the bedroom. It started off small and then built.

Abraham ran for the bedroom and flung open the door. The midwife was holding a crying baby boy. The remedy man was leaning over Hester, his needle flying up and down over her stomach. There was blood everywhere.

"What the hell?" Abraham cried.

"A miracle. That's what it is," the midwife said. "He cut her stomach open and took the baby out."

Abraham crumpled to the floor.

Anna-Marie giggled. "Men." She dipped her hand in a bucket of water and flicked it on Abraham's face.

When he came to, Abraham looked around for a minute, bewildered. Then he struggled to his feet and walked to Hester's side. Her eyes were closed. Her breathing was shallow. Her skin was pale, and sweat beaded her brow.

"She's been through a lot," the remedy man announced, checking to make sure that the stitches were spaced exactly right. "She'll be out for a few hours. When she comes to, give her some more of that to drink." He pointed to the potion he had mixed earlier. "Just a little every time she wakes up for the next three days. She needs to sleep."

"Is she going to be okay?" Abraham asked, staring at Hester fearfully. "Is she going to…?

"Live? Yes," the remedy man said. "A few more minutes and she…, but yes, she will live. Just keep this area around the cut clean and dry and let her sleep. She'll be in some pain when she awakens, but she'll be all right."

"She would have died," the midwife piped in, turning around to hand the baby to Abraham. "I've never seen anything like it. If he hadn't of been here, she'd be dead, and so would the baby."

"Shush," Anna-Marie said, gently. "It's not the time. Let's clean up this mess as best we can."

Abraham stood next to the bed, trembling, holding his tiny son in one hand. "Will he be okay?" he asked.

"Yes. He's early, and he's small, so you'll need to keep an eye on him. Find a wet nurse to feed him until his mother is well, and give him a drop of this every morning and every night for a week," the remedy man said, pulling a small bottle from his bag.

Abraham didn't argue. He watched as the remedy man put a dropper in his son's mouth and squeezed. He smiled when the baby sucked, wanting more.

"That's good." The remedy man handed Abraham a small blanket. "Keep him wrapped up and get a wet nurse here as soon as you can."

"I know one," the midwife said. "Can you give me a ride?" she asked Anna-Marie.

"Of course," Anna-Marie said. "The horse and buggy are right outside. We'll be back as soon as we can."

After Anna-Marie and the midwife left, Abraham sat down in a chair near Hester while the remedy man gathered his things.

"What is your name?" Abraham asked. "I feel like I should know your given name so I can thank you properly."

"My name is Sanon. Sanon Estilien Duveillaume, but I don't require anything from you."

"Nonsense. I thank you from the bottom of my heart, Sanon."

Abraham held his fist to his chest for emphasis. "I owe you a debt that I cannot repay."

"You owe me nothing." Sanon leaned over to listen to Hester's breaths. He placed two fingers to her neck and counted. "Her pulse is stronger now. The potion is working. Good. Very good."

"Hester told me about you, but she didn't say that you were a doctor. She just called you the remedy man."

"I'm not a doctor. I'm a healer. I usually heal through potions. My ancestors were Haitian. My father was a healer and his father before him," Sanon said.

"Have you done this before?"

"No," Sanon admitted. "I've heard about it, but this was the only way. These were extraordinary circumstances."

Abraham looked down at his son, and his eyes filled with tears. "Thank you for having the courage to save my wife and son. I will not forget what you did, and as I prosper, you, too, shall prosper."

Sanon smiled. "No need for all that. The Lord provides. My payment will be watching your son grow and knowing your wife is alive and happy. That's all I need in this life. Now, tend to your family. I must go."

Abraham sat in that chair for a long time after Sanon departed. He stared down at his son. Isaac. Isaac Sanon Jackson, he decided, knowing Hester would agree. He reached for Hester's hand and sat there, quietly thanking God for the gifts he had been given this day.

CHAPTER 9

November 1917

"How are you, doing?" Anna-Marie asked, when she saw Hester walk into the store.

"I'm fine, but I'm scared. And worried,"

"Me, too," Anna-Marie said. "We just have to stay strong and believe they will be fine."

"I know, but it's difficult. I haven't had a letter in a month."

Anna-Marie grinned. "Well, let me remedy that for you." She reached under the counter. "I knew you'd be in, so I put it right here. May I?"

"Yes. Please."

Anna-Marie had been teaching Hester to read, but they had only begun the lessons the previous month, so Hester had asked Anna-Marie if she would read Abraham's letters to her.

Anna-Marie unfolded the letter and began reading aloud:

September 5, 1917

My Dearest Hester,

I cannot express how much I miss you and Isaac. At night, when all is quiet, I look at the stars and think about how far away you are, but distance cannot take me from you because I hold you both so close in my heart. It's cold at night in France, but I like it because it reminds me that I am alive and have much to live for. Do not fear for me. Claude always looks out for me, and I him. We have become very close. War has a way of doing that. We watch out for each other for you and Anna-Marie. I hope you are taking care of each other, as well. I miss you and love you with all my heart. Kiss my son for me.

Forever yours,
Abraham

Anna-Marie placed the letter back in its envelope and handed it to Hester. "I really hate this," she said.

"Me, too," Hester agreed.

"I know it's harder for you with the baby and the farm. How are you doing? Are you really doing well? Do you need anything?"

"I'm fine," Hester said. "Poopdeck helps around the farm, and Abraham's mother has been coming over to sit with me and Isaac. She always puts on a brave front, but I know she's worried, too."

"We all are," Anna-Marie said. "I don't even read the newspaper anymore. It's too depressing. Downright scary, really. Who would have ever thought we'd be caught up in a world war, or that our husbands would be in France? I'm glad I have Claude Jr. and Charlie to keep me busy. And the store. Otherwise, I'd go stark-raving mad. You know, in his last letter, Claude said I should ask you to help out around here. I didn't want to ask until you got your strength back. You could bring Isaac with you. Claude Jr. and Charlie are always here, although Claude Jr. doesn't make it easy. He's always into something. Between the two of us, it would be easier, but only if you want to."

"Of course. I'd love to help you," Hester said. "It might make the time go by faster, and you've done so much for us."

Anna-Marie smiled at her. "It's settled then. You can start tomorrow. Nine sharp. I'll teach you everything you need to know, and between customers and babies, we'll do your lessons. In a few months, you'll be reading Abraham's letters yourself."

"I don't know how to thank you for everything you've done for us."

"My pleasure. I'll send Spit to get you in the morning."

"Oh, no, I can walk."

"You don't need to be walking that far carrying the baby," Anna-Marie said. "Spit will be there. Besides, I have to keep him busy or he gets into trouble. I have to keep an eye on that one, especially when he's cleaning the saloon."

"He's still hitting the bottle?" Hester asked.

"Not around me, he's not. I put the fear of God into him." Anna-Marie grinned mischievously.

"Good for you," Hester said. "He needs that."

"I bet he can't wait until Claude gets back so he doesn't have to answer to me anymore. Oh, look. Here he comes now. His ears must have been ringing," Anna-Marie said as Spit walked into the store.

"Miss Anna-Marie. Miss Hester," Spit said. "I came by to see if you ladies need anything."

"Can you give Hester a ride home?" Anna-Marie asked. "And take these groceries with you," she added, pointing to several sacks on the counter. "They are for you, Hester."

"Oh, no. I don't take no charity. You know that," Hester said, firmly.

"It's not charity. You work here now. It's part of your pay. Ask Spit. He always gets groceries."

"It's true," Spit said. "I get paid in food and money. A good thing when I'm out on a bender, for sure, or I'd never eat."

"Well, I'll bring you some oranges tomorrow," Hester said. "And I made some night shade. I'll bring that along, too."

"That sounds lovely." Anna-Marie turned to wait on Mildred, who had been lurking nearby, listening to the conversation.

When Hester and Spit were gone, Mildred leaned over the counter and whispered, "You're going to let a Mulatto work in the store with you, ringing up the cash register and everything?"

Anna-Marie's eyes narrowed. "Mildred Barrington. Talk like that could get you banned from a store if it was mine. Oh, wait. It is mine. That's right. I'm married to the owner, and he left me in charge. It's a long walk to the next store, but I'm sure you'll get along fine."

Mildred's chubby cheeks turned beet red. She sputtered for a moment, and then she grabbed her bags and stormed out of the store.

"'Bye now," Anna-Marie called out, laughing as she watched her go. "That's what you call a busybody," she said to Claude Jr., picking him up. "Yes, she is. A busybody if ever I've seen one."

"If I never see another ditch again, it'll be too soon for me, and I grew up in Louisiana where ditches are everywhere," Abraham muttered, as he pushed his shovel into the muck and threw mud and water out of the trench.

"Stay low," Claude cautioned. "Them snipers are deadly accurate. Look at this," he continued, rolling up his sleeve and showing Abraham his arm. "You see those teeth marks? Damn rat bit me last night while I was sleeping."

Abraham laughed quietly. "I know. I heard some men down the line talking about it. They said you woke up everyone with your cursing. I didn't know you could curse like that. They said you damn near got everyone killed. You're lucky no one was out in No Man's Land last night."

"Look down there." Claude pointed between the duckboards that lined the bottom of the trench. "They just scurry about like they own the place. I swear, when I get home, I'm going to shoot every rat I see. And now I've got lice." Claude unstrapped his helmet and began to scratch. "My head is on fire, and scratching don't help nothing. God, I hope I don't get trench fever."

Abraham put his hand on Claude's shoulder. "Put your helmet back on. It's not safe. You're going to be all right, man. Hang in there. We'll get home soon enough. This war can't go on forever."

"Can't it? Here we are in godforsaken France, hiding in a trench, getting eaten by rats and God knows what other kind of vermin down here. And getting shot at day and night."

Abraham looked at Claude with concern in his eyes. "That boy dying yesterday really got to you, huh?"

Claude leaned back against the sidewall of the trench. "Yeah, man. Name was Flounder, seeing as how he loved to eat them. I heard tell that he would fish all day until he caught one. He was from Dime just down the river from us, only twenty-one years old. Still a baby. His parents are good, God-fearing people. Don't deserve what they're fixing to have to deal with. Yeah, it got to me."

"You can't let it, man. You've got to shrug it off, or you'll never survive out here. Men are going to die. All we have to do is make sure it's not us. You hear me, Claude? It ain't gonna be us." Abraham reached out and grabbed Claude's arm. "You gotta keep your head right."

Suddenly, gunfire rang out. "Get out of here!" Claude yelled above the din. Black men were not allowed to engage in combat. They were in service—cooks, trench diggers and maintainers, first aid workers. It had been a fluke that a rainstorm a few days before had brought Abraham into the same trench where Claude was assigned. Claude grabbed his weapon and got into position to return fire, while Abraham held back, angry as always that he could not fight alongside his friend. All around them shrapnel rained down, causing them to duck and cover before Claude jumped up to shoot back as fast as he could. The attack lasted more than an hour before the tanks rolled in. As quickly as it started, the gunfire stopped, and the enemy retreated into their trenches.

When Abraham looked up, Claude wasn't there. He looked around and spotted him about three feet away, lying on the ground, blood spreading across his chest. "Jesus Christ, Claude. Oh no, you don't." Abraham dropped to his knees and pressed his hands into Claude's shoulder, desperately trying to stem the flow of blood. "I need a medic!" he screamed. He ripped open Claude's shirt and then pulled off his own, pushing it into the wound and then pressing down with all his might. "Medic!" he screamed again.

Finally, a medic came and worked on Claude for a few minutes before a gurney arrived to take him away.

Abraham slid down the wall of the trench and just sat there in the muck staring straight ahead. None of the other soldiers said a word. No one ordered him to get back to work. They knew. They had all lost a buddy. And every night, when they lay down in their sleeping bags, they all, white and black alike, stared up at the starlit sky and prayed that they'd make it through another day.

It was a week before Abraham learned that Claude had lived. He was informed that his quick action had kept Claude from losing too much blood. Abraham was thankful that Claude was alive, but he was angry—angry that a good man like Claude had been shot and angry that he had been unable to do anything about it. For the first time in his life, Abraham began to understand his place in the world. Living by the river had not fully prepared him for what it meant to be white and what it meant to be black. He could shoot better than any man in the trench. At home, they called him Trigger because he could ready his gun faster than anyone, and he was deadly accurate. Abraham could kill a rabbit or a squirrel from a great distance, but here, when his friend had needed him, he had been unable to protect him. That thought weighed heavily on Abraham as he shoveled more muck from the trench.

"Anna-Marie, I'm not going to argue about this." Claude watched the storm clouds rolling into Anna-Marie's eyes. He knew this would be a fight, but he was determined. He had been home recuperating for a month, but it was time to go back. "I've made up my mind. I cannot in good conscience leave Abraham out there alone. What kind of man would I be?"

"A smart one," Anna-Marie said. "Do you really think Abraham would go back for you?"

"Yes, yes, I do. You weren't there. Abraham saved my life, and I can't leave him there on his own."

"You know my papa has pull. You don't have to go back. You've already been shot once. Do you really want to get shot again?"

"No, I don't. And I'm not going to lie. It's miserable there. But again, I'm going. I've already notified my superiors."

"But what about Claude Jr. and Charlie? Do you want them to grow up without a father? Charlie won't be a baby anymore by the time you get back."

"That's not fair. I want them to know their father had honor and a heart, that he loved his country and he was a good friend. That's what I want them to know. I'll come back, Anna-Marie. I promise."

"You can't make that promise. You can't even promise me that you'll be able to walk if you do come back. You don't know what's going to happen, but we all know what could happen. You can't even shoot with your right arm."

"I've been practicing with my left," Claude said. "I'm getting pretty good."

"Oh really? When?"

"At night after you're asleep. I've been shooting rabbits in the marsh for practice."

"You can't see at night," Anna-Marie argued.

"With a head light you can."

61

Anna-Marie was so mad she stomped her foot. "Well, if you go back, you deserve what you get." She burst out crying and ran into the bedroom, slamming the door behind her for good measure.

A week later, she sat on their bed and watched Claude pack his bags. Last time, she had packed them for him. This time, she refused. She had barely spoken to him during that week, but as she watched him pack, she realized that she might never see him again.

"I'm sorry for what I said," she ventured. "I didn't mean it. I'm just so scared, that's all."

Claude dropped the shirt he had been folding and sat beside her. "I know. I'm scared, too, but this is something I have to do." He reached out and pulled her into his arms. "I love you so much, woman. You have no idea. I used to stare up at the stars at night and see your face smiling at me. It's what kept me sane, kept me going. I promise I'll come back to you."

"You swear?"

"I swear."

A week later, Claude sloshed through a front-line trench in the south of France, passing soldier after soldier looking for Abraham. When he spotted him, he snuck up behind him and grabbed his shovel from his hand. Quick as lightning, Abraham knocked him to the ground.

"What the hell?" Abraham roared before realizing who it was that he was about to pummel. As recognition dawned, he pulled Claude up and hugged him tight. "Are you crazy, man? That's a good way to get yourself killed. What are you doing back here? You had a pass."

Claude slapped him on the back. "I couldn't leave you out here alone. I just couldn't do it."

"You are river rat crazy for sure. I would have left you here in a heartbeat."

"That's what Anna-Marie said right before she quit talking to me," Claude said, laughing.

"Ooh wee. I bet she was some mad."

"You have no idea, but she's okay now. She even kissed me good-bye."

"How's the shoulder?"

"Still bothersome, but I've been practicing shooting with my left hand, and I'm getting pretty good."

"Did you see Hester? How is she? The baby must be getting big."

"I brought you something." Claude reached into his pocket. "Anna-Marie had this made for you." He handed Abraham a photograph of Hester holding Isaac on the front porch of their home.

Abraham looked down at it for a long moment. He had tears in his eyes when he looked up and said, "Thank you, Claude. Thank you." Later, he carefully tucked the photograph into his sleeping bag.

Claude and Abraham would spend almost another year in France, dodging bullets and living in trenches, doing their best to protect each other above all else. Finally, guns fell silent on November 11, 1918, after Germany signed an armistice effectively ending the fighting, although World War I would not be officially over until the Treaty of Versailles was signed on June 28, 1919. Nine million soldiers on both sides of the conflict had lost their lives. For the first time in history, airplanes, tanks, machine guns, bombs, and flamethrowers had been used in warfare, culminating in a massive loss of life. It was the end of an era. The romanticism of previous decades was gone, and stark realism was left in its wake.

Although they had witnessed far too much bloodshed and had lost many friends in the trenches, Claude and Abraham returned to Louisiana with happy hearts, eager to see their wives and children. They had witnessed the worst of humanity, and they were more than ready to return to the good life on the river.

CHAPTER 10

April 1922

Claude looked up when he heard the tires squealing outside of the general store. He saw the cloud of dust first, and then he saw Abraham running toward the door.

"You keep driving like that, you're going to tear up that truck I sold you in no time," Claude said when Abraham entered.

"Get Anna-Marie and the children, and come with me," Abraham said, urgently. "Hurry. We've got to get to the boat."

"What are you talking about? I can't leave the store in the middle of the day." Claude looked at Abraham like he was crazy.

"We don't have time for this," Abraham said. "I heard that the levee at Poydras broke, but Albert said it broke at Caenarvon in St. Bernard Parish. He said his cousin saw it with his own eyes. Poydras, Caenarvon, it doesn't matter. The river is rising fast. Come on, Claude. We have to go."

Claude ran into the storeroom to get Anna-Marie and the children and then threw some provisions into a bag. "Let's go," he said.

Anna-Marie sat in the front seat with her two daughters, Madeleine and Jeanne, born after the war, and Claude, Claude Jr., and Charlie rode in the back of the truck with Florence and Emmanuel, Abraham's parents, whom Abraham had picked up on the way. Abraham drove as fast as he could toward Fucich Bayou, keeping an eye on the levee along the Mississippi River as he drove. He knew they would be okay as long as he didn't see water spilling over the top. He had brought Hester and Isaac to *The Pearl* as soon as Poopdeck had informed him of the breach, and then he had tied a pirogue to a tree on top of the levee at Fucich Bayou before he left to get his parents and Claude and his family.

"Be careful," Hester had warned him.

Abraham kissed her quickly, watching the water rising rapidly. "I will. I'll be back soon. I promise," he added when he saw the worry on his wife's face. Then he jumped into the Model T and sped away.

Now, he saw the same worry on Anna-Marie's face. "We'll be okay once we get on the boat," he reassured her.

"I know, but will we make it in time?" Anna-Marie said, watching the levee as intently as Abraham had.

"We'll make it," Abraham said, pressing down on the accelerator. "We have to. I can't let Hester go through this alone. Not after what happened in that hurricane." Suddenly, he slowed down. "Wait a minute. Where are Claude's parents? Do we need to get them?"

Anna-Marie shook her head. "No. They're up north visiting with kinfolk."

"And your parents?"

"They're in New Orleans."

Abraham sped up again. "Thank the Good Lord. I don't know that we would have had enough time."

By the time they reached Nestor, Fucich Bayou had already risen halfway up its small earthen levee. "How are we going to get to the boat?" Anna-Marie cried when Abraham slammed the truck into park on top of the levee.

Abraham didn't have time to answer. He jumped out of the truck and ran to untie the pirogue. "The landing is covered. We'll have to use the pirogue to get to the boat. Y'all stay here," he told his parents. "We'll get the children first."

Abraham and Claude pulled the pirogue to the bayou's edge and hurried back for the children. They ran down the levee, Claude carrying the two girls, and Abraham carrying the boys. They placed the children in the bottom of the pirogue, and then they climbed in, paddling furiously against the current of the swelling bayou. When they reached *The Pearl*, Abraham climbed onto the rope ladder that Hester had thrown over the side, and Claude handed him the children one at a time, girls first, then the boys. When the children were safe, Abraham got back into the pirogue and motioned for Claude to get out.

"I'll go with you," Claude said.

"No. That won't work." Abraham shook his head adamantly. "This pirogue can only hold four adults, and that's pushing it. Go on, now. I'll bring her to you." He didn't add that he wanted a man on board *The Pearl* with Hester in case something happened.

Claude reluctantly climbed up the rope ladder, and then he watched as Abraham paddled back to the levee.

By the time Abraham made it back to the truck, the bayou had climbed almost to the top of the levee. Abraham saw the fear in Anna-Marie's eyes and in his parents' eyes. He knew it must have been terrifying to watch the water rise inch-by-inch, foot-by-foot, toward them. He hurried them into the pirogue and began paddling again. A few minutes later, he and Claude helped his mother, then Anna-Maria, and then his father climb onto the rope ladder and into the boat. Abraham tied the pirogue to the ladder and climbed aboard.

"Thank you," Claude said. "We didn't even get a telegram about the breach. We had no idea the flood was coming."

Abraham smiled when Hester barreled into him, wrapping her arms around him like she would never let go. "It's okay. I'm here. We're going to be okay," he reassured her.

And they were. They, along with boats filled with neighbors riding out the flood, watched as the bayou washed over the levee. They couldn't see what was happening on the other side of the levee, but they knew. They all knew. It took several days for the water to retreat, and the bayous and the river once again filled with debris scooped from the homes of people. The 1922 flood garnered a 21.27-foot reading at New Orleans on April 25, the highest reading to date. Because of the levee breach, the East Bank of Plaquemines Parish was devastated. Politicians denied that the Poydras levee had been deliberately broken to save New Orleans, but no one down the river believed them. No one cared about them—their homes, their culture, their contributions to the rest of the state through the seafood industry and farming. New Orleans had to be protected at all costs, even at the cost of lives and livelihoods.

After the flood, the people of Plaquemines did what they always did. They surveyed the damage and set about cleaning and rebuilding with stoic determination. The river gave plenty and the river took plenty. That was understood—an accepted consequence for the privilege of living alongside the Mississippi River.

CHAPTER 11

July 1922

Jefferson Davenport was in a particularly good mood as he waited for his friends to arrive for a Sunday jazz brunch at Arnaud's restaurant on Bienville Street in the French Quarter. He ordered a coffee, black, although some folks might wonder why anyone would drink coffee on such a sweltering hot summer day. It was common in the French Quarter, where tourists filled Café Du Monde to sip on creamy café au lait twenty-four hours a day, no matter the heat. When his coffee arrived, Jefferson winked at the waiter and pulled a flask from his pocket, adding a healthy measure of whiskey. Although Prohibition had begun in 1920, it meant little in the French Quarter when there was money to be made under the table. Arnaud's was too upscale to risk its reputation by breaking the law; however, eyes were averted and backs were turned if, by happenstance, customers brought their own liquor. Most speakeasies and restaurant owners in the Quarter had created workarounds that meant business went on as usual, and if federal agents showed up to raid their establishments from time to time, that was simply the cost of doing business.

Pierre and Sal were late, as usual, but even that couldn't put a damper on Jefferson's spirits. Mother Nature had dealt him a winning hand, and he knew it was time to roll the dice. He had spent years studying the lay of the land, consulting with engineers, and generally plotting how he would get his hands on what he was confident was oil-rich land in Plaquemines Parish. Jefferson was an excellent planner, always had been.

As he waited for them, Jefferson sipped on his coffee and read a report about the oil field in Jennings, Louisiana, and how much it was producing. A few minutes later, he saw Pierre and Sal weaving their way toward him.

"Gentlemen." Smiling, Jefferson stood up and shook their hands.

"What are you so happy about?" Sal asked. He rarely saw Jefferson smile.

"Sit down, and we can discuss that," Jefferson said. He waited while the two men ordered drinks and Shrimp Arnaud—shrimp marinated in Remoulade sauce—and then he jumped right in. "We have had the greatest stroke of luck we could have been given. That flood was a gift, a blessing, really."

"How's that?" Pierre asked. "It may have escaped your attention, but the people down in Plaquemines Parish and St. Bernard got hit hard."

"Be that as it may, New Orleans was mostly spared, and gentlemen, we are in the business of ensuring that New Orleans doesn't go under," Jefferson reminded them. "And on that note, it's time to put our plan into action. The flood should help bolster our case if anything will."

"You believe that?" Sal asked.

"I do. We speak with engineers all the time. We know exactly how spillways function. Those folks at the Capitol in Baton Rouge probably don't know anything about how a spillway operates. Hell, half the members of the levee districts don't understand the ins and outs. And after the cost of this last flood, our representatives will be open to any cockamamie story we give them. All we have to do is convince them that this is in the best interest of New Orleans. I've already got people whispering in their ears, and there are a few senators I know who will vote our way. It's all about greasing pockets. We all know that, and I'll grease as many as I have to. The promise of oil revenue will take us where we need to go."

Pierre, although he had agreed to go along, still had reservations. His cousin, Antoine, was powerful. He certainly didn't want to upset that apple cart. "What about the people who live down there? What happens to them?"

"I already told you they'll be compensated. We'll buy the land from them at a fair market price," Jefferson explained patiently as their soup arrived.

"And if they don't want to sell?" Pierre asked.

Jefferson waited until the waiter left before he answered. "We'll cross that bridge when we come to it. You may want to keep in mind what happened with that well near Beaumont in 1900 or was it 1901? It was 1901, I believe, the salt dome up on Spindletop Hill. It had so much oil that it blew up when they first drilled into it, spread crude all over the place. Before long, they were pulling a hundred thousand barrels out of that salt dome every damn day. I don't need to translate that into dollars for you, do I? Use your imaginations. Now eat up, gentlemen. It's time for us to take a ride down the river. I want to show you what I'm talking about."

Two hours later, the three men arrived in Pointe á la Hache. "We'll have to hop on a boat from here. The flood washed away parts of the road farther down, and it's not drivable. Don't worry," Jefferson said, observing the concern on the faces of his friends. "We'll catch a packet boat near the ferry."

The men walked a short distance to the landing, and climbed aboard the packet boat. "Let us know when we get to where Bohemia Plantation is located," Jefferson instructed Captain Henry.

A short while later, the captain pointed to his left. "It should be right across the levee there. It's not a big plantation, but in its day, it produced a lot of sugarcane. Looks more like a cottage really. Big wraparound porch. Lots of latticework. Chimneys on either side anchor it, which is why it hasn't been blown away in a hurricane yet."

"Can you let us off here?" Jefferson asked. "You can pick us up in three hours in Nestor. I'll make it worth your while," he added, noting the look of aggravation that appeared on Captain Henry's face.

Jefferson, Sal, and Pierre climbed off the boat and began to walk through a rice field and then up the levee.

"This is where the spillway should begin," Jefferson said when they got to the top of the levee. He pointed across the road. "That's the plantation."

"Looks a little small," Sal observed.

"Not all plantations were mansions," Jefferson said. "There are a lot of smaller plantations down here, like Bethel and Martin just below Pointe á la Hache. I've spoken with our engineers, and this is the perfect spot. The spillway will extend south for eleven miles or so. Our plan includes turning this whole area into a natural spillway, which means tearing down some of these artificial levees. It won't be easy. When the river rises, the water will spread out into the marsh." Jefferson pointed toward the east. "Those back levees will have to come down to give the river the room to spread out. Some of these levees have been here for hundreds of years. The people down here have maintained them using whatever was at their disposal. Some are even filled with clam shells, like that road right there, if you can call it that."

The men began walking along the levee, discussing Jefferson's plans.

"It's hot," Sal complained after about fifteen minutes. "I wouldn't have worn a suit if I'd have known we were going hiking."

"Look, there's a store. We'll go down there and get something to drink, but let me do the talking." Jefferson walked down the levee. "I want to test the waters a bit."

Jefferson, Pierre, and Sal walked into the store, each dressed in a business suit, shiny shoes and stylish hats, and each wiping beads of sweat from their faces. They reeked of New Orleans.

The lady behind the counter looked at them and smiled. "Nobody told me the city was coming to town. I would have dressed up," Anna-Marie said.

Jefferson, struck by the woman's beauty, smiled his best smile, which was, in reality, only a small upward twist of his lips. "Good afternoon, ma'am. I'm Jefferson Davenport. Is the owner here?"

"Yes, she is." Anna-Marie watched the three men struggle to mask their surprise. "I'm Anna-Marie Bertaut Couvillion. How can I help you?"

"Anna-Marie," Pierre exclaimed. "Antoine's daughter? You've certainly grown up. You were but a teenager the last time I saw you."

"And who's fault is that?" Anna-Marie asked, recognizing her father's cousin. "I invited you to my wedding, but you didn't come. Papa said you can't be bothered much with the poor side of your family."

Pierre turned red and sputtered, "That's certainly not true. There's nothing poor about your father. As a matter of fact, we were going to visit him at the mill today."

"He's not there," Anna-Marie said. "He drove up to Baton Rouge today to talk with some senator friends about appropriating some money to the Grand Prairie Levee Board to build up our levees. The flood really did a lot of folks in."

"You don't say," Jefferson piped in. "Your papa has a lot of friends over there?"

"Oh, yes. They always come to his parties." Anna-Marie directed her statement to Pierre, who shifted uncomfortably.

"Where's your husband?" Jefferson asked. "May we speak with him?"

"Of course. I'll go get him." Anna-Marie hurried into the storeroom to get Claude, warning him about their visitors. "There's something about them I don't like. One is my second cousin, and I definitely don't like him. Papa says he's a big city, highfalutin' politician with no regard for family, but see what you think."

Claude laughed, enjoying the way his wife didn't mince words. "I'll let you know what I think," he said, as they walked into the store.

"You must be the owner?" Jefferson reached out to shake Claude's hand.

"When she allows it." Claude nodded toward where Anna-Marie was standing.

"Yes, she's quite a young lady," Jefferson observed.

"Yes, she is," Claude said. "When she's not running this place, she's helping folks clean out their homes or bringing them groceries or fixing them up with something or the other."

"This is Pierre, my cousin," Anna-Marie said.

"I've heard a lot about you." Claude ignored the giggle that escaped Anna-Marie. He shook Pierre's hand before turning to Sal. "And you are?"

"Sal Ragliosi," Sal said, shaking his hand.

"And what brings you folks to Union Settlement today?" Claude asked. "It's not often that suits from the city drop by."

"We're on a fact-finding mission," Jefferson said. "Studying the damage from the flood. Trying to see how we can make life better down here."

"Oh, you're with the Corps of Engineers?" Claude prompted.

"Something like that," Jefferson said.

"I thought Papa said you were on the Orleans Levee Board," Anna-Marie said to Pierre.

Jefferson shot Pierre a warning look.

"I was. I am," Pierre said.

"And you gentlemen? Are you on the board, as well?" Claude asked.

Jefferson nodded.

"We heard tell that the levee at Poydras was deliberately broken when the river started rising." Claude said. "Is that true?"

Jefferson was caught off guard. He cleared his throat. "You know how rumors fly around, son. Every time there's a hurricane or a flood down here, we get blamed for it. We're in the business of building levees, not breaking them."

"I see. Well, how can we help you gentlemen?"

"We'd like some information if you can sit with us for a minute."

Claude led the men outside to a picnic table. "How can I help you?" he asked again, once they were seated.

"How high was the water here?" Jefferson asked.

"High," Claude said. "Some homes and businesses had upwards of five feet. Down the river, it could have been higher."

"Your father-in-law, did he get a lot of damage at the mill?" Pierre asked.

"Yes. Nestor was hit as hard as anywhere. We're usually prepared, but this time, there wasn't much warning. We knew the river was going to rise, but we had no idea how high it would get. There was no telegram. Nothing. If it weren't for Poopdeck, we would of drowned. He heard about the levee breach and warned us."

"Poopdeck?" Jefferson asked, and then shook his head. "Never mind. That was a rumor, son, like I told you."

Claude stared at him and waited. He sensed that all of this was building toward something.

"You spend time in Nestor?" Jefferson asked.

"Of course. It's just down the road a ways," Claude said.

Jefferson leaned forward and looked at Claude earnestly. "You ever see that salt dome down there?"

"Yes sir. Can't help but see it. Comes right out of the river," Claude said.

"Ever see strange folks, out-of-towners, surveying it?" Jefferson continued.

Claude shook his head. "Why would they?"

"No reason. Just heard some talk and got curious." Jefferson realized it was time to change the subject. "No one in your family was harmed in the flood, were they?" he asked, feigning concern.

"No. A friend got us to safety. Most folks rode it out on boats like they always do."

"Good to hear that." Jefferson stood up. "We don't want to take up too much of your time, and it's god-awful hot out here, so we'll be on our way. Bid your wife a good day."

Claude stood up and shook hands with the men, then watched them walk down the road toward Nestor.

"City folks," he murmured aloud. "Sure don't know how to dress for a Louisiana summer. By the time they get to Nestor, folks will think they got sprayed by a skunk."

CHAPTER 12

Claude was still standing there a moment later when Abraham and Hester rode up on their horses.

Abraham helped Hester and Isaac down and then grabbed a sack he had tied to his saddle.

"Good heavens, this boy is getting bigger every day," Claude said when Isaac ran up to him. Claude picked him up and swung him around. "You're almost too big to pick up anymore." He turned to Hester. "What do you feed this child?"

Hester laughed. "It's hard to believe how little he used to be. I swear he grows an inch every month. He's going to be a giant, just like his daddy."

Abraham handed Claude a sack of shrimp he had boiled that morning. "I know Anna-Marie said she was frying up some trout, but I thought I'd bring these along. Did you see those men in suits walking toward Nestor?"

"Oh, yes. I saw them. Come on in, but be warned, Anna-Marie is probably in a tizzy." Claude followed Abraham and Hester into the store.

Claude was right. Anna-Marie was waiting for him. "What did they want?" she asked. "Why wouldn't they talk in front of me? I didn't like them. Not one of them. Did you notice that Jefferson Davenport's eyes? I've never seen such cold eyes. And the way his thin lips stretched across his face, like he's not capable of a real smile. And what was my cousin doing with those men? They are obviously in cahoots with each other. What did they want from you? What did you talk about? Hi, Abraham. Hi, Hester. Isaac, the children are in the back. You can go play with them."

Claude, Abraham, and Hester burst out laughing.

"You did warn us," Hester said. "He said you'd be in a tizzy."

"Well, I have a right to be. My papa's cousin comes in here like he owns the place, doesn't even have the decency to inquire after my health, and doesn't apologize for missing my wedding. They wanted something, that's for sure. What did they want, Claude?"

"I'm not sure. They were looking at the levee, almost measuring it with their eyes. I'm sure about that. They seemed interested in Nestor, in that salt dome. They asked if I had seen it. Strangest thing. Why ask about that? That salt dome was there long before our ancestors got here. It takes thousands of years for one that big to grow."

"What would they want with salt?" Abraham asked.

"I don't know, but I don't like it," Claude said. "Whenever city folks dressed in suits come calling, it's never good. They're up to something."

"And I want to know what it is," Anna-Marie said. "When Papa gets back, I'm going to talk with him. If anybody can find out, he can."

"That's a good idea," Claude said. "You should visit him tomorrow. See what he knows."

"Well, now, who is this?" Anna-Marie said, looking out the window as another man in a suit walked up. "What in the world is going on?"

Claude and Abraham turned at the same time. Abraham let out a snort. "That's the judge," he said, as Leonus Lozano walked into the store. "I saw his picture in the newspaper."

"Twice in one day," Claude muttered. "Something's definitely afoot."

"Can we help you?" Anna-Marie eyed the newcomer up and down, not at all impressed with his powder-blue suit and his big white hat. He looks like a giant ball of cotton candy, she thought.

"Howdy, folks," Leonus said. "I'm Judge Lozano, Leonus Lozano, but you can call me Judge. That's what everyone calls me." He shook hands with Claude but ignored Abraham.

Anna-Marie bristled, and Claude's back stiffened.

"I'd like to talk to these folks alone," the judge said dismissively to Abraham and Hester.

"That won't happen," Claude said. "Anything you have to say to me will be said with my friends standing right here, or you can be on your way."

"We can leave," Abraham said, not wanting to interrupt any business Claude may have.

"No. You most certainly will not leave," Anna-Marie said. "I invited you for dinner, and you're staying."

Leonus stood there for a moment, deciding. "My apologies," he said.

"Didn't mean to offend you good folks. Listen here, I just stopped in to introduce myself and see if you've had any strange visitors lately. Anybody from New Orleans nosing around?"

"We have people in and out all day long," Claude said. "Anyone in particular of interest?"

"This would be three businessmen. They'd stand out. One's tall with a pointed nose. The other is shorter, Italian, with a big belly, and the third is French, rather homely-looking man, related to those Bertauts in Nestor."

"Oh, you mean my cousin, Pierre?" Anna-Marie said. "I'm Anna-Marie Bertaut Couvillion."

Leonus tried to cover his faux pas by lighting his cigar and blowing a cloud of smoke toward Abraham. "Good to meet you, Miss. You must be Antoine's daughter. Good man, your father. Brings a lot of jobs to Plaquemines Parish. Yes, that would be the fellers I'm talking about. Have you seen them?"

"We have," Abraham said. "Saw them walking up the road a while ago. Looked like they was in a hurry, like they had to be somewhere important. Went that way," he added, pointing back toward Pointe á la Hache.

Anna-Marie hid a smile. "If you hurry, you might catch them," she added.

"That way, you say," Leonus said. "Funny I didn't see them on my way in."

"It's been a while. They probably already made it to Pointe á la Hache," Claude said. "Or maybe they hopped a packet boat. I don't know."

The judge nodded. "I best be on my way then. Good day."

"So that was Judge Lozano," Anna-Marie said when he was gone. "Papa says he's a crook."

"He looks like a crook," Hester agreed.

"Judge or not, crook or not, next time he disrespects you, I'm going to show him what this man is made of," Claude said.

"I'd be careful with that one," Abraham said. "He don't like blacks. I could see he didn't like you defending us like that. You can always see it in their eyes. Like that Mildred."

"Mildred don't come around here much anymore," Anna-Marie said. "Her husband taught her to drive, so she's doing her shopping in Nestor or Point á la Hache. I can't imagine what she's doing now that the road is out."

"That don't bother me none," Claude said. "It's nice not having her listening to every conversation we have. Remember Anna-Marie? She was in here that day you told me I was going to marry you. The whole town knew before you even had a chance to tell your papa."

"That was the luckiest day of your life, Claude Couvillion, and you know it," Anna-Marie said.

Claude grinned at her. "And yours." He placed his arm around her shoulder and drew her near.

"When you two are finished, maybe we can get back to the issue at hand," Abraham said. "Who were those men that were here, and why did the judge show up looking for them? It seemed like he wanted to know what they were doing. Something is up. You agree?"

"Yes, indeed." Claude jumped out of the way as Charlie chased Isaac behind the counter. "You boys go outside if you're going to run all over the place. Go out in the front and pick all the ripe pears you see. Tell Claude Jr. to bring a ladder to the tree. And be careful."

When the boys were gone, Hester said, "I feel a bad wind coming. Something about this doesn't sit right. Maybe we should talk to Sanon. He has a way of knowing things that others don't."

Abraham nodded his head. "We should go see him tomorrow after church."

Claude agreed. "Between Antoine and Sanon, maybe we'll be able to figure it out."

"You don't think they want to mine salt?" Hester asked.

"No. That would have happened years ago," Claude said. "Something else is going on. Those city slickers are up to something, and the judge wants to know what it is. That much is clear. We just have to figure out what they're up to."

"We will, but for now, I've got to fry some trout," Anna-Marie said. "I've been dying to try that new Crisco shortening everyone's talking about. Y'all will have to let me know what you think about it. Miss Penny swears by it and asked me to buy some to sell in the store. I wanted to try it for myself first."

Hester gathered the children and sat them at the picnic table. Claude spread newspapers over it, and poured the river shrimp Abraham had brought on top. "Y'all peel this shrimp while we get the fish ready. And don't eat it all before we get back. Separate those potatoes and corn and sausage. And don't eat all the garlic. Save some for us." Claude grabbed a head of garlic and squeezed a clove into his mouth.

"Man, that's good," he told Abraham. "Seasoned perfectly. Spicy but doesn't burn."

"That's Hester," Abraham said. "She has all these secret herbs and spices she puts in everything. I'm afraid to ask what they are. She gets them from Sanon."

"Whatever they are, your shrimp boils are always so much better than mine."

"You can ask her, but I don't think she'll tell you her secret."

"By the way, are you still having those nightmares?" Claude asked.

"Are you still trapping muskrats?" Abraham responded.

Claude grinned. "Touché."

"Why don't you and the boys come with us tomorrow? We'll go by boat. We can visit Sanon and get some crabs while we're down there. Crabs are usually plentiful near Ostrica if the Takos haven't gotten to them first. I'll bring the hoop nets, and we can leave right after church."

"I'm sure Anna-Marie won't mind. She's been telling me to take some time off. Let's go ask her," Claude said. "It'll be good for the boys."

The next afternoon, Claude met Abraham at the landing at Fucich Bayou and helped him load the boat with food and supplies for the trip. Abraham's boat, thirty-feet long and made of cypress that had been carefully carved and bent, had been built by his father around 1900. Emmanuel had named her *The Pearl*. "This sure is a fine boat." Claude watched Abraham raise the lugsail that adorned the front of the boat.

"My mama sewed that," Abraham said proudly. "I don't know how many cypress trees my daddy had to pull from the river, but with that big deck aft, it holds as many oysters as I can pull from a bed. It's not as big as the luggers, but daddy did that on purpose so that we could easily navigate in and out of the bayous." Abraham pointed to the built-in storage containers. "Those hatch covers on the cockpit keep the oysters fresh. *The Pearl* also doubles as a trawler. Those are otter trawls. They're new. Heard about them from a boat captain who spends his off-time shrimping. He sold them to me dirt cheap." Abraham pointed to the nets suspended in mid-air along the sides of the boat. "You should come out shrimping with me sometime."

"I'd like that," Claude said. "Most of the shrimp we get comes from the shrimp boxes I had the boys hang from some willow trees on the bank of the river near the house. Those are always small, but they're sweet."

"Yes, they are," Abraham said. "But the ones I catch are much larger. They like the bays and bayous because the water there is brackish. Albert usually helps me because operating this boat is a two-man job."

"Why don't you call him Poopdeck like everyone else?" Claude asked.

"Seems disrespectful. I ain't got nothing against nicknames, mind you. Hell, mine's Trigger, but that one just seems wrong."

"Never thought about it like that," Claude said. "I don't know the given names for half the fishermen that come in the store."

"Yeah, the river has a way of spawning names for folks." Abraham steered the boat away from the dock.

"How long will it take to get there?" Claude asked.

Abraham let out a snort. "You've lived here all your life, and you don't know how long it takes to get to Ostrica by water?"

"I've lived in that store all my life," Claude retorted. "Don't get out on the water much. You know that."

"We need to fix that. Does a man good to be on the water. Heals the soul. The bayous are easy, but you have to understand the river to navigate her. She has moods, just like a woman. She demands respect. She puts obstacles in your way. That's why those big ship captains can't navigate her. Those sand bars at the mouth of the river require skill, but I sure wouldn't want to be one of those bar pilots. They have to jump on and off of those ships in any kind of weather, no matter how bad, just to maneuver ships over the sand bars. In South Pass, it used to be really bad when the river was only eighteen feet deep. Then there's the mud lumps."

"Mud lumps?" Claude repeated.

"Yeah, they spring up out of nowhere. The Indians were afraid of them. It's lumps of mud and clay that rise up from the bottom of the river, sometimes overnight. They have funnel-like tops that spew mud and water out like a geyser. One minute you're riding along and nothing is in front of you, and the next minute, a huge mud lump could be blocking your path. They don't happen often, but when they do, it's something to see."

79

"I've heard about that, but I've never seen one," Claude said.

"Have you ever seen the swamp balls?" Abraham asked. "Those are really something. I read that a lot of Indian tribes stayed out of South Louisiana because of the mud lumps and swamp balls. I've heard only one tribe settled here, not because they were braver than the others, but because they were poor and could eat well off the river."

"I've never seen a swamp ball."

"I have," Abraham said. "A big ball of fire shooting across the marsh at lightening speed. Those come out of nowhere, too. That's why the Indians thought evil spirits were inhabiting the underground here."

"What are they?" Claude asked.

"I don't know. Some kind of gas or something bubbling to the surface and then igniting and taking off till they burn out. Hester says they are God's way of reminding us that hell is real. Like hell rises to the surface and a small piece tries to escape."

"Hester has a colorful way of looking at things, doesn't she?"

"She sure does, but I've learned not to doubt her. Too many times, she's been right in what she thinks. Like yesterday, when she felt a dark wind. That's worrisome. Ever since Sanon saved her life, she's had these feelings, and they always come true. Something evil is coming. I hope Sanon can shed some light."

"Me, too," Claude said.

As they made their way through the bayous, Claude began to see the landscape through Abraham's eyes.

"Nicholls is over that way." Abraham pointed to his left. "You can't see it from here. Did you know that Dime got its name because its founders decided that a dime was better than a nickel? For a long time, Nicholls had the only post office around this area of the river, so Dime had to get a post office, too. The folks in Dime are always trying to keep up or be better for some reason."

"No. I didn't know that," Claude said. "But it sounds about right."

Abraham pointed again. "When the river's low, ponds form over that a way between the levee and the river. That's where fish go to spawn. You have to be careful when you swim or fish along the batture, though, because there could be drop off of fifteen or twenty feet out of nowhere."

While Isaac, Claude Jr., and Charlie chased each other around the boat, snapping at each other with metal oyster tongs, Abraham educated Claude about each village, each new bayou or bay they entered, each bird that flew overhead. "Life on the water has a way of getting under your skin," Abraham said, sounding the horn as another oyster lugger passed nearby. *The Pearl* rocked in its wake, and the men laughed when the boys lost their footing and tumbled across the deck.

"When you see another boat, hold on to something," Hester yelled at them.

"They'd be holding on all day," Abraham said.

A little while later, Abraham said they were near Point Pleasant and Daisy, and then Quarantine Island. "That's where they used to send seamen who had yellow fever," Abraham said. "A lot of good men died on that island. No one around here will go near that place. They say diseases still live there."

Finally, Abraham steered *The Pearl* into Cuselich Canal and informed Claude they were almost there. "Peter Cuselich founded this town back in the late 1800s. His family owns the grocery store, which is connected by a wooden plank to the Big House, what folks around here call it, where they live. Cuselich Canal was built specifically so that oyster boats could traverse it."

"Is there anything you don't know about the people down here?" Claude asked.

"Not much," Abraham said, grinning. "Ostrica means oyster. I bet you didn't know that. Mostly Austrians settled down here. Not sure why folks call them Takos, but they don't seem to mind. Came in by boat to New Orleans like everyone else and scattered down the river, then settled here. Did well for themselves, as you'll see, but they're territorial. And they don't like Mulattos, mostly because of their religious practices. They call it voodoo. The Mulatto camp is just outside of town, but the Mulattos rarely go into Ostrica. They get their food from the river and their gardens, or they go to Point Pleasant if they need something. They don't need doctors because they have their own remedy man."

"That's sad in this day and age," Claude said. "I don't know why some folks are like that."

"They're afraid of what they don't understand," Hester, who had been sitting quietly, listening to their conversation, said. "Lucky for us, it's the only place on this side of the river that's like that."

"Won't be for long," Abraham said. "Not if that judge who came in the store yesterday has anything to do with it. Did you see the way he looked at us?"

"I saw," Claude said, "and I was mighty offended. I thought Anna-Marie was going to bite his head off."

Abraham and Hester laughed. "He'll learn soon enough not to rile her up," Abraham said. "Pardon me for saying it, but that woman has no idea how to hold her tongue."

"You don't say," Claude said, laughing.

A few minutes later, Abraham had maneuvered his way through Cuselich Canal and had docked the boat. "The camp is that way," Abraham said, pointing north.

CHAPTER 13

"What a surprise," Antoine said in French, when he opened the door of the three-story antebellum home where Anna-Marie had grown up. "You look wonderful."

"Hi, Papa. I brought the girls to see you."

"Madeleine. Jeanne. Give your grandpére a hug." Antoine stooped down and held his arms open wide. "You girls are prettier than ever."

"Is *Maman* here?" Anna-Marie asked.

"No. You know your *maman*. She's gallivanting in New Orleans with her sister as usual. Been there for a week. Come in. Come in. Let's go sit on the back porch. I'll have Frita fetch us some iced tea. It's hotter than a bull in heat out there."

"Is *Maman* still mad? It's been years. I thought she'd be over it by now." Anna-Marie sat in a rocking chair her grandfather had built for her grandmother decades before.

"You know your *maman*. She'll come around."

"When?"

"That I don't know. Sooner rather than later, I think. Especially now that the girls are getting bigger. You know she won't be able to resist dressing them up and teaching them manners. I know she'll be happy when I tell her how well you're looking. Still as pretty as ever, child. How are things with the storekeeper?"

"Oh, Papa. His name is Claude. When are you going to call him by his given name?"

"When I get over being mad at him for stealing you from me. You know you could have done so much better. That rich gentlemen in New Orleans. You'd have been the rage of society there."

Anna-Marie laughed. "I'm the rage of society on the river in more ways than one."

"I bet," her papa agreed. "Now what brings you here on a Sunday afternoon without advance notice? You're lucky you caught me. I was supposed to play golf with the governor this afternoon, but he canceled at the last minute. He's been busy ever since the flood."

"I did want to talk to you about something. There are some strange things going on." Anna-Marie told him about the three men who had visited the store.

"And Pierre was with them, you say? Without telling me he was coming down? That doesn't bode well. What did they want?"

Anna-Marie explained that they had asked about Nestor and the salt dome in the river.

"Why in the world would they be interested in the salt dome? That sounds fishy to me."

"I don't know, but a few minutes later Judge Lozano showed up. He's never come to the store before, and he was asking about those men."

"That means something's definitely up. The judge has been trying to get land redistricted all along the West Bank lately. Rumor has it that he's going to run for district attorney after this term. I don't like that man. Not at all. He's dangerous. Got a lot of friends in high places. I don't get it. He's as sneaky as a snake, and always puffing on that god-awful cigar. Can't even smoke a cigarette like a man of class. He was asking about Pierre and the others?"

"Yes. He wanted to know what they were doing at the store. After he insulted Abraham and Hester, of course."

"Oh, it's no secret. He don't like people of color. He's going to be trouble for them. Of that, I'm sure."

"Not in my store, he's not. Claude put him in his place."

"Good. At least the storekeeper has spunk."

"Papa," Anna-Marie exclaimed. "Really?"

Antoine smiled and patted her knee. "I still can't fathom why they'd be asking about that salt dome."

"Madeleine, get back here now," Anna-Marie yelled, watching her daughter running too far out and getting close to the marsh.

"She's fine." Antoine said. "You used to do that all the time. I can't count the times you came home soaking wet."

"Exactly," Anna-Marie said.

"I'm heading into the city soon. I'll ask around. See what I can find out. If that doesn't work, I'll talk to Pierre myself, not that he wouldn't lie to me. You can pick your friends, but you sure can't pick your family."

"Thanks, Papa. I thought it was too coincidental that they all showed up in one day."

"Yes, child. You were smart to let me know."

Antoine and Anna-Marie spent the next hour playing with her girls. Anna-Marie enjoyed watching her papa giving them piggyback rides across the back yard. Finally, she stood up. "I hate to say it, Papa, but we have to go. I left Spit at the store, and I can't leave him there too long by himself. He's probably been sipping on his flask all day."

"That's what happens when you marry low," Antoine said, and then he laughed when Anna-Marie turned away in a huff and gathered the children.

"One more comment like that, Papa, and you'll see me about as much as you see my *maman*," she said, before storming through the house, children in tow.

"My apologies," Antoine called after her, still laughing. "You know how I love to get your goat."

"Let's sit here," Sanon said when he saw Claude, gesturing toward a long table on his front porch. He knew better than to ask a white man to enter his home, although he had seen Claude's wife inside of Abraham's home. "Hester, my dear. How are you? And Isaac? Is he well? Yes, I can see that he is." Isaac hugged the man whom he had come to know as his godfather.

"We are all well," Hester said. "Thank you. How are you, Sanon? Are you well?

"I am." Sanon said. "I have good health. Then what brings you so far down the river? Do you need some more of my herbs?"

Hester's face clouded for a moment.

"Yes," Abraham said. "Please, but you must let us pay you this time."

"Nonsense." Sanon walked to a table that was filled with herbs of every kind in labeled containers. He scooped a handful out of a blue container and placed them in a bowl. He looked at the labels on several more bottles before he found the right one, then he added some of its contents to the herbs. He murmured something indistinguishable as he crushed the mixture, breaking the stems into minuscule pieces.

Claude observed this with interest. "What is that for?" he asked.

Abraham shook his head, warning him to be silent, before looking at Hester, whose eyes were spitting fire at him. She had been upset ever since Abraham had first asked Sanon to make the potion. Hester desperately wanted more children, but there was no way Abraham was going to let that happen. He had come too close to losing her once. He wouldn't risk it again. He had asked Sanon years before if he could make a potion to keep Hester from getting pregnant. Sanon had honored his request, understanding why Abraham was so concerned. At first, Hester had taken it without balking. She knew then that it was much too soon to try again after what had happened with Isaac. But as time went on, she began to want more children, and she had objected each time Sanon made a new batch.

"You were unconscious, child," Sanon told her once. "You don't remember what it was like. Abraham saw the blood. He counted your breaths. He was scared to death. You can't expect him to go through that again."

"Can I have children?" Hester had asked.

"I don't know. The way I cut you, I don't know what will happen. I can't promise that you or the baby would come through it."

Still, Hester wanted to try, but Abraham adamantly refused. It was the only point of contention in their marriage. "I can't lose you," Abraham said every time the subject came up.

"You won't," Hester argued.

"You don't know that. I'm not willing to take that risk. We have Isaac. He is enough."

The argument would usually end with Hester crying and then not speaking to him for a day or two, but Abraham felt like that was a small price to pay to keep her by his side.

Sanon handed Abraham the potion and sat down. "That's not all that is required of this visit," he said.

"No," Abraham said. "There's more."

Hester told Sanon about the men who had come from New Orleans and then about the judge. "I had such a feeling of foreboding while they were there. Like a darkness all around me," she explained.

"Come here." Sanon said, gesturing for Hester to stand in front of him. He took both of her hands in his. He closed his eyes for a few moments and then looked up at her. "You are right to be worried, child. Trouble is coming. The kind of trouble that will change everything for all of us."

"What kind of trouble?" Abraham asked.

"The kind you don't come back from," Sanon said. "It comes from forces beyond our control. Powerful forces we can't fight."

"We're strong," Abraham said. "We can fight anything."

"Not this. The most we can do is make the best of it."

"What does that mean?" Claude interrupted.

"It means, son, that life has a way of changing the order of things when we least expect it. Forces beyond our control are destined to exert their will, and we are powerless to fight them."

"When will the trouble come?" Abraham asked.

"Soon. The wheels are already in motion."

"Is there nothing we can do?" Hester asked.

"No, child. There is nothing."

After thanking him, they made their way back to the boat with a hot, southerly wind whipping around them.

"Did you understand any of that?" Claude asked Hester.

"Not really. No, but I know it wasn't good. I still have no idea what's going to happen, but something is. I'd stake my life on that. Sanon is never wrong about these things."

"We'd better hurry," Abraham said, pointing to the sky. "Looks like a storm is coming in from the Gulf. I don't think we're going to get any crabs today. If we hurry, we can sail the wind and beat it."

Abraham scooped Isaac up and set a fast pace for the boat. In no time, they were back on the canal, traveling with the wind as quickly as they could to Nestor. By the time they docked, the afternoon thunderstorm had caught up with them, and they rode it out in the cabin. When it was over, Claude said, "I best be getting home. Anna-Marie went to visit her papa today, and I'm eager to hear what he said. Come by the store tomorrow, and I'll fill you in."

"Papa doesn't know anything," Anna-Marie told Claude later. "But he's going to find out. He's going to New Orleans tomorrow to nose around."

"Sanon predicted trouble, the kind you don't come back from," Claude said, "but he couldn't be specific. He said we won't be able to fight it. Something about it being destined and out of our control."

"That sounds sinister," Anna-Marie said.

"It did. I could almost feel that bad feeling Hester was talking about. Whatever it is, somehow we need to find out and prepare. He said the wheels are already in motion."

"How do we do that if we don't even know what it is?" Anna-Marie said, moving closer to Claude. He wrapped her in a hug.

"I don't know," he said. "Maybe your papa will find out something tomorrow. Until then, let's not worry. What will be will be, *ma chérie.*"

Claude and Anna-Marie spent the rest of the evening worrying.

CHAPTER 14

January 1923

Antoine Bertaut strode into the building that housed the Orleans Levee District like he owned the place. He didn't have an appointment, but he didn't care. He was there to see his cousin. He had spent the past months making subtle inquiries among his friends at the Capitol, and today he was here to verify what he had heard. If what they said was true, his cousin was aiming to take away his livelihood, a livelihood that had proved profitable year after year and afforded jobs to many in lower Plaquemines Parish. He located Pierre's office and walked in without knocking.

"What the ...?" Pierre said when he saw his cousin.

"You know why I'm here," Antoine said.

"No, I don't," Pierre said, motioning for Antoine to sit.

"I'll stand." Antoine reverted to their native French. "What's this I hear about a spillway in Nestor?"

Pierre couldn't control the rise of color that suddenly stained his cheeks. "A spillway?" he repeated.

"Yes, a spillway. Running right through my property."

"I don't know nothing about no spillway." Pierre shuffled some papers on his desk.

"Of course, you don't. Why would you know, being on the levee board and all? And what good's a spillway down there going to do for New Orleans? It's fifty miles from Algiers Point across from the Quarter to Nestor, much too far to be of any significant help to New Orleans. It's the craziest thing I've ever heard," Antoine said, his voice rising.

"Antoine, sit down. Calm down," Pierre said. "You're overwrought."

"I have cause to be. Word is that the levee board has been lobbying for a spillway to start at Bohemia and run down through Nestor. What do you know about that, cousin?"

"You should be talking to the Grand Prairie Levee Board if that's what you heard. Plaquemines is not in our jurisdiction. Grand Prairie oversees the levees down there. If they're planning a spillway, it has nothing to do with me."

"That's bullshit, and you know it," Antoine said. "You can go anywhere you want and do anything you want. Now tell me, is what I've heard true?"

"I don't know, but I can make some inquiries if you'd like," Pierre said.

Antoine snorted. "Inquiries? You'll make some inquiries? That tells me everything I need to know." Antoine stared at him for a long moment, watching Pierre as he shifted uncomfortably in his seat. "Your papa will hear about this and the rest of the family. So much for blood being thicker than water."

"Antoine, wait," Pierre said, as Antoine headed for the door.

"What?" Antoine said. "What do you have to say?"

Pierre sat there for a moment, silent. Finally, he took a deep breath. "You'll be paid fair market value."

"Like that makes a difference. And when were you going to tell me? What about my daughter? You know she owns that store in Union Settlement. When were we going to find out? When they come to kick us out?"

"It won't be like that," Pierre said. "We don't know yet if the Legislature will approve the spillway. You're being premature. This may not happen."

"Oh, it'll happen. After the last flood, you'll have carte blanche. The state will do anything to keep from having to pay for flood damage, but it doesn't make sense. Why Plaquemines Parish? Why not nearer to the lake or upriver? That would make sense."

Pierre explained how that area could easily give the river an outlet to keep it from rising so high and flooding New Orleans. "It's simple math," he said.

"More like hocus pocus," Antoine retorted. "Something else is up. What is it?"

"Look, I shouldn't have said as much as I have. You're my family, so I'm letting you know that it's a possibility but no more than that."

"Family," Antoine repeated. "You don't know what that word means."

Antoine took his leave, slamming the heavy wooden door behind him, and then walked down the hallway, listening to the sound of it echoing through the building.

Antoine walked to his car feeling defeated for the first time in his life. He knew all too well that there could be no fighting the levee board on this particular issue. The Louisiana Legislature was hurricane- and flood-weary. His friends up there would buy into anything at this point. But why the lower East Bank? There had to be a reason. He knew that a spillway down there would do nothing for New Orleans. It was too far south of the city. There had to be something else, a motive known only to his cousin and his cronies. He had to find out what it was. Only then would he be in a position to stop it. Until then, he knew he had to start making plans, and he had to let Anna-Marie know. This would affect her, as well.

Antoine took his time on the drive back down the East Bank. He had driven that same road so many times, but this time was different. He took note of everything—the grand oak trees laden with moss, the cypress trees tall and strong with cypress knees sprouting up around them, the birds flying with abandon from tree to tree, the wooden shacks interrupted only occasionally by a plantation home built on mounds, most surrounded with wide verandas across the front facing the river. He drove past bayous and canals and bays—some manmade, some carved out by the Mississippi River. Fruit orchards spread across the landscape to his left with the marsh ever present in the background. He could hear the crack of bullwhips on the other side of the levee to his right as farm hands tried to stave off the ricebirds that attacked their crops.

At Pointe á la Hache, the courthouse, the seat of parish government that doubled as a source of refuge during hurricanes, rose up against a sapphire blue sky. Antoine turned into the parking lot. It was here, he knew, that hope could be found.

"Where's the judge?" he asked the receptionist at the front desk.

"Court is in session," the receptionist informed him.

Antoine picked up a notepad and began writing, "I need to see you now," and he signed his name. "Get this to the judge," he said, handing the note to the receptionist, and then "Quickly," when she sat there staring at it undecided. She didn't want to anger the judge. Everyone was leery of his quick temper, and she had experienced it more than once. "Now." Antoine barked, making her jump to her feet.

While he waited, Antoine paced back and forth in the lobby. A few minutes later, she came back. "The judge will see you in his office," she said. She led Antoine up some stairs and down a hallway, and then opened a door. "He'll be here in a few minutes."

Antoine sat down and waited, noticing a law degree from Tulane and another degree from Louisiana State University hanging on the wall behind the judge's desk. A picture of Leonus' wife, Amelia, sat on a side table under a long window, and numerous newspaper articles about the judge were thumbtacked to a corkboard on the other side of the room. Antoine rolled his eyes. But as much as he held Leonus in disdain, he recognized that Leonus was becoming a force with whom to be reckoned. He also knew he had good friends on the Grand Prairie Levee Board.

Ten minutes later, the judge entered the room, shrugged out of his robe, hung it on a peg behind the door, and seated himself behind his desk.

"I do not appreciate you yanking me out of court in this manner," he said, reaching inside his desk drawer for a cigar. "This had better be important. I've got criminals in there who require swift justice."

"It is," Antoine said. "I just verified through my own cousin, who is on the Board of Commissioners of the Orleans Parish Levee Board, that they are planning to build a spillway down in Bohemia. I thought that might be of interest to you."

"A spillway? Why on God's green earth would they want to do that?" Leonus said, his face expressionless.

"I don't know. It doesn't make sense. That's why I wanted to talk to you."

"How am I supposed to know? Those boys up there look at us as second-class citizens. They don't share their plans with me."

Antoine stared at Leonus. He noticed there had been no surprise in his reaction, that his eyes had barely twitched when he shared the news. He already knows, Antoine thought. He's plotting something of his own.

"I thought you knew everything that went on around here," Antoine said. Everyone knew that the judge had spies everywhere.

"Oh, I do," Leonus assured him. "But the levee board, that's a little different. Them boys don't like me at all. Nobody in New Orleans shares

any news with me. Apparently, I'm not up to snuff with them city folks."
He stubbed out his cigar and stood up. "Is that all?"

Antoine stood up. "Apparently so," he said, watching the judge don his robe.

"Don't make the mistake of pulling me out of court again," Leonus said as he walked out the door.

Antoine saw himself out and got back into his car.

The judge is in this thing up to his neck, he thought. Leonus doesn't do anything that isn't to his benefit. Why wouldn't he be raising the roof about this? There's a piece missing. Something I don't see.

Antoine drove past several mills where sugar and rice were packaged and shipped around the country. What will happen to all of this if they build a spillway? What aren't they telling me?

When he got close to Union Settlement, he slowed his speed. He did not want to have this conversation with his daughter. He knew her temper better than anyone, and this was sure to set her off. He hoped the storekeeper was there to take some of the heat off. When he pulled into the parking lot of the general store, he took a deep breath before he got out of the car.

Anna-Marie smiled when the bell hanging on the door clanged, announcing his arrival. "Papa! What a surprise." She took off her apron and ran from behind the counter to greet him. "It feels like I haven't seen you in a month of Sundays."

"*Bonjour, ma chérie,*" Antoine said, kissing her cheek. "Is your husband around?"

"My husband? Not the storekeeper? Uh oh. What's up?"

"I'd like to talk with you both," Antoine said.

Anna-Marie took note of his serious tone and hurried to find Claude. She found him on the side of the store, drawing water from their large cistern. "Papa's here," she said. "He wants to talk to us."

"He wants to talk with me?" Claude said. "This can't be nothing good. Your papa never talks to me. He ignores me like I'm not there."

"That's what he said, so hurry," Anna-Marie said impatiently. "Something's weighing on him. I can see it."

Claude poured some water on his hands and washed the sweat from his face before wiping his hands on the back of his pants. Together, he and

Anna-Marie walked into the store to find Antoine holding their daughters, one in each arm. "I swear they look just like you," Antoine said to Anna-Marie. "They get prettier every time I see them."

"Thank you, Papa." Anna-Marie took them from him and settled them in a corner with some old newspapers and crayons.

"Anna-Marie said you wished to speak to me," Claude said, holding out his hand.

Antoine hesitated, and then shook it. "To both of you," he said.

"We can sit over here." Claude pointed to some barstools by the counter.

"We've got a problem. A big one," Antoine began. "I cornered Pierre at his office today, and now I know why those men were here. Remember when the city slickers came calling?"

"Yes. What's the problem, Papa? What's going on?" Anna-Marie asked.

"They're planning to build a spillway down here. Right through here," Antoine said. "I have no clue as to why. We're so far south of New Orleans that it couldn't possibly do them any good, but here we are. And there's more. I stopped and spoke with the judge about it, and I'd swear he already knew. He didn't seem too concerned, which worries me. Tells me there's more to this than a spillway."

"That judge is worrisome," Claude agreed. "I heard tell that he's been redistricting land across the river. He's been down here a lot lately, nosing around and already campaigning to be district attorney next year. Word is he'll do anything to win an election."

"I heard that, too. Not surprising. In the last election, there wasn't a politician in Louisiana who supported him, but he won anyway," Antoine said. "That district attorney position would give him all the power he needs to do anything he wants down here."

"What are we going to do, Papa?" Anna-Marie asked.

"I don't know yet. We've got to do something. We've got to stop this, but I don't know how. I'll talk to some attorneys I know. First, we need to find out if they can actually do this. From what I gather, I think they can, but I'm not positive. Before we get any more worked up, we need to get the answer to that. I also need to get the particulars about what exactly they are planning and where. My friends in Baton Rouge say they're talking about starting it at Bohemia Plantation and going south from there, which includes Union Settlement, Nestor, Point Pleasant, and Daisy, maybe all the way to Ostrica. That's a lot of area."

"But what does that mean, exactly?" Anna-Marie said.

"It means you can say good-bye to this store and your home, and I can say good-bye to the mill and our family home. That's what it means. It means everyone down here will have to move. They will buy up all the property, and my guess would be for pennies on the dollar."

"We won't sell," Claude said, looking at Anna-Marie. "Do you agree?"

"Of course we won't," she responded.

"You won't have a choice. That's the way of things," Antoine said. "You will sell, or you'll be forced off your land."

"How do you know this?" Claude asked.

"I've been around a long time son, and I know the inner workings. The government will always get what the government wants."

"So what can we do?" Anna-Marie persisted.

"I can try to fight it at the state level, but honestly, after this last flood, I think that would be wasted effort on my part."

"So we just give up our land and move somewhere else?" Anna-Marie asked.

Antoine switched to his native French. "Don't worry. You know I'll take care of you. I know you've extended a lot of credit around here. If you don't have the money, I'll make sure you are able to buy a home and start another business."

"I speak French, you know," Claude interrupted. "I can take care of my own family."

"Not in the manner to which your wife is accustomed," Antoine shot back.

"Papa. Stop it." Anna-Marie ordered, fire flashing through her eyes. "Thank you, but we'll be just fine."

Antoine stood up. "Well, on that note I'll bid you *adieu*. Start putting away as much money as you can. If you take care of your nickels, your dimes will take care of themselves."

"What does that even mean?" Claude asked his wife after Antoine was gone.

"It means if you keep your nickels, they'll grow into dimes, and on and on," Anna-Marie said, giggling. "Are you sure you're French?"

Claude grinned. "Yes, madam. I'm sure. Now where is Spit? I think we should send him to fetch Abraham and Hester. They need to know this."

"I'll find him," Anna-Marie said, walking outside.

After asking Spit to go fetch the Jacksons, Anna-Marie sat down at the picnic table in the front facing the river. She could see the tall mast of a passing ship. She could hear the men on board barking orders. She could smell the river and feel the ever-present breeze that flowed from it. When she looked across the roadway, she could feel the tears welling in her eyes. There, nestled between oaks whose branches swept the ground, sat the home she had built with Claude. An oak alley led from the highway to the bricked steps that widened to the veranda. She had selected every piece of furniture and had it all shipped from New York City. She had made the heavily brocaded curtains herself from fabric Claude had ordered from his distributors. Claude had pieced the oak floors together and then shined them to a sparkling finish. The walls, high and painted an off-white, held pictures of her life. Her wedding picture. Claude in his Army uniform. Baby pictures of Claude Jr., Charlie, Madeleine, and Jeanne. Her children playing on the levee. Claude's mother and father. Her *maman* and papa. She and Claude behind the counter at the store. The house held so many memories that hurricanes and floods had not been able to take from her. As she sat there, she realized that the life she loved may well be over.

Furiously, Anna-Marie wiped the tears from her cheeks with the back of her hand. "It's not over yet," she said aloud. With determination, she marched into the store. "We have to fight them, Claude. We simply must."

CHAPTER 15

What is this?" Claude asked Hester. "It's delicious."

"Thistle salad, made from that pesky Russian thistle that's grows everywhere," Hester said. "I clean it real good and add some berries and oranges and chicken, and it becomes a meal. And my special seasonings, of course."

Everyone laughed because they all knew that Hester could make anything taste good with her special seasonings, but no one dared ask what they were made with. It was dusk, and they were sitting on the front porch at Anna-Marie and Claude's house, watching the sun go down over the river.

"I love your special seasoning," Anna-Marie said. "I always feel better after eating anything you cook."

"Me, too. I eat way too much of her cooking and then feel better for it. That's why I have to work so hard, or I'd be big as a house," Abraham agreed.

"Hester said you're teaching Isaac to fish oysters. How's he doing?" Claude asked.

"I'm just teaching him to coon oysters right now," Abraham replied. "That's why I ordered those little gloves for him. He's picking it right up."

"How do you coon oysters?" Anna-Marie asked.

"You get them just like a raccoon does. You reach in the water and pluck them right from the bottom, one at a time. It takes a while, but you can feel around for the biggest shells that way. It's best to go oystering in months that have an R in them. In the other months, the oysters have a tendency to be milky. We were down near Ostrica today, and you should have seen Isaac in the water plucking those oysters. He loved it. He was so proud each time he came up with one." Abraham saw the concerned look that appeared on Anna-Marie's face and said, "Don't worry. I'm right there with him."

Anna-Marie smiled. "I know, but he's just a child."

"I was younger than him when my father started teaching me," Abraham said. "It'll make him a good living when he gets older. Hester and I worry about nothing between the oranges, figs and pears, and the rice, shrimp, and oysters. What we can't get, the river provides. Albert sits out at the river sometimes just waiting for those packet boats. You wouldn't believe what he brings us. Sometimes, the crates on those boats are stacked so high that when the current is strong, the ones on top tip over and fall into the river. They're fair game after that because the captain isn't going to turn around to retrieve them. As much cargo as they lose, you'd think they'd come up with a better way to transport goods up and down the river. At least, they don't stack the mail like that, or we'd never get any. Sometimes I think Captain Henry jerks his boat around on purpose when he sees Albert."

"That's how I got this dress," Hester said, twirling around. "I had to take it in, of course, but it's pretty. Poopdeck brought me a whole crate of clothes that I was able to sew to fit us. I made some for him, too."

"That's why you've been looking so fancy," Claude said to Abraham. "I thought you struck it rich."

Abraham stood up and turned around in a circle with his arms outstretched to show off his new suit. "I do clean up good, don't I? Next thing you know, I'm going to start drinking scotch."

"Speaking of drinking," Claude said. "There's a reason we sent Spit to fetch you, and the news is not good." He explained what Antoine had told them earlier about Pierre and the judge. "So that's the crux of it. We were right to be suspicious of those men."

"Sanon was right," Hester said. "He warned that trouble was coming, and that we would be powerless."

"We're not powerless," Anna-Marie said. "We're going to fight if I have to march right up to the State Capitol myself. Those men can't take what is ours if we don't want them to have it."

"I'm afraid they might be able to," Claude said. "You can't fight the government."

"Are you telling me that they can take our farm? Hester's grandfather was awarded that land for his service in the War of 1812. Earned that land fair and square," Abraham said. "Her father put in the orange grove and made a decent living for his family. How can they just take it away?"

"They won't take it," Claude said. "They'll buy it. Antoine says for pennies on the dollar."

Abraham jumped up and strode away. Hester moved to go after him.

"Let him go." Anna-Marie placed her hand on Hester's arm. "He needs a minute. I was mad like that earlier. I still am."

"We would have to move?" Hester asked.

"Yes," Claude said.

"But this is our home," she said.

"I know how you feel. We feel the same way," Anna-Marie said. "The question is, what can we do about it?"

"Your Papa didn't seem to think much could be done if they have a mind to do this," Claude reminded her.

"My Papa, smart as he is, doesn't know everything," Anna-Marie retorted. "There has to be a way to stop this, and I'm going to find it."

Claude leaned back in his chair and laughed. "If anyone can, woman, it will be you. Now, I'm going to find out where Abraham went. We might be gone a while. I think we'll go out into the marsh. You ladies enjoy your coffee."

Claude went inside and came back with two headlamps. "Nothing like a little twilight trapping to take a weight off your mind," he said, kissing Anna-Marie on the cheek.

"You'd better bring a mosquito brush." Anna-Marie picked one up from beside her chair and handed it to him. "I can't believe the mosquitos are still out when it's this cold," she said to Hester. "There's one by your chair if you need it."

"My daddy used to make these all the time," Hester said. "He'd strip the leaves quicker than all get out, and then he'd braid rope to make the handle. Nothing like it to get mosquitoes off of you. Of course, Mama found another use for them when she didn't have a switch handy. My brother thought they really were switches. I remember one time, I pulled one out when the mosquitoes were biting, and Isaac took off. He thought I was going to use it on his backside." Hester laughed at the memory, and then her smile disappeared. "I can't leave my home. My parents, Isaac, they are still there. I feel them. I can't leave them."

"I know," Anna-Marie said. "I was sitting outside at the store earlier just staring at this house wondering how I was going to leave it. All of my memories with Claude and the children are here. We've got to think of something. Maybe the men will come up with something out there in the marsh. I wonder if Claude found Abraham yet."

Claude spotted Abraham on the other side of the general store, sitting on the ground, leaning against the wall, flask in hand. When Claude walked up, he took a long swig.

"What are you doing, man?" Claude asked.

"I'm thinking about how that judge and those other men are going to look after I give them a good beating," Abraham said.

Claude laughed out loud. "Now, you know you can't do that. You'd spend the rest of your life in that prison they built next to the courthouse."

"I don't care," Abraham said. "How can they just make us leave our homes?"

"Like I said. We don't know yet what's going to happen. Come with me. Let's go get some muskrats. That'll ease our minds."

Abraham laughed when Claude pulled him to his feet. "All right. Let's go. I've been wanting to see what you're doing with those muskrats. Every week, I see new pelts hanging on those hooks in the barn."

Abraham and Claude spent the next hour checking the traps Claude had put out near all of the muskrat runs he could find. "See, they make trails." Claude pointed to a worn path. "If you place traps near the runs, you'll catch plenty. I can't believe you've never done this before."

"I'd rather just put out my rabbit boxes. It's easier. You just wait for a rabbit to wander in, and when it hits the stick in the back, the door closes. Nothing to it," Abraham said, looking at the animal trails. "You have to be careful when you open that door, though, because if he can, he'll run away. You have to reach in, grab his hind legs, and pull him out. Then you give him a rabbit chop behind the head. And you know, Hester can cook up a mess of rabbits in all kinds of ways. Nobody wants to eat a river rat."

Claude leaned over the pirogue and retrieved a trap that had captured a muskrat by its hind legs. When the muskrat wriggled, he picked up a sturdy stick from the bottom of the boat and whacked it on the back of its head.

Abraham looked at Claude and grinned. "Now I get it." He took a sip from his flask and reached down and retrieved a muskrat for himself. "You're making these rats pay for what the ones in the trenches did to you."

"I hate 'em. With a passion, I do." Claude pulled out his own flask. "I'd shoot them, but the pelts fetch a pretty penny."

For the next two hours, Claude and Abraham drank their whiskey and whacked muskrat after muskrat. After each kill, they reset the traps, driving wooden stakes into the ground to hold the traps in place. When they finished, they paddled their way back to dry land, and then they stumbled the rest of the way to the house, dragging the pirogue behind them.

They went behind the house and skinned the muskrats and then hung the pelts on the hooks that lined the side of the barn.

"You boys look like you had fun," Anna-Marie said when they finally walked onto the porch.

"We did," Abraham said. "I've always made fun of him for chasing down those rats, but I won't anymore. Next time, I'm going with him."

"It's going to stink around here for days until those pelts dry," Anna-Marie commented.

"Yes it will, but nothing makes a man feel better than killing a rat," Claude said. "I've been telling Abraham that for years."

"I believe it now. I feel good," Abraham said. "Come on, Hester. Get Isaac, and let's go. We'll worry about that other mess tomorrow."

CHAPTER 16

By the end of 1923, folks all along the East Bank of the river had heard that that their lives might be changing soon. News like that travels on the wind, whispering through the willows from town to town. In the general store, that's about all that was discussed.

"Anything new with the spillway?" Nikolas Jankovic said, before he got through the door with his mail sack. He limped up to where Claude was standing and threw it on the counter.

"Nothing new since yesterday," Claude said, watching his Tako friend rummage through his sack before handing him a stack of mail.

"It's sorted," Nikolas said, as he did every afternoon.

"Thank you. I don't know how you manage to row across that river twice every day."

"Keeps me in good form." Nikolas smiled when Anna-Marie walked up and handed him a slice of blackberry pie. "Thank you, ma'am."

"Made it fresh this morning," Anna-Marie said. "I know it's your favorite. Those blackberries you picked for us gave me a hankering to make one."

"I was sure hoping that would be the case." He turned to look at Claude. "That's a mighty fine woman you have there."

"Don't I know it," Claude said. "Have you heard anything new?"

"Nothing more than we already knew. Momentum is building in the city. Those levee men are smart. They started telling folks how this spillway could save them from flooding, and nobody thinks to ask a single question. Even *The New Orleans Item-Tribune* is favoring it. That Jefferson Davenport is so popular right now that the Rex Krewe will probably make him king of the Rex parade. Wouldn't that be something? Of course, we won't find out until Mardi Gras day. That's the best kept secret in the city."

"Oh, it would be something, all right. About like having the judge riding on that float waving his scepter," Claude said.

"Don't say that man's name," Nikolas said. "Of all the scurrilous, ill-begotten…"

"Yes sir," Claude interrupted, looking at Anna-Marie.

"Oh, sorry ma'am, but that man just rubs me raw."

Anna-Marie laughed. "Me, too. How's Marta? Is she well?"

"Still as ornery as ever," Nikolas said. "That woman will surely be the death of me if one of those ships in the river don't get me first. By the way, give these to Miss Hester for me. I cut them out for her." Nikolas handed Anna-Marie a stack of coupons.

"That's very kind," Anna-Marie said. "You always take such good care of her."

Nikolas blushed and hung his head for a moment. "I won't ever forget that time I fell down by the river, and she came to my aid. I hurt my good leg and skinned both my knees. She fixed me right up and then sat with me 'til I felt like I could walk again. She's a good woman, that one. Not like my Marta, who told me to quit whining when I told her about it."

"You win some, you lose some," Claude said, laughing.

"Trust me. I'm losing more than I'm winning. Only God knows why I didn't marry a good woman like your wife or Miss Hester."

"Shush now." Anna-Marie said. "You shouldn't speak ill of your wife. I'm sure she has some wonderful qualities."

"So do rats if you look hard enough, I guess."

Anna-Marie laughed when she saw Claude shudder. "Here, bring Marta a piece of pie. She deserves it after all your talk."

Nikolas reached for the pie, put it in the side pocket of his sack, and waved as he limped out the door. "See you tomorrow," he said.

"I bet that pie don't make it to the river." Claude pulled Anna-Marie close to him. "He's right, you know. I am one lucky man. Thank you again for telling me I had to marry you," he added, grinning and backing away from her.

Claude ducked when Anna-Marie scooped some pie out of the pan, threw it at him and then ran off. He was still tying to sponge the dull purple blackberry stain from his shirt when Mildred walked in. "Why hello, Mildred," he said. "Haven't seen you in a while."

"Well, if truth be told, your wife was rude to me," Mildred said, a pained look on her face. "But the Good Lord says to forgive, so I'm forgiving her."

"I'm sure she'll be right pleased to hear that." Claude couldn't resist. "Anna-Marie, Mildred's here. She wants to tell you something." Claude loved nothing better than watching his wife's temper rise, and this one was sure to do it.

Anna-Marie emerged from the schoolroom that, before Prohibition, had been the saloon. Now she used it to teach her children, Isaac, and a few other children arithmetic, reading, and writing.

"Hello, Mildred," Anna-Marie said. "I see you've come back."

"Yes, yes, I have. I've decided to forgive your rudeness," Mildred said, "although it took me a while. Like I was telling your husband, the Good Lord says to forgive, so I'm forgiving."

Claude sat down on his stool and watched the color flow into his wife's cheeks. "Why that's just downright sweet of Mildred. Isn't it, Anna-Marie?"

He almost laughed out loud when she glared at him. Anna-Marie took a deep breath and plastered a smile on her face. "What brings you here?"

"I was hoping that you had some of those delicious biscuits you make."

"Oh," Anna-Marie said, smiling brightly now. "I don't make those. My friend, Hester, that's her recipe. She brings them by twice a week. How many would you like?"

Mildred turned red. "Just, just one," she said.

"Are you sure? I have plenty." Anna-Marie reached for the pan of biscuits.

"No, no. One's fine," Mildred said.

Anna-Marie tucked the biscuit into a thin leaf of tin and then placed it in a paper bag. "Can I get you anything else?"

"No, that's all I needed. Have y'all heard about the spillway? It's supposed to come right through here from what I hear. The judge was telling me about it just the other day. He's such a nice man. He's doing so much for the people down the river. He tells me he's going to run for district attorney next year. You should vote for him. He wants to stop taxes. That's what he told me yesterday. Did you know that some people are running down to the tax office to pay their past-due land taxes so they can sell their land when the government comes calling? Some folks are excited about that. It's no never mind to me either. I was planning to move across the river to live closer to my son anyhow. He lives in Buras. He's a bar pilot, you know. Makes a lot of money, he does."

"Isn't that something?" Claude said, waiting for Anna-Marie to explode.

She didn't say a word. She stared at Mildred for a moment and then walked back into the schoolroom.

"Well, I never. You really need to get your wife in hand," Mildred said to Claude.

"That's what I hear," Claude said.

Mildred turned and walked out with a huff.

When Anna-Marie was sure that Mildred was gone, she stormed back into the store. "Claude Couvillion, I should box your ears."

"Yes, you should. I'm sorry, *ma chérie*. I couldn't help myself. I needed a good laugh today."

Anna-Marie giggled. "Did you see her face when I told her Hester made the biscuits? There was nothing she could do. She had to take one."

"I could hardly contain myself," Claude said. "That was funny. So am I forgiven?"

Anna-Marie kissed him on the cheek. "I guess if Mildred can forgive me, I can forgive you."

They were still laughing when Abraham and Hester arrived to pick up Isaac. Anna-Marie told them about Mildred's visit.

"You should have seen her face. It was priceless," Claude said. "And you should have heard her talking about the judge and the spillway. She loves the judge, and she doesn't have any issue with the spillway coming through. Says she going to live in Buras. I thought Anna-Marie was going to explode."

"At least something good's coming out of all of this. That busybody's leaving," Abraham said. "Nobody else has treated us the way she does, excepting the judge. Them two are cut from the same cloth."

"That's certainly true," Anna-Marie agreed. "I've always loved living on the river because most folks don't have all those snobberies that other folks have. Folks down here are just folks. We have more kinds of folks here than anywhere else, I think, and we all get along just fine."

"Yes, we do, but Sanon says change is coming, and it's coming fast,"

Hester said. "He was out on the boat with Abraham earlier. Tell them, Abraham."

"Sanon worked with me today," Abraham said. "He's an oysterman, too, when he's not healing folks. Sometimes he speaks in riddles. I'm not sure what he meant, but he said that a blood moon is coming soon. With it will come change like we've not seen before. More than any war, more than any invasion could accomplish, our very culture will give way to greater pursuits. He said that what we have known here will forever disappear, living only in memory of days gone by."

"I don't like the sound of that," Claude said.

"It's downright scary," Anna-Marie agreed. "Is he talking about the spillway coming in?"

"I'm not sure, but could be," Abraham said. "I believe we should heed his words. We should accept what cannot be fought and start preparing."

"Papa says there's still a chance. He's been planting seeds at the Capitol, asking everyone why they don't build it closer to New Orleans," Anna-Marie said.

"I'm not sure that'll do much good," Claude said. "I think there's a reason they want this land, something we don't know about. It's the only explanation."

"I know there's a lot of activity on the river. Between the bootleggers and the men in fancy boats gathering around Nestor, the river's extra crowded these days," Abraham said. "I've seen those same men walking along the bank on both sides of the river."

Claude nodded his head. "Something's not right, and if we don't figure it out before long, it'll be too late."

"What did Sanon mean about the blood moon bringing change?" Anna-Marie asked.

"We were talking about that on our way here," Hester said. "We can't figure it out."

"It is baffling," Claude said. "Any idea when we'll see that blood moon?"

"Soon was all he said," Abraham said. "I'll surely be watching for it, though."

The Bohemia Spillway

CHAPTER 17

February 1924

"Gentlemen," Jefferson Davenport said loudly, convening a meeting of the Orleans Levee District. "Your attention, please."

When everyone was seated and quiet, Jefferson sat down at the head of the long table. "I am happy to report that everything is on track. All of the engineers' reports have been submitted, and we have enough members of the Louisiana Legislature on board to push the spillway through. As you are aware, the river levels during floods have been rising higher, and our levees have been built as high as we can safely build them. We have been tasked with protecting half a million lives along our twelve-mile riverfront. Relief measures must be taken. This spillway will mitigate the river levels at New Orleans."

"Do you have the reports on projected costs?" Sal Ragliosi asked.

"Yes." Jefferson reached for a stack of papers. "The breakdown is included in the estimation. A copy for each of you." He handed the stack to Pierre, who took a copy of the report and passed the rest down.

When everyone had a copy, Jefferson explained. "As you know, Judge Leonus Lozano has been causing problems. Says the land down there belongs to Plaquemines Parish, and we have no legal right to put the spillway in place. He's wrong, of course, but he and his cronies have been placing obstacles in the way of this project the whole way through. He has some good friends in Baton Rouge, as you know." Several of the men nodded.

"The first item on the list deals with the levee districts down there," Jefferson continued. "They are in serious debt. Don't have enough money to maintain the levees that are there, much less run day-to-day operations. I figure we can take care of their debt and pave the way for the spillway.

The cost should run about $140,000. Additionally, it will cost an estimated $360,000 to buy up all the property from individual property owners down there. We should expect some resistance. Antoine Bertaut and his daughter have been kicking up quite a fuss, even going door to door warning folks about the spillway and telling them not to sell, from what I hear." Jefferson looked pointedly at Pierre.

"I warned you," Pierre said.

Jefferson ignored him and continued, "That won't make a difference in the long run. We'll get all of that property one way or another. The way we've framed everything will include expropriation for those who refuse to sell. From what we've gathered, there are 256 private tracts that are owned by 168 individuals. Keep in mind that this covers an eleven-mile stretch along the river and includes 33,000 acres. If everything goes as planned, the state, which owns about fifty-eight percent of the land down there, will deed that to us at no cost."

"So we just force these people off their land if they won't sell?" Joseph Gaspard, a newcomer to the board, asked.

"We've been over this," Jefferson said. "The answer is yes. We are talking about protecting the lives of a half million people, so yes, they will be offered a fair price and if they refuse, they will be forced off their land. Now enough of that. It will cost an estimated $55,000 for the removal of eleven miles of river levee to create a natural spillway. Removal of the back levees so that the water will flow into the marsh will cost another $18,000. We also want to extend the lower Bohemia levee another 25,000 yards, which will cost approximately $5,000. Then we will need to strengthen the rear levees from Pointe á la Hache to Bohemia. That will cost another $5,000. We have included drainage provisions for $15,000, and engineering costs are expected to run $70,000. We have also put in $75,000 for contingencies, but I don't foresee that being used up. The total cost is estimated at $743,000. However, if it becomes necessary to replace any of these levees, the cost will increase considerably to almost a million dollars, but we are confident that we can keep our expenditures within this range. The only possible additional expense would be if we have to build a cross levee below Nestor."

"How long will all of this take?" Sal asked.

"We have projected it will take two years. If all goes well, we should

110

have the governor's signature on it sometime this summer. Assuming the legislature acts quickly, we should be finished with construction by the end of 1926."

For the next hour, the commissioners went over the report from the engineers, reviewed the numbers in front of them, and suggested friends who should be awarded the contracts to conduct the work. Finally, Jefferson stood up.

"Let me remind you, we have a lot of work to do. We need to be ready to go. We'll meet next week to go over more particulars."

When the meeting ended, Jefferson pulled Sal and Pierre to one side. "Meet me in the front parlor at the St. Charles Hotel in a half hour. There is much left to discuss."

Exactly thirty minutes later, Jefferson sat in a picturesque parlor in the St. Charles Hotel, located on St. Charles Avenue just two blocks from Canal Street, waiting for his fellow commissioners. When they arrived, he directed them to an office on the second floor.

"I love this hotel," Sal said, as they walked. "You know, it's burned down twice. The original hotel was considered the grandest hotel in the country. It had Corinthian columns and a huge cupola, like the U.S. Capitol Building. Presidents used to stay here when they came to New Orleans. My father used to have an office here when I was young, He would bring me to work with him sometimes, and I'd spend the day wandering around looking at everything."

"That's fascinating," Jefferson said. "Now, let's get down to the business at hand. I had a meeting yesterday with a representative from Humble Oil. A friend of mine put me in touch. It's been a year or so since I last spoke with him, and I was getting worried. He promised me he would speak with some engineers at the oil company and ask them to look into the salt dome in Nestor. It seems he kept his word. He said they've been doing some research, and they might be interested in testing the area. He's agreed to wait until we get the okay for the spillway before he takes any further action."

"That's good news," Pierre said.

"Yes, it certainly is. I know they are going to find oil."

"What if they don't?" Sal said. "What if there's nothing there?"

"I can't entertain that thought," Jefferson said. "It's there. I feel it in my bones."

"Yes, but what if it's not?" Pierre asked. "I've alienated my whole family over this."

"You gentlemen worry too much. There's oil in that dome. I'd bet there's oil all over the place down there, and come summer, that land will be under our control," Jefferson said, pulling a flask from his pocket.

"For a spillway," Pierre reminded him.

"For whatever we want." Jefferson passed his flask to Sal. "Drink up, gentlemen. We have much to celebrate. Everything is falling into place nicely."

CHAPTER 18

On February 20, 1924, Abraham bounded up the steps that led onto the porch that encircled Claude's home and banged on the door. It was late, almost nine in the evening, and Claude was not expecting him.

"What's all this ruckus about?" Claude said, opening the door. "Oh, Abraham. I wasn't expecting you."

"Apologies," Abraham said, "but this is urgent. Follow me."

Claude followed him down the steps and into the front yard. "Look," Abraham said, pointing to the sky above the river. "Look at that."

Claude looked up and stared at the huge blood-red moon suspended eerily in the sky.

"Sanon's blood moon," Claude said, still staring, mesmerized by what he was seeing. "I've never seen a moon that red."

"Me either," Abraham said.

"I'm going to fetch Anna-Marie. She needs to see this." Claude turned and walked back toward the house.

While he waited, Abraham sat at the top of the stairs and listened to the sounds of the river. A foghorn signaled that a ship was approaching. Abraham could see its mast, high above the levee, gleaming in the moonlight. He could hear the scurrying of night creatures and the quacking of ducks that had not yet bedded down for the evening. The breeze, rustling through the trees, added a chill to the already cold February air, but Abraham didn't mind. The cold had always made him feel more alive. When he heard the door open, he turned sideways and leaned against the column on the edge of the porch. "Look out there," he said, pointing.

Claude pulled Anna-Marie with him down the steps. "Have you ever seen the likes of that?" he asked.

Anna-Marie looked up. Like Claude, she simply stared for a moment.

"It's just like Sanon said, a blood moon." She had tears in her eyes when she looked at Claude. "What will we do?"

Claude had no answer.

They walked back to the porch hand in hand and sat in their rocking chairs.

Abraham cleared his throat. "I've talked it over with Hester, and we're not selling. They'll have to drag us off our land, kicking and screaming. I'm not sure there won't be bloodshed."

"Don't talk like that, Abraham." Anna-Marie cried. "We need to be calm about this."

Abraham and Claude looked at each other. It began small, just a snicker from Claude, and then Abraham and Claude were laughing so hard they had tears in their eyes.

"What's so funny?" Anna-Marie asked.

"You? Telling us we need to be calm. You've never been calm a day in your life," Claude said, laughing harder.

Anna-Marie began laughing with them, and then her smile disappeared when she looked up and the moon reminded her. "We should begin making plans," she said, resigned now to the fact that this was a fight she couldn't win. Her papa had been telling her that for months. Seeing that moon was the final straw. "I've been thinking about where we could go. Maybe Ronquillo Settlement or Homeplace. Maybe Diamond or Nairn or Happy Jack."

"There's hardly anything there," Claude said. "Most of the mills and factories are on this side of the river. It would be like starting from scratch."

"I'll have to start all over, too," Abraham said. "Over here, I know where I can dock my boat and where to find oysters, crab, shrimp, and fish. Across the river, I have no idea. And I won't have the oranges to fall back on in the off-season and probably not rice either. What about you? Will you open another store, Claude?"

"I don't know. Going out on the boat with you makes me realize what I'm missing working in the store every day. I've lived here all my life, and I don't know half as much as you do about the bayous and bays around here."

"Maybe not," Abraham said, "but being in that store, you know more about the goings on around here then any of us. Folks count on you. We need the general store, no matter where we go."

"That's true," Anna-Marie said, her tone defeated. "We could open another store. I have that money Papa put away for me if we need to use that to build it."

"That's your money," Claude said. "If it comes to that, I'll take care of building the store."

"I'd help," Abraham said. "Between me and you and Poopdeck and Spit, we could throw it up in no time."

"It sounds like we're putting the cart before the horse," Anna-Marie said. "We don't even know for sure if that spillway will be built down here."

Claude and Abraham looked out at the moon. "It will," Abraham said. "No doubt in my mind."

"Where would you go, Abraham?"

"Wherever y'all go. Me and Hester already discussed it. If we're forced to leave, we want to live near y'all. That way, Isaac can continue with his lessons, and if y'all need help, we'll be nearby."

"And vice versa," Claude said. "What about your parents? Have you talked to them about this?"

Abraham nodded. "They feel the same way I do. My granddaddy sharecropped their land till he owned it. By the sweat of his brow, he earned every inch of that ground, and my daddy's not going to go easy. He couldn't care less how much they offer him."

"Can they really just kick us off our land?" Anna-Marie asked, probably for the hundredth time since she had first heard about the spillway. "Just like that?"

"Yes. There's this thing called eminent domain," Claude explained patiently. "For example, if the government wants to build a road and that road will come right through our property, the government can seize the land if we refuse to sell it. In our case, they want to build a spillway, but the same principle applies. If we don't sell, they can seize it. States have just as much power as the federal government when it comes to eminent domain."

"Like what happened to those Indians on the Trail of Tears." Anna-Marie said.

"Yes, but in that case, it was the federal government who used the military to force them off their land," Claude said. "You can bet if there is an uprising over this, the governor wouldn't hesitate to send the Louisiana National Guard."

"We ain't scared of no Louisiana National Guard. Those guys were nowhere near the front lines in the war," Abraham said. "We're United States Army, and folks don't call me Trigger for nothing."

"Whoa there, Trigger. There won't be any uprising. Most folks down here are peaceful. And some of them actually want that money."

"Yeah, but most don't," Abraham said. "The Takos down in Ostrica are none too happy. They don't think the spillway will include them, but no one knows for sure yet. The Italians down in Daisy aren't happy either. Everywhere I dock, folks are talking. They wonder what this is going to do to our seafood industry. We all depend on it for survival."

"I'm not sure what it will do to the seafood, but I know what it will do to our crops. It'll put the Mississippi River right on top of them. Think about it. If the orange groves survive, there will be nobody here to pick the oranges," Claude said.

"This is all too much to think about," Anna-Marie said.

"I know it is, *ma chérie*," Claude agreed. "But we have to think about it, or we'll get caught by surprise if it happens, with no plan in place. We should start looking for land across the river. From what I hear, that judge is moving the property lines around for some reason, scooping up more and more of the land from the state by calling it 'new swampland.' We have to be careful when we make our choice."

"It has to be as close to the river as we are now. Maybe right across the river." Anna-Marie stopped and thought for a moment. "But then I'd stare out my front door, and I'd know our home and store was on the other side of the levee. I don't think I could do that. I'd cry all the time."

"Maybe you can take the house with you," Abraham said. "If it comes down to it, maybe I can take mine."

"How would we do that?" Claude asked.

"Timbers. Roll it on timbers to the river and put it on a barge. We could have mules pull it to the river, and then I could pull the barge across with the boat."

"Are you sure that would work?"

"Yes, I've seen it done. Folks pull all kinds of thing across the river."

"Papa was telling me about some new contraption folks out west are using for farming. It's called a tractor," Anna-Marie said. "They're real expensive, but they can pull anything. Maybe we could get one of those."

"I'd have to speak with him about that," Claude said. "I'm not of a mind to spend a lot of money on something that might not work when mules would do the trick. Especially now when our future is so uncertain."

"I think we could do it," Abraham said. "I have a stack of logs that we could use ready to go behind the outhouse. Don't know why I never cut them up, but now I see it was a good thing. We may need them."

"If you think we could do it, then I trust that," Claude said. He reached over and patted Anna-Marie's knee. "See, you can stop feeling so sad. If nothing else, we may be able to save our home. And yours, Abraham. When I look for land, I'll look for enough for both of us. We can live side by side. You're sure your boat can pull our homes?"

"I think so," Abraham said. "My daddy built that boat strong. I've pulled large boats, weighing eight tons or more upriver when they broke down. Surely, I can pull a house."

Anna-Marie smiled. "Thank you, Abraham. Sometimes I swear I don't know what we'd do without you. You and Hester and Isaac, you are our family. You always will be."

Abraham smiled and stood up. "I feel the same," he said. "I best be getting on home. Don't want Hester to worry. And Claude, why don't I bring Hester to help Anna-Marie in the store tomorrow and you come oystering with me? Would that be okay, Anna-Marie?"

"Of course. Claude always comes back so relaxed after a day out with you."

"It's settled, then. We'll see you in the morning," Claude said.

Claude walked with Abraham to the road. "Thank you," Claude said. "This may have eased Anna-Marie's mind a bit. She's been very anxious. I've never seen her so upset. You have given her some hope."

Abraham patted Claude on the shoulder. "That moon up there tells me that this is going to happen, and we may have no choice. Come what may, I'm still not selling. They will have to force me to leave."

"Let's just wait and see what happens," Claude said. "Wheels turn slow in government. Maybe we have some time."

"I don't think so. There's been too many strangers down here snooping around, measuring this and that. It doesn't bode well."

"Well, there's nothing we can do tonight. Be careful going home, and don't stay outside all night staring at that moon."

"I'll see you tomorrow," Abraham said, climbing into his truck. "Bright and early."

CHAPTER 19

March 1924

Leonus slammed his fist down on the conference table. "You can't just come into my parish and force my people off their land," he said. His rounded cheeks were stained red, and his eyes were flashing. "You know just as well as I do that spillway ain't going to do a damned thing for New Orleans. I know why you're doing this, and you're not going to get away with it. I will sue you to kingdom come and back."

"Careful, Judge." Jefferson leaned back in his chair nonchalantly. "I know what you've been doing, as well, although how you think you are going to profit from state lands is beyond me. There's a whole lot of redistricting going on down there. You've moved property boundaries from here to there to everywhere that suits your purpose. And new swamplands? What is that? Swampland just sprouting up everywhere and on dry land. But don't you worry yourself none. We're going to pay off all the debt down there. Those levee boards have been operating at a deficit for years, no matter how much they get in tax dollars."

"The parish is poor. You know that. Not enough tax money to go around."

"Or maybe too many sticky fingers in it. Your own included."

The judge turned red again. "Watch yourself, Jefferson Davenport. You don't want me spreading the word about what's really going on here, now do you?"

"Say what you will," Jefferson said. "It matters not to me. I'm in the home stretch. The ball is in motion, and the pendulum is swinging my way. Not much you can do to stop it now."

"We'll see about that." The judge stood up and shoved his hat on his head. He hated to admit it, but he knew Jefferson was right. At this point, there wasn't much he could do. He had spent years making friends who could influence the vote, but those friendships meant little when it came to the protection of New Orleans, one of the country's busiest ports. He already knew the governor would sign off on it. Anything for New Orleans. Even a spillway in the wrong location on the river.

As he drove through the French Quarter toward Canal Street, Leonus reflected on his meeting with Jefferson. He had known that it wouldn't change anything, but he had hoped Jefferson would slip and accidentally reveal more of his plan. The judge had heard that Jefferson was already meeting with oil companies, but he had wanted to verify that and learn which ones were interested in the salt dome. Thirty minutes of arguing with his nemesis had not accomplished his goal. Jefferson had revealed nothing new. There's a reason they call them city slickers, the judge thought, turning his attention to the construction he saw along the way. New businesses were springing up everywhere. Warehouses and grain elevators lined the river. New Orleans had rebounded tremendously after losing so much economically during the Civil War, most notably the slave trade. The slave ships had been commonplace for more than one hundred years before the Civil War.

Even now, in the midst of the Roaring Twenties in New Orleans, segregation was common, but in Plaquemines Parish, the residents had formed their own unique culture where people from all over Europe— France, Croatia, Italy, Spain—mingled with blacks and whites. Yes, there were restrooms labeled "White only" and "Colored only," and yes, there were separate water fountains at the courthouse, but in the hierarchy, each group respected the next and accepted their customs. The whites happily fed and clothed their black workers whenever it became necessary, and blacks attended church with the whites, although they sat in a separate section. Leonus didn't like that at all. Not one bit. He much preferred the way things operated in New Orleans, where people kept the races more segregated. Here, Leonus thought, blacks knew their proper place. That's the way it should be, he thought as he drove down River Road.

At thirty-three, Leonus had a mind to change things in his parish, but he knew he needed two things to accomplish that—wealth and power. He had already begun accumulating some wealth through various legal and questionable means, and he was confident there would be a lot more. Oil was coming, and he was already setting the stage for his piece of that pie through buying as much land as he could downriver. But power, that had to be earned through respect, and he intended to have it. He knew that he had to win the race for district attorney by any means necessary—whatever he had to do. In Plaquemines Parish, there were no mayors presiding over towns. There were no parish presidents. A police jury form of government enacted the laws for the parish, and the district attorney was the legal advisor to the police jury. Leonus was determined that the district attorney position would be his before the end of the year. Of that, he was sure.

He was almost to Pointe á la Hache when an idea began to form. Since there was nothing he could do about the spillway, he needed a workaround. As the idea began to take shape, Leonus smiled. Forty-five minutes later, he sat at his desk and compiled a list of oil companies that had already begun drilling in Texas. Then he pulled some old maps of Plaquemines Parish from a cabinet. He studied them carefully, looking for land that his parish owned. He marked each location, and then he marked which land was state-owned. Next, he arranged a meeting with the Grand Prairie Levee Board for the following day. He wasn't happy about bringing the board members in on his plan, but it was the only way.

The next morning, Leonus waited for the members to be seated.

"Gentlemen, I have good news," he announced. "As you know, the Orleans Levee District has decided to encroach on our parish land to build a spillway that will do nothing for New Orleans. I say, as I've said before, that we should not stand for this, but our efforts have been useless. I spoke with Jefferson Davenport yesterday, and the spillway legislation is about to come to fruition. There's nothing more we can do to stop it."

Leonus stood up and placed his hands on the table, leaning forward. "Gentlemen, there is something else afoot here, something much bigger than a spillway. I am asking for your leave to represent you, free of charge, in beating the Orleans Levee District at its own game."

"What exactly are you proposing, Judge?" asked Christopher Davies, president of the Grand Prairie Levee District.

"I am suggesting, sir, that we go into the same business as those city slickers. The oil business."

Leonus observed the confused looks on the faces of the men in the room. He lit his cigar and then continued. "Several years back, I overheard a conversation at a restaurant between three commissioners of the levee board in New Orleans. They were talking about that salt dome down by Nestor. They were saying that in Texas and West Louisiana, oil companies were drilling around salt domes. They were plotting a way to get their hands on the land down there, land that belongs to the folks who live down there. They don't need that spillway, gentlemen. They want that land for the mineral rights."

"Are you sure about this, Judge?" Christopher asked. "Seems a bit farfetched to me."

"Seemed farfetched to me at the time, too, but lo and behold, the levee district is about to own all of the land. For what? Everyone with half a brain knows a spillway this far downriver will do nothing to stop New Orleans from flooding. The river runs north to south. It's ridiculous. No, they want to lease that land to oil companies. I say we lease that land first, and we don't have much time. We need to buy up as much as we can."

"Maybe you haven't heard, but we have no money," Christopher pointed out.

"There are always ways to get money when there's a chance it will make more. In this case, a lot more," Leonus said. "Leave it to me. I'll reach out to representatives with Humble Oil and Standard Oil to let them know we're interested. I'll speak with friends in Baton Rouge about transferring more state lands to the parish. As you know, that has been in the works for a while. If the Orleans Levee District can lease that land, why can't we? All we have to do is lease it to an oil company first. It's a brilliant plan, don't you agree?"

Leonus watched as the men looked at each other and then back at him. "Would you gentlemen like a few minutes to discuss this amongst yourselves?"

"Yes, if you don't mind," Christopher said.

Leonus stood up and walked to the door. "I'll be back in five minutes," he said. He wasn't worried at all. He knew people. If they thought there was money to be made, they would be amenable to his plan. He waited a few minutes and walked back into the room.

"Well?" he said. "Are you gentlemen ready to make some real money instead of operating in arrears?"

"Are you sure about this, Judge?" Christopher asked.

"As sure as I'm standing here."

"Then the answer is yes. You can represent us."

Leonus slapped his hand on the table. "Gentlemen, today you have made a wise decision. I will keep you posted on my progress. I bid you good day."

Leonus smiled all the way to his car thinking about how mad Jefferson Davenport was going to be when he learned that he had been beaten to the punch.

CHAPTER 20

April 1924

Abraham eased his boat next to the dock not far from the Ostrica Lock and waited while Claude dropped the anchor. He reached for a rope and tied off to the nearest piling.

"That channel there leads into Breton Sound, which meets the Gulf," Abraham said, pointing.

Claude observed the wooden miter gate that was situated near a row of houses. "I imagined something much grander," he said.

Abraham laughed. "You've been spending way too much time around Anna-Marie. She sees everything bigger and better than what it really is. Hester surely enjoys that. She told me once that Anna-Marie taught her how to imagine, how to hope. My family says we don't even speak like black folks anymore because of the way Anna-Marie taught us."

"She's the best thing that's ever happened to me, that's for sure," Claude said. "I hate to see her so upset right now. I've never seen her like this. She's losing hope that she'll be able to stop this spillway, and she doesn't want to move. I've tried to tell her that everything will work out, but she doesn't want to hear it."

"I know. Hester's been the same way. Inconsolable, even though I told her I would move the house. That land is what she has left of her family, and she doesn't want to leave it."

Hearing a horn, Abraham looked up and saw a boat heading toward them. "It's Captain Henry," he said, waving.

The captain pulled up alongside of *The Pearl*, and Claude and Abraham watched as he made his way to the side of the boat. "What are you boys doing?" Henry yelled. "Aren't you supposed to be at the store?" he directed to Claude.

"Came down with Abraham to get a few oysters," Claude said.

"So that pretty wife of yours is all alone?" Henry asked, grinning.

"Yes, but she has a good right hook, so I'd mind my manners if I were you," Claude shot back.

"And Hester's with her," Abraham added.

"Well, damn. I guess I'd better mind my manners then. How is Hester?" Henry said.

"She's fine," Abraham said. "Doing just fine."

"Glad to hear it."

"Where's your packet boat?" Abraham asked.

"I'm off today. Just doing a little fishing," Captain Henry said. "You boys heard about that spillway? I can't believe it. Of all the nonsensical, ludicrous, preposterous, asinine things to do. What good is a spillway down here gonna do? I couldn't believe my ears when I heard about it."

"Yes, we can't believe it either. What business does the levee board in New Orleans have disrupting things down here? It's ridiculous," Claude said.

"Maybe they think this area's dying," Captain Henry said. "A lot of folks left after the flood. Got tired of having to rebuild every few years."

"A lot of folks did leave," Claude agreed, "but there's plenty of us left who've grown up on this river and don't want to leave it."

"Word around the Port of New Orleans is that this spillway is gonna keep the city safe. All the folks there are talking. They seem excited about it." Captain Henry shook his head and rolled his eyes. "They don't realize what it's going to do to the seafood industry, sugar cane, rice, oranges, and every other crop that's grown down here. Nobody's thinking about how fertile this land is, being in the Delta and all. That spillway's gonna put everybody down here out of business."

"They don't care none about that," Abraham said. "Nobody there ever gave much of a care about what goes on down here. They just enjoy what we bring them and go about their lives."

"You got that right," Claude said. "This is going to put me out of business. My father opened our store more than thirty years ago. That store is a part of who we are."

"Just like the farm. It goes back two generations," Abraham said. "It's survived hurricanes and floods and everything Mother Nature could throw at it. Now, we just have to pick up and walk away. And for what? A spillway that ain't gonna do anyone any good."

"Well, I'm not happy about it at all," Captain Henry said. "I love the folks down here. It's the only place where people wait on the side of the river for me to ride by. They wave their arms like I'm some kind of float in a parade, just waiting for something to drop into the river, or they want to hop on for a ride up- or downriver. I know just about everyone down here, how many babies they have, what kind of boat they have, who they're mad at. I don't want to see all of that get swallowed up in some damn cockamamie nonsense. And where these poor people gonna go?"

"A lot of oystermen are talking about going to Biloxi," Abraham said. "Lots of oysters in the Gulf with easy access. Some of my people are talking about moving up north. Folks there treat black folk different than down here."

"It's true," Captain Henry said. "I've seen that with my own eyes. The further up the river I go, the more I see it. Black folks up there are almost treated like they're white."

"It's not that bad here," Abraham said. "Everybody has their place, and everybody knows it. Excepting Claude here and Anna-Marie. She don't know nothing about nobody's proper place. They treat us like we're white."

"Well, your wife's half-white. That's for sure. I couldn't believe it when I heard she married you. Not that there's nothing wrong with you, mind you, but Mulattos don't usually marry blacks from what I heard."

Claude watched Abraham's face to see if he was taking offense, but Abraham just grinned. "I know. I'm a lucky man, finding her in that tree like that and taking care of her. How could she resist?"

The captain started laughing. "Indeed," he said. "You've taken good care of her from what I can see. Her father would have been appreciative. Big Jake loved that little girl. He used to bring her out on the boat with him when she was just a tot. I'd hear her just a giggling at something he said whenever they rode by me. I still can't get over what happened to him. Sad indeed. Gave me a soft spot for the girl, losing her family like that."

"It's been hard on her," Abraham said, "but I try my best to make up for it."

"You do a good job," Claude said.

"Well, I best be getting on up the river," the captain said. "Ain't no rest for the weary these days. Here, give this to Hester." The captain threw a small box to Abraham. "Tell her it's from ol' Henry. This way, I won't have to stop when Poopdeck rows out to meet me."

"Mighty kind of you, sir," Abraham said, setting the box down. "She loved the material you dropped into the river. Made some pretty dresses with it."

"I had nothing to do with that," Captain Henry said, grinning, before he saluted and sounded his horn. Abraham and Claude watched as he maneuvered his boat back into the middle of the canal.

"That's what I'm going to miss," Abraham said. "Folk like him. Folks taking care of other folks."

"I know," Claude said. "Just seems like everything's going to be different on the other side of the river."

"At least we'll still see the packet boats, just from a different angle. I'm just worried about how this spillway is going to affect the oysters. Oysters need brackish water. They always talking about diverting water here and diverting water there. They don't know what they're doing. All that fresh water is gonna mess up our seafood."

"That spillway is going to mess everything up," Claude said. "Just think about it. Where's Miss Penny going to go? We won't get to have any more of her redfish court-bouillon. And what about old man Hank? He's always cooking up something or other and bringing it to the store. And those beignets Miss Hannah makes. They taste just like they came from Café Du Monde, and we don't have to go to the city for them. Where are all these folks going to go?"

"Yes, and what about Sanon? What about everyone in the Mulatto camp? Where are they gonna go?" Abraham asked.

"I heard tell there's some remedy men living over near Nairn. Maybe they could go there. That's just a hop, skip, and a jump from Homeplace, if that's where we land," Claude said. "Maybe you could suggest that to him. For some reason, I'd like to keep Sanon close."

"Yeah, me, too." Abraham reached for his tongs. "Come on. We've been lollygagging long enough. Can't go home with no oysters."

Abraham and Claude spent the rest of the afternoon talking and fishing oysters, ending up with a good haul.

"Looks like you could get twenty dollars for all this," Claude said, tying up the last sack.

"If I do, you'll get half," Abraham said.

Claude shook his head. "No," he said. "This is just fun for me. It gets me out of the store and onto the water. You keep it. You know, I've been thinking. If we do have to move, I might go out and work with you for a month or two before I open a new store, if you'll have me. You've made me realize what I've been missing all my life by working day and night in the store. Just for a while, mind you."

"I'd enjoy that," Abraham said, "but you'll have to take your cut then. I won't have it otherwise." Suddenly Abraham started laughing.

"What is so funny?" Claude asked, when Abraham continued until the sound of his laughter ricocheted across the canal.

"You do realize that this could be the first time in the history of the United States that a white man works for a black man, don't you? You'd better not let anyone know that you're actually working on this boat."

"I won't," Claude said, laughing. "And we have a deal. At least that gives me a little something to look forward to. I know the next months are going to be hard if this thing passes. I don't want to think about what Anna-Marie's going to be like."

"And Hester," Abraham said. "It won't be nothing nice, but we'll get through. It looks like we won't have a choice in the matter."

The following day, Anna-Marie threw the morning newspaper down on the counter of the store. "Did you see this?" she said to Claude.

"What is it?" he asked, noticing that her cheeks were already red.

"It's a notice of intent from the Orleans Levee District that they want to build a spillway here. It's official now. They are really going to do this."

"Let me see." Claude picked up the newspaper. When he finished reading, he turned to Anna-Marie, his eyes reflecting the hopelessness that she felt. "I'm so sorry. I was praying that it wouldn't happen, just like you were. But this, this does make it official. It still has to pass the legislature, but if they've come this far, far enough to put this in the paper, we have to accept that it's going to happen."

"What are we going to do?" Anna-Marie cried.

"We're going to do just what we discussed. We can move our home across the river."

"But what about our oak alley? What about the levee where our children play? What about our store and all of our customers? It's all going to be gone."

"I know, *ma chérie*. I know," Claude said, pulling Anna-Marie close. "I don't know what to say."

Anna-Marie looked up at him. "There's got to be something we can do, someone we can talk to, someone who can stop this. There just has to be."

"You've talked to everyone from here to Baton Rouge," Claude said. "That Jefferson Davenport almost threw you out of his office, if you recall. I don't think there's anything more you can do."

"Don't you worry, Claude Couvillion. I'll think of something. I have to."

With that, Anna-Marie stormed out of the store and began walking toward Nestor to see her father. There had to be something he could do. There just had to be, she thought.

Less than two hours later, she returned feeling dejected. Her father seemed to have given up hope, too.

CHAPTER 21

May 1924

Antoine Bertaut stomped into the store looking none too happy. Anna-Marie and Claude were sitting on stools by the counter across from Hester and Abraham. Hester had fried some green tomatoes, and Abraham had made rabbit stew for their lunch.

Without as much as a greeting, Antoine pulled some papers from the inside of his jacket. "It's done," he announced.

"What's done, Papa?" Anna-Marie said.

"The spillway. It's as good as done." Antoine said. "The Senate voted on it yesterday."

"What does it say?" Claude asked.

"Here, I'll read it to you." Antoine unfolded the papers and began reading aloud. Claude, Abraham, Anna-Marie, and Hester gathered around him to listen.

"*May 12, 1924,*" Antoine began.

Act No. 99

Senate Bill No. 226

By Mr. P.H. Gilbert, Substitute for Senate Bill No. 180 by Mr. P.H. Gilbert

An Act

To authorize the Board of Levee Commissioners of the Orleans Levee District, in order to reduce flood levels and to better protect from overflow by high water of the Mississippi River the City of New Orleans; to create in the Parish of Plaquemines a spillway or waste wier, or other means to that end; to authorize said board to acquire by expropriation the necessary property for such purpose, and to contract with the Board of Commissioners for the Grand Prairie Levee District and the Board of Commissioners for the

Plaquemines Parish East Bank Levee District to pay and retire the bonds and other indebtedness of said levee districts; to remove the levees in the area affected by the work contemplated, to provide the necessary funds therefor, and to repeal all laws in conflict herewith. Notice of the intention to introduce this act has been published in the localities where the matters or things affected are situated, all in the manner required by Section 6 of Article IV of the Constitution of the State, and evidence thereof has been exhibited to the Legislature."

"So they will expropriate our land?" Claude asked.

"Absolutely, they will," Antoine said. "Notice how slick they were, retiring the debts of our levee boards here. Eliminating obstacles. That's what they were doing. Probably negotiated that with the judge."

"Keep reading, Papa. I want to hear every word," Anna-Marie said.

Antoine continued, *Section 1. Be it enacted by the Legislature of Louisiana, that the Board of Levee Commissioners of the Orleans Levee District be and it is hereby authorized in its discretion in order to reduce the flood levels of the Mississippi River and to better protect the city of New Orleans from danger of overflow by the high waters of the Mississippi River, to construct or cause to be constructed on the east bank of the Mississippi River in the Parish of Plaquemines a spillway or waste wier, or other works, so located and designed according to plans and specifications as shall have been approved by the State Board of Engineers and the Mississippi River Commission.*

Section 2. That the Board of Levee Commissioners of Orleans Levee District be and it is hereby authorized to acquire by purchase, donation, or expropriation the lands or other property necessary for the construction of such works. It shall also be authorized to receive and expend for said purpose any funds contributed to it by the United States Government or any of the Levee Districts of the State benefited by said works, which said Levee Districts be and they are hereby authorized to make such appropriations for that purpose as to them seem proper.

Section 3. The Orleans Levee District is hereby required, as a condition precedent to removing any levees or taking possession of any property, to acquire by purchase or expropriation and to pay for all lands and property privately owned within the area covered by the proposed plan from the upper to the lower limits thereof and from the Mississippi River to the sea.

"What do they mean to the sea? Are they talking about building a spillway all the way down to the Gulf?" Claude asked.

"I'm not sure what they're planning, but it looks like they covered all their bases," Antoine said. "This truly is the most ridiculous thing I've ever seen. Just wait. It gets better."

Section 4. That the State Board of Engineers be and it is hereby directed to cooperate with the said Board of Levee Commissioners of the Orleans Levee District in the preparation of the necessary plans and the construction of necessary works; the cost thereof to be paid by the Orleans Levee District.

Section 5. That the Board of Levee Commissioners for the Orleans Levee District be and it is hereby authorized and directed to arrange with the Board of Commissioners for the Grand Prairie Levee District and the Board of Commissioners for Plaquemines Parish East Bank Levee District whereby the bonded and other indebtedness of said two levee districts, as to the area to be affected by the proposed works, shall be acquired by said Orleans Levee District, to be paid for by it, at values as of June 17, 1924, and cancelled; and said two levee districts be and they are hereby authorized, upon the completion of the plans and after their approval by the State Board of Engineers and the Mississippi River Commission, to consent to the removal, at the expense of the Orleans Levee District, of the Levee systems of these two districts in that portion of the levee systems thereof as may be determined by the Orleans Levee District shall be removed.

Section 6. That the Board of Levee Commissioners of the Orleans Levee District be and it is hereby authorized, for the purpose of raising the funds required under the provisions of this act, to levy annually for such length of time as it may determine, such taxes, within the constitutional limitation, as may be required; and those taxes, and other revenues may be by it funded into bonds or other evidence of indebtedness, bearing not more than six (6%) percent per annum interest, the proceeds thereof created by a sale at not less than par and accrued interest, to be used for the purpose of the acquisition of the property and the construction of the works herein authorized.

"Now they're going to raise taxes to pay for it," Antoine said. "Maybe not ours, but surely the people within their district."

"We're the ones who are going to pay," Anna-Marie said. "With our way of life."

Section 7. That all laws or parts of laws in conflict herewith be and they are hereby repealed. In case any section or sections or part or any section or sections of this act shall be found to be unconstitutional, the remainder of this shall not thereby be invalidated, but shall remain in full force and effect. As this act is designed to meet an emergency, it shall be broadly construed.

"An emergency?" Anna-Marie couldn't believe what she was hearing. "What emergency? This river has been flooding the land here for centuries. We're still here. New Orleans is still there. What's the emergency?"

"You're right, child. There is no emergency. That's how I know something else is going on here. For the life of me I can't understand why they want this land, but there's no escaping it now. There will be a final vote in July when the House meets for the second regular session, but there's no doubt it will pass. I can't find a single representative who's dead set against it. They will have the right to take our land, our businesses, our homes. And it gets worse."

"Worse? What can be worse?" Claude asked.

"To my knowledge, they will have to pay us fair market value, but, if you remember, our land was reassessed after the 1915 hurricane for a much lower value than before. Almost seventy percent lower, if I recall correctly, so we'll only realize about thirty cents on the dollar of what our land is really worth."

"Oh, no, Papa! Are you serious?"

"I'm afraid so. Fortunately, I have reserves, but most folks down here have nothing more than last week's pay. What they get for their land will be hardly enough to start over."

"What about all the oystermen who rent those cabins from Old Man Fucich? He's always kept rents low for them. Where will they go?" Abraham reached for Hester's hand. "I'm sorry, sir, but I've heard enough for one day. I have to relay this news to my family." Abraham pulled Hester toward the door.

Anna-Marie followed them out. "Don't worry, Hester. We'll help you and Abraham when the time comes."

"I've done told you, Anna-Marie. I don't accept no charity," Hester snapped.

"Forgive her," Abraham said. "She just so upset by all of this."

"I know. I am, too," Anna-Marie said. "We all are."

Anna-Marie walked back into the store and sat down, looking over the papers her papa had laid on the counter.

"It's really over, Papa? Is there nothing you can do to sway votes in the House?"

"I can try, but truly, there's nothing more that can be done."

Claude placed his hand on Anna-Marie's shoulder. "We'll be okay," he said. "I promise."

"How can you promise such a thing? We'll never be okay!" Anna-Marie said, running from the room.

"Let her be," Antoine said when Claude moved to follow her. "She needs a little time."

Claude wanted to go after her, but he knew Antoine was right. She needed time. So did he. Time to process the fact that the life they had always known would soon be over.

CHAPTER 22

"What do you mean? We will have to sell our land?" Florence asked when Abraham told her the news. "They can't make us sell what we've worked our whole lives for. I know you know how many times we've rebuilt this house, how many times we've suffered floods and hurricanes. All of that mess couldn't make us leave, so how are some politicians gonna make us?"

Abraham, Hester, Emmanuel, and Florence were sitting outside on the front porch, or "gallery," as Florence called it, of Abraham's childhood home in Union Settlement. Emmanuel and Florence could imagine nothing worse than this news their son was bringing them.

"Your mother's right, son," Emmanuel said. "My daddy sharecropped this farm and earned every inch of it fair and square. Ain't nobody got the right to take it from us."

"It's not set in stone yet, but the final vote will come in July. Mr. Bertaut says no one up there in Baton Rouge is against it. They will buy our land, or they will take it," Abraham said. "It don't make them no never mind. Mr. Bertaut says we'll only get about thirty cents on the dollar because of that last hurricane. We won't have a choice. If we don't sell, they will force us off. It's called 'expropriation.'"

Florence snorted. "I don't give a care what it's called. Of course, they won't pay a fair price, but why are we bothering with that? I'm not selling, and that's that."

"I agree," Hester said.

"You'll have to, Mama, or they will come here and make you leave," Abraham said. "We're mad as hell about it ourselves. Hester's land has been in her family for over a hundred years. We don't want to sell either, but I don't know what else can be done. Neither does Claude. If Anna-Marie's father can't do anything about it with all his money and clout, I know we can't do anything."

"They'll drag me off by my hair or my legs or whatever, but I ain't going nowhere," Florence said, a rare tear spilling down her cheek.

Abraham saw it, and wiped it away with his thumb. Florence swatted at his hand. She was a strong woman, stronger than most, and she had experienced her fair share of trauma and sadness in her life. She had lost three children in childbirth before she had Abraham and two more after. Five children she grew in her belly only to lose them in the end. She had fretted for months when Emmanuel contracted yellow fever, afraid when he left for Hotel Dieu that he would never come back. Her father had died of yellow fever, and her mother had worked herself to death after her father died. She knew what loss felt like, but this, this was different. This was her home, the home where she had raised Abraham, the home she shared with her husband, the home she loved.

Abraham leaned over and placed his arm around her shoulder. "This isn't going to happen tomorrow, but we must get ready because it's going to happen. We can stand on our principles and refuse to sell. That's one choice. The other choice is to sell to them. There's no in between. It's going to have to be one or the other."

Florence stood up and, without saying another word, she went into the house.

Emmanuel stared after her for a moment, and then he turned to Abraham. "What are you and Hester going to do, son?"

"Our first instinct is to fight, but who can we fight? We're already considered second-class citizens. No one cares what happens to us, so we don't stand a chance. We're luckier than most, you and I. We own our property. Most folks like us down here don't. I've talked to Claude, and we've discussed moving our homes across the river, but still, it won't be the same. If you want, we can take yours, too."

"How you gonna do that, son? That's plumb crazy."

"It won't be easy, but I've seen it done. All we need are timbers, mules, and a barge. Captain Henry should be able to arrange the barge for us. I thought about using my boat, but the captain advised against it," Abraham said. "And Claude is already looking for land. He plans to move somewhere around Homeplace and open up another store. There's not much there— just a bunch of small farms. Used to be a big orange grove by Nairn, but the hurricane wiped that out. Like I said, not much of nothing, but it's someplace to go."

"How much time do we have?" Emmanuel asked.

"Not sure. Government moves slow, so I don't know. If we hold out, maybe a year."

"That's a long time, son. Anything could happen in a year."

"That's true," Abraham agreed. "I wanted to warn you because we don't know when these people will show up at our door. I'm sure Claude will find out how this is going to work, but until we hear from them, we don't need to do anything yet, except prepare our minds for the move."

"This is going to be very hard on your mother," Emmanuel said. "I'll talk to her, but I don't think it'll do much good. She's stubborn as a mule."

"So is my wife," Abraham said, smiling at Hester. "I guess we'll see what happens."

"I'm as sure of that as the day is long," Emmanuel said.

"We have to go. We're going to the Mulatto camp to speak with Sanon," Abraham said. "Tell Mama we said good-bye."

"I will." Emmanuel patted Abraham on the back. "Damn those politicians."

Abraham gave his father a hug, and then he and Hester walked to the landing where he had tied his boat. As he steered it out into the bayou, he took a deep breath. He steeled himself for his visit with Sanon. He really couldn't bear any more bad news.

"At least we'll still be close to the river," he said when Hester walked up to stand beside him. He put his arm around her. "I know how hard this is for you," he added.

"I lost them once," she said. "Now, I'll lose them again."

"No, you won't. You'll carry them with you. That's what you'll do," Abraham reminded her.

"Let's stop by the house before we go to the camp. I want to collect some soil to bring to Sanon," Hester said.

Abraham wasn't sure why she wanted to do this, but he knew whatever the reason, it might make her feel better, so when they reached Nestor, he pulled into the landing on Fucich Bayou and helped her from the boat. Together, they walked to their home and then to the barn to retrieve a bucket. With a small shovel, Hester dug up the earth near an orange tree until her bucket was almost full.

"This will be plenty." She handed the bucket to Abraham.

They walked silently back to the landing and then headed back out into the bayou.

When they reached the Mulatto camp, Sanon was outside waiting for them on his porch. "I knew you were coming," he said, greeting them with a hug. "Those clouds up there, covering the sun, they look threatening, no?"

"I noticed them earlier, but I don't smell rain," Abraham said.

"You won't," Sanon said. "There will be no rain this evening. Only clouds settling over this place."

"Tell us," Hester said. "What do you feel?"

Sanon sat down and gestured for them to join him. He pointed to Hester's bucket. "What is this you bring me?"

"It's my father's land," Hester said. "I want to carry it with me."

Sanon smiled and took the bucket from Hester. "You shall, child. Leave it with me. Now tell me why you came."

"It is happening," Abraham said. "Everything you predicted. The Senate voted to take our land to build a spillway. From the river to the sea, it says. The House votes in July, but I don't see them doing anything different."

"Yes, we will be gone, tossed away into the wind to scatter across the land," Sanon said, "but we mustn't let them take our spirit because, when the time comes, that's all we will have left." Sanon looked pointedly at Hester. "You, child. You must pull from within. You have lost before, and you shall lose again, but you must stay strong. I know you want to fight, but this is already determined. Look at those clouds. In them, you will find truth. There is no stopping the forces that plot against us."

"But why are they doing this?" Hester asked.

"There is a greater reason," Sanon said. "This land has value to them, a value we cannot see. All will be revealed in time, and then a great fight will commence. A fight that will be won and lost at the same time."

"Pardon me, but you speak in riddles, Sanon, "Abraham said. "I don't understand."

"Then you must simply accept that which you cannot understand. Do not fight them. You cannot win. Accept what they offer and begin anew with an open spirit. Take the past with you and keep it close. When the time comes, we shall be victorious, but that time is not now."

"What will you do?" Hester asked.

"I will cross the river, as well. It is not to my liking, but there is nothing I can do. My power lies in healing. Like you, I will have to find my way. Now excuse me for a moment while I take care of this." Sanon pointed to the bucket of soil.

While they waited, Abraham reached for Hester's hand. "We will get through this together," he said. "It won't be easy, but I'm sworn to care for you, and I will."

Hester looked up at him. "You have taken good care of me, husband, but even you can't make this better."

"We have to make the best of it, Hester. If we don't, they win."

"Then they win because I see nothing good in this. We can't just go buy new land."

"Claude will buy it using our money and then deed it to us. We've already discussed it," Abraham reassured her.

"Claude and Anna-Marie do too much for us already. Folks talk about it, you know."

"Let them talk," Abraham said. "Claude and Anna-Marie sure don't care, and neither do I. They could never understand what Claude and I went through in the war or that Anna-Marie doesn't think like others do. We are lucky to have them, and we should always remember that."

Hester nodded. "Yes, we are. Look at Isaac. Already, he can read and write. Anna-Marie says he's very smart. She treats him as well as she treats her own children."

"That's because we're family. That's how she sees it."

"I wonder how the folks across the river are going to see it."

"We can worry about that when the time comes," Abraham said. "Until then, we must ready ourselves and make our plans."

Abraham stood up when Sanon returned and handed a large piece of damp clay to Hester. "What is that?" he asked.

"It is to place in a sacred spot on your new land," Sanon said. "I have mixed the soil with the clay. This stone now carries the spirit of Bernice and Big Jake and Isaac. You will take their spirits with you."

Hester placed the stone on the railing of the porch and walked out into the yard, searching until she found the perfect stick—thin, but sturdy. She carried it back to the porch and began carving her parents and brother's names into the stone. Underneath their names, she drew a cross. When she finished, she turned to Sanon and gave him a hug. "Thank you, my friend. Now I can take them with me. I will forever cherish this gift you have given me."

"Your parents were strong, and now you, too, must be strong," Sanon said.

"I will be. I will make you proud. I will make them proud."

Sanon smiled. "That is all you can do, child."

Hester and Abraham said their good-byes and walked back to the landing with Hester tightly clutching the stone to her chest. Along the way, Abraham noticed that his wife had a new spring in her step. The dark mood that had engulfed her for months seemed to have lifted. And when she smiled at him—not the half smiles she had attempted for a long time, but a bright, sunny smile—his heart soared. His Hester was back.

He said a silent prayer of thanks. Together, they would get through this. Together, they could get through anything.

Still sitting on his porch, Sanon stared at the storm clouds gathering in the dreary sky. Worry furrowed his brow. He had said so little, but he knew so much more. Troubled times were coming. Troubled times indeed.

CHAPTER 23

On June 30, 1924, Act 99 was received in the Louisiana House of Representatives. On July 1, it was read in session by title. Then it was read a second time and referred to the Committee on Public Works, where, on July 2, it was given the go-ahead. On July 3, it was referred to the Legislative Bureau, which returned it with an amendment. On July 7, the act was read with the amendment, and on July 8, the final reading predicated the vote. Seventy-three yeas were recorded when the roll was called. There were zero nays. Not one legislator opposed the act that would create a spillway so far south of New Orleans. Not one questioned its effectiveness. Everyone thought they were doing what was best for New Orleans. The spillway was necessary, and the people who lived and worked on the East Bank of the river would be compensated. On July 14, 1924, Governor John M. Parker signed the act into law. The members of the Board of Commissioners of the Orleans Levee District had done their job well. It was done, set in stone, and reaction from New Orleans and on down the river was mixed.

In the coming months, folks who had left after the 1915 hurricane and the 1922 flood rushed back to pay unpaid taxes, happy at the prospect of making a few dollars off of their forsaken land. Folks who did not have clear title to their land showed a renewed interest in obtaining it. Other folks checked to see what their land was worth, only to discover that it had been devalued after the hurricane. But most folks just scratched their heads, wondering how this could be happening, wondering why the Orleans Levee District wanted their land, and hoping that it was all just a bad dream. In New Orleans, folks were pleased that the government had finally done something good to protect their city. The Bohemia Spillway would solve all of their flooding issues, or so they thought.

In Nestor, Antoine Bertaut convened a meeting to discuss Act 99 with his company executives to determine what next steps were necessary to preserve his milling company. "I want numbers," he said. "I want to know exactly what this mill is worth, every last dime. They might take what is mine, but they are going to pay for it. We have to decide where we will move and what area will be most advantageous to the company. We must also consider our employees, or more precisely how many employees we will have left once all is said and done. There is much to consider indeed."

In the Mulatto camp near Ostrica, Sanon gathered his friends and informed them that they must find a new place to make camp in the coming months. "We don't know for sure yet how far down the spillway will come, but I'm not willing to wait around and take a chance on being flooded out one day. It's time to move. Those who wish to leave the area may do so," he said, "but those who wish to move across the river with us are welcome. We will move upriver where we will be a little safer from the elements, maybe around Nairn or farther north near Happy Jack. Soon, I will cross the river and travel its course until I see a sign of where we should land. I will let you all know then where we are led to go. Until then, cast your eyes around and decide what you will take and what you will leave. We have some time, but we should be prepared."

In Union Settlement, the general store was abuzz with talk about the spillway.

"I'm going wherever Hester and Abraham go," Poopdeck told Claude, one afternoon in August. "I have to take care of them, you know. They've always taken such good care of me."

"I feel the same," Claude said. "Wherever we go, they must be nearby."

"Where you gonna go?" Poopdeck asked.

"Don't know yet. Abraham and I are going across the river next week to look at what's available. We have to have enough arpents to accommodate our house, Abraham's house, and maybe even his parents' home. We also have to see how much we are offered for our land. That's certainly a factor. We don't even know how much money we'll have. We also don't know exactly where this spillway is going to be. I've heard they are going to take about 33,000 acres for eleven miles along the river. It's supposed to begin at Bohemia Plantation, but I'm not entirely certain of that yet. We'll have to wait and see."

"Golly, that's Nestor and Grand Prairie and Point Pleasant, Daisy,"

141

Poopdeck said, counting on his fingers as he named each village and settlement. "And Nicholls and Dime, too. Almost to Ostrica. Where all those people gonna go? The Takos sure won't be happy if they have to move. They are very set in their ways. What's gonna happen to them?"

"I don't know," Claude said. "I just don't know."

"And what's gonna happen when the river rises up and just flows across the land? Everything we've built will be destroyed."

"Yes, it will," Claude agreed.

Poopdeck pulled a flask from his pants pocket and took a long swig. "If this ain't the most god-awful thing I've ever heard," he said.

"Yes, it's quite ridiculous." Claude watched as Poopdeck swallowed the last drop from his flask before walking toward the door.

A few minutes later, Mildred walked in, positively beaming. Claude looked around to make sure Anna-Marie was not in the store. Mildred was the last thing his wife needed right now.

"Hello, Mildred," he said, trying to form his lips into a smile.

"Did you hear that the spillway passed? I can't believe it. I'll get a tidy sum for my land, and then I can go live with my son. He's so excited about it."

"I bet," Claude said.

"Of course, you'll have to give up the store, but I'm sure you'll be just fine. Although, how you're going to support all those kids without this income, I have no idea. Of course, your wife's daddy will probably help. And you'll get money for the store, so you'll be okay, I guess. Where's your wife, anyway?"

Claude's eyes were glittering dangerously, but Mildred was oblivious. "What's she doing now? That girl is always up to something. How you picked her out of all the eligible girls down here has always been beyond me. She's pretty, for sure, but oh my, she does have some funny ways about her. Where is she?"

Claude couldn't help himself. "Hiding would be my guess. She must have seen you coming."

"Well, I never," Mildred said. "I'm accustomed to your wife's rudeness, but you, Claude Couvillion, you should be ashamed. I will certainly have a talk with your daddy about this."

"Please do," Claude said, moving from behind the counter to escort her out of his store. "Just leave those groceries. You won't be doing business here anymore. In fact, when you see me or my wife or my children, please look the other way. We have no further need of your acquaintance."

Mildred's cheeks turned blood red. She huffed and puffed for a moment and then hurried out of the store. Claude watched her stomp her way down the road, and then he heard laughter. He turned to find Anna-Marie bent over holding her stomach. "That was the best thing I've ever seen you do," she said, trying to catch her breath.

Claude burst out laughing, too. "That felt downright good." He picked Anna-Marie up and twirled her around. "At least we don't have to bother with her anymore."

"Thank goodness," Anna-Marie said. "At some point, I was going to have to forget my manners and flatten her."

"Flatten who?" Hester, who had just walked in, asked.

"Mildred. You should have seen Claude. He just gave her what for and kicked her out," Anna-Marie said. "It was the funniest thing I've ever seen. She was flabbergasted. With all her airs and butting her nose where it don't belong, she couldn't say a word. She just turned flush and stormed out."

"I wish I could have seen that," Hester said. "That woman does not like me or my kind. Never has."

"Well, she doesn't like me or my kind, either, and now she doesn't like Claude. After this, we won't have to worry about her again."

"Oh, I don't know," Hester said. "Everyone will hear about this."

"And everyone will understand why Claude did it."

"I hope so," Claude said.

Just then, Miss Penny walked in, a basket in her hand. "Good afternoon," she said, handing the basket to Claude.

"Good afternoon. What's this?" Claude asked.

"Just a little something for you good folks to nibble on," Miss Penny said. "My boys butchered a pig yesterday and roasted it. They cooked up everything but the squeal. I couldn't watch. I don't know who started the custom of drinking the blood, but it's disgusting. Mighty fine eatin', though, so I thought I'd drop some by."

"Thank you," Anna-Marie said. "We'll surely enjoy this."

"I saw Mildred down the road. She seemed none too happy. I take it you've lost your manners, Claude," Miss Penny said.

"He sure did," Anna-Marie said. "I've never been so proud."

Miss Penny started laughing. "Well, if anyone deserved that, I'm sure it was Mildred. One thing about this spillway coming through—we won't have to deal with her anymore. I heard she's moving further down the river on the West Bank. Can't be too far for me."

"Me, either," Anna-Marie agreed. "But that's about the only good thing coming from this. What are you going to do, Miss Penny?"

"I don't have a clue. I've been praying to the Almighty that this wouldn't happen, but the Good Lord has his own plans, it seems. Now I don't know what to do. Ever since my Benjamin passed away, the boys have been helping out on the farm, but if we have to give up the farm, I don't know what will happen. It's all so worrisome."

"Yes, it is," Anna-Marie said. "But don't you fret overmuch. Claude and Abraham are going to scout around next week across the river, and we'll let you know what they find. We're friends, and friends take care of friends. Maybe we can find you a nice spread near us. Claude can do the negotiating. He's real good at that."

Relief washed over Miss Penny's face. "Thank you, Anna-Marie. I've been fretting something awful. You know, the boys, bless their hearts, do everything they can, but they're just barely becoming young men, and they don't know the first thing about up and moving. They know how to hunt and chase rice birds away and milk the cows, but they don't know nothing about finances or the business side of the farm, or even how to pay for a new farm."

"Well, don't you fret no more. We'll figure something out for you and yours, won't we, Claude?" Anna-Marie said, looking at her husband.

"Yes ma'am. We sure will," Claude said.

Later that evening, Claude and Anna-Marie sat on their front porch with Abraham and Hester while their children played on the levee.

"I'm worried," Claude said. "There's so many folks who just don't know what to do. Everything is up in the air, dependent on what some politicians think the land down here is worth. And then there's folks like Miss Penny. She's had a bad turn of luck since Benjamin passed on, and now she's wringing her hands about what to do."

"We've got to help her," Anna-Marie said. "We've got to do what we can to help everybody."

"Y'all already do help everybody," Abraham said. "You'd be wealthy if everyone paid the credit you've extended at the store. How are you going to collect that if everyone's gone?"

"I don't know," Claude said, "but we can't worry about that right now on top of everything else."

"Sanon said we would lose, but we would be victorious in the end," Hester said. "What do you suppose he meant by that?"

"I couldn't make heads nor tails of it," Abraham said. "All I know is he kept looking at those dark clouds. They didn't look good."

"No matter what happens," Anna-Marie said, "we have our family and our health and each other. We'll figure the rest out."

"Yes, we will," Claude said, hoping Anna-Marie was right. "Now let's gather the children and take a walk along the river. We need to try to enjoy ourselves as best we can right now."

As they walked, each couple hand in hand and the children running ahead, Anna-Marie and Claude and Hester and Abraham breathed in the scent of the river, listened to the sounds that had been the rhythm of their lives, and observed the stunning scenery that had been the backdrop to everything that had ever happened to them.

A tremendous sense of loss settled over each of them.

CHAPTER 24

July 1924

Jefferson leaned back in his chair, placed his feet on his desk, and puffed away on a Camel cigarette. He couldn't have been more pleased. Everything had gone exactly as he had planned. In fact, it had been easier than he'd expected. The 1922 flood had helped. That had been a gift, he thought. A perfectly-timed gift. Now all he had to do was wait until the land was under his control, and he could begin the leasing process. He had no doubt the mineral rights to that land would fund the Levee Board and whatever projects he deemed necessary for decades to come. He was still daydreaming when his secretary informed him that Sal and Pierre had arrived.

"Gentlemen," he said when they walked in. "Please, sit. It's time we get all of our ducks in a row, and that's why I called you here today. We need to act swiftly. I figure it will take about six months to buy up all the property down the river, barring any stubborn homeowners. We'll pay them according to the latest property assessment. I hear it's much less than the previous assessment from before the hurricane, but that's that. It does give us some negotiating room with anyone who balks, like I'm presuming your cousin and his pretty daughter will do," he added, looking at Pierre.

"Oh, we can count on that," Pierre said. "He was none too happy when he came to see me a while back. In fact, he was madder than a hissing snake. Damn near got me disowned."

"That's why I fought so hard for the "under threat of expropriation" clause to go into Act 99. I knew that some of those people, especially the wealthier ones would try to fight this," Jefferson said. "They'll never win, though. It's set in stone now."

"Are you sure there's oil down there?" Sal asked.

"As sure as I'm sitting here, boys. I've already had a few meetings with some oil executives, and they will be onboard. As soon as we own that land, they'll begin testing. All of this might take a few years, but trust me, in the end we'll be rolling in the dough."

"You seem very confident," Pierre said.

"I am. We'll be able to do so much with all that money. Things that now we can only dream about," Jefferson said.

"Like what?" Sal asked. "What kind of dreams are you having?"

"That airport, for one. The one Abraham Shushan keeps talking about. He wants to build it as a land and seaplane terminal. That's never been done. How they're going to do that is beyond me, though, because where they want to build it is partially in Lake Pontchartrain. Wouldn't that be something, though? If we could fund it, that would be even better. Just think of it—the Jefferson Davenport Airport."

"Well, that's nonsensical," Pierre said. "How can you build an airport in a lake?"

"I don't know, but they're hell bent on figuring it out. Best to keep an eye on Shushan, boys. He's been sniffing around our plans for the spillway. He's smart, and he suspects something. He knows that spillway ain't gonna do as much for New Orleans as one that was built closer would," Jefferson said, lighting another cigarette. "He's ambitious, about as ambitious as that judge down the river. If we're not careful, he'll try to remove us from our positions. We can't let that happen. But never mind him. We've got some celebrating to do. And some planning. There's money to be made, gentlemen, and we are now in the business of making it."

"How much do you think that land is worth?" Sal asked.

"Millions," Jefferson said. "Millions and millions and millions. Just look at what's going on over there in Jennings, Louisiana. Ever since Standard Oil discovered oil around that salt dome there, they've been sniffing around all of Louisiana. When I've spoken with their representatives, they seem very interested."

"You really think so?" Pierre asked.

"I know so. I feel it in my gut. That's why we've done all this."

"But what if the people down there won't sell?" Pierre asked. "What about my cousin? What if he won't sell?"

"Oh, he will. If not, we'll send the authorities to escort him off the property." Noting the worried look on Pierre's face, Jefferson added, "But he's smarter than all that. He'll sell."

"I hope so," Pierre said. "I really don't need this kind of upheaval inside my own family."

"It will all be worth it. I promise," Jefferson said. "Now let's get to work. We need to go over those assessments and decide what we're going to offer those folks. There are 33,000 acres in the proposed eleven-mile area, and fifty-two percent of that is owned by the state. That will be deeded to our levee district, so we don't need to worry about that. That leaves forty-eight percent, roughly 15,000 acres we'll have to purchase. This includes everything from Bohemia Plantation to the Forty Arpent Line—Union Settlement, Grand Prairie, Nestor, Dime, Nicholls, Daisy, and Point Pleasant. From what I gather, there are 168 property owners with homes or businesses. Further down, Fort St. Phillip is nothing to worry about because it's been out of commission since the 1915 hurricane. The Austrians, or should I say Yugoslavs now? I can't keep up with the changing climate overseas. Anyway, they won't be happy down there in Ostrica, but they won't cause trouble. Of that, I'm sure. They've always kept to themselves. I imagine they'll eventually pick up and move, especially when the drilling starts, only they won't be compensated."

"It sounds like this is going to change the whole landscape down there. What will be left?" Pierre asked.

Jefferson let out an exasperated sigh. "A spillway, gentlemen. And big oil wells. Big, huge money-producing oil wells."

"Somehow this don't seem right," Pierre said. "It's not sitting well with me."

"That's because your cousin has your whole family mad at you," Jefferson said. "Trust me, a few years from now, you'll see things in a different light. Now where are those assessments?"

"Right here," Sal said, pulling a stack of papers from his briefcase.

"I want you to give those to the Real Estate Committee, and tell them to begin researching who holds title to each and every arpent of land down there," Jefferson said. "Tell them it's urgent, as we need to begin work on the spillway as soon as possible. Make sure they understand the urgency. As a matter of fact, call a meeting with everyone on that committee so you can reiterate that. I would like them to report back to me by the end of the year. I want the report to include each titleholder and the amount of the assessment of the property owned, so that we will have some idea of exactly what our expenditure on the land will be. I know we've had estimates, but I want solid numbers. By January of next year, I want to begin procuring the land."

"That's not a lot of time," Pierre commented.

"You're right. It's not," Jefferson agreed, "but we need to move as quickly as possible. My goal is to have the spillway finished by 1926. We're going to name it the Bohemia Spillway, and from here on out, the whole area will be referred to as Bohemia."

"Bohemia? After the plantation?" Sal asked.

"Why not? It's as good a name as any, and the spillway starts below it," Jefferson explained.

"So none of the settlements or townships will keep their names?" Pierre asked.

"Why would they? They'll be gone. What the people don't take, eventually the river will. It just makes sense to call the whole area Bohemia, but enough of that. Pierre, the Corps of Engineers has given me the report they intend to submit to the Mississippi River Commission. I'd like to go over the finer points with you. We need to know this information like the back of our hand."

Jefferson began to read aloud from the report:

"To whatever causes it may be attributed, it is a fact that flood heights in the Orleans District have been constantly rising, and are dangerously approaching the ultimate height to which the levees in this district can be built with safety.

"The protection of nearly half a million lives, and a billion dollars worth or property, on a river front of twelve miles, demands relief measures, supplemental to levees, be provided for the earliest date possible."

"We know all of this already," Sal grumbled.

Jefferson ignored him and began to flip through the report. "Ah, here we go. Actual plans...'Before undertaking this work, of course, the Orleans Levee Board will acquire all the property, lands, and improvements contemplated to be required for the project as a whole, and would further be in a position to protect the lands upstream from the effects of back water. The only extra expense to this Board being the construction of a small cross levee* *one mile below Nestor. In short, this experimental spillway would be, as to construction and cost, part and parcel of the Pointe á la Hache project, but would be undertaken during this coming high water, in order to afford us the only opportunity we have so far had, or will ever have again, of obtaining data about which the engineering profession has been divided for the past seventy years.'"*

"So they are designating this as an experimental spillway?" Pierre asked.

"Seems that way," Jefferson said, "and really, isn't that what it is? No one can say for certain that it will work, but let's continue. *The back levee from Pointe á la Hache to Bohemia will be strengthened in its weak spots and the section brought to an 8 foot crown, Elev. 28.0 C.D. and 3 to 1 slopes; likewise the cross levee on the lower line of Bohemia, from the river levees to the back levee will be brought to same section but crown at grade 29.0 C.D. The borrow pit paralleling the back levee, and on its east side, will be dammed at the lower line of Bohemia by extending the existing cross levee across the said borrow pit, and into the prairie as far as practicable, approximately half a mile, and at a slight angle pointing downstream, as shown on the plan. It is thought that the expansion of this cross levee will tend to divert water in a more southerly direction, and materially reduce the flow of back water upstream.'"*

"Essentially flooding everything south of the spillway during hurricanes and floods?" Pierre asked.

"Yes. We'll remove all of the levees with the exception of those we just talked about, so, of course, everything in the spillway and south of it will flood. That's the point. Doing that should keep the river at Carrollton under a gage of twenty," Jefferson said. "Y'all can read the rest for yourselves. My secretary will make you both a copy of this document. I want you to understand it completely. I want everything coordinated perfectly, so that by the time we obtain the land, we are ready to proceed. Understood? I want the waste weir in operation by 1926 in the event of high water. This has been a long time coming, and I want it finished as soon as possible."

Pierre nodded. "What about the contractors? When are we opening it up for bids?"

"We can start immediately. It's time to give our contractor and engineering friends some work. As you both well know, there's always a few bucks to be made in construction, but that's peanuts compared to what we'll make in the end," Jefferson said. "We have $1.2 million projected for our 1925 budget for levee construction and maintenance, so there should be no financial issues. Oh, and one more thing. Keep the planning as close to your belt as you can in the coming months. That judge is becoming more powerful down there and is running for district attorney. He's got his hands in so many pies, and I'm sure he'll cause as much trouble as possible for us. From what I hear, he's got spies everywhere, so watch what you say, and watch who you say it to. Not one word about oil to anybody. Not yet. That's still a ways away, and I'd prefer to have signed contracts in hand before they know anything. Agreed?"

"Agreed," Sal and Pierre said in unison.

"But do you really think the judge has that much power?" Sal asked.

"Not yet, but he's aiming for it. I've been keeping an eye on him for years, and I don't like what I see. All he needs to do is align himself with someone powerful enough to promote his agendas, and he'll become a problem. Trust me on this one, gentlemen. I think I've mentioned before that he could become a burr in our backsides. That time is now," Jefferson said. "The minute we begin working in what he considers his territory, anything could happen. He's sneaky and tricky. I don't trust him as far as I can throw him."

"I didn't like him the moment I met him," Pierre said.

"Me either," Sal said.

"Well, mind your P's and Q's around him and his friends, and we should be okay. Just remember, mum's the word," Jefferson said. "Now go on. Get out of here. Let's get this ball rolling."

After Sal and Pierre left, Jefferson lit another cigarette, leaned back, and smiled. These are the good times, he thought.

Mighty fine times indeed.

Daisy

People coming from the neighborhood of Harris' Canal Sunday morning were astonished by seeing water one foot deep on the public road. Thinking the levee had broken, they spread "the alarm of crevasse", but were assured by the residents that this was nothing unusual; Mr, John Roberts was only flooding his rice field.

This notice in the Lower Coast Gazette depicts how fearful residents were of flooding in Daisy.

The packet boat RWCarter carried goods and passengers up and down the Mississippi River in 1902.

Plans for the Louisiana and Southern Railway that would run down to Bohemia Plantation began in 1910. (Lower Coast Gazette)

Hon. Simon Leopold and Sheriff Mevers are busy getting signatures to the Right-of-Way for the extension of the Louisiana and Southern Railway to Bohemia plantation. This extension is now an assured fact and as soon as all of the signatures are obtained to the Right-of-Way the work of surveying and construction will begin.

Mrs, G. Favret, and son Clarence are visiting friends and relatives in New Orleans.

El Rito Sold.

The Power Boat El Rito was sold on Thursday in New Orleans by the U. S. Marshall. The Spicuzza Bros. Transportation Co. being the successful bidders for $9350.00.

DEPARTMENT OF THE INTERIOR
UNITED STATES GEOLOGICAL SURVEY
GEORGE OTIS SMITH, Director

BULLETIN 429

OIL AND GAS IN LOUISIANA

WITH

A BRIEF SUMMARY OF THEIR OCCURRENCE
IN ADJACENT STATES

BY

G. D. HARRIS

WASHINGTON
GOVERNMENT PRINTING OFFICE
1910

This geological survey published in 1910 describes the salt dome near Nestor, giving politicians the indication that there should be oil in the area.

The road that ran along the river in Pointe a lá Hache in 1915

BOHEMIA PLANTATION SOLD.

One of the Richest Estates in Plaque- mines Parish Auctioned.

POINTE A LA HACHE, LA., July 27.—The Bohemia plantation, owned by Marcus Waltzer & Co., was sold at public auction here to-day as a result of a partition suit among the co- owners. This plantation, which is among the most valuable in the parish, measures 18 2-8 arpents fronting on the river by a depth of 40 arpents. It is adapted to truck, orange and rice culture. It was adjudicated to Chris Reuter for $10,000. The new owners intend to con- tinue to develop this property, the orange cult- ure on a large scale forming part of their plans for the future.

Bohemia Plantation was sold at auction in 1912. (Times-Picayune)

The train schedule for the Southern Railroad from New Orleans to Pointe a lá Hache in 1916

SCHEDULE

LOUISIANA SOUTHERN R. R.

Daily except Sunday

Leave		Arrive	
New Orleans	7 a m	P'te-Hache	10:50 a m
"	5 p m	"	7:25 p m
Pte-Hache	6:30 a m	New Orleans	9 a m
"	1 p m	"	5:45 p m

SUNDAY

New Orleans	7:30 am	Pte-Hache	9:50 a m
"	5 p m	"	7:25 p m
Pte-Hache	6:30 a m	New Orleans	9 a m
"	4:15 p m	"	6:40 pm

Folks who lived along the river used mules to carry products across the levee to the river.

A typical home in the Bohemia area

The church in Union Settlement

Thriving Lower State School
Pupils' Work Elicits Praise

POINT PLEASANT, La., Feb. 22.— The Point Pleasant school, of which Miss Norma Buras is teacher, is one of the most thriving in lower Louisiana. It is one of the two schools in the parish, and under the careful guidance of Miss Buras the 28 pupils have attained a standard in their studies which has called forth the commendation of the parish school authorities.

ER ITEM FROM MRS. RAVEY'S scrapbook is the above clipping. It is believed to have
ed sometime in the early 1900's.

This school in Point Pleasant in the early 1900s was one of only two schools in the parish.

Many East Bank residents traveled to Pointe a lá Hache on Sundays to attend St. Thomas Catholic Church.

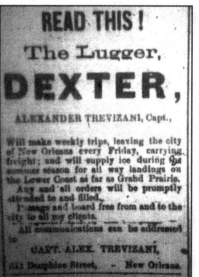

READ THIS!
The Lugger,
DEXTER,
ALEXANDER TREVIZANI, Capt.,

Oyster luggers like Dexter also carried goods and people down river from New Orleans.

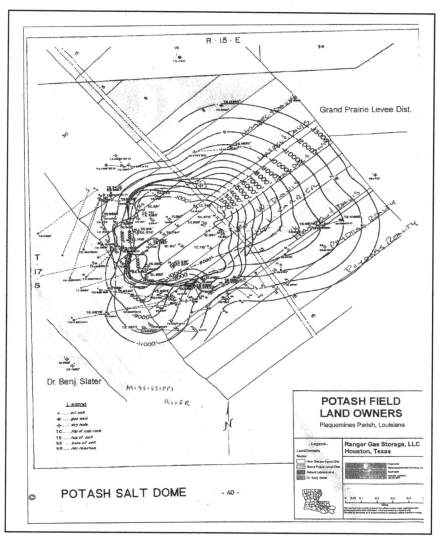

Grand Prairie Levee Dist.

R · 15 · E

Dr. Benj. Slater

MISSISSIPPI RIVER

N

Legend
o ....oil well.
✳ ....gas well.
✧ ....dry hole.
TC....top of cap rock.
TS....top of salt.
BS ...base of salt.
NR ....not reached.

POTASH SALT DOME   - 60 -

POTASH FIELD
LAND OWNERS
Plaquemines Parish, Louisiana

Legend
Land Owners
Name
☐ New Orleans Levee Dist.
☐ Grand Prairie Levee Dist.
☐ Robert Lobrano et al
☐ Dr. Benj. Slater

Ranger Gas Storage, LLC
Houston, Texas

0 0.05 0.1   0.2   0.3   0.4   1
Miles

The Potash Salt Dome that inspired the Orleans Levee
Board of Commissioners' interest in Bohemia

Most of the people who lived in Bohemia farmed their lands.

The Union Settlement cemetery before the Bohemia Spillway made the area uninhabitable

All of the homes in Bohemia had outhouses because there was no indoor plumbing.

21, 1928.
Oil, Gas & Mineral Lease.
By
of Commissioners for the Orleans
District - To-
Oil and Refining Company

FOLIO:

OIL, GAS and MINERAL LEASE

THIS AGREEMENT made this 8th. day of November, 1928,
between - BOARD OF LEVEE COMMISSIONERS OF THE ORLEANS LEVEE DISTRICT,
Lessor, and

HUMBLE OIL & REFINING COMPANY, Lessee - WITNESSETH :

1 - Lessor in consideration of twenty-seven thousand,
three hundred thirty-six and 83/100 Dollars ($27,336.83), of which
the sum of thirteen thousand and fifty-three and 75/100 Dollars
($13,053.75) is in hand paid to the Lessor, and the balance, the
sum of fourteen thousand two hundred eighty-three and 08/100
($14,283.08) dollars has been placed in escrow in the New Orleans
Bank & Trust Company of New Orleans, La., under an escrow agreement
entered into this day by and between the parties hereto and the
said bank, of the royalties herein provided and the agreements of
lease herein contained, hereby grants, leases and lets exclusively
unto Lessee for the purpose of investigating, exploring, prospecting,
drilling and mining for, and producing oil, gas, and all other
minerals, laying pipe lines, building tanks, power stations, telephone
lines and other structures thereon to produce, save, take care of,
treat, transport and own said products, and housing its employees,
the following described land in Plaquemines Parish, Louisiana, to-
wit:

A certain tract of land, situated in the Southeastern
Land District of Louisiana, east of the Mississippi River
in the "Spillway Area" of the Parish of Plaquemines, La.,
containing 3644.91 acres more or less, and consisting of
the following sections :

That portion of Radiating Section or River Lot No. 53 -
68 acres more or less, lying south of a straight line, being
the extension of the northern boundary of Radiating Section
or River Lot No. 13, Township 17, South, Range 15 East, to
the point where the township line dividing Townships 17 and
18 South, Range 15 East, meets the east bank of the Missis-
ippi River.

All of Radiating Section or River Lot No. 13 -161.67 acres
more or less.

All of Radiating Section or River Lot No. 14 -210.62 acres
more or less.

All of Rear Fractional Section
33 -189 acres, more
or less.

*The Orleans Levee Board of Commissioners signed this mineral
lease with Humble Oil on November 21, 1928.*

159

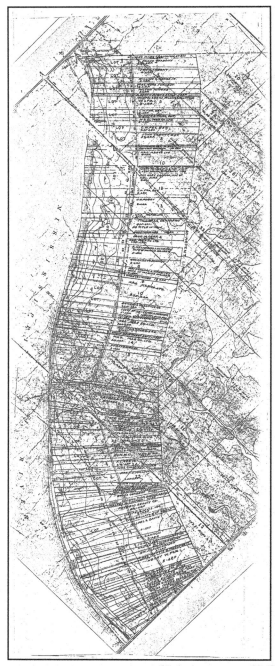

This map depicts the first eighty-five lots bought for pennies on the dollar or expropriated for the Bohemia Spillway.

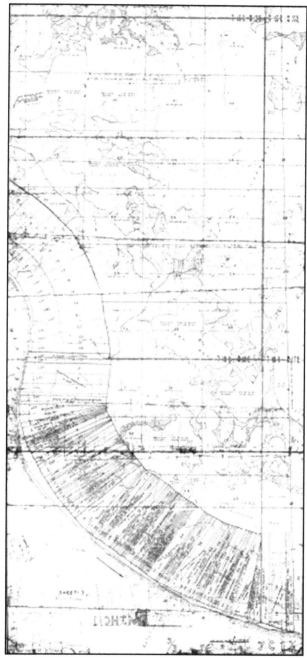

This map shows the rest of the lots that were bought or expropriated for the spillway.

We procured One Hundred thirty (130) options, covering one hundred sixty-three (163) tracts, representing Four Hundred (400) arpents front, by approximately forty (40) arpents in depth, amounting to Sixteen Thousand (16,000) square arpents, as will more fully appear by reference to the detailed maps attached hereto and forming part hereof.

The total value of the land covered by these options being Two Hundred Twenty-Eight Thousand, Five Hundred Seven and 20/100 dollars---- $228,507.20

The total value of the improvements included in options obtained---------------------------- 93,956.00

The average price per arpent front being---------------------- 570.00

The average price per square arpent being---------------------- 14.28

[handwritten: 1 sq. arpent = 0.85 acre]

VALUE OF ALL LANDS, EXCLUSIVE OF STATE LANDS, AS FIXED BY YOUR COMMITTEE-------------------- ~~$282,843.70~~ [handwritten: 274,413.50]

VALUE OF IMPROVEMENTS-------- ~~146,818.50~~ [handwritten: 151,231.00]

TOTAL VALUATION-------------- ~~429,662.20~~ [handwritten: 425,644.50]

The average price per front arpent on all land being----------- ~~$552.43.~~ [handwritten: $535.96]

This document, part of a report from the Orleans Levee District, shows some of the monies spent by the Board of Commissioners to create the spillway.

-5-

COST.

The cost of the project has been estimated as follows:-

1.	Bonds to be redeemed. Grand Prairie Levee District	$ 35,000.00
2.	East Bank Plaquemines Parish Levee District about 2/3 of $155,000.00	105,000.00
3.	Purchase or expropriation of lands and improvements (undetermined by Board as of January 23rd, 1925, but be- lieved will not exceed).	360,000.00
4.	Work to be done. Removal of 11 miles of river levee, 550,000 cu. yds. @ 10¢	55,000.00
5.	Removal of 11 miles top of rear levee, 180,000 cu.yds. @ 10¢	18,000.00
6.	Extending lower Bohemia Levee, 25,000 cu. yds. @ 20¢	5,000.00
7.	Strengthening rear levees Bohemia to Pointe-a-la-Hache	5,000.00
8.	Drainage provision	15,000.00
11.	Engineering and experiments including provision for emergency in case of threatening gap	70,000.00
12.	Contingencies	75,000.00
	Total Cost	$ 743,000.00

In the event replacing of levees is necessary,

9.	Replacing 11 miles river levee, 750,000 cu. yds. @ 25¢	187,500.00
10.	Replacing 11 miles rear levee about 400,000 cu.yds. @ 15¢	60,000.00
	Total	$ 990,500.00

It is confidently expected to keep the expenditures well within the figures given above.

FINANCIAL AND LEGAL ASPECT.

A special report is being submitted jointly with this report by the Legal Counsel of the Orleans Levee Board, Mr. Benj. T. Waldo, discussing fully the legal and financial aspects of the project. It may be said briefly here, however, that ample provision has been made by the Louisiana Legislature

Another page from the report notes the total cost of the spillway.

U. S. TO RESERVE SPILLWAY LAND MINERAL RIGHTS

Levee Board's Proposal for Expropriation Strikes Snag Quickly

A government counter-move to retain mineral rights to more than 450 acres of marsh prairie in Plaquemines parish, within the scope of the Pointe a la Hache spillway, may block a proposal by the Orleans levee board to expropriate the land held by the United States. A suit filed by Deutsch and Kerrigan, attorneys for the board, alleges that title to the land is needed by the board to satisfy the terms of the act of 1924 providing for the spillway.

The latter element in the suit is interpreted in some quarters as indicating that the board does not intend to abandon the Plaquemines project since the beginning of federal spillway work at Bonnet Carre and Laplace. In government circles, however, it is understood that activities of oil exploration interests which already have sought leases of board lands in the Pointe a la Hache area may be linked with the levee board move.

U. S. Moves for Right

United States Attorney Edmond E. Talbot, who was to be served with a copy of the petition Friday, could not be reached for an expression in the matter, but it is understood that department of justice officials have

Continued on Page Two

U. S. TO RESERVE SPILLWAY RIGHTS

Continued from Page One

already taken steps to protect the government's rights in the matter of potential petroleum deposits. The question of the board's right to sue the government for expropriation of the lands may also be raised thus referring to Congress the question of transferring the lands.

The board's suit lists three tracts, one of which was retroceded to the government after having been patented to J. C. Pendergast in 1839. The remaining two tracts, which, like the first, lie between the lower line of Bohemia Plantation and the Cuselich canal, have remained continuously in the possession of the government since the Louisiana Purchase.

Would Change Status

The approval of the Mississippi River Commission given the spillway project will make the proprietary rights of the government on the spillway area amenable to the terms of the 1924 statute of the Louisiana Legislature, in the opinion of the board's attorneys, who brought the suit against the government as the proprietor of lands held only in a proprietary sense and unused for any government works or as potential defenses.

Mr. Talbot is expected to make recommendations to the attorney-general for action in the matter which will protect the government interests, and may, it was said, advocate granting the levee board flowage rights to the lands or terrain title with a reservation of mineral rights to the government. The fact that oil companies are said to have leased other lands in the area "will complicate the issue," government officials said.

Times Picayune 1928-10-27-1 and 2

This 1928 Times-Picayune article discusses how the U.S. government tried to reserve mineral rights and stop the expropriation in the spillway area.

Many men in Bohemia made their livings by fishing oysters.

Fishing oysters was hard work, but oystermen could earn one to two dollars per sack.

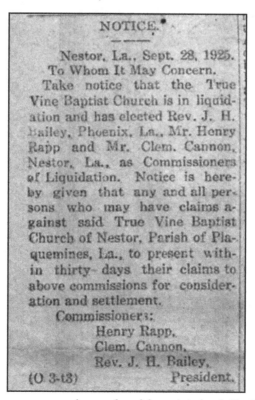

NOTICE.

Nestor, La., Sept. 28, 1925.
To Whom It May Concern.

Take notice that the True Vine Baptist Church is in liquidation and has elected Rev. J. H. Bailey, Phoenix, La., Mr. Henry Rapp and Mr. Clem. Cannon, Nestor, La., as Commissioners of Liquidation. Notice is hereby given that any and all persons who may have claims against said True Vine Baptist Church of Nestor, Parish of Plaquemines, La., to present within thirty days their claims to above commissions for consideration and settlement.

Commissioners:
Henry Rapp.
Clem. Cannon.
Rev. J. H. Bailey,
(O 3-t3)   President.

After so many people were forced from their land, The True
Vine Church in Nestor went into liquidation.

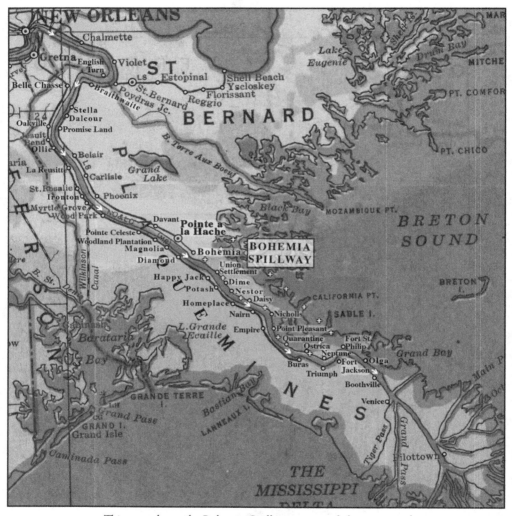

This map shows the Bohemia Spillway area and the towns and villages that lined the Mississippi River.

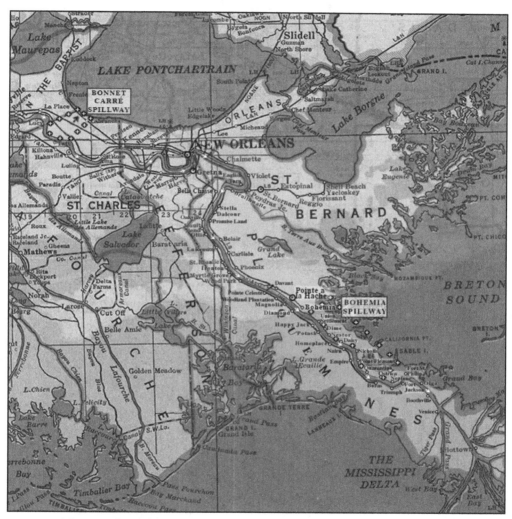

This map shows the Bonnet Carré Spillway in relation to New Orleans and the Bohemia Spillway. The Bonnet Carré Spillway proved much more effective at protecting the city because it was upriver and much closer to New Orleans.

Susan D. Mustafa and Charles J. Ballay

ILDERS ELAND TODAY

FOUR ARE NABBED WITH STOLEN AUTO

Released on Bonds of $1000 Each on Theft Charges

Four young men were arrested by policemen at St. Mary and St. Thomas streets late Saturday night, charged with grand larceny of an automobile and with having stolen property in their possession.

Those arrested were: Roy Daigre, 22 years old, 2241 Magazine street; Thomas Burns, 24, 714 Seventh street; Herman Spearing, 24, 2038 Camp street, and Andrew Castay, 27, 2314 Laurel street.

The automobile belonged to Mrs. A. T. Jackson, 2312 Octavia street, police said. The four accused were released on bonds of $1000 each.

JUDGE WESTERFIELD TO ADDRESS SOCIETY

Judge William W. Westerfield of the court of appeal will be speaker of the evening at the annual meeting of the Orleans Parish Medical Society tonight at Hutchinson Memorial building. Canal and Villere streets. Dr. J. Birney Guthrie, retiring president, and a committee

Daughter of Nobleman Marries Titled Athlete

—P. & A. Photo.

LADY MARY SCOTT, daughter of the Duke and Duchess of Buccleuch, married Lord Burghley, titled Olympic hurdling champion, in London recently.

TRANSFER OF U. S. HOLDINGS FOUGHT BY LEVEE BOARDS

Lake Borgne and Grand Prairie Officials Protest Orleans Plan

By Paul Wooton

Washington, Jan. 13.—Strenuous objection has been raised by the Lake Borgne levee board and the Grand Prairie levee board to the passing of pending legislation proposing to vest title in the Orleans levee board to certain lands in the Bohemia plantation area below New Orleans. The legislation pending before the public lands committee of the House would convey to the Orleans levee board all lands of the United States between the lower line of the Bohemia plantation and the Cuselich canal, which are needed in

connection with the Bohemia spillway.

A request has been filed with the public lands committee that representatives of the Lake Borgne and Grand Prairie levee boards are granted a hearing before action is taken on the bill. These levee boards challenge the ownership by the United States of the lands in question. They want the matter investigated to determine if these lands are not sovereignty lands belonging to the state of Louisiana and subsequently transferred to the levee boards of the locality.

It is contended further by the Plaquemines parish levee board that the Bohemia spillway is functioning haphazardly and that the flowage of water has been impeded to such an extent by the deposits of silt and debris as to render it worthless. The lands in the spillway area under present conditions are valuable, it is contended, for trapping and for pasturage and there is a prospect that they may possess mineral rights of value.

BENEFIT CONCERT PLANNED

A benefit concert for the Women's Dispensary building fund will be held tonight at 8:30 o'clock at 5003 Spruce street with Mrs. Eugenie Wehrmann-Schaffner at the piano.

Levee boards in Plaquemines Parish challenge the Orleans Levee District's right to take the land in Bohemia. (Times-Picayune)

The courthouse and jail in Pointe a lá Hache were often used as a refuge during hurricanes.

*The Fox homestead, one of the many farms along the
Mississippi River, bordered the spillway area.*

CHASSE, LA.

The Plaquemines Gazette

Original lattice work adorns historic home.

The
Bohemia
Plantation

History, Charm Reflected In Old Home

Withstands Time And The Elements

*by Roxanna S. Giordano,
Publicity and Landmarks
Chairman*

Nestled peacefully below Pointe-a-la-Hache for over a 100 years one will find Bohemia Plantation, a charming one story cottage framed with delicate lattice work, the individuality of its builder.

Bohemia Plantation is the home of Mr. and Mrs. Lawrence Tabony, a charming young couple with talent and patience. They restored the home, which was in a state of ruin, to the picturesque place it is today.

A unique feature of the home is, that according to belief, the lumber had been cut out in New

York and barged down the river to the present site, for the large timbers in the roof were meant to hold snow by New York standards.

The Tabony family acquired the property in 1925 from Mrs. Chris Reuther of Reuther Seed Company in New Orleans, and the home has remained in the Tabony family ever since. The original furnishings in the home were stolen in late 1950 and disappeared without trace.

Rice was planted on the plantation and one can still see the levees built to hold water in the rear of the land.

During renovation of the home the Tabony's found written on

one of the old doors this inscription, "R. N. Moores, Hudson, December 29, 1852, Bettwel Turnin," probably affording a date for its construction.

Bohemia Plantation has stood serenely through the ravishes of hurricanes and abandonment, and now it faces a bright future with a lovely young couple.

News is the life-line of a newspaper. News of yourself and friends is welcomed. All news must be signed, but if you do not wish your name used, just say so. Send news to THE PLAQUEMINES GAZETTE, 1901 Belle Chasse Hwy. North, Belle Chasse, La. 70037, or dial 394-1901.

The spillway began right below Bohemia Plantation. (Plaquemines Gazette)

Canal at Ostrica, Louisiana

Ostrica Canal was a popular waterway for fishing for oysters.

Oyster Cannery at Ostrica, Louisiana

The oyster cannery that was once located in Ostrica

This cemetery in Point Pleasant is the final resting place of many Bohemia residents.

Legislation will dangerous precedent

Just a little less than one year ago, your newspaper recommended that voters reject proposed constitutional amendment No. 2 because of the broad application and lack of legislative guidelines for returning expropriated public land to original owners, when the land is no longer used for its original purpose.

As you know, the Bohemia Spillway land owned by the Orleans Levee Board, though not specifically mentioned, was the target of the constitutional amendment which passed despite the warnings of every major newspaper in the state.

What most experts feared is now occurring in the Louisiana Legislature. The House of Representatives has already passed and the Senate is now considering legislation to return the Bohemia Spillway land to the descendants of the original owners, arbitrarily and capriciously ignoring the fact that the spillway has protected New Or-

leans from Mississippi River flood waters 16 times since 1928. In fact, the Bohemia Spillway is currently diverting Mississippi River flood water into the Gulf of Mexico, and twice last year automatically kicked-in as a natural overbank spillway to protect New Orleans.

If this legislation passes, the Orleans Levee Board believes the Louisiana Legislature will be establishing a dangerous precedent. Last year, when discussing the ramifications of this constitutional amendment with opinion leaders around the state, we learned of some interesting situations which parallel the Levee Board's situation regarding the Bohemia Spillway.

For instance, in Alexandria, the city's new multimillion-dollar City Hall and civic center complex has been constructed on land orginally expropriated for construction of a bus barn. If the Bohemia Spillway legis-

lation passes, precedent will be set for the descendants of the original landowners to initiate proceedings to regain the land on which the Alexandria Civic Center now sits.

The same would apply in Calcasieu Parish where long-abandoned school board property now is revenue producing oil and gas lease land, unoccupied by school buildings or school yards.

As the Senate prepares to debate this issue, the Orleans Levee Board hopes you will examine the issue, and if you agree that the legislation sets a dangerous precedent, urge your subscribers to ask their senator to vote against HB No. 1196.

EMILE W. SCHNEIDER
President
Board of Levee
Commissioners of the
Orleans Levee District
New Orleans

The president of the the Board of Levee Commissioners writes an editorial to sway public opinion in the matter of the return of the land in Bohemia. (Times-Picayune)

In 1983, Louisiana Governor Dave Treen met with a concerned citizens group to discuss how former landowners in Bohemia could get their land and mineral rights back. (Plaquemines Gazette)

TALK WITH TREEN — New Orleans attorney Bill Quigley (left) and state Rep. Frank Patti (second from right) stand with Gov. David Treen and a delegation from the Plaquemines Fishermen and Concerned Citizens group last week in the governor's office. The group asked for Treen's help in researching the legality of a 1924 act of the state legislature which allowed 57,000 acres of land in Lower Plaquemines Parish to be expropriated by the Orleans Levee Board for a flood control structure many of the group say is unnecessary. (Photo by Terence Adams)

New Legislation On Bohemia Spillway

A bill passed in both the House the Senate will enable some claimants of property along the Bohemia Spillway to legally regain their lands.

The bill, introduced by State Representative Frank Patti, amends prior legislation and orders that tracts of land expropriated from their owners by the Orleans Levee Board be returned to their original owners. The previous bill said that lands would only be returned if they had been taken by expropriation or threat of expropriation. Patti's change says land will be returned no matter how it was acquired by the levee board.

"The properties were acquired by the board for public purposes which no longer exist," says Patti. "The manner of acquisition should make no difference," he says.

Patti says that some of the property acquired by the levee board was sold for taxes and not expropriated as was the requirement under the original legislation. They were then considered a transfer, but not a purchase. The owner still had a right to redeem it, he says, and the new amendment allows this.

The previous bill also said that lands subject to litigation were not ordered to be returned. Patti's new bill says those lands can now be returned.

The Bohemia Spillway, about 33,000 acres of oil-rich lands on the east bank, was taken by the Orleans Levee Board from its original owners nearly 6[] years ago. The lands were originally intended to be used for flood control, but instead the levee board used the property for its mineral rich lands and collected the revenues. It awarded its first oil lease in 1927.

Today, it is estimated that annual revenues from the land are at about $2 million.

Descendants of the families who were made to leave their lands have struggled to reclaim them. Heirs to some of the spillway's 219 tracts between Pointe a la Hache and Buras have been battling the levee board and the government to take their lands back for their families.

The bill has passed both the House and the Senate and is now awaiting a signature from Governor Edwin Edwards.

The Bohemia Lands

P. Pache

Bohemia
Spillway
location

P. Sulphur

Buras

Venice

A bill passes in the Louisiana House of Representative and Louisiana Senate to give the land in the Bohemia Spillway area back to its former owners.

Governor Edwin Edwards signs the legislation to return the land in Bohemia. (Plaquemines Gazette)

Court Throws Out The Bohemia Spillway Law

Plaq. Gazette April 5, 1985 P.!

Action by former owners or their heirs to reclaim land in the Bohemia Spillway was stalled abruptly last week by a district judge's ruling in Baton Rouge.

Judge Frank Foil found the state law requiring return of the land the Orleans Levee Board took over in 1924 to be unconstitutional, and issued an injunction barring the state from enforcing the law.

The Department of Natural Resources began only last week to accept applications from people who believed they had a claim on some of the thousands of acres of land comprising the 22-mile long spillway on the east bank of the Lower Mississippi River.

Included in that number was the lawfirm of Broadhurst, Brook, Mangham, Hardy & Reed, hired just last week by the parish commission council to push what the parish officials believe is a legitimate claim to substantial portions of the mineral-rich spillway land.

The Louisiana Legislature passed a law in 1984 requiring the Orleans Levee Board to return the land to its former owners after a 1983 constitutional amendment authorizing the action was approved by Louisiana voters.

The levee board has resisted the return of the land because it derives about $5 million annually from oil and gas discovered after the spillway was created in the 1920's.

The parish began its legal action in hopes of gaining a portion of that mineral wealth for itself.

Attorneys for the state said Attorney General William J. Guste Jr. will appeal the ruling of the state Supreme Court, an action permissible when a court declared a law unconstitutional.

The 1983 amendment allowed the legislature to return to private owners land taken for a public purpose that no longer exisits under terms and conditions set by the Legislature.

But Foil said no terms and conditions exist and that the law ordering the levee board to return the land without compensation amounted to a gift.

Foil also said he is not of the opinion that the spillway has ceased to exist. Critics of the spillway contend that it has never served its avowed purpose of flood control and that the levee board is concerned only with the potential loss of 25 percent of its income.

Last week's hearing was called at the request of the levee board, which asked the state court to halt enforcement of the law.

In 1985, a district judge challenges the law that gives Bohemia back to its former owners. (Plaquemines Gazette)

Spillway Land Will Be Returned To Heirs

The Louisiana Legislature's authorized return of the Bohemia Spillway land to the original owners and their heirs has withstood its second test of the Louisiana Supreme Court with a ruling to that affect Monday by the state's high court.

The Orleans Levee Board has held the land since 1925 when most of it was purchased under the threat of expropriation under the pretense of constructing a spillway at the site to protect the City of New Orleans. Over 30,000 acres was acquired, much of it land farmed by poor residents of the parish.

Shortly after the acquisition, oil was discovered on the land and the Orleans Levee Board has derived millions of dollars of income over the past 50 years from the property. Currently almost 40 percent of the Board's income or $3 million annually comes from Bohemia.

Former landowners and descendants of landowners began attempts to regain the land winning significant victories during the past three years. In 1984, legislation ws approved which allowed the return of land taken for a public purpose but no longer needed for such purpose. In 1985, the Legislature decided the spillway was no longer needed and ordered the land returned to the original owners according to the prior year's legislation.

The return was challenged in a Baton Rouge District Court by the Orleans Levee Board and eventually ruled constitutional in February by the Louisiana Supreme Court. At the request of the levee board, the court agreed to reconsider the matter with its final decision being the same as in February.

Levee board officials have vowed to continue to fight return of the land to the federal courts or appeal to the U.S Supreme Court. A suit in federal court was filed at the time the suit was filed in state district court but was not acted on pending the state court's decision.

Representative Frank J. Patti who pushed the legislation through the house and senate on behalf of the claimants said he was very pleased with the decision of the court. "It's a personal feeling of great satisfaction and happiness for everyone affected by act 233 and all the people of Plaquemines Parish," Patti said citing that the parish may have a claim to some of the land. "I hope this decision finally and once and for all clears way for the return of the spillway."

Patti said he would be meeting next week with officials in Baton Rouge to coordinate his staff and the staffs of the Attorney General's Office and the Department of Natural Resources to begin processing the claims. "We plan to re-open the offices at Belle Chasse and Buras to accept applications and help people to file their claims."

Patti said he hopes to keep the offices open for six months. "In the general appropriations bill, I set aside funds to staff these offices. We will let the people know when the offices will open as soon as the office space can be arranged and staffing completed," Patti said.

Patti said although claimants who have already filed a claim at one of the offices during the prior application period will not need to reapply, they will be able to check at the offices to be sure their applications are still pending. "I know how important this is to our people and I want them to be able to rest assured that their application are on file. If they want to check at the offices when they're open, that's fine with me. In fact, I would suggest that they do so," Patti said.

Patti said while he will not rest until the land is finally returned, he is optimistic that an attempt at relief from the federal courts by the Orleans Levee Board will not drag on too long. "I believe the federal courts will say this is a state matter and throw it out," he said.

Bohemia residents and their descendants experience another win when the Louisiana Supreme Court rules that their land must be returned. (Plaquemines Gazette)

174

Hundreds in Louisiana Regaining Family Land
By FRANCES FRANK MARCUSSpecial to The New York Times
New York Times (1923-); Oct 25, 1986; ProQuest Historical Newspapers: The New York Times
pg. 6

Hundreds in Louisiana Regaining Family Land

By FRANCES FRANK MARCUS
Special to The New York Times

BOOTHVILLE, La., Oct. 23 — Sixty years ago, when Adeline Pinkins was a teen-ager, a stranger went to her family's house and told her father they had to leave.

"Move where?" her father asked, according to Mrs. Pinkins. "Where am I going to go with my family?"

"Well, you're going to have to go," the stranger said, Mrs. Pinkins related, "because we're going to make a spillway here and you can't live under water."

"I'll never forget it," Mrs. Pinkins, who is 79 years old, said today, smiling on her front porch, after the Louisiana Supreme Court handed down a decision upholding a 1984 state law that orders the return of the land taken by state government decree. Mrs. Pinkins's parents received $700 for two acres.

Mrs. Pinkins's account is one of hundreds like it in south Louisiana's oil-rich Plaquemines Parish, or county, an isolated peninsula of marshy land south of New Orleans.

$3 Million in Annual Revenue

The land in dispute is producing about $3 million annually in oil and gas revenue, which has been going to the state agency that took it over. The heirs of the land are entitled to the mineral rights from 1984. But the state said it would continue its fight to retain the land.

Like their neighbors, poor black and white fishermen, trappers, oystermen and rice farmers, all poor people, the same order, Mrs. Pinkins and her family picked up and left their house for the other side of the Mississippi River. They navigated the swift current in a skiff, carrying their clothes and mattresses.

Her father came back later, took apart their house and carried it across the river in pieces, on the skiff, Mrs. Pinkins said. The house lay on the ground until he could get some help to rebuild it.

In the meantime, a friend offered the family the use of an old house downriver. "There were all kinds of insects in that house and all kinds of snakes," Mrs. Pinkins recalls. "They had to run them out. We lived there for a while."

Livestock Left Behind

The family had left behind their horses, chickens and hogs. "We had nothing to bring them in," Mrs. Pinkins said.

The area has rankled residents here since the mid-1930's when they were forced to leave their homes on the river's east bank, cultivated with rice and orange gardens, for what they regarded as inferior land on the west bank. They were told the spillway had to be created "to save the city of New Orleans," 58 miles upriver, from flooding, Mrs. Pinkins said.

George M. Edgerson, who is 80 and lives in New Orleans, has one poignant memory. He received a news about the spillway in a letter from his mother when he was attending the Fisk Institute in Brooklyn. "My mother was upset at first but after they came out with the story that New Orleans would be flooded, she agreed to do it," he said. "Everybody had to get out." A retired teacher, he recalls that the cattle and cows were driven away from the other side. They were driven away from their churches, their rice farms, their cemetery and now there is an oil well in the center of it."

'Facts Are Very Murky'

Exactly why the Plaquemines Parish land, specifically land in the Grand Prairie Levee District, became a spillway is not known, according to William P. Quigley, a New Orleans civil rights lawyer who worked with the Fishermen and Concerned Citizens Association in Plaquemines Parish for five years to lobby for the state legislation making it possible for the land to be returned.

Mr. Quigley says, "The facts are very murky."

These facts are known: In 1924 the State Legislature ordered the creation of a spillway, or weir, for flood-control, to protect New Orleans, and ordered the Orleans Levee Board to acquire the land situated in the Plaquemines Parish Grand Prairie Levee District. The Orleans Levee Board was to purchase or expropriate the land for the spillway, which was named Bohemia, after a plantation existing on the site, and are responsible for a network of devices for flood protection.

The Bohemia Spillway turned out to be a good deal more costly to the property taken from the land owners. The court said that from 1950 to 1981 the oil and gas revenue from the entire spillway totaled almost $43 million. About half of the 33,000-acre spillway had been public land owned by the state.

Owners Paid $359,500

The State Supreme Court decision handed down Monday says, "The owners of the private property taken or acquired for the spillway were compensated $359,500."

Since the state law was passed in 1984 the state board has been keeping the oil and gas revenue from the disputed property in escrow, should it lose its Plaquemines case, should it lose the State Supreme Court for another review of the case or reactivate a case it has filed in Federal court.

Mr. Edgerson, a retired engineer,

Mrs. Pinkins and others whose relatives were forced off the land, insist that the area's real estate spillway. They assert that the spillway story was a sham concocted by politicians to get the land and the minerals beneath it.

The Orleans Levee Board contends that. "The spillway works and its worked 19 times since it was originally constructed," according to a spokesman for the board, who said in simple terms is lower the water level at the city of New Orleans by close to half-a-foot when it's in operation.

"Oh, yes, Mr. Edgerson, was there was a Grand Prairie Levee District in Plaquemines Parish and the spillway didn't work, and it went broke. The State Legislature asked the Orleans Levee Board to pay off the debt and to buy the land for the spillway."

Five Years of Meetings

Among those celebrating the State Supreme Court decision this week were Elizabeth Taylor of Boothville, president of the Boothville chapter of the Fishermen and Concerned Citizens Association, and her friend Muriel Burus of Venice. They have attended five years of meetings and rallies to get back the land.

Mrs. Taylor's great-grandfather was a slave in Virginia. Mrs. Burus's great-grandfather was a slave owner in Louisiana. Neither woman remember when blacks and whites have worked together in a common cause of such magnitude as the Bohemia Spillway dispute.

Ronald V. Chisom, a New Orleans so-cial activist who organized the Fishermen and Concerned Citizens Association in the 1970's, who is not an heir to spillway property, said of the prospective heirs: "A lot had lawyers over the year or so to no avail. Basically, we just kept fighting."

Mr. Quigley said that "about 4,000 people have put their family names on record" with the State Department of Natural Resources, which is forming rules for returning the property. "Based on that," he said, "16,000 people could be impacted and receive some benefit."

Muriel Burus, left, and Elizabeth Taylor, head of Boothville, La., chapter of Fishermen and Concerned Citizens Association. They have attended five years of meetings and rallies to get back land in Bohemia Spillway dispute.

The New York Times/David J. Farrell

Dispute over land taken for Bohemia Spillway began in mid-1920's.

Adeline Pinkins was a teenager when her family was forced to leave their home 60 years ago.

Bohemia makes national news when the New York Times publishes an article about the return of the land to its former owners.

Susan D. Mustafa and Charles J. Ballay

Public notices inform claimants about the process for the return of the land in Bohemia.

Lawsuit May Be Needed To Get Bohemia Land

Senator Sammy Nunez warned that it probably will take court action for the Orleans Levee Board to give up the land and mineral royalties from the Bohemia Spillway even though the Louisiana Legislature has ruled the land rightfully belongs to the landowners it was expropriated from.

Nunez, when addressing the Plaquemines Parish Council recently, said the legislature has said, "Give the land back," and the courts have upheld that ruling after the Orleans Levee Board (OLB) challenged it.

Nunez said both Representative Frank Patti and he had worked toward a compromise with the OLB so that a $175.00 processing fee, that needed to be paid by people claiming to be heirs of the land would be reimbursed by the OLB. The money would come from funds the OLB has received from the Bohemia Spillway

land since the Legislature voted to return it to its rightful owners. However, the OLB has fought the return of the land saying it would strip the agency from operating money. Nunez said if he and Patti would have signed papers the OLB was trying to compromise with, it would have significantly threated the return of the land to its owners.

Claimants launch fight against the fee to reclaim land. (Times-Picayune)

176

Board keeps grip on spillway land despite '84 law

Times Picayune April 17, 1989 p1-A

By MICHAEL PERLSTEIN
Staff writer

The concept was as simple as it was popular: Since the Orleans Levee Board was no longer using 33,000 acres of oil-rich Plaquemines Parish bottomland for flood protection, return the land and its mineral rights to the families forced off the property more than half a century ago.

That was 1984. Today, five years after a state law ordered the return of the Bohemia Spillway 45 miles below New Orleans, not a square foot has been transferred. Moreover, Levee Board officials acknowledge they have spent the $15 million in oil money Bohemia has yielded during that time — money that the law's author says was intended for the heirs to the land.

Instead of riches, the attempt to right what many call a decades-old injustice has brought nothing but frustration, confusion, and most of all, litigation.

Consider:

► For most of the past five years the Levee Board, determined not to lose the steady oil and gas income, has been fighting the legislation in court. The board finally quit after a federal appeals judge ruled that a subdivision of the state cannot sue the state to reverse a state law.

► The state Department of Natural Resources, responsible for sorting out the ownership of the spillway, has received about 40,000 claims for the spillway's 219 tracts of land. A department official estimated that only about 3,000 of those claims will be authenticated. Furthermore, those with good claims may end up dividing their land with dozens of family members.

► Individual heirs hoping to share Bohemia's $3 million in annual oil and gas royalties probably will be disappointed. Less than a third of the acreage is

See SPILLWAY, A-4

George Edgerson, 93, born and raised in the spillway, has waited years for the land's return. *STAFF PHOTO BY MATT ROSE*

Senator Sammy Nunez warns that residents may need to file suit to get their land back. (Plaquemines Watchman)

BOHEMIA SPILLWAY
Land Ownership Inquiries

Please contact the Louisiana Department of Natural Resources (phone: 225-342-4508, mail: P O Box 2827, Baton Rouge LA 70821, E-mail: gerryT@dnr.state.la.us) if you have any information regarding the identities of heirs and/or successors of individuals, organizations and/or churches that in 1925, were the owners of the following tracts of land within the Bohemia Spillway. The Bohemia Spillway is located on the East Bank of the Mississippi River, Plaquemines Parish, Louisiana.

Tract 17 Bethlehem of Judea African Baptist Church
Tract 18 Albert Ramsey, Ben Ramsey, Robert Ramsey, Joseph Simpson, Lawrence Patterson
Tract 22A Seymour Perry
Tract 24 Meyer Morris
Tract 34 Mrs. Valentine Wagner
Tract 38 Union Benevolent Association
Tract 48 True Vine Baptist Church
Tract 59 Second Mount Zion Church
Tract 78 Charles Ursin (Eusan), Carter Ursin (Eusan), Joseph C. Ursin (Eusan)
Tract 85 Mrs. B.S. Roberts

Tract 100 Clem Cannon
Tract 106A Lucus G. Spencer
Tract 107 Eugene Ahearn
Tract 110 Phillips Land Co.
Tract 111 William Connell
Tract 113 C.A. Ranson
Tract 117 Union Title Guarantee Co.
Tract 119 Phillips Land Co.
Tract 126 Claud Flora
Tract 131 W.G. Gahan
Tract 137 Geo. Knopp
Tract 167 1/2 Mt. Zion Baptist Church
Tract 179 Clem Ricouard
Tract 182 Peter LaFrance
Tract 206 Emma Herwig
Tract 217 Mary O'Donnelly O'Neil

PG: July 28, 2000

By 1989, residents are still waiting for their land to be returned. (Times-Picayune)

177

Feb. 21, 1987
p. B-6

NOTICE OF RETURN OF BOHEMIA SPILLWAY LANDS, PLAQUEMINES PARISH

1. Act 233 of the 1984 Louisiana legislature directed the return of land expropriated or purchased under the threat of expropriation for the construction of the Bohemia Spillway to its former owners or their successors.

2. Beginning February 9, 1987, copies of the list of original owners of property and other information will be available for public inspection and review at the Plaquemines Parish Public Libraries located in Buras, La., and Belle Chasse, La., the Plaquemines Parish Clerk of Court's Office in Pointe-a-la-Hache, La., the Belle Chasse Council Office, Belle Chasse, La., the Buras Auditorium, Buras, La., and the Orleans Levee Board Office, Administration Building, Lakefront Airport, New Orleans, La.

3. Beginning March 9, 1987, persons claiming ownership pursuant to Act 233 of 1984 can obtain an application form and a copy of existing rules for the return of the land by appearing in person either at the Belle Chasse Council Office, 106 Avenue G, Belle Chasse, La., or the Buras Auditorium, Buras, La. Also, an application form may be obtained by sending a written request and a self-addressed, stamped envelope to:

BOHEMIA
POST OFFICE BOX 44121
CAPITOL STATION
BATON ROUGE, LA. 70804-7121

4. No application for return of the land or property will be accepted unless received on or before September 4, 1987. All completed applications shall be mailed to the address listed on the form.

5. A similar public notice concerning application forms and procedures for filing claims was published in the Times-Picayune on March 25 and 29, 1985, and in the Plaquemines Gazette on March 22, 1985. The processing of applications filed in 1985 was terminated by court order, and Act 233 of 1984 was amended in 1985. Any person who filed an application in 1985 must submit a new application, using the 1987 forms, to insure that all claim information is current as of 1987.

B. Jim Porter, Secretary
Dept. of Natural Resources

In 2000, the Louisiana Department of Natural Resources was still searching for the heirs of people who once owned land in Bohemia.

The Bohemia heirs are awarded $21 million. (Plaquemines Gazette)

The Times-Picayune

METRO

AND THE METRO AREA

SECTION
B
Wednesday,
November 22, 2006

Board offers to settle Bohemia case

Plaintiffs would get about 50%

By Bruce Eggler
Staff writer

Faced with a federal court judgment that it says it cannot afford to pay, the Orleans Levee Board offered Tuesday to settle the claim for a little more than 50 cents on the dollar.

The board voted 5-0 to offer plaintiffs in the long-running Bohemia Spillway case $13 million over the next 19 months. Board President Michael McCrossen said that is the best offer the agency can make.

A federal judge last month ordered the Levee Board to pay a $17.4 million judgment to the corporations and families that own land inside the mineral-rich Plaquemines Parish tract. With interest and legal fees, the board figures the total debt at about $24 million, a figure it says it cannot pay.

A resolution approved by the board said it also "does not have the ability, either financially or legally," to post a bond equal to 20 percent of the judgment to prevent seizure of its assets while it would appeal U.S. District Judge Marcel Livaudais Jr.'s Oct. 10 ruling.

McCrossen said the board has enough money, either on hand or expected, to pay the $13 million on the timetable it has offered. But he said it intends to ask Gov. Kathleen Blanco for some assistance anyway.

Attorneys for the plaintiffs could not be reached Tuesday for comment on whether they will accept the latest offer.

However, in July 2005, the plaintiffs had agreed to settle the dispute for $10.1 million, with the money to be paid by Jan. 21, 2006, the board's resolution noted. That agreement dis-

See **BOHEMIA,** *B-2*

In 2008, the Orleans Levee Board admits it can't afford to pay the amount awarded to plaintiffs and offers to settle the case. (Times-Picayune)

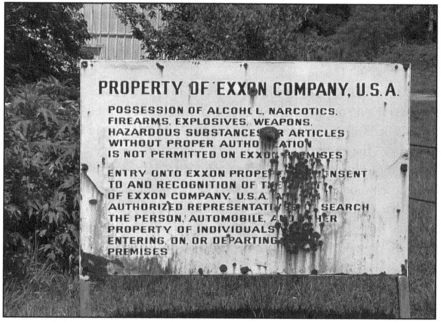

Today, this sign is located near a fenced-off stretch of road that leads into Bohemia.

CHAPTER 25

April 1925

Claude and Anna-Marie were sitting on their front porch discussing the offer they had been given for their land when Hester, Abraham, and Isaac walked up. It was late afternoon, almost dusk, and the mosquitoes were already out in full force.

"How are you all doing?" Anna-Marie asked, handing Hester a mosquito brush. "You're going to need this. They're eating us alive. Have a seat. I'll run in and grab some lemonade."

"I'll get it," Hester said.

"Make mine a whiskey, if you don't mind," Abraham said, noticing the glass sitting on the arm of Claude's chair. "It's been one of those days."

While Hester was fetching the drinks, Anna-Marie told Isaac to go to the back. "The children are in the back playing. If you want, you and the boys can go check the rabbit boxes," she said. "I know it's not winter, but I'm in the mood for some rabbits smothered in onion, garlic, and gravy."

"That sounds delicious," Claude said.

"Let us know when you cook them, and we'll bring some turnips to throw in the pot. Hester has some ready to pick in her garden," Abraham said.

Hester returned with a tray and poured a tall glass of lemonade for Anna-Marie and herself. She had chipped a small chunk of ice from the block of ice in the icebox to cool the drinks. She handed Abraham a glass of whiskey Claude had bought from a bootlegger on the river.

"Thank you." Abraham pulled out his handkerchief and wiped sweat from his face. "I really needed this today."

"What's the matter?" Claude asked. "You seem out of sorts."

"I am," Abraham said. "We got the offer for our property today, and I'm not happy about it."

"It's a travesty," Hester said.

"We got ours, too," Anna-Marie said. "It's laughable."

"What did they offer?" Claude asked.

"We have two arpents, so they offered $600, plus $200 for the improvements, which I assume means the house and the barn. It's ridiculous. Eight hundred dollars total. That house and the property are worth a lot more than that. And there's an orange grove."

"They don't care," Anna-Marie said. "Papa warned us they were going to do that—offer us about thirty percent of what it's really worth."

"We have six-and-a-half arpents, with the store, the house and a barn, and you wouldn't believe what they offered us," Claude said. "I'm almost embarrassed to tell you."

"What?" Abraham said. "It should have been at least $20,000."

"Six thousand two hundred," Claude said. "This property was assessed at about $20,000 before the hurricane. My father paid more for it than they offered."

"I couldn't believe it when I saw the offer," Anna-Marie said. "I swear I know I turned red in the face. I've never been so mad."

"Me either," Hester said. "We couldn't believe it. That's hardly enough to build another house nowadays. Not a decent one anyhow. And certainly not enough to buy the land to go with it."

"They said it was a fair market value offer," Claude said. "Anna-Marie was so mad when she saw it that she tore it up into little pieces."

"That's what I felt like doing, too." Hester said.

"And they act like they are doing us a favor," Abraham said. "Like they're being generous."

"Well, I'm not accepting this offer," Claude said, downing his drink. "I'm going to haggle. I couldn't hold my head up in public if I accepted this. Not considering the income I'm losing from the store. This is nowhere near enough to rebuild and restock a store."

"Maybe all the folks who owe you money will pay you when they get their check," Hester said, hopefully.

Anna-Marie reached over and patted her hand. "That's a sweet thought, but not likely. Folks are going to need every penny to rebuild their lives.

We understand that, so we're not expecting to be repaid. That's a chance you take when you extend credit, but for the life of me, I'm not sorry about that one bit. It was the right thing to do, and I'd do it again."

"So would I," Claude agreed, "but it does seem like if you live your life to do right by people, others would have the same values. That levee board sure don't. We're just going to hold out and haggle with them and see where it all lands."

"I can't do that," Abraham said. "Either I accept the offer, or I get nothing. They don't care about no black families. Honestly, I'm surprised they offered us that much. My parents were only offered six hundred and sixty six dollars, and they have more land than we do."

"That's such a shame," Anna-Marie said. "I don't understand why things are the way they are."

"Me neither," Abraham said. "My mother swears she's not selling, so they will end up with nothing. I told them they could come live with us, but she's so proud that I'm not sure what they're going to do."

"You want another drink?" Claude stood up and walked toward the door.

"Yes, thanks," Abraham said.

"I'll bring the whole bottle."

When he came back, he handed Abraham a stiff drink. "I checked on the children. They're in the back chasing the chickens," he said to Anna-Marie and Hester. "The children seem on edge, too, probably because we're on edge. I told them not to chase them too far."

""They've been doing schoolwork all day. Yes, let them run off some steam," Anna-Marie said. "Charlie loves chasing the chickens."

"I just don't know what to do," Hester said. "I want to turn down the offer. I swear I do, and I always thought I would, but if we have to move anyway, that doesn't make sense."

"No, it doesn't," Claude said. "We all have to take what we can get so we can start over. Have y'all decided where you want to move?"

"Whatever you decide is fine with me," Abraham said. "I can work from anywhere as long as I'm near the river. No matter where we go, I'll have to learn the bays and bayous before I can begin to find any oysters. Hopefully, we get land that is fertile so I can plant some orange trees."

"Yes," Hester said. "I like having my oranges."

"I don't think the land on the West Bank is as fertile as ours is, something about the way the river deposits sediment, but I think the land further down the river in Homeplace might be good. If we bought the land we saw in Diamond, that would be right across the river, but I don't know that I want to stare at our old life every time I walk out the door," Claude said. "Of course, Homeplace is closer to where y'all live. I'm just not sure what to do. Maybe we should go look again. Try to find someplace in the middle, maybe in the Happy Jack area."

"We can do that," Abraham said, "although I'm not sure how much it will cost, and now that we know we don't have a lot to spend, I'm not sure what to do."

"Don't you worry none about that," Anna-Marie said. "Wherever we go, you'll go, and that's settled. And don't go talking about no charity, Hester, because this isn't that. Claude and I want you both near us, and Isaac. Y'all are our family, and we'll figure it out. No use fretting over it when there's nothing that can be done."

"Let's go scout Happy Jack tomorrow," Claude said to Abraham.

Abraham was about to agree when they heard Claude Jr. screaming. "Dad! Mom! Madeleine got bit by a snake. Hurry!"

All four adults took off running toward the back of the house. They found Madeleine sitting on the ground, crying, while Isaac frantically sucked venom from her swollen hand. Anna-Marie sat down next to her, and held her other hand, while Claude looked around for the snake.

"There it is," Abraham said, pointing to a pile of brush about twenty feet away. "It's a water moccasin. I'll get it."

"Charlie, run and fetch a hatchet from the barn," Claude instructed. "I'll take over here, Isaac." Claude began sucking on Madeleine's finger and then spitting venom on the ground while Abraham hacked the snake to bits.

When he was satisfied that the snake was dead, Abraham put it in a gunnysack. "It's dead," he said. "How is she?"

Claude held up Madeleine's hand. Her hand was three times its normal size, and the venom was traveling up her arm. Abraham immediately understood the fear he saw in Claude's eyes. He took off his belt and wrapped it tightly around Madeleine's upper arm. "Keep that tight," he said. "And get her inside and comfortable. This is going to be painful. Maybe

183

you could give her a drop of laudanum and put some Mercurochrome on the wound for now. I'm going to get Sanon. I'll be back as soon as I can."

Claude scooped his daughter up and carried her into the house. Anna-Marie gave Madeleine a sip of laudanum while Claude cleaned the puncture wounds. "This is going to sting," he said, before applying the Mercurochrome. When Madeleine started screaming, Anna-Marie hugged her tight.

"I'm sorry, baby. I'm so sorry. I know this hurts," she crooned.

Claude and Anna-Marie sat together on the bed with their daughter, holding her, wiping her tears, watching as her breathing became labored, and praying that God would have mercy. By the time Abraham returned with Sanon, an hour had passed, and Madeleine had progressed to vomiting violently.

Claude and Anna-Marie stood up when Sanon entered the room. "It was a water moccasin," Anna-Marie exclaimed.

"This is what Abraham told me," Sanon said, examining Madeleine— her arm, her shoulder, her eyes. He began mixing a potion of dried leaves and herbs with a red liquid and then spread it across her shoulder and down her arm. "You gave her laudanum?" he asked.

"Yes," Claude said.

"Give her some more," Sanon instructed. "This is going to be painful."

"What? What is going to be painful?" Anna-Marie cried.

Sanon gestured for her to come closer. "You see this?" He pointed to Madeleine's arm beneath her elbow. "These red streaks? This swelling? I think if I cut here, that should take care of most of the venom."

"What do you mean, 'cut?'" Claude asked, moving to see what Sanon was showing his wife.

"I mean that I must remove most of her arm if she is to live," Sanon said. "Immediately."

"Is that the only way?" Claude asked, reaching for Anna-Marie's hand.

"It is," Sanon said. "The venom has spread. When it reaches her heart, she will die. We have to take the arm now."

"No!" Anna-Marie cried.

"It is the only way. Look, she is fading. I will need a sharp saw. Put it in boiling water before you bring it to me."

Anna-Marie looked at Madeleine, whose ragged breaths seem to be torn from her small body. "But she's only five years old."

"Leave now," Sanon urged. "Let me save her."

Claude and Abraham gently pushed Anna-Marie from the room while Hester gathered towels and started a fire in the wood-burning stove. When the fire was roaring, she put a big pot of water on it to boil. Abraham hurried to the barn to fetch a saw. He rubbed the blade back and forth across a large stone as fast as he could and then ran inside to sterilize it. By the time he brought it to Sanon, Madeleine was unconscious.

"This is good," Sanon said, when Abraham asked if she was still alive. "She in a deep sleep, which will make this easier for her. Go over there and hold her down. Do not let her body move."

Abraham did as he was instructed, holding the young girl's body in place while Sanon prepared to amputate her arm. Hester brought in the towels, and Sanon placed them under her arm and shoulder.

"Do not let Anna-Marie back into this room until I have sent for her," Sanon said.

Hester nodded and hurried from the room. She wanted to help, but she couldn't bear to watch.

A few minutes later, Claude and Anna-Marie heard their daughter's screams. Anna-Marie began to run toward the bedroom, but Claude caught up to her and blocked her path.

"You can't," Claude said. "You will only upset her. You shouldn't see this. Let Sanon do what he must do." He pulled Anna-Marie back into the kitchen and stood there holding her close for what seemed like hours, but was only about fifteen minutes. Then they heard screams again.

"What is going on in there?" Anna-Marie cried.

"I can't think about that," Claude said. "Not now. I just can't think about it."

Finally, Sanon and Abraham emerged from the room, both men covered in blood.

Anna-Marie fainted when she saw them. Claude caught her right before she hit the floor. He carried her to the sofa and asked Hester for a wet cloth.

Hester hurried to get it, and then gently stroked Anna-Marie's forehead with the cloth until she awakened.

"Madeleine?" she asked, looking around the room. "Is my baby still with us?"

"Yes, she is," Abraham said.

"She is living now," Sanon said, "but the next few days are crucial. You must keep the wound clean and spread this over it for thirty days." Sanon handed Claude a bag and a bottle. "Use ten drops for every five tablespoons of herbs. Mix it fresh each time, and spread it three times per day. It will help kill any residual venom."

"And she will live?" Anna-Marie asked again.

"You must watch for infection, and if you see signs of it, send for me," Sanon said. "If infection doesn't set in and the venom didn't spread too far, yes, she will live, but you must keep the wound clean. And before you go see her, there's something you should know."

"Let me," Abraham said. He turned to face his friends. "Sanon had to take her whole arm. There was no other way. He tried below the elbow, but the venom had spread too fast, and her arm was useless to do anything but cause her death."

Anna-Marie buried her face in her hands and began crying, her shoulders shaking.

"You must pull yourself together," Claude said. "We must go see her for ourselves."

Anna-Marie took a deep breath and dabbed at her eyes with a handkerchief. "You're right, of course. Hester, will you go outside and take the children for a walk? I'm sure they are very upset. They've been on the veranda this whole time. Calm their fears, please, while Claude and I sit with Madeleine."

Hester went outside to tend to the children while Abraham removed the bloodied towels from the bedroom. He didn't want Anna-Marie to see them.

"Let me check on her first," Sanon said.

When Sanon returned, he nodded. "She is the same. That's good. There's been no turn for the worse. Go see her, but do not awaken her. She needs to sleep."

Anna-Marie and Claude walked fearfully toward the bedroom, holding tightly to each other's hands.

Madeleine lay there, unconscious, but breathing softly. It took everything Anna-Marie had to contain herself when she saw her daughter. Her right arm was gone. Her shoulder was wrapped in a huge wad of gauze and bandages. Her other arm lay limply across her chest. Her face was deathly pale. Anna-Marie reached for her hand, but Claude stopped her.

He shook his head and put a finger to his lips. Then he tucked his wife's hand in his and led her to a chair. Together, they watched over their daughter for a long while, listening for every breath. Finally, they left the room to find Abraham and Hester outside with the children.

"Where is Sanon?" Claude asked.

"I already brought him home," Abraham said.

"But I didn't get a chance to thank him."

"He doesn't require gratitude," Hester said. "Remedy men only seek to heal. Their reward comes in the next life."

"I feel I must do something for him," Claude said.

"I know how you feel," Abraham said. "Remember when he saved Hester and Isaac? I felt the same way, but he would not accept any gifts I tried to give him."

"There must be something we can do," Anna-Marie said.

"There is," Hester said. "When you and Abraham go scouting land, find some for him, as well. I'd like to keep him close, closer than he is now."

"Yes," Claude said. "That's a good idea. And you're right. We must keep him close. Now where is Isaac?"

Abraham called for his son, and Isaac came bounding up the stairs that led to the porch, taking them two at a time.

"Come here, son," Claude said, motioning for Isaac to come closer to him. The other children had followed Isaac, and they, too, gathered around. "Madeleine will be okay, but we must take very good care of her in the coming weeks. You will all be able to go in and speak to her once each day when she awakens, but there will be no horseplay around her. Is that understood?"

The children nodded. "Is she going to be okay, Papa?" Jeanne asked.

Anna-Marie picked her up and settled her on her lap. "Yes, she'll be okay, but Sanon had to take her arm."

"He took her arm?" Claude Jr. asked. "What did he do with it?"

Claude smiled at his oldest son. "I honestly don't know. I think he must have taken it with him."

"Why did he want her arm?" Charlie asked.

"He didn't want it, son. He had to take it off because it was full of poison from the snake. It was the only way to save her life."

"How did you know that you were supposed to suck the venom and spit it out?" Anna-Marie asked Isaac.

"My mama told me to do that one time when I saw a snake in the orange grove. She said, 'If a snake bites you, suck the poison out and then spit it out.' I always see snakes, so I think about that a lot," Isaac said.

"Well, I think you might have saved Madeleine's life. Thank you, son," Claude said. "And you Abraham, for everything you did. I can never repay y'all for what you've done this day."

Abraham put his hand on Claude's shoulder. "That's what family's for," he said.

For the next few weeks, Claude and Anna-Marie spent every waking moment tending to Madeleine. By mid-June, she was playing outside, running around with the other children, and learning to utilize her left arm for everything.

Isaac, fearful that something terrible would happen to her, watched her every move.

CHAPTER 26

On June 9, 1925, the Board of Levee Commissioners, meeting at its headquarters in room 201 of the new courthouse in New Orleans, resolved that it would authorize the issuance of $500,000 in bonds, "bearing interest at the rate of four-an-a-half percent per centum per annum from date of issuance, the said interest being represented by coupons payable semi-annually," according to commission minutes. Then-president Peter J. Flannigan presided over the meeting as the board prepared to move quickly on the Bohemia Spillway project. The funds were deposited into several banks across the city, including Canal Commercial Trust & Savings Bank, Hibernia Securities Company, Interstate Trust & Banking Company, Marine Bank & Trust Company, and Whitney Central Bank & Trust. These bonds would be used to pay for land options in Bohemia.

After the meeting, Jefferson and Sal went to lunch at Tujague's Restaurant on Decatur Street in the Quarter. Once they were seated, Jefferson handed Sal a cigarette. He waited while Sal lit it and then said, "Everything is coming together splendidly, don't you think?"

"Yes, it is, but why didn't you invite Pierre?" Sal responded.

Jefferson leaned forward and spoke quietly. "I'm getting a little worried about him. You were in that meeting last week when the engineer asked if owners with businesses could stay even after we own the land. Did you see the way that engineer kept looking at Pierre?"

"No, I didn't see that," Sal said.

"I did, and it made me a mite uncomfortable. Pierre has family in Bohemia, and he's trying to look after them. They have spoken to him only once since they got wind of our project, and to my understanding, Antoine Bertaut was none too happy. Now, it looks like Pierre's doing everything he can to minimize the damage to his family. Granted, the engineer did recommend that we charge the owners rent to stay there, but still. I feel that Pierre is becoming cumbersome, that he's not completely on board with our agenda. He wants to have his cake and eat it, too. He wants the mineral leases and the money, but he wants to appease his family, as well. He can't have it both ways."

"Do you want me to talk to him?" Sal asked.

Jefferson shook his head. "Let's see what happens. I'm keeping an eye on him. I know that he's aware that he can be removed from the board if he takes it too far. However, I don't think we should keep him in the loop of our progress with the oil companies. For now, the less he knows the better. From my standpoint, he knows too much already. I don't want the word 'oil' to come up in any conversations related to the spillway until we have leased the mineral rights, and that's still a few years away, based on conversations I've already had. These things take time, and I don't want anyone to try to thwart our plans."

When the waiter arrived, Jefferson ordered Oysters Bienville and Sal ordered escargot for appetizers. Both men ordered turtle soup for their entrées. It was almost mid-June, already much too hot and humid to eat big meals in the middle of the day, so they passed on their usual filets.

After the waiter left the table, Jefferson continued, "We should also keep an eye on our fellow board member, Joseph Haspel. He's always been on board with the building of a spillway down there, bought into the idea of it saving New Orleans from floods and hurricanes, but he's got pretty powerful kinfolk in Bohemia, too. Haspel & Davis is one of the largest milling companies down there, and they own a lot of property on the river, especially around Nestor. From what I hear, Joseph's kinfolks are none too happy. We made sure they got a fair offer for all their property and holdings, but still, blood is thicker than water, so keep your ears open when it comes to Joseph and Pierre."

Sal nodded. "I'll do that." Then he leaned forward. "Between you and me, is this spillway really going to stop the city from flooding?"

"Who knows? It's possible. Theoretically, it could help when hurricanes come in from the Gulf. But when the flooding comes down the river, I doubt it. There's not much it could do, really, when the water comes from the north."

"How on earth did you sell the legislature on it?"

Jefferson smiled. "I'm good at what I do," he said. "It helped that the

1922 flood was still fresh on the minds of our legislators, and everyone was desperate for a solution."

"Are you satisfied with the way options are progressing?"

Jefferson leaned back in his chair and lit another cigarette. "No, I'm not. According to our attorney, those people down there are plain greedy, all of them haggling and trying to get more than their land is worth. They all have an inflated sense of what they should get. I don't understand it. We are offering them a fair market price based on the latest assessment of their property, yet they want more. There are quite a few who are refusing to even entertain our offers, including the Poydras Realty Company, and some of those poor folks that live down there. It's not like they can't just move somewhere else with the money we're doling out. We should have expected they would get greedy, though. People always do when there's money to be had. Even our chief engineer is asking for a raise. We'll be taking up that measure at the next meeting. Everybody wants a piece of the pie."

"Ironic, don't you think?" Sal noted.

"We're not doing this for us," Jefferson said, frowning. "We are doing it for the city. One day, we'll be able to lower the taxes we collect and use the money we make down there to fortify our own levees. It will all be worth it in the end, and everyone will benefit."

"Everyone in New Orleans, you mean," Sal said.

"Yes, that's exactly what I mean. Everyone in New Orleans, including you. I'm sure that once that oil revenue comes rolling in, we'll be able to vote for hefty raises for all of our board members. Imagine what we can do—build an airport, build a seawall around the lakefront, invest in our own levees. There's so much we'll be able to do. And, I don't know if you know this, but the legislature is considering an act that will allow us to benefit personally from land under our control. Tomorrow, when we go down there to do our inspection of the properties we've optioned, I want you to keep your eye on the prize, no matter how sorry you may feel for those people. Remember, there's a bigger picture, and you're part of it."

"I will," Sal said, "and I am grateful to be a part of it. Thank you for including me."

"That's better," Jefferson said. "That's where we all need to be. We've come this far. Now we just need to get those people out of there and get started on the spillway. Then we wait. I'm guessing we'll be leasing that land in a year or two."

"That soon?" Sal asked.

"Maybe. Those oil companies are going to want to explore around that salt dome, and once they find even traces of oil, they will want to lease that land. And the best part—we'll own every bit of it. As you know, I've had meetings with them. They are definitely interested. It will just take time, and now, we have all the time in the world."

"We just have a few hurdles to get through first," Sal said.

"Yes, the options and the Grand Prairie Levee District. We'll need to keep an eye on Leonus Lozano, as well. Since he became district attorney last year, he's been exerting his power all over the parish. He's greedy. He's dangerous. And he's hungry. That's a dangerous combination. Did you know that he had men at the polls asking those folks who they were voting for? I heard he has a way of getting the results he wants. He will stop at nothing. I spotted that in him when he was just a young pup."

"I remember. You warned us about him."

"Yes, now, I'm warning you again. He's been fighting us tooth and nail on this spillway. He's none too happy, although he likes that we're going to pay off the debt of those levee boards. That puts him in a better position to do whatever he wants. I hear he's buying up land on the West Bank of the river and the East Bank below where the spillway will go. I swear, I've thought about it, and I'm sure he knows about the salt dome and oil."

"Of course, he does. You don't remember? He was sitting at the next table the first day we discussed it. We didn't notice until he got up to leave. I bet he overheard every word."

Jefferson nodded his agreement. "That was careless of us," he said. "Never mind, though. There's nothing he can do to stop us either. Act 99 sets our plan in stone."

"That was brilliant of you," Sal commented.

Jefferson smiled. "Yes, it was. Now let's get back to the office. There is much to do."

The next morning, seven members of the Board of Levee Commissioners boarded the Dock Board's yacht and headed down river to Pointe á la Hache. From there, they began their inspections of frontage property all the way down to Ostrica. They did not return to New Orleans until 9:30 that night.

CHAPTER 27

"Anna-Marie, why, your hair is a mess," Grace Bertaut said when she opened the door.

Anna-Marie stood there for a moment, shocked. It had been more than a year since she had seen her *maman*, and she wasn't expecting her to be there when she knocked on the door. As usual, Grace's black hair was flawlessly coifed, her lipstick perfectly applied, and her bright yellow linen dress fitted to her trim body.

"Well, don't just stand there. And where are the children? Why didn't you bring them? I haven't seen them in ages," Grace said.

Anna-Marie cleared her throat. "I left them with Claude. I didn't know you were home, *Maman*."

"Oh, that storekeeper? I hope he watches them. Where was he when Madeleine was losing her arm? That's what I'd like to know."

Anna-Marie's face turned red. She took a deep breath and counted to ten like Hester had taught her to do. "He was sitting right next to me on the porch," Anna-Marie said. "When did you get home?"

"Yesterday," her *maman* said. "I certainly wasn't going to leave it to your papa to pack up this house. Oh, no. That would have been a disaster, everything thrown haphazardly into boxes. No. I'm here to make sure this move goes smoothly."

"Yes, she is." Antoine walked over and kissed Anna-Marie on the cheek. "Hello, *ma chérie*. What brings you over?"

"Claude took the children out on the boat with Abraham and Hester, so I thought I'd come by to see if you've settled on a new place for your mill."

"Your *maman* has talked me into moving everything to the city," Antoine said. "Although, I think I'm not going to go as big as what we have here. I'm not sure what's going to happen yet. All I know is that your *maman* wants to live in New Orleans, and who am I to argue with her?"

"But papa, I won't be able to see you as often," Anna-Marie said.

"Don't fret. We'll see each other plenty. You can bring the children to visit, and I'll come here as often as I can."

"You never seem too worried about coming to see me when I'm in the city. You could get on the Southern Louisiana Railroad at six-thirty in the morning in Pointe á la Hache and be in New Orleans by nine," Grace said to Anna-Marie. "I haven't seen you in a year. I imagine the children are almost grown by now."

"You could come see me," Anna-Marie said.

"Not while that shopkeeper is there. I still can't get over why you married so far beneath you. I just don't understand it. We sent you to finishing schools, for mercy's sake. We raised you to know your place in proper society, and off you go, marrying the first poor man you could find. We had such a nice man, a proper husband, picked out for you," Grace said.

"That's enough, *Maman*! I won't stand here and listen to any more of this." Anna-Marie turned to leave.

"Wait," Antoine said. "Don't leave. We've much to discuss. Come sit out on the porch. Frita will fetch some tea. Your *maman* won't say another word about Claude, right, Grace?" he said, looking sternly at his wife.

Grace reluctantly nodded and led the way outside. Frita brought iced tea, and they sipped on it while they watched a ship pass by on the river.

"Have you found some land on the West Bank yet?" Antoine asked.

"That's what Claude and Abraham are doing today. Claude wanted to bring the children in case they saw a particular spot they liked. It's important that it's where Hester and Abraham will feel comfortable, too."

"You're taking those heathens with you?" Grace asked, sniffing delicately.

"That's enough," Antoine said.

"Yes, Abraham and Hester are coming with us, and maybe Abraham's parents. They're like family to us."

"Of course they are, dear," Grace said, rolling her eyes ever so slightly.

"Were you able to get any more money for your store?" Antoine asked.

Anna-Marie laughed. "If you call it more. A few hundred dollars. I can't believe they can get away with what they are doing to folks down here."

"Oh, they'll get away with it," Antoine said. "It's pitiful. I was talking with Charles Ballay the other day. You remember him, Grace? He once owned a nice parcel of land, but years ago, in 1904, I think, he sold some of his land so that the Second Mt. Zion Baptist Church could have a home. Of course, the church was destroyed in the 1915 hurricane, but that didn't stop those Christian folks. Sister Alice Raphael Simpson hosted worship services in her home until the new church was built. Now they have to move that church across the river. I think they are taking it to Nairn. Anyway, they only offered Charles $2,000 for two arpents fronting the river. Very fertile ground there, and that's all he's getting. And the church, they got offered $2,200 for the worship building and four houses on the property. It's a shame. I swear it is."

"Frank Tabony told me he got $4,000 for his land. He had two-and-a-half arpents," Anna-Marie said.

"I know. It doesn't make sense. It's like they pulled these numbers from thin air," Antoine said. "Samuel Fucich over by Fucich Bayou got offered more than $20,000 for his land, but he has all those cabins he rents to the oyster fishermen on his property, along with the canal and levees that run through. He's been the postmaster since 1916 or so."

"Yes, I know. Abraham was telling us about those cabins. Where are all those people going to go?" Anna-Marie said.

"Somewhere," Grace said. "They will go somewhere. They don't have a choice in the matter. Sometimes in life, you have to stop complaining, put your chin up, and deal with the hand fate gives you." She had not shed a tear over the proposed move. In fact, she was happy that she would now be able to live full-time in New Orleans.

"This hand isn't fair," Anna-Marie said. "Taking people's home and livelihoods like this?"

"It will all work out in the end," Grace said.

"For who, *Maman*? You?"

"Don't get smart with me, young lady," Grace warned.

"It's not fair. We're not getting anywhere near what our land, our home, or our business is worth. Neither is anyone else," Antoine said.

"I worked all these years, and now I'll have to take a loss and start over somewhere else. This is hard on everyone."

"I don't know," Anna-Marie said, looking at Grace. "*Maman* doesn't seem to mind. She's been trying to get you to move to New Orleans for years. The rest of us, we love it here."

Antoine reached over and patted Anna-Marie's shoulder. "This is hard on everyone, even your *maman*. The only ones really making anything worth having are Haspel & Davis. I heard they got offered almost $50,000 for their holdings down here."

"They have a lot of land," Anna-Marie said. "Don't they have that seagull farm down the river, too?"

"Yes, that's true, but I have a mill and a lot of land, and I got less than half of that. It's what I've been saying. None of these offers make sense," Antoine said.

"We're better off than some," Anna-Marie said. "Abraham and Hester were only offered $800, and you wouldn't believe what the folks in the store have been telling us. Joseph Jones Jr. received a $500 offer, and so did Saxon Taylor. Nelson Taylor was offered $750. They only offered poor Gus Jones $200 for his half arpent when Anioins Jones' widow was offered $1,025 for one-and-a-half arpents. It's ridiculous. Artead Gains was offered $700 for one arpent. They are all refusing to give an option on their land, so I don't know what's going to happen to them. Oh, and Mr. Franesevich, whose property is near Ostrica, was only offered $450 for one-and-a-half arpents. Can you believe that?"

"It's like I've always said, a little money is better than none. I don't know why they're holding out," Grace said. "They'll be forced to leave anyway, so why bother being stubborn?"

"It's the principle of the matter," Anna-Marie said. "They feel like nobody has the right to force them to sell their land for peanuts. For any amount, really, but certainly not for peanuts. I know that's how Florence, Abraham's mother, feels. I still don't know what she's going to do. I wish I were that brave because I agree with them. I wouldn't mind punching your cousin, Pierre, in the nose."

"Anna-Marie! Have you completely lost all of your manners? Your father and I spent a fortune to make sure that you would be a proper lady, and look at you now. Talking like a farm girl." Grace stood up. "I can't bear any more of this." She turned and walked back into the house.

Antoine laughed out loud, and then, looking toward the door, he reigned his laughter in. "Oh, Anna-Marie, you are going to be the death of her. I can't say that I haven't thought about punching my cousin more than once over the past year."

"Do you think *Maman* is ever going to approve of anything I do?" Anna-Marie asked.

"No, but don't you fret. She doesn't approve of anyone or anything. Even me. It's sad, really, because when she was young, she was so carefree, like you are. I don't know what happened to her—maybe New Orleans society, maybe all those clubs she belongs to where all of the women only look down their noses, maybe it's her friendship with that Mildred. You know, your *maman* keeps tabs on us through that woman, and I'm sure she has nothing nice to say."

"I'm sure of that," Anna-Marie said, giggling for a moment before picking up their conversation. "Claude says the smart thing to do is to sell, but I wish I could stay and make them force me off our land. At least I would know I had fought for it."

"Claude's right," Antoine said. "I tried, but even with all my friends and money, I couldn't do anything. Nobody can. You have to sell."

"I know, but it hurts, Papa. It really hurts."

"It does, child, but you will make your way. Of that, I'm certain. And you're not alone in your thoughts. John Edgecomb is refusing to sell, from what I hear. You know, the men in his family have always been handy, and he just built that big, beautiful house. He saved for that for years. He told the Real Estate Committee that under no circumstances or conditions would he consent to give the option or to sell at any price. And he meant it. They will have to drag him off his land. I heard they only offered him a little over $4,000."

"It's a travesty," Anna-Marie said. "Mr. Cahan told us they offered him $1,000 for his property, and he told them that for sentimental reasons, he could not and would not sign the option."

"Everyone wishes they could do that," Antoine said. "I'm rather surprised that some folks aren't putting up more of a fuss. John Ormond over by Bayou Lamouque was offered $12,500 for his land, which, of course, includes the bayou and its levees, and he signed the option. I was surprised. He loves his property, and he doesn't usually take things sitting down."

"I heard that Whitney Central Trust and Savings Bank was only offered $1,600 for the bank, plus four arpents of land," Anna-Marie said. "I couldn't believe that one."

"Well, the Poydras Realty Company is refusing to sign the option, too. They've had several meetings with the Real Estate Committee, and now, the company is refusing to meet with the committee. They own seventeen-and-a-half arpents, and they were offered roughly $9,500," Antoine said. "And you know that cannery down the river, Dunbar Dukate Co?"

"Yes, sometimes they buy oysters from Abraham," Anna-Marie said.

"They're only getting $12,500. Do you realize how much money they are going to lose per year when they have to move?"

"I know. I think about that a lot—how much me and Claude are going to lose. We're the only store for quite a spell, and there's a lot more people who live here than across the river," Anna-Marie said. "We've worked hard to give our children a good life, and a percentage has always gone to Claude's father to sustain him. We don't know what's going to happen now."

"No one does. That's why everyone is so frightened," Antoine said. "When you've worked so hard for something, it's never easy to pick up and start over."

"And I'm worried about what's going to happen to the oyster industry," Anna-Marie said. "I heard Louisiana Navigation & Fisheries signed the option for $12,500. They only had one arpent but those locks down there are on the property, and a canal. All the oyster fisherman use those locks, and we don't know if they will still be able to. And John Dymond, you know, the owner of Gulf Coast Oyster Company? He's signing, too, he said. He was offered $12,500, but he has more than 1,600 arpents. That's not a lot for the amount of land he has, but the Real Estate Committee seems to like that number."

"They like low numbers. That's what they like," Antoine said. "And then there's those folks who paid their taxes and sold as fast as they could. Some marked their name with an X, I heard."

"Don't look down on people who can't write, Papa, please. Not everyone is as fortunate as we are."

"I know, *ma chérie*. My apologies. I'm just frustrated, that's all,"

Antoine said. "So frustrated. And now your *maman's* here taking charge of things, and I have to move to the city. It's not a good time for anyone."

"No, it's not." Anna-Marie stood up. "Tell *Maman* I said good-bye. I have to get back. I left Spit running the store, and that always ends in some kind of catastrophe."

Antoine said good-bye and watched his daughter walk toward the levee. As he observed how the sun turned her hair from brown to auburn, he smiled. At least I will always have her, he thought.

By the end of that summer, residents whose families had lived and worked along the river for decades, some for more than a century, began to pack up their belongings in preparation to leave their homes and their way of life behind them. Some had plans to move to the Mississippi Gulf Coast where the seafood industry was thriving, some left for New Orleans or further north across Lake Pontchartrain, and those who couldn't bear to leave the area bought land across the river on the West Bank. Some oystermen and fishermen stayed on the East Bank, choosing to move to Pointe á la Hache because of their familiarity with the bayous and the marsh. They knew where to fish, where to shrimp, where to find oysters, where to hunt and trap. They did not want to invest the time it would take to find new spots across the river.

Thirty-three thousand acres comprised the area the Orleans Levee District needed to build the spillway—eleven miles of home sites, businesses, churches, and farms that started at the lower line of Bohemia Plantation and went to Fort St. Phillip just past Ostrica at the forty arpent line. Fifty-eight percent of the land that fronted the river was owned by the state and deeded to the Orleans Levee District. From 168 property owners, who owned 256 tracts of land, the Real Estate Committee secured 130 options. Thirty-eight remaining property owners were not secured for a variety of reasons—ownership of some of the land could not be determined after title searches were conducted, some heirs to the land could not be located, and some refused to sell. They could not abide settling for paltry amounts for the most fertile land in the country.

After all of the land purchases were finalized, the residents who refused to sell comprised three percent of the total landowners. The Orleans Levee District forced these residents to leave their homes, their land, and their way of life behind with not a penny in their pockets.

CHAPTER 28

"I don't give a damn what the state said the Orleans Levee District can or cannot do," Leonus pounded his fist on his desk. "That land should belong to the Grand Prairie Levee District. They have no right to build a spillway or anything else in my parish. For God's sake, that's why we have parishes in this state—to separate who can do what where. I know why they want that land. I've known it all along."

For the past few years, Leonus had been buying land of his own from whoever would sell it, but he could not get his hands on the land on the East Bank, and he wanted it. Badly.

"You're my realtor. Go down there and buy some land, especially around that salt dome," Leonus said.

"Leonus, it's simply not possible," Marcus Williams explained. "By rights, sooner or later, it will all belong to the levee district. Even if you buy it, you'll eventually have to sell it to them. There's nothing that can be done."

"Well, maybe I can lease the land to the oil companies before that happens," Leonus countered.

Marcus laughed. "They will take you to court if you try something like that, and you'll lose. Be satisfied with what you've acquired on the West Bank. You've got a lot of land near the salt dome, and in other spots along the river. I'm sure you'll get good money from leasing that land."

"It's not the same," Leonus said. "It's the idea that they can just come in here, force my people off their land, and offer them a third of what it's worth. It just don't sit well with me."

"Mostly because you want the land," Marcus said, not flinching a bit when Leonus turned red and glared harshly at him.

"Maybe I need another realtor—one who will do my bidding," Leonus said.

Marcus stood up and reached for his hat. "Go ahead then, but I doubt you'll find anyone who can put up with your tantrums on a daily basis."

"You've made a lot of money off of me, you ungrateful little…" Leonus sputtered.

"And you will make a lot more off of me," Marcus retorted.

Leonus thought about that for a moment and then gestured toward the door. "All right then. I expect to see you next week at this time with a full report of my holdings and their proximity to that salt dome. Understand?"

Marcus nodded and swiftly made his exit.

Leonus leaned forward and stared at his copy of Act 99 on top of a stack of papers on his desk. He picked it up and read it one more time. "Damn it!" he yelled, and then he threw the Act across the room.

Leonus got up and began pacing back and forth. Nobody gets to come into my parish and do whatever they want, he thought. Nobody. I'm the one who runs this parish and St. Bernard Parish, as well. People do what I tell them to do.

After a few minutes of furious pacing, he sat back down and lit a cigar. It was time to strategize, he decided, to maximize his advantage. He already had the people of two parishes fearful of him. It was time to put the fear of God into the Orleans Levee District. But how? I need a friend in the governor's office, he thought. I need a friend to be governor of this state, someone who owes me. He contemplated that for a few moments, and then he smiled.

Leonus called for his secretary. "Get Huey Long on the telephone," he said.

"Huey," he said, when the chairman of the Louisiana Public Service Commission answered. "It's the judge. I have some information that I'm sure you will find mighty useful. Let's meet in New Orleans."

The following week, Huey P. Long and Leonus Lozano met at Leonus' civil law office in the Hibernia Bank Building in New Orleans.

Leonus poured Huey a fine bourbon he had bought off a bootlegger the previous week and then sat down to observe him. Huey was young, thirty-two, only two years younger than Leonus. He had dark hair and a friendly face. His personality matched his looks, and he was always smiling. People trusted him instantly because he was so likable. Underneath all that, Leonus recognized a schemer when he saw one, a man after his own heart, a kindred spirit. Whereas Leonus could be charismatic when he chose, it was not his nature to be charming. He preferred authoritarianism and brute force to smiles and charm. Huey was naturally charismatic, and people across the state had already begun to fall under his spell, even though he had lost the last governor's race by 7,000 votes. Leonus had watched him since he first appeared on the political scene, and he knew that Huey was going places.

"I hear you've got your eye on the presidency," Leonus said.

Huey laughed. "I have to become governor first, then a U.S. senator. After that, we can talk about the presidency."

"Ambitious. I like that," Leonus said. "And sure of yourself. Both traits you'll need."

"So I'm told." Huey took a sip of his bourbon. "This is good."

"Only the best," Leonus said. "There is one more thing you'll need. Friends. Powerful friends. Friends who can help you get to where you want to go."

Huey put his glass down and looked at Leonus, trying to ascertain where this was going. "I take it you could be one of those friends?"

"I could," Leonus responded. "Friendships are best when they are mutually beneficial, don't you agree?"

"I do," Huey said. "Most certainly. So, tell me, how are we to be beneficial to each other?"

"I am going to help you win the governorship. I'm sure you are aware that two parishes are under my control—St. Bernard and Plaquemines. The people down here vote the way I tell them to vote, so my endorsement can do wonders for your aspirations."

"Yes, I am aware," Huey said. "I am planning to run again."

"That's what I'd hoped," Leonus said. "The sooner you start making friends who can help you, the better. I want to be that friend. The one you turn to in times of need. The one who advises you. The one you know you can trust. It's hard to know, once you get into office, who you can trust."

"Trust is indeed a valuable commodity," Huey said. "But how do I know you are the one?"

"Because I am about to make you a very wealthy and powerful man," Leonus said.

Huey leaned forward, more interested now. "How's that?"

"Oil," Leonus announced confidently. "Mineral leases."

"But we don't have much oil in Louisiana," Huey said. "They're finding it in Texas."

"Oh, it's here. They haven't discovered it yet, but it's here."

"How do you know that?"

"Are you familiar with the Bohemia Spillway project the Orleans Levee District just got passed through the legislature?"

"I've heard of it. Don't make much sense to me, but I am somewhat familiar."

"You're right. It makes no sense. None whatsoever. But nonetheless, the project is moving forward. Do you know why?"

"Why?"

"Oil. That's why."

"They've found oil there?" Huey asked.

"Not yet, but they will. That's why those folks over in New Orleans want that land."

"How do you know this?" Huey asked.

Leonus told him about the conversation he had overheard at Antoine's several years before. "They've been planning this for years. Everyone down here knows this spillway will do little to protect New Orleans, but they want their greedy hands on that land around the salt dome. That's where oil companies are finding oil in Texas."

"Well, I'll be," Huey said, leaning back to digest this. "Now it makes sense. If there's oil there, that will mean a whole lot of money."

"Yes, it will."

"You know, there are salt domes all over Louisiana," Huey said. "I've heard Avery Island was created by a salt dome, and Jefferson Island, as well. The McIlhennys own Avery Island, the whole island. That's where they make Tabasco. There's another one in the Red River by the border to Texas and Oklahoma. From what I hear, we have quite a few in the state."

"Yes, but this one down in Nestor is the one that matters right now." Leonus said. "Before the end of the year, that salt dome and all those mineral rights will belong to the Orleans Levee District. Even though I'm mad as hell that they got away with this, that Jefferson Davenport is one smart feller, and he wouldn't be doing this if he didn't believe that there is money to be made."

"Interesting," Huey said. "They're as corrupt as it gets over there in New Orleans."

Even while he spoke, Leonus could see that Huey was mentally calculating just how much money could be made. "You see how friendship works now?" he asked.

Huey nodded. "Yes, yes I do. Mutually beneficial friendships."

"I have just made you a very wealthy man," Leonus said. "I can also help you become governor."

"And what do you require in return?" Huey was well aware that this information would come with a huge price tag.

"Consideration. Any time I need it," Leonus said. "Consideration for my needs and the needs of both of the parishes under my control. We just got kicked by the legislature, basically robbed for no good reason. I don't want something like this to ever happen again."

Huey nodded. "I will do what I can."

"Good," Leonus said. "Then we are in agreement. I suggest you set up a corporation and begin buying as much land as you possibly can. Also, send me a list of every salt dome in the state."

"I can do that," Huey said. "It will be on your desk next week."

"Good," Leonus stood up, indicating the meeting was over. "We'll talk soon." He reached out to shake Huey's hand.

When Huey was gone, Leonus walked to his window and looked out over the city. His prospects had just become a lot brighter. He had no doubt Huey would become governor in the next term. He also knew he would be right there behind him, pulling the strings.

CHAPTER 29

July 1925

Anna-Marie, Claude, Hester, and Abraham got out of Abraham's truck and stood at the railing as the ferry made its way across the Mississippi River to West Point á la Hache. Claude and Abraham were nervous. Today was the day when they would show their wives the sites of their new homes, and neither man was certain about what the reaction would be. Anna-Marie and Hester stood quietly, each feeling a sense of fear about what awaited them on the west side of the river. Anna-Marie reached over and squeezed Hester's hand, the gesture a reminder to be strong.

When the ferry had docked, Claude turned the key in the ignition. "Here we go, ladies," he said as cheerfully as he could. "Your new home awaits."

No one said a word.

Claude drove the eight miles to Homeplace, and then he pulled over when he came to a curve in the road.

Abraham opened the door and helped the ladies out. "This is it," he said. "They call it Homeplace. Captain Henry knows all about this area. He said that this settlement got its name from a man who used to live around here. He came down the river on a packet boat, and when the captain asked him where he wanted to get off, he pointed over there and said, 'My home place.' The name stuck. I asked Captain Henry and Sanon to meet us here, so they should be on their way."

Hester and Anna-Marie looked where Abraham was pointing—a stretch of land decorated with oak trees, whose branches were laden with Spanish moss. "It is pretty, just like y'all said," Anna-Marie said, begrudgingly.

"I don't see an orange grove," Hester said.

"No. There's no orange grove, but we can plant one," Abraham said. "We could grow one in a few years. Usually, it takes three to five years before they start producing, though."

"That's true, Hester. We could make our own. And look, you can grow rice down there close to the river," Anna-Marie said. "It won't be home, but we might be able to replicate it somewhat."

"Yes, we can try," Claude said, pointing to a spot near the road. "We could build a store right there. The closest store is a few miles away in Nairn. George Lincoln owns it. He's a good man and well-liked, so it might take us a while to build a regular clientele like we had on the East Bank."

"I don't know if this will work," Anna-Marie said. "The population over here is much smaller than ours, too."

"Yes, it is," Claude said, "but I have a feeling that will change once everyone starts moving. I think the West Bank is going to become much more populated."

"We also have the issue of finances," Anna-Marie said. "Claude haggled with the Real Estate Committee until they agreed to pay him $7,000, but will it be enough to build a store and bring our home across the river? And then we would have to restock the store."

"This is a nightmare. We couldn't wrangle another dime for our land," Hester said. "It's a crying shame. What are we going to be able to do with $800?"

"We are going to buy that piece of land right over there," Abraham pointed to his left. "Claude has already negotiated the price for us and the deposit. He is going to buy it and then deed it to us. We'll be able to pay for it on time," Abraham didn't mention that the property cost twice what they were receiving from the levee district. He didn't want Hester to worry. "There's enough room for our house and a cabin for my parents, and Claude said we can use his barn if I help him build it. And I'll be able to dock the boat in Bay Lanaux, according to Captain Henry. It's on the other side of those woods and leads into Bay de la Cheniere."

"How are we going to get our house over here?" Hester asked. "We can't afford to have it brought over on a barge now."

"I'm going to take it apart log by log. Albert said he would help."

"I'll help, too," Claude said. "We'll have it taken apart in no time."

"I'm building a raft to load the logs onto, and I'll pull it across the river myself," Abraham said. "We can use mules to get everything over the levee. It will be a lot of work, but at least we'll still have our own home. We also have to take apart Miss Penny's house. Her boys will help, and they are strong, so that's good. We sure have a lot of work ahead of us."

"Yes, we do," Claude said. "That's why it was so important to find our new homestead now, so that we have time to do everything we need to do. I'm going to rebuild the store, too, although that might be costly because some of the metal on it is rusty and needs to be replaced, and some of the wood is rotten."

"My papa said he would help us," Anna-Marie reminded Claude.

Claude frowned. "No thanks. Pardon me, but we don't need charity from him. He thinks poorly enough of me, and if your *maman* got wind of it, you'd never hear the end of it."

"That's true. She met Claude that one time at our wedding, and Papa had to drag her there kicking and screaming. I don't know how she suffered through it. She was some mad," Anna-Marie said to Hester. "She said I was a disgrace, and after everything she did to make me a proper lady. She's barely spoken to me since and only does so she can see the children." Anna-Marie turned to look at Claude. "You're right," she said. "We should take nothing from them."

"What about your father, Claude? And your aunt? Have they decided what they are going to do?" Hester asked.

"They are selling, or course, but they only got $1,200. My aunt wants to go to Mississippi—Biloxi—where the land is not as expensive as New Orleans and they can buy a piece of land with a house already on it. We have kinfolk up there. My father doesn't really want to go, so I've told him he can move in with us. He's thinking on it, but he is not well and doesn't want to be a burden."

"He wouldn't be a burden at all," Anna-Marie said. "Families take care of their own."

"I know, but that's how he feels. He's lived with his sister for so long that he knows no other life. I don't think he wants to separate from her. I told him that whatever he decides will be okay with me," Claude said.

"Please tell him I'd be happy for him to move with us," Anna-Marie said. "I think he'd get a lot of joy from being around his grandchildren."

"Yes, he would, but the decision is his. We have to worry about how we're going to get all of this accomplished in a short period of time. If we all work together, we can do it," Claude said. "but it won't be easy. Just the opposite, in fact."

"We don't have much time," Abraham agreed. "That levee board already has people and equipment down here taking levees down on the land they already bought. They are moving fast. Makes one wonder why."

"It sure does," Claude said. "I still think something else is afoot. Just can't place my finger on it. We'll find out in good time, I'm sure."

"Maybe so," Abraham said."

"Did you find land for Miss Penny?" Hester asked.

"Yes, I found her a nice piece a few miles upriver in Happy Jack," Claude said. "If she needed us, we could get to her easily."

"That's good," Abraham said. "She'll need as much help as we can give her."

"Yes," Anna-Marie said. "We have to look after everyone who moves across the river. So many of our customers are worried about what they will do, about what will happen to them and their families. We'll have to help everyone we can. Some people still don't know what they are going to do. Do you know Peter Pelitire? He had just started working for my papa at the mill when all this happened. Since Papa began moving the operation to New Orleans, he hasn't had a job. He's our age, but he already has seven children. His wife, Christina, she had them back-to-back. Papa really liked him so he gave him a stipend, of course, but with all those kids, that's not going to go far."

"I told him we'd try to hire him at the store once we get up and running," Claude said.

"I do know him. He's a right fine man," Abraham said. "And his wife, Christina, she's a proper young lady. Always has something kind to say, and sometimes she gives us their son's hand-me-downs. She saves Hester a lot of pricked fingers from sewing all of Isaac's clothes. They're Italian, right?"

"Yes, came here straight off the boat. We should help them, too," Claude said. "Peter knows rice milling, but he's no handyman, as God is my witness. We should help them find land and move their home."

"Find something for them nearby," Anna-Marie said. "I'd like to keep them close. Christina could help with the children while we build the store, and y'all could teach Peter a thing or two about carpentry."

"I'm sure he'd catch on," Claude said, liking the idea. "He's certainly not dim-witted."

"No, he's not," Anna-Marie said. "Papa always said he's real smart and willing to learn anything. That's why he was sorry to let him go."

"It's settled then," Abraham said. "But the list is long. We'll move as much of the store as we can and your house. We'll move our house and my parents' house. And we'll move Miss Penny and the Pelitires. We'll also need to move Sanon. It won't be home, but it will be as close to our old life as we can make it."

"Can we really do all of this?" Hester asked.

"Yes," Abraham said. "We'll do it because we have to, and because it's the right thing to do."

"Come on, Hester," Anna-Marie said. "Let's go see what Claude and Abraham have picked out for us."

Carefully, Anna-Marie and Hester began to inspect the property.

"It does have possibilities," Hester admitted grudgingly. "I can see where we can plant oranges and where our house could go."

"And ours could go back there," Anna-Marie said.

"The barn could go in between in the back," Claude said, walking up behind them. "It's not as much land as we are accustomed to, but we can make do."

"Hester, we could put the rock Sanon made for you under this tree," Abraham said, walking toward a huge oak with limbs that bowed and twisted almost to the ground.

"Yes," Hester said. "That looks like a good enough spot. Still, it's not the same."

"It's not, of course," Anna-Marie said. "But my papa always says that when life hands you lemons, you have to make lemonade. That's what we are going to do, is it not? Make lemonade?"

Hester nodded. "If we must."

"We must," Anna-Marie said, firmly.

"Here comes the captain and Sanon," Abraham said, before walking over to greet them.

"What do y'all think?" Claude asked.

"It's a fine piece of land." Captain Henry looked around for a moment. "Lots of willows by the riverbank for collecting mushrooms and shrimp and room enough here for everyone."

"Yes, and Bay Lanaux is just past those woods," Abraham said.

"They call those Guenard Woods," Captain Henry said. "Quite a history in those woods."

No one but Hester noticed that Sanon was staring at the woods intently. She moved closer to him and whispered, "What do you see?"

"Evil has lived in those woods," he said. "I can feel the spirits."

"Legend has it that years ago a murderer lived in those woods," Captain Henry said. "In the olden days, peddlers used to use those woods as a route from the river to the bay. They usually traveled into the woods around sundown. Some of their bodies were found strewn about here and there."

"We don't need to talk about that in front of the ladies," Claude interrupted.

"Oh, yes, we do," Anna-Marie said. "Go on, Captain."

"Well, one day after a particularly gruesome murder, a group of men banded together armed with axes and knives and rifles, anything they could find, and they hunted the killer."

"Did they find him?" Hester asked, hanging on every word the captain said.

"No, they couldn't find him. Not then, but he soon struck again. A hunter found another body in the woods. This time, they scoured every inch of it and found the killer in a deep hole covered with tin and branches. I don't know what those men did to him, but his hideout became his grave from what I heard. They say the spirits of those murdered men still wander around the woods at night."

"It's true," Sanon said. "They are still there." When he saw the fear in Hester's eyes, he added, "But they will not harm you. They were good men who happened upon evil."

"I don't want to live here," Hester announced, turning to walk away.

Sanon put a hand on her arm to stop her. "You are safe, here, child. This happened long ago, and these spirits will not harm you. I would tell you if you were not safe."

Hester stood there for a moment, thinking about what Sanon had said. "There's nowhere else we can go?" she asked Abraham.

"There's nowhere that suits our needs like this land does," Abraham said. "It has everything—room for all of our homes and a store and access to the bay, which I need. And we can afford it. That's the biggest consideration."

"Well, you're not going to catch me anywhere near those woods," Hester said.

"They're a fair distance from where our homes will be," Claude reassured her, "and you'll have Abraham and me around. You'll have no need to fret."

"He's right, child," Sanon said. "You will be protected. I will bring a special potion next time I visit. I will sprinkle it in the woods and over your land. You will be safe."

Anna-Marie put her arm around Hester's shoulders. "I will be here with you, as well. We will be fine."

The following week, Abraham and Claude signed the papers agreeing to the option on their land with the understanding that they would have three months to move. Anna-Marie and Hester couldn't hold back their tears when Claude showed them the signed copies of the option.

"How long do we have before we have to have everything moved?" Anna-Marie asked.

"We've got to start right now and be settled by winter. We've got a lot to do and not much time," Claude said.

"It doesn't seem real," Hester said. "We've been hearing about this for a long time, but now it's here. It's now."

Abraham squeezed her hand. "It will be okay," he promised. "We will build a new life close to home."

"It won't be the same," Anna-Marie said. "It will never be the same."

"At least we have each other and our children," Claude said. "That's a lot."

"Oh, they'd take them, too, if they wanted to," Hester said. "I don't trust no government. Never had. Never will. I feel like we're being exiled."

"I don't blame you for feeling like that," Anna-Marie said. "Not after this, but I know you have much more reason not to trust them than I do."

"Fortunately, we live in an area where people treat us with more dignity than in some places. That's why I don't want to leave. But then my people certainly have it better than Abraham's," Hester said. "We are Mulattos, and some of us can pass for white. Abraham's people haven't been so lucky."

"That's true," Abraham said. "I could tell you horror stories, but I prefer not to dwell on that. That's why my mama is refusing to sell. My daddy worked hard for his land, earned it fair and square, and she feels that nobody has the right to take it from him."

"They are going to take it one way or another," Claude said.

"I know, but she'd rather lose it fighting for it. I completely understand," Abraham said.

"So do I," Anna-Marie said. "If it weren't for the children, I might have done the same thing."

"Has anyone thought about where we are going to live once we begin tearing our houses apart?" Hester asked.

"Yes, we've thought about it," Abraham said. "Samuel Fucich said we can rent three of his cabins until we get our homes together. Some of his cabins are near Nestor Canal, so I can easily go out on the boat to bring money in while we're working on everything. He said he'd charge us little to nothing. I spoke with him about it yesterday."

"That's mighty nice of him," Claude said.

"Yes, that's quite a relief. I was worried about that, too," Anna-Marie said.

"They're small," Abraham said. "He usually rents them to oystermen, but some of them have already moved on to Biloxi. He said he's going to wait until the last possible moment to sign the papers, so we have a little time."

"What do you think? A few months?" Claude asked.

"Thereabouts, but not much more."

"Then we'd better get busy," Claude said. "You ladies can start packing up the children's things and personal items to take to the cabin. Abraham and I will determine the best way to move forward with moving our homes and the store. And we'll need to buy that land as soon as possible. A lot of folks are looking for land across the river. I don't want to lose it."

"We'd better get going," Abraham said, looking at the sky. "I see some clouds rolling in, and the water can sure get choppy just before a storm. If it's too choppy, the ferry won't run."

As they drove away, Anna-Marie looked back at the levee that hid their future home. I have to be strong, she thought. For everyone. This is not going to be easy.

Still, her heart was heavy as they docked and then made their way back to Union Settlement. She looked at Hester and knew that she, too, was feeling the ache that comes with change.

Two weeks later, Claude purchased four arpents of land in Homeplace. As he placed his signature on the contract, he angrily swiped at an errant tear that sprang to his eye.

CHAPTER 30

August 1925

"This is certainly intimidating," Claude said, staring at Abraham's home and wondering how they were going to take it apart piece by piece.

"It won't be as bad as you think," Abraham said. "Hester's father built this house using mortise and tenons. Every log and board is carved and wedged together perfectly kind of like a puzzle. All we have to do is pull them apart. Once you get the first one loose, it becomes easier. You'll see."

"Hester's father was a fine carpenter. This house is solid, more solid than mine," Claude said.

"Her father had many talents." Abraham inspected a corner of the house, searching for the best place to begin unraveling it. "He's one of the reasons Hester is having such a hard time right now. He built this place from the ground up with his own hands, with the exception of the room in the middle that was built by his father. It's the only connection she has left to him, and that connection is being ripped away from her."

"It's a travesty. A downright shame." Claude wiped the sweat that was dripping down his face. He and Abraham had spent the morning finishing the raft to transport the house, using logs Poopdeck had pulled from the river after the last flood. The August heat, simmering and humid, had done Claude in. He wasn't accustomed to working outdoors. On this day, the usual breeze from the river had dissipated, and the hot August air was suffocating.

"Isaac," Abraham called. "Fetch Mr. Claude some more water. Fill a whole pitcher. He's not used to this."

Isaac ran to the cistern to do his father's bidding. A few minutes later, he returned with a pitcher of water for Claude.

"Drink that, but not too much," Abraham said. "A little at a time,

214

otherwise you'll get sick." He didn't like how red Claude's face had become. "Sit down for a spell until you get your bearings back."

"Do you think this is going to work?" Claude asked a few minutes later when he started feeling better.

"Yes, it will work. The hardest part will be getting those mules up the levee with each load. A mule can only pull about eighty pounds. I've got four we can use—that's 320 pounds for each trip. We'll have to be careful about how much we load onto the raft."

"How do you know so much about mules?"

"The military. The Army did a study once. We used mules to carry provisions from time to time, and the sergeant was always on us about how much we could load."

"And how are we going to keep all this wood on the raft in the river's current?"

"Captain Henry gave me some steel wire rope we can use to tie all of the wood together."

"Captain Henry is mighty good to you," Claude noted.

Abraham grinned. "That's because I married Hester. He's got a soft spot for her after what happened to her family."

"Everyone loves Hester," Claude said.

"I'm a fortunate man," Abraham agreed. "Finding her in that tree was the best thing that ever happened to me. I worry about her, though. She's so distraught about this move. I'm trying to make it as easy as possible for her."

"I know. Anna-Marie is none too happy herself. She's been moping around ever since we showed her the new property. It's become real for her, and now with her papa moving to New Orleans, she's even more distressed."

"Did he get a good value for his property?" Abraham asked.

Claude shook his head and laughed. "Twelve thousand five hundred. I know that seems like a lot, but considering all the land he owned and the house and mill, it's laughable. Anna-Marie said he went down to that levee office and raised the roof."

"Somebody needed to," Abraham said. "We all should have. There's more power in numbers."

"Wouldn't have done no good," Claude said. "Once the legislature voted, it was a done deal. We didn't stand a chance."

"I'm almost afraid to move across the river," Abraham walked over to a nearby tree, picked a newly ripened pear, and bit into it. "The Good Lord only knows what will happen when we get there." He picked another pear and handed it to Claude.

"I know what you mean," Claude said. "Living below New Orleans comes with a mighty big price tag. Who knows what they'll conjure up next?"

"Maybe we could talk Sanon into conjuring up something for them," Abraham said.

"Wouldn't do no good. His powers are minimal compared to those politicians and the power they wield. Hopefully, they got what they wanted, and they'll leave us alone now."

"Hopefully," Abraham repeated, and then he walked toward the barn. He found a ladder and leaned it against the side of the house. "We work top down. We'll tear the roof off first. It's metal, so that won't be a big deal."

Abraham, Claude, and Poopdeck climbed onto the roof and began disassembling it piece by piece. Most of the metal was still good, as it had been replaced after the hurricane. Claude lasted a half hour before Abraham insisted that he climb down and take a break.

"You'll catch a heat stroke if you don't, and that won't do anyone any good," Abraham said. "Drink some water, rest for a few minutes, then come back up."

For two days, the men worked in the sweltering heat, with Claude taking breaks every thirty minutes or so. Finally, the roof was off and stacked neatly near the raft.

It was nearly dusk by the time they finished, and Claude, Abraham, and Poopdeck sat under a tree to relax with cold glasses of lemonade. Finally, a breeze began to stir.

"I hope that doesn't mean rain," Abraham said. "I don't think we should get any for a few more days. I sure hope not. We've got most of the furnishings out, but there are still a few things inside that I don't want to get wet."

"Afternoon thunderstorms can pop up anytime," Poopdeck said.

"Maybe we should cover it with a canvas tarp or something," Claude said.

"I think we'll be okay for tonight," Abraham said. "Maybe tomorrow. I'm pooped."

"Me, too," Claude said, laughing. "I'm certainly not used to this, but I must say, it feels pretty good. I'm sore all over and heated to the core, but something about working like this makes a man feel good."

"That's why I like working on the boat rather than working for someone else indoors," Abraham said. "Hard work is good for the soul."

"Well, my soul must be doing pretty good right about now because this is the hardest I've worked in years," Claude said.

"Just wait." Abraham looked at his house. "The real work begins tomorrow." He laughed when Claude groaned.

The next morning, the three men began taking the house apart log by log, wooden slat by wooden slat, window by window, door by door. Each timber was wedged tightly, a tribute to Big Jake's skill. "See that room in the middle?" Abraham said from atop the ladder. "The one with the wood-burning stove? This house used to be just that room. Hester's grandfather built that in the 1800s, and then her daddy started adding on. I bet that room is built differently from the rest."

"There sure is a lot of history in this old house," Claude said,

"Sure is. Hester's grandfather served in the War of 1812 and was awarded this land for his service. He became a free man after the war. I guess it helped that he could pass for white, and some of his children actually did. Hester does have some family left—an auntie and two uncles—but they decided they were white and moved up north to have a different life than they could here. Can't really blame them, I guess, but who turns their back on family like that? Hester hasn't ever seen them. She's only heard about them back when she was very young. I guess they didn't hear about what happened in the hurricane, or they didn't care. I don't know, but there's quite a few Mulattos up north and even in New Orleans who live the life of a white man."

"Doesn't Hester want to find them?" Claude asked. "After all, they are family."

"They're no family of mine," Hester said, catching the tail end of the conversation. "Never once did they visit us or even send a letter. My daddy said they left and never looked back. Forgot where they came from, who they were, and the color of their bloodline. Why would I want to find people like that?"

"I guess you wouldn't," Claude said.

"Besides, I have all the family I need. I have Abraham and Isaac, and Florence and Emmanuel, and you and Anna-Marie and your children. What more could I ask for? The Good Lord has blessed me in abundance."

"You're right about that," Claude said.

Hester balanced a tray of lemonade on two makeshift workhorses. "Y'all come get something to drink. Fresh lemonade will give you a boost. Hurry now. I ain't got all day. There's plenty that needs doing around here."

The men gathered around while she poured each one a glass.

"Look," Claude said. "Here come reinforcements."

Everyone turned to see Peter Pelitire and his two oldest sons, Victor and Rocco, walking through the orange grove. Peter waved and hurried the boys toward them.

"What brings you to my humble home?" Abraham asked after greeting Peter. It was highly unusual for a white man, especially an Italian or a Tako, to visit a black man's home.

"Claude told me you were taking the house apart and that you needed all the help you can get," Peter said. "My boys are big and strong, and I can fetch and carry. Many hands make light work, my daddy always said."

Abraham bowed his head for a moment to hide the tears that sprang unbidden to his eyes. "Thank you kindly, sir," he said. "Your help is appreciated indeed and that of your boys."

For the next three weeks, the men and children worked side by side, carefully removing the walls of the home that Hester had lived in since she was born. Hester kept them supplied with drinks and food while Anna-Marie worked at the store so that Claude could help their friends.

Sometimes Hester sat under a large oak, the same oak whose branches she and her brother had climbed as children. As room by room disappeared into a stack of wood, she said good-bye once again to her father, her mother, and her brother.

At times, she smiled broadly to hide her pain, but other times, sitting under that tree watching, she felt like the weight of the world had settled onto her shoulders. She tried to tell herself that it was just a house, but that didn't ring true. It was here that she had formed her character, learned to laugh and cry, played with Isaac, and learned the value of hard work. Here, she had listened to her mother sing. She had listened to her father's stories about the river and his experiences on it. Here, she had learned about God and what was right and what was wrong. She had learned about her place in the world and not to step outside of those boundaries. Anna-Marie had changed some of that for her, but the lessons she had learned in this house about the hierarchy of race lived within her. "You will take them with you," Abraham had told her one night when he found her on the porch crying quietly. To a degree, she knew that was true. They would rebuild the house, of course, and the spirit of her parents and Isaac might still be there, but one never really knew such things. She would not be able to sit under Isaac's favorite tree. She would not be able to go into the barn and imagine conversations with her father. She would never again imagine her mother picking oranges from the trees in their yard or filling their socks with candies and fruit at Christmas before hanging them on the old stove. Hester knew she would carry those memories with her, but she would never again be able to sit outside, look around, and relive those happy times.

Anna-Marie kept telling her that they must make the best of it, but she knew her friend couldn't really understand the depth of her loss. Anna-Marie still had her *maman* and papa.

"Rocco," she heard Peter yell. "Quit trying to carry so much at one time. You're going to drop those boards, and they might crack."

A small smile came to Hester's face. In the midst of all of her turmoil, she realized she still had much for which to be grateful.

CHAPTER 31

September 1925

"Claude, this is Captain Richard Johnson," Captain Henry said. "He's been pushing barges on this river all his life. He's the best there is in these parts, and he's the one who should move your house across the river."

Claude shook hands with the captain, observing his weathered face and hearty smile. "It's good to know you, sir. I'll be frank with you. My wife and I are very nervous about this."

"No need to worry, son. I moved the Second Mt. Zion Baptist Church over to Nairn just last week. The trick is to time it carefully when the currents aren't moving too swiftly. We have to minimize sudden jolts that could loosen nails or screws. Other than that, it's just like pushing any barge loaded with goods. A barge can carry up to 1500 tons of cargo, so the weight of your house shouldn't be an issue. Getting the house to the river and then onto your land will be more difficult than getting it across the river."

"You're in the best of hands," Captain Henry said. "I'd do it, but packet boats operate differently than tugs, and I don't want to take a chance with your home."

"I appreciate that. What about this store? Could we move this, too?" he asked Captain Richard, hopefully.

Captain Richard looked around for a few minutes and then walked back inside. "We could, I guess, but I couldn't guarantee it will arrive in one piece. Henry showed me your home, and it's built solidly. This store looks rickety in places. It could fall apart just getting to the river. If I were you, I'd take the store apart before trying to move it."

"That will be a chore," Claude said. "We just took my friend's house apart, and it wasn't easy."

"No, it's not," Captain Richard agreed. "For your house, you'll need men, and mules and timbers to roll it on."

"I can arrange that. What will the cost be?"

"If I could, I wouldn't charge you anything, seeing as you're Henry's friend, but I have to pay to use the barge, and there are other expenses associated with using my tug." Captain Richard noticed the look of concern that appeared on Claude's face. "Don't worry, the charge will be minimal compared to what other captains are charging to move houses. I'm waiving my normal fee and charging you only for my expenses."

"I'm much obliged," Claude said. "That's mighty kind of you."

Captain Richard shook Claude's hand. "After the way you folks were treated by that levee board, I'm happy to do all I can. From what I hear, y'all are leaving with much less than you had before."

"Truth be told, I don't know how some folks are going to manage," Claude said.

"Me neither," Captain Henry said. "I've always tried to do my part to help the folks down here—giving them rides and dropping goods into the river, but what's happening now is beyond belief. I can't figure how they can force people to sell for next to nothing like this. It's legal thievery. That's what it is."

"Yes, and people are scattering like the wind. Some folks have already moved to other parts of the state, or they've moved in with relatives across the country because they can't afford to buy land with the money they got. My business is already down about eighty percent."

"That's such a shame," Captain Richard said.

"I was hoping to take a few months off after the move to go out on the boat with Abraham, but I don't think that's going to happen. I didn't realize what this move would entail and how many people we'd have to build homes for. It will take months and months to get everyone settled. It's a nightmare, really."

"I can imagine," Captain Richard said. "I'll do as much as I can to help."

"Thank you, sir. When do you think we'll be able to move the house?"

"In about two weeks if the weather holds up. And if we don't get a hurricane. As you know, September is unpredictable."

"Yes sir."

After the two captains left, Claude hurried to tell Anna-Marie to prepare the house for the move in two weeks. She had already begun packing up their possessions in crates and had already moved some of their things to the cabin they had rented in Nestor. "We won't be there long," Claude had assured her. "Just long enough to get the house moved and to run water to it."

"We're going to have indoor plumbing? A real flush toilet?" Anna-Marie had asked.

"No, not a flush toilet. We'll still have an outhouse, but we will have running water in the kitchen *zink*."

"I can't wait to tell Hester," Anna-Marie had said.

"Maybe you should wait. I know they can't afford to do that, and I don't want to rub their noses in it. We must be considerate."

Anna-Marie had nodded. "You're right, of course."

On September 17, 1925, one day after their twelfth wedding anniversary, Anna-Marie watched as her home was placed on timbers and rolled away. Claude and Abraham went with Captain Richard, while Anna-Marie, Hester, and the children stayed behind to stack the debris that had built up through the years under where the house had stood.

"I can't believe it's gone," Anna-Marie said to Hester. "It looks so barren."

"That's how I felt when they took our house apart. I cried and cried," Hester said.

"It was bad enough when they took the store down. Now this. It's just too much. Will you watch the children for a few minutes? I need to be alone."

"Of course," Hester said. "Take your time. We'll be fine."

Anna-Marie walked toward the levee across the uneven road that had not been fixed since the last flood, and then she climbed to the top of the levee. Sitting down, she surveyed the land that had once housed her life. She saw the rope swing that Claude had made for the children hanging from an oak tree, slightly moving in the breeze. The barn was still standing and the stable, but Claude and Abraham were going to tear those down, as well. They were salvaging everything they could. She saw the cistern that had provided them with water and thought about how many times her family had made the trip to that cistern—for boiling water, for baths, for cooking. The galvanized washtub, where everyone bathed and clothes were washed, barely noticeable before, stood out like a sore thumb, sitting just behind where the house had been. The gardens she had planted around the house, lush and filled with flowers, were still blooming, although now the flowers hugged the earth, trampled when the house was moved.

Anna-Marie had always been an optimistic person, and in her heart she knew they would survive this move, but sitting there, staring at what remained of the memories she had built, she experienced a grief unlike anything she had felt before. After today, she knew she must plaster a smile on her face and help everyone else cope, but today, just for a few moments, she allowed herself to feel her loss. She had been happy here, happier than she had ever been. No matter what her *maman* said about what her life could have had, she loved her life with Claude and the children. Hers was a life that had meaning. It had love and kindness and faith in all things good. That was what hurt the most. What had happened here was not good for anyone who lived along the river. She felt like a way of life was being wiped away, erased, forced into extinction. Theirs had been a diverse culture filled with numerous nationalities who lived and worked together in harmony, who had adapted to each other and accepted each other's differences. Here, most people accepted her relationship with Hester and Abraham. Even if they didn't approve, they rarely made mention of it, with the exception of Mildred, who had always made her feelings known. She didn't know what it would be like on the West Bank. Folks were different there. Everything was different there, even though it was just across the river.

Anna-Marie watched Hester and the children as they picked up large sticks, remnants of old furniture, and small items that had made their way under the house, and moved each item to the burn pile. She felt like her whole life would go up in those flames when the match was tossed onto the pile. Feeling a tinge of guilt for not helping, she started to get up and then sat back down. She needed this time to feel the enormity of what was happening. She could hear the sounds of the river, the ship horns blowing, the tide washing up on shore behind her. She watched the sun set behind the levee in a cloudless sky, a sight she had cherished for many years. She couldn't count the times she and Claude had sat on their front porch, talking about their days, making decisions about the store, while they watched the sun go down together and just enjoyed each other's company.

Sometimes they had danced on that porch, playing music on their battery operated tube radio—songs like "When My Baby Smiles at Me" by Ted Lewis and his orchestra or "Hold Me" by Art Hickman. Sometimes, they had sat there quietly watching the children play after all schoolwork was completed and chores were done. Anna-Marie knew they would do all of these things in their new life, but still she sat there, staring at the land that had brought her such happiness.

Finally, she roused herself. Stop lollygagging, she told herself. There is work to be done.

Anna-Marie took a deep breath, squared her shoulders, and walked down the levee with determination. Claude and Abraham would not be back until tomorrow, and she must have everything that had been left behind cleaned and ready to go. In the coming days, they would move the barn, the stable, and the horses. When she got within earshot, she told Claude Jr., Charlie, and Isaac that they should clean the stable the next day. "The girls will pack up the barn tomorrow, but tonight, we'll sleep in there."

"Poopdeck is bringing the boat to take me and Isaac to the cabin," Hester said. "He should be here any minute now. I told him to bring a basket of food for y'all. He'll bring me back first thing in the morning."

"Thank you, Hester. I've been so distraught, I didn't even think about food," Anna-Marie said.

"We'll get through this somehow," Hester said.

"I know. It's just a bit overwhelming."

"It is," Hester agreed. "But we'll get through. We have no other choice."

After Hester and Isaac left, Anna-Marie fed the children and then led them to the barn. Together, they turned the hay into makeshift beds. "Get a good night's rest," she said, kissing each child good-night. "There's a lot of work to be done tomorrow."

After the children fell asleep, Anna-Marie sat outside the barn listening to the croaking of the bullfrogs as they sang their nightly chorus. She stared at the stars, shimmering and blinking in the night sky. The moon, a waning crescent, seemed more distant than usual, barely illuminating the sky. She took a deep breath and said her farewells, silently listing the people she knew who had already left and those who would be gone soon.

Tomorrow would be the beginning of a new life just a short boat ride away, a life that would be similar yet so different.

And while her children slept, Anna-Marie replayed in her mind the happy and the sad times she had experienced on this land amid a chorus of frogs. When exhaustion finally set in, she lay right there in the grass and inhaled its sweet scent before she finally fell into a restless sleep.

CHAPTER 32

October 1925

Leonus sat at his desk preparing for the conference with the Board of Commissioners scheduled for late October. As he flipped through the account ledgers, he verified that the board owed his parish a lot of money. He had heard stories of delayed payments to homeowners, as well, and he prepared to hash that out with them. To his mind, they had stolen enough from his parish, and he was going to see to it that every penny owed was paid. He had called for this conference that would include representatives of the Grand Prairie Levee Board, the Plaquemines Parish East Bank Levee Board and the Board of Commissioners of the Orleans Levee District, including Jefferson, Sal, and Pierre. Attorneys and engineers would also be present.

On that Friday, October 23 at 3:00 p.m., the meeting convened. President Peter J. Flanagan acted as chairman of the conference. Leonus began by quoting Section 3 of Act 99 before informing participating commissioners that the Orleans Levee District owed the Plaquemines Parish East Bank Levee Board $155,000 in bonds and owed the Grand Prairie board another $35,000 as well.

"I recommend that the Supervisor of Public Accounts should be called in to verify the assets and obligations of both boards," Attorney James Gremillion suggested.

"I don't understand why payment has been delayed," Leonus said. "The Grand Prairie Levee Board is bankrupt. Some of the homeowners have not been paid for their bonds. This is ridiculous."

"I do believe that Mr. Lozano's position has merit," Gremillion said.

"Everything is held up at your attorney's office," Leonus said. "Settlements have not been paid, but the people are expected to move.

Our levees are getting worn down, and you are sitting on the money we need to fix them."

"That's not true," Gremillion said. "The only question is that of unredeemed lands. We are not required to pay for them. A massive amount of faulty titles have been submitted. This is why there have been delays. We have no control over that. Perhaps we could deposit fifty-three percent of the outstanding bonds in escrow with the treasurer or at a bank. We could create a committee, three people, who can work out a final settlement for all levee boards in Plaquemines Parish."

"I don't have any objection to that," Leonus said.

The state engineer, Alexander Crandall, stated that the area of land along the spillway that belonged to the Plaquemines Parish East Bank Levee Board was fifty-three percent. "This includes fifty-seven percent of the levee line."

"Before, your office said that two-thirds of the land would be taken," Leonus said.

"That was merely an estimation," Alexander said. "Since then, we have determined that the area is fifty-three percent."

Leonus shook his head in disgust. "What about accrued interest from this date to when the bonds mature?" he asked. "And you should be aware, the Plaquemines East Bank Board and the Grand Prairie board have employed legal counsel at the rate of $5,000 each for the services required to settle matters regarding the spillway. I would like that included in your adjustment of monies owed to these boards."

"An adjustment can be made," Alexander said.

"Don't overlook the settlement of your debt to private individuals, too," Leonus cautioned. "Now I would like to make a statement about my position regarding this matter. Can you bring in the stenographer?"

Once the stenographer was ready, Leonus stood up and read his prepared statement:

"I desire to state that as district attorney of the Parish of Plaquemines, and ex-officio attorney for the Plaquemines Parish Levee District, that I will call a meeting of the Board of Commissioners of these two levee districts as soon as the Orleans Levee Board furnishes these two boards with copies of the necessary resolution touching upon the matter of retiring the outstanding bonds and unbonded indebtedness of the Grand Prairie

Levee District and the outstanding bonds of the Plaquemines Parish East Bank Levee District in proportion to the area affected in the spillway."

Leonus went on to state that, "After the Orleans Levee Board has submitted proof of proper showing to these two levee boards that it complied with whatever conditions precedent as set forth in Act 99 of 1924, known as the Spillway Law, I shall urge the two levee boards to take the necessary action by formal resolution to give its consent for the Orleans Levee Board to cut whatever levees of these two levee districts which may be included in the area of the spillway plan."

When he was finished, Alexander explained that he would create the resolutions and would present them to the Orleans Levee Board. "I request a meeting for Saturday, the 24th, and a copy of these resolutions be furnished to Mr. Lozano as soon as possible," he said.

When the meeting was over Leonus returned to his office, not quite happy with the results. He had believed the levee districts would get two-thirds of the bonds based on the projected amount of land that would be used. At fifty-three percent, the districts had just lost thirteen-and-two-thirds percent of those funds.

I did what I could, he thought. But now, I have other things that need my attention.

Leonus picked up a map of the East Bank of his parish, focusing on the land below the Bohemia Spillway area. He knew he needed to buy as much as he could in the coming months. People might be more eager to sell now that the levees further up river were being taken down, making them even more vulnerable to floods. Leonus thought of Jefferson Davenport and smiled. Davenport might have gotten eleven miles, but he had no claim to the rest.

After the meeting, Jefferson walked outside with Pierre and Sal. "I told you he was going to be a burr in our backsides," he said. "I have a feeling this is just the beginning. Keep an eye on him, boys. I don't trust him as far as I can throw him."

"What can he do now?" Pierre asked. "Everything has been finalized, and the spillway is in progress."

"There's plenty he can try. He's an attorney," Jefferson said. "He'll think of something. I don't like the way he's changing property lines and buying up land. I've been thinking, maybe we should try to extend the boundaries of the land we need. The federal government has a lot of land holdings down there. Maybe we could try to get that transferred to us. Think on it, boys. We need a good reason for the transfer."

"Is all of this going to be worth it?" Sal asked.

"Ask me that again in a few years," Jefferson replied, "when our coffers are full and we can do whatever we want."

After Sal and Pierre left, Jefferson returned to his office feeling very pleased with himself. Yes, the board would have to pay off the debts of the other levee boards, but he knew without a doubt that it would all be worth it in the end. His board would be flush with money and able to achieve the lofty goals he had planned. And there will be enough to go around for all of us, he thought, smiling.

The West Bank of the River

CHAPTER 33

Fall 1926

On September 26, 1926, *The Times-Picayune* published a letter in the "Aunt Jane's Letter Club" column from a young girl who lived in Nestor:

Dear Aunt Jane—I would like to join your letter club if you will let me. I am 8 years old and live at Nestor Canal, La., which is the center of the spillway, but we will soon have to move away because our levees have been torn down and the next time the Mississippi River rises, we may get flooded and drown.

I was born in New Orleans and went to kindergarten at La Salle School. Then we moved down here, and my mother taught me the first and second reader. Last April and May, I attended the Buras school and was promoted to Third B. I made my first communion at the Buras church on May 30.

I can handwork a little and have just finished a pillow cover with a back stitch. My sister, who teaches at Chautauqua in Colorado has sent me a lovely book of little Richard Headrick who preached out there this summer. He is called "The Little Minister." I wish I could read this book alone: my mother helps me to read a part each day. Aunt Jane, if you wish I will lend you this book.

When my sister returns she will take me to Buras for our school opens next Monday week. She is a teacher in the high school down there. Buras and Nestor are just a few miles above Fort Jackson and Fort. St. Phillip that Edith Earnest told about in her prize letter of last Sunday.

Aunt Jane, please excuse my writing; I am left-handed and can't do as well but I am trying to use my right hand, too.

Your new niece,
Gloria Delta Subat Nestor, La.

Anna-Marie showed the letter to Claude. "Look at this. Even the children are being affected by the spillway. This poor little girl lives in Nestor and thinks she might drown. Bless her heart."

"It's a shame. She'll probably have to move soon. The spillway is finished from what I hear," Claude said.

The Bohemia Spillway had been completed at a reported cost of $1,083,000. Included in that amount was approximately $425,000 that had been paid to all of those who owned front arpents on the river—$65,000 more than originally projected. Eleven miles of riverfront levee had been removed, along with back levees. The lower Bohemia levee had been extended, and the back levees between Pointe á la Hache and Bohemia had been reinforced.

From the river, Claude and Abraham had watched as the artificial levees that had protected the East Bank for generations were removed, oyster shell by oyster shell, mound of dirt by mound of dirt, until you could see clear across the marsh. Houses that had once been lovingly attended fell into disrepair or were removed by the Orleans Levee District. The spillway began just below Bohemia Plantation, but the plantation was left untouched. Other houses in a weakened state because of neglect were damaged when a hurricane the month before had tracked through the Gulf, grazing the East Bank before making landfall in Houma, Louisiana, with winds of one hundred fifteen miles per hour. The empty houses on the East Bank had sustained some damage, contributing to the ghostly atmosphere of abandoned towns for eleven miles. About halfway through the construction, Abraham had begun to look the other way when he traveled on the river, his gaze always away from the East Bank. He couldn't bear to see the destruction. Claude had the opposite reaction. He wanted to see everything. He wanted to be able to inform people if they asked about the progress or if their home was still there.

Hester had not adjusted well to living on the West Bank. She had placed the stone Sanon had given her under a tree before they rebuilt the house and had said a prayer for her family. Sometimes she sat by that tree for hours trying to feel the presence of her family, but it didn't work. Even after the house was built, she no longer felt them near her. They were across the river. That's where they would always be, and she could no longer visit with them. She tried to adjust, but the people on the West Bank were different, with their own customs and traditions, their own belief systems, less tolerance. Only a few of her former neighbors lived within ten miles of her home, and they were busy trying to make their way, too.

She knew Anna-Marie had been parrying questions about why she and Abraham lived so close to them, about their unusual friendship, and why they didn't live in the Mulatto camp. They didn't understand that, aside from Sanon, the Mulattos no longer accepted her. She had married a black man. Anna-Marie had not said a word to Hester about it. Isaac had heard it from Madeleine, and he had told Hester. Isaac said that Madeleine had asked him why white people don't like black people here. Hester had been very upset by this. Yes, on the East Bank, there had been rules, boundaries that had been in place since the slaves had been emancipated, but there had been little overt bigotry, aside from Mildred and that judge. Most people of every nationality had been kind and treated them with respect as long as the rules were followed. There was a hierarchy—the French, then the Austrians, then the Italians, and at the bottom of the list, the Mulattos and then the blacks. She knew her place.

Hester understood that she could not sit in the same pews at church with white people. She knew that she couldn't visit just any white person's home. She always drank from the "Colored" water fountains and did not go inside restaurants. She knew that if she wanted to go to a picture show, she must sit in the top balcony, but the way Anna-Marie and Claude had treated her had changed the way she thought about things. They, through example, had given her family an elevated stature that most black people did not enjoy. Hester had grown accustomed to that. People on the West Bank did not see things the same way. It was like moving backward in time, and Hester did not like it one bit.

She worried about Isaac. Her son had not been exposed to many other black children. The Couvillion children had been his only friends. That had never been a problem before, but Hester realized that it might become a problem in their new surroundings. She didn't want that for her son. He was Mulatto, but he could never pass for white. He looked more like his father. People here were already questioning their friendship with their neighbors. She worried what they would say when they saw Isaac playing with Anna-Marie's girls, especially Madeleine. Since the snakebite incident, Isaac and Madeleine had become very close. At nine years old, Isaac had taken upon himself the role of her protector. Wherever Madeleine played, Isaac could always be found nearby, keeping an eye out for anything that could hurt her. For the first time, Hester questioned the wisdom of allowing Isaac to grow up within this unusual friendship she and Abraham had with Claude and Anna-Marie.

When she mentioned her concerns to Abraham, he brushed them aside. "You worry too much," he told her. "Yes, it's different here, but everything will be fine. Claude and certainly Anna-Marie will put anyone who speaks out of turn about it in their place. Of that, I'm sure."

After weeks of chewing on it, Hester finally brought her concerns to Anna-Marie one afternoon when they were outside scrubbing their clothes on the washboard.

"People sure treat us differently here," Hester said. "There are a lot more rules for one, and they don't smile at us like they did across the river. I can feel the difference. They aren't ugly, but they don't go out of their way to say a kind word either."

Anna-Marie, hearing the seriousness in her friend's voice, sat down and patted the spot beside her, indicating that Hester should sit with her. "I've noticed it, too," she said when Hester was settled. "I'm sorry. I wish it were different. I think it's got something to do with that judge. He has a lot more influence on this side of the river for some reason."

"Isaac said that Madeleine overheard you and Claude talking about it."

"Yes, we were, although I didn't realize Madeleine was listening. Folks have stopped by when we're on the porch acting like they wanted to welcome us, but it always ends with questions about y'all living so close and why you didn't move to the Mulatto camp. I think Claude's getting a little tired of it because he surely put the last one, that Mrs. Dubonette, in her place. I don't understand it. Most of these people are French. They know better. It's like they've adopted the attitudes of the South instead of staying true to their roots. But don't you never mind. They'll get used to it."

"I sure hope so. I worry about Isaac playing with your girls. People can get real ugly about things like that."

"They won't get ugly with me for long," Anna said. "You know me. I don't put up with much from those sort of folks."

"But I don't want to cause problems for you and Claude. Y'all have been too good to us."

"That's a two-way street," Anna-Marie said, standing up. "We do for each other. That's what best friends do. Now stop your fretting. We've got to get these clothes washed. We'll worry about things when they happen. Not before. Worry does no one any good, and we've got enough worries without piling more on top. Everything will be fine."

Hester stood up and put one of Abraham's shirts in the washtub they were sharing, not for a minute thinking that even that wasn't done. She swirled it around in the Lux bubbles before she began scrubbing. "You sure have a way of easing my mind," she said.

Anna-Marie giggled, reached her hand into the washtub, and then flicked some water at Hester.

"You did not!" Hester reached her hand in and flicked water back.

A moment later, whole handfuls of water were being tossed back and forth until they were laughing uncontrollably and soaking wet. That's how Abraham and Claude found them.

"What in the world are you girls doing?" Claude asked.

"She started it," Hester said, pointing at Anna-Marie.

"No, she did," Anna-Marie said, still laughing.

"I don't care who started it," Abraham said. "It's mighty good to see you girls laughing." He had hardly seen Hester smile since the move.

"Sure is," Claude said. "We've got to get back to work. We just came to get some whiskey for the men helping us at Miss Penny's. You girls try to stay out of trouble."

Anna-Marie stuck her tongue out at his back as he walked away.

"Don't think I don't know what you're doing," Claude said.

"I swear that man has eyes in the back of his head," Anna-Marie said to Hester.

"He just knows you well," Hester said.

Later that evening, Anna-Marie asked Claude to take a walk while the children played outside. She told him about her conversation with Hester. "She's really fretting about it," Anna-Marie said.

"I can't say that we can truly understand how she feels, but she has good reason to fret. Things are different here. I know you've noticed."

"But what can we do about it?" Anna-Marie asked.

"There's not much any one person can do. It's just the way it is. People think what they will. We'll just go on like we always have, and if they don't like it, well, they can just lump it. That's what my father always says."

"Do you miss him?"

"Yes, I do, but I understand why he moved to Mississippi. My aunt has always taken care of him, and it's natural he would have gone there with her."

Anna-Marie tucked her hand inside of his. "I sure do love you, Claude Couvillion."

"And I you, *ma chérie*."

"Now what are we going to do about Hester? She's also worried about Isaac playing with our girls. She says people will talk."

"Let them talk. You're the one who taught me that," Claude said. "I don't care. Abraham is my best friend. He and his are family to us, and we couldn't ask for better. I don't care what other folks have to say about that."

Anna-Marie was quiet for a moment. As they walked, she listened to the sounds around her. "Have you noticed? We can still hear the river. The sounds just come from a different direction. They have the same birds— the blue herons, the brown pelicans, the mourning doves. The squirrels still chatter, and the bullfrogs sing at night just like they did across the river. Maybe things will be okay. Maybe once the store is up and running, everything will be okay."

"Yes, everything is going to be okay. It will just take time. We must be patient," Claude said.

CHAPTER 34

The general store Claude and Anna-Marie had planned to rebuild still wasn't open by the fall of 1926, one year after they had made the move across the river. There simply wasn't enough time in a day. Abraham and Claude had spent that year helping everyone they knew get situated and into a home. Anna-Marie knew it was the right thing to do, and she agreed wholeheartedly, but she worried about their funds, which were rapidly dwindling. They needed to hold onto the money from the sale of their land to stock the store. To supplement their income, Claude and Abraham went out on the boat on weekends, plucking oysters from reefs in Lake Washington, Bay Chicot, Bay Baptiste, and Grand Bayou. It wasn't much, but they made do. During the week, they built homes.

First, it had been Abraham's house. Then they had helped set up the much smaller Mulatto camp in Happy Jack about eight miles upriver from Homeplace, and they built a cabin for Sanon there. Then it was Miss Penny's house not far from the Mulatto camp, and then the Pelitires' house next door to Miss Penny's. They had also helped build a home for Captain Richard in the township of Empire to the south. Claude felt like he owed the captain for taking their home across the river without damaging anything and charging him next to nothing.

Abraham's mother, Florence, had waited to move until the last possible moment. For her, it was the principle of the matter. She didn't care about the paltry amount she was offered. She waited until she got the letter that stated that she and Emmanuel's land had been expropriated and that they must vacate the premises. Only then did she begin to gather her belongings. Abraham, Claude, Poopdeck, Spit when he wasn't drinking, and Peter took their house apart and then put it back together behind Abraham's house in Homeplace. After the move, though, Florence was never the same.

She felt defeated, robbed, broken.

She understood now how her ancestors had felt when they had no control over their own lives. She didn't cry or scream or whine. For the most part, she was silent, too silent. That had never been her way. She spent most of her days sitting on her front porch rocking in her chair and staring across the river. Emmanuel, Abraham, and Hester did everything they could to ease her despair, but nothing worked.

Abraham sat with her often, just talking without much of a response. He hoped her malaise would pass, but on Thanksgiving Day, he became more concerned. Every year of his life, his mother had prepared Thanksgiving dinner. This year, she did not even come into her house to help.

"Mama, are you okay?" Abraham said, sitting down next to her on the porch. He took her hand in his. He could feel a quiver running through her fingers. "Why don't you come in and eat? Hester prepared a feast for us."

Florence looked at him through vacant eyes.

"Please, Mama. You need to eat. Join us in giving our thanks."

"I'm not hungry," Florence said, her voice shaking and low. "Not much to feel thankful for these days."

"Of course there is," Abraham said. "We still have our homes, and we have each other. We should give thanks for that."

Florence didn't respond for a moment, but then she patted his hand. "You've been a good boy, Abraham. A fine son. Don't you ever forget that."

"I won't, Mama. How could I not be? You taught me how to live life."

"You are a good father to my grandson. Teach him about his past. Teach him to be strong. You have to be strong in this life."

"You've been the strongest one of us all," Abraham said.

Florence managed a small smile. "I've tried, but I think I've finally been beaten. I can't seem to shake these doldrums."

"You will, Mama. You'll be fine in no time."

"We'll see," Florence said.

"Will you come in and eat with us?" Abraham stood up and reached out his hand to help her up.

Florence stood up and allowed Abraham to lead the way inside. She sat in her usual spot to the right of her husband. For a moment, she seemed more like herself. She bowed her head with the others when Emmanuel said his prayer of thanks. She passed the gravy to Abraham. She smiled when Isaac announced that he was thankful for his family. She thanked Hester for cooking dinner. And then she went back outside to stare at the river, rousing herself long enough to tell Abraham, Hester, and Isaac good-bye after the dishes were washed, dried, and put away.

That night before she went to sleep, Florence placed her hand on Emmanuel's chest and told him she was grateful for the life he had given to her.

Emmanuel lay next to her smiling, feeling relieved. His Florence was coming back.

The next day, she simply disappeared.

Abraham and all of his friends searched everywhere for her, even the neighboring plantation, but they could not find her.

One week later, a muskrat hunter discovered her remains curled up underneath an oak tree on her former property. No one had thought to look for her there. Abraham could never figure out how she had crossed the river. The nearest ferry was in West Pointe á la Hache ten miles away.

On a dreary, cold, early December evening, Abraham and Claude buried her in that same spot. Her family prayed for her soul and then left her there to rest peacefully surrounded by the land that she loved.

Abraham carried that pain with him, along with a burning anger that he could not hide. Hester tried to console him. She understood how deeply a loss such as this could cut, but for weeks Abraham lashed out at anyone who dared to mention the spillway. Finally, Claude suggested that they take a trip out into the gulf for a few days to catch some shrimp. Hester thought that was a great idea and pushed Abraham to go. To pacify his wife, he reluctantly agreed.

Claude and Abraham left just before the shrimp season ended. There was a chill in the air, but it wasn't too cold. The sky was clear as Abraham steered his boat out of Bay Lanaux. "I'm going to stop on the way at Ben Ballay's place," he told Claude. "He makes the best cast nets around. I need to get a new one, and we can use it to catch bait or shrimp."

When they reached Ben's home, Claude noticed snipe that had been de-feathered and gutted, hanging on the clothes line. Abraham followed Claude's gaze and said, "They're aging them. Makes for some tender meat. They cook them with turnips, carrots, onions, and garlic. That's some good eatin' there. Ben's wife, Miss Suzanne, can make anything taste good."

"We'll have to try that," Claude said.

"Ben will be in the back," Abraham said, calling out as he made his way behind the house. "Ben Ballay. I've come for one of your cast nets."

An old man emerged from a work shed holding a large net in his hand. "Good day," Ben said, handing the net to Abraham to inspect.

"Your reputation speaks for itself," Abraham said. "I don't need to inspect it."

"You boys heading out for some shrimp?" Ben asked.

"We're going out for a few days," Claude said after introducing himself.

"You'll catch a lot with that," Ben said, nodding toward the net. "Stop in on your way back, and I'll have the missus send you home with some of those snipe on the line. We have plenty."

"Thank you, sir." Abraham said. "We'll do that. I was just telling Claude here about how tender the meat is when you age them like that."

"Sure is," Ben said. "Ain't nothing better."

Abraham paid Ben, and the two men headed back to the boat.

Abraham didn't talk much on that first day, and Claude left him to his thoughts as he steered out of Bay Lanaux toward Halfway Bayou and Lake Washington. On the second day, after they had hauled in about a hundred pounds of shrimp, Claude handed Abraham a glass of orange wine and sat down next to him.

"We've been through a lot together," Claude began. "Isaac's birth, the war, Madeleine losing her arm, hurricanes, floods, losing our land, and now the death of your mother."

Abraham sat there staring ahead silently.

"You've got to come to terms with that," Claude continued. "Remember all those nights I spent in the marsh whacking muskrats on the head?"

Abraham nodded.

"That's how I came to terms with the war. Remember how the nightmares stopped when you started killing muskrats with me?"

Abraham nodded.

"Well, you've got to find something that will ease this pain, this anger you are carrying. I don't know what that something will be, but you've got to find it. Hester needs you. Isaac needs you. Your father needs you. Hell, I need you."

Abraham looked over at Claude. "I can't fix this," he said. "That's what kills me. My mother sat on that porch staring across the river, and I couldn't help her. Now she's gone because I did nothing."

"That's not true. You took her home apart and put it back together for her. That's not nothing. You tried to ease her mind. You did everything you could do, but her spirit was broken. That's not your fault."

"She was always so strong. It killed me to see her like that."

"I know. This whole thing has been hard on everyone."

"Yes, but everyone else is still here, and she's gone."

"That's true," Claude said. "But maybe you could look at it differently. We are still here angry about what happened, worried about what will happen, and struggling to rebuild our lives. Out of all of us, she alone is at peace. She will spend eternity on the land she loved. She doesn't have to worry anymore."

Abraham thought about that for a moment. "I'd like to kill a few people, namely everyone on the Orleans Levee Board," he said.

"Wouldn't we all? I don't know a person who sold their land who doesn't wish them harm, and you, certainly, have more reason than most."

"That I do," Abraham said.

"You should go visit Sanon. Maybe there's some wise words he could give you or some herbs that would ease your mind."

"I'll do that when we get back home. Sanon seems to have something for any ailment, even those of the mind and heart," Abraham said. "I remember when Hester first told me about him. I was dead set against her visiting with him because I didn't understand his way of life. Now I couldn't imagine my life without him. He's done so much for all of us. I wish I had brought him to see my mother. Maybe he could have done something for her."

"Your mother is right where she always wanted to be. Try to remember that," Claude said. "And when the time comes, I'll help you bury your father next to her."

The two men drank orange wine and talked late into the night. Even after Claude turned in, Abraham sat at the helm and watched slivers of light, sent from the moon, dancing across the water. Finally, the rocking of the boat lulled him into a deep sleep right where he sat.

The next morning, Abraham seemed more like himself. The light was back in his eyes, and he laughed and joked with Claude all day.

When they were satisfied with the amount of shrimp they had caught, Abraham steered the boat toward Bay Lanaux.

"I can't believe how much we got," Claude said, when hours later they docked the boat.

"This haul will fetch a pretty penny," Abraham said. "And most of them are jumbos or bigger, at least eleven/fifteens."

"Lord knows we can all use the money right now," Claude said.

"Ain't that the truth," Abraham said. "I'll keep them on the boat overnight. Help me ice them down before we go, and I'll take them to old man Angus tomorrow. He pays a fair amount and then sells them to the restaurants in the Quarter."

After they had iced the shrimp, Abraham shook Claude's hand. "Thank you, man. I needed that. After I get rid of these shrimp. I'll come over and we'll start rebuilding the store. We've got to get you back in business."

"Much obliged, Abraham. Anna-Marie will be happy to hear that. It's time."

"Yes, it is. Maybe once that's done, we can all get back to normal."

A few days later, Hester approached Claude while he was laying the foundation for the store.

"I'm not sure what you did, but thank you," she said.

Claude took off his hat and bowed toward her. "My pleasure. That's what friends are for."

CHAPTER 35

Spring 1927

By March of 1927, Claude and Abraham were finished building the store. Anna-Marie began the work of purchasing goods, and the children helped with stocking sliced bread, preserves, Quaker oats, tea, coffee, and canned vegetables, along with flour, sugar, and paper goods. Hester cleaned the meat counter until it sparkled while Anna-Marie arranged cigarettes and trinkets on the counter near the brand new cash register. They wanted everything to be perfect. By March 15, they were ready to open.

"I never thought it would take this long to reopen the store," Anna-Marie said to Claude the night before they opened.

"I didn't either." Claude pulled her close to him. "I'm glad this day is finally here."

"Me, too. I missed our store and talking to folks. It was never like a job, more like a visit with friends all day every day."

"It was always like that, even when my father ran it. When I was a boy, I used to sit and listen to the old men talk. They gossip just as much as women, you know."

"Oh, I know," Anna-Marie said, giggling. "About different things, though. You'd never hear them talking about a woman's choice for a Sunday dress, but if someone was letting their boat go to ruin, you'd hear all about it."

"I hope we get some good customers," Claude said.

"We will. The women will always come to see you no matter where we have a store."

Claude laughed. "That's probably the other way around, but however it works, I hope we will be successful."

"We're due for something good to happen, so I don't think we should worry overmuch about that. Let's just go to sleep and wake up to our new store. Claude Couvillion, I do believe we are back in business."

"Yes, we are. And it only took a year-and-a-half."

The next morning, Anna-Marie and Claude flipped the "Open" sign around together and waited for the bell to ring signaling their first customer. It didn't take long. No one who lived on the river could resist a "Sale" sign, and Anna-Marie and Hester had plastered them across the front of the store along with a bigger one that announced the opening date.

As they waited on customers—Anna-Marie at the cash register and Claude helping people carry purchases out—occasionally, they would look at each other and smile. Each felt a sense of pride that they had done this together. At the end of the day, they sat together and counted what they had made.

"I'm plumb worn out," Anna-Marie said, stacking bills in like denominations and handing Claude the coins to count.

"I'm not," Claude said. "This is much easier than building a house in the hot sun, trust me. Would you like me to do the counting?"

"Oh, no. That's the fun part," Anna-Marie said. "Count your coins, and I'll let you know what the bills come to."

A few minutes later, Anna-Marie glanced at Claude. "You're not going to believe this."

"How much?" Claude asked.

"One hundred and twenty-six dollars," Anna-Marie announced.

"You're pulling my leg."

"No, I'm not. Count it yourself." Anna-Marie handed the bills to Claude.

"Well, I'll be. That's better than I expected. I have eighteen dollars and fifty-two cents in change, so what is the final tally?"

Anna-Marie did the math in her head. "One hundred forty-four dollars and fifty-two cents. Almost one hundred fifty dollars, Claude."

Claude pulled her up and swung her around. "We did it. Every day won't be like this, but we won't have to worry anymore," he said, hugging his wife to him.

Anna-Marie sighed a happy sigh. Finally, things are getting back on track, she thought, hugging Claude close. Maybe our life here won't be so bad after all.

For the next month, Anna-Marie and Claude worked in the store, meeting their neighbors and learning more about the West Bank. There were a few curious stares whenever Hester and Anna-Marie joked back and forth or when Isaac was spotted outside playing with the other children, but no one said anything.

Their friends from the East Bank—Captain Henry, Captain Richard, Peter Pelitire, and Miss Penny stopped by to wish them well. And Nikolas, who had always delivered their mail, showed up with his mail sack on his back. "At least I don't have to cross the river to get this to y'all anymore. That's one good thing," he said. "Oh, and give this to Miss Hester." He handed Anna-Marie a slice of blueberry pie, carefully wrapped in a cloth napkin.

"Funny how you never bring pie for me," Anna-Marie teased.

Nikolas turned red. "No offense meant, ma'am. It's just that Miss Hester, she's special. She really took care of me that one time."

"I'm just teasing you," Anna-Marie said. "I'll make sure she gets this."

After he left, Anna-Marie asked Claude to take over while she checked to see how the children were doing with their lessons. Hester normally watched them while Anna-Marie worked, and she helped teach them arithmetic and reading. Anna-Marie had taught Hester well, which had been easy because Hester loved learning.

A few minutes later, Abraham came into the store.

"I thought you were out on the boat this morning," Claude said.

"I was, but then I ran into Captain Richard." Abraham looked around for Anna-Marie.

"She's with Hester at the house," Claude said.

"Good, I don't want to worry her."

"What's going on?" Claude asked.

"Have you been listening to the radio? Have you heard how those radio folks are talking about the river, about how it's been flooding folks farther north?"

"That's been going on all year. Should we start worrying?" Claude asked.

"I'd say so, yes," Abraham said. "All that water is heading straight down here. Used to, the river could escape through natural drainage areas all along its tributaries. That Mississippi River Commission built levees all the way up the river, and now it has nowhere to drain, so yes, I am very worried. I don't know what makes politicians think they can control a river, especially one as big as this one. I saw Captain Richard on the river today. He said he's been upriver, and it's bad. He's worried. He said more than a hundred people died in Arkansas when the flood reached them. What do you think's gonna happen when it reaches us?"

"You remember what Mark Twain said in that book we read? Something about 10,000 river commissions not being able to tame that lawless stream? Twain sure knew what he was talking about. Anyhow, I thought that's why they built the spillway, to stop the flooding," Claude said.

Abraham laughed. "They didn't build that to save us. They built it for New Orleans, and I'd be willing to bet my horse that it's not gonna work."

"Good Lord," Claude said. "We just got the store stocked and opened."

"I know. That's why I wanted to warn you. We've got a little time, I think, but not much. If I were you, I'd put everything in the attic. I'll help, of course, and I'll get Albert. Maybe we could get Spit to help. Between all of us, we should be able to get everything that can be saved moved up high. I don't even think we should ride this one out in the boat. I'd feel better if we headed north away from the river. I don't think my father—you know his health has gone down since my mother died—could make it through another flood on the boat. What do you think?"

"I don't know." Claude looked around the store. "Anna-Marie is going to be so mad. We're going to lose milk, eggs, fruit, vegetables. Oh, she's going to be mad. We just bought all of this."

"I know. I'm sorry," Abraham said. "If we must, we can go to the boat, but this time I'd rather not. Maybe I should speak with Sanon. He'll be able to advise us."

"Good idea. You do that, and I'll find Anna-Marie. How much time before we would have to leave?"

"A week or so would be my guess. I'll let you know when I get back."

Abraham went outside and jumped on his horse, and then he raced toward the Mulatto camp as fast as he could. When he arrived, he stroked the horse and gave him some water before knocking on Sanon's door.

"I had a feeling you were coming," Sanon said when he saw Abraham. "I know why you're here. Come, let's sit outside." Sanon pointed to the bench—carved like a church pew—that Abraham had built on his porch along the front wall of the cabin.

Sanon sat quietly for a moment and then pulled out his pipe, filled it with herbs, and struck a match and lit it. "I had a dream about this last year. Back when they were having all that rain up north in Kansas, Iowa, and Illinois. Then rains in Oklahoma, Arkansas, and north Louisiana started raising the Arkansas and Red Rivers. In my dream, the winds began blowing south. I saw explosions, huge bursts of fire like bombs in a war, but I could never make heads or tails of what was happening. I saw ships wrecked and people running for their lives. To be honest, it was frightening, and I haven't been able to shake it, even after all this time."

"What does all of that have to do with this?" Abraham asked.

"I'm not sure. I wish I knew. All I can tell you is something bad is about to happen, something that will be of great significance and will affect many people."

"Are we going to flood like in 1922?" Abraham asked. "That was mighty bad."

"It's possible. Look what's already happened. We got all that rain in February, and just last week New Orleans got fourteen inches of rain. The levees kept all that water in the city. I don't know what kind of people dream up all these ways to keep people from flooding, but they all seem to backfire, do they not?"

"Yes, they do," Abraham said.

"The river's already high, has been for months," Sanon said. "I fear there will be nothing left of our old homes on the East Bank. The water will escape through the spillway, and everything will be gone."

Abraham hesitated, then he asked, "What about over here?"

"Logically speaking, if the river goes into the spillway like they said it would when they built it, our levees should protect us. That's logically speaking, of course. I'm feeling far too unsettled for that to be true. I can hear the whispering of the wind, and it's telling me that more change is coming, I'm afraid."

"What are you going to do?" Abraham asked.

"It is undecided. It's a chore to move the whole camp, but I'm thinking we should pack up and leave this god-forsaken place. I will send word to you when I decide."

"How much time do we have?"

"The decision should be made within days. Take care of your family, Abraham, above all else."

"I will. Thank you, Sanon."

Sanon nodded his head and watched Abraham ride away. He wished he could shake the darkness that had settled over him.

CHAPTER 36

"Can you take over for a few minutes?" Claude said to Anna-Marie when he saw that Abraham had returned and was waiting for him outside. "Abraham's here, and I'd like to see how he's doing. I've been so busy in the store, I haven't been able to speak with him at any length for a while."

"Of course," Anna-Marie said, walking behind the counter. "Take your time and visit."

Claude walked outside and led Abraham to the side of the building. "What did Sanon say?"

"As usual, it was a bit hard to decipher. He seems worried, but he has not decided what to do yet," Abraham said.

"What were his exact words?"

"He said he had a dream last year that seems connected to this. He saw explosions, big bursts of fire like bombs in a war, and ships wrecking."

"What does that have to do with whether it's going to flood?" Claude asked.

"I don't know, but he seemed very unsettled. He's thinking about packing up the Mulatto camp. He said he would send word of his decision in a few days."

"Do we wait to hear from him?"

"I don't think so. I think we should start putting our things up higher and get the store in order," Abraham said. "I'll get the boat ready in case we decide to ride it out. I'm not sure where we can go if we decide to leave."

"We could go to my aunt's home in Mississippi. My father is there, and she doesn't live anywhere near the river."

"Would they welcome me and my family?" Abraham asked.

"I believe they would. Remember that time you took your boat to the Mulatto camp to get healing herbs when my father was in such pain? He's never forgotten that. Of course, you and your family would be welcomed."

251

"Let's prepare but wait to hear from Sanon. I am worried, though. Captain Richard said they have thousands of men shoring up the levees around New Orleans, and that he heard they've ordered six million sandbags. Obviously, the city officials are worried. Sanon looked worried, too. He said change is coming, and that this could be as bad as or worse than 1922."

Claude put his hands in his pockets and stared across the street at the levee. "After you left, a customer told me that levees are breaking upriver."

"I heard that, too," Abraham said. "Do you think our levees will hold? The river is already swollen."

"I don't think I want to stick around and find out. Remember how afraid our wives were during the last flood? I don't want to put them through that again. Or our children. What do you think? Should we leave?"

"I think Anna-Marie and Hester have been through enough. I will never ask Hester to go through another flood or hurricane in a boat. I say we start preparing to leave," Abraham said.

"Agreed. We can tell our families tonight."

Claude walked back to the store with a heavy heart while Abraham went to find Hester.

Later that evening, while the children were doing their chores, Claude invited Anna-Marie to sit with him on the porch.

"It's a beautiful evening," Anna-Marie commented.

"Yes, it is," Claude said, wondering how he was going to break this news to his wife.

Anna-Marie could see that Claude seemed preoccupied, so she sat quietly, waiting for him to share his thoughts.

"I have news," Claude said, taking her hand. "It's not good news."

"What is it? Tell me." Anna-Marie leaned toward him, listening intently.

"We have to leave for a while," Claude said, his tone deflated. "A flood is coming, and I don't think we should stay here."

Anna-Marie studied Claude's face. She saw something she had not seen before—resignation. "It's going to be bad?"

"I think so. Abraham said Captain Richard said it's real bad upriver. If it's bad farther north, it will be worse here. Abraham also talked to Sanon.

He didn't understand much of what he said, but Sanon is considering packing up the whole Mulatto camp and moving north. He wouldn't do that if he weren't concerned."

"Will there be a blood moon?"

"He didn't mention it," Claude said.

"Well, if the captain and Sanon are both worried, that's good enough for me," Anna-Marie said. "Are we going to Abraham's boat?"

"Not this time. The captain said more than a hundred people died in Arkansas. We don't want to take that chance with you and the kids. Or Hester, after everything she's been through. I was thinking we should go visit my father. It would be safe there."

"Can they come?" Anna-Marie asked.

"Of course, they can. My father has a cabin for guests. They can stay there."

"That's good. What do we need to do to prepare?"

"We'll have to put everything we can salvage into the attic of the store. We can give away the perishables. Better to give them than to waste them. We can caution everyone who comes in the store to leave. Then we'll pack up our house, Abraham's house, and his father's house. Before we go, we'll help whoever needs help. We've got a few days, I think, so we'll need to start first thing in the morning. We need to warn Miss Penny and the Pelitires and anyone who comes into the store, as well."

Anna-Marie bowed her head and stared at the ground for a while. Finally, she looked at Claude with tears in her eyes. "When will it stop? We just got the store opened."

"I know, *ma chérie*," Claude said. "I know."

At the house next door, Abraham was having a similar conversation with Hester.

"If Sanon is worried, then I am worried," Hester said after Abraham broke the news. "What do you think is best?"

"I think we should leave. Captain Richard said the river is higher than he's ever seen it farther north, and he's been on the river for thirty years. Claude said we could go with them to visit his father."

"Will we be welcomed? Don't they live in Mississippi?"

Abraham smiled. "Yes, we will be welcomed. Claude has assured me of that."

"Does Anna-Marie know? She's going to be so upset. They just opened the store. If it floods, what will they do?"

"We're going to try to save what we can. I think Claude is more concerned about his family than anything he owns. He wants to go."

"Then we should go. I certainly don't want to ride out another flood in the boat."

"I understand why you feel that way. I don't want you to have to do that ever again," Abraham said. "It's settled then. Tomorrow, we will start to prepare. Now I must speak with my daddy. I'll be back soon." He leaned over and kissed Hester. "Try not to fret. We will get through this together."

When he was gone, Hester walked to the oak tree where she had placed the stone Sanon had made for her. She picked it up and carried it into the house. She didn't know what was going to happen, but she knew she could not leave it behind.

The next morning, April 19th, Jefferson Davenport sat at a table in a conference room at City Hall in New Orleans waiting for everyone else to arrive. He had invited local politicians, a few bankers, some business owners, and other influential people, anyone who he thought could help his cause, anyone who had the governor's ear. He knew he would need all the help he could get. Noticeably absent were any representatives from St. Bernard Parish or Plaquemines Parish.

Jefferson greeted each guest as they arrived and invited them to have a seat. When everyone was seated, he began, "As you know, I am here to represent the Board of Commissioners of the Orleans Levee District. Gentlemen, let me be frank. We have a looming disaster on our hands, one that could possibly be the greatest challenge we have ever faced. The Mississippi River is higher than we've ever seen it. Levees are breaking all along the river, in Arkansas, in Mississippi, and the death toll is mounting. We all bore witness to what happened here just days ago when the pumps failed after fourteen inches of rain. New Orleans cannot withstand a major flood, and there is a whole lot of water heading straight for us. I am sure we are all in agreement that we cannot let that happen. Already, pressure is building on the levees. The river is rising rapidly. That rainstorm this week did not help matters. Our people are out there buying boats. They are afraid. I have spoken with Governor Simpson about a plan that could save the city, but he is unwilling to go along. I need your help to convince him."

"Aren't we already doing everything we can?" Joseph Martine, a local banker, said. "I know that levees are being shored up and sandbags are everywhere."

"Unfortunately, contrary to our best efforts, levees can breach. If even one of our levees breaches, we could be in a world of trouble," Jefferson said.

"But what can we do?" Joseph asked.

"I have had my engineers go over my plan, and it could work, but there are drawbacks," Jefferson said.

"What is this plan, and what are the drawbacks?" Sam Impastato, a prominent businessman in New Orleans, asked impatiently.

"My plan is to blow up the levee at Caenarvon," Jefferson said. "If we do that, we will flood St. Bernard and Plaquemines Parishes, but New Orleans will not flood."

"You can't be serious," Sam said.

"I'm very serious. What is the alternative? New Orleans going underwater? All of your businesses destroyed, your banks? Everyone in the city left homeless? You've seen what this flood has done further north."

"I thought that spillway you built down there in Plaquemines Parish was supposed to protect us from this very thing," Joseph said.

"Nothing can protect us from this. We have no choice but to divert the water before it reaches us," Jefferson said. "I have contingencies in place for the people of our neighboring parishes. We can offer them compensation for their losses. We can send trucks down there to get them to safety before we blow the levee. Gentlemen, this really is the only way, and I need your help to convince the governor. I'm asking you to help me save our city."

The meeting lasted for several hours. No one in attendance liked this plan, but everyone knew what would happen to New Orleans if the Mississippi River overtopped or breached its levees. In the end, everyone concurred. It was the only way.

The next morning, the pressure on the governor began.

Governor Oramel Simpson had a difficult decision to make. He had consulted a meteorologist and an engineer and asked them if New Orleans would flood. They said no, that the levees would break further upriver in Louisiana and New Orleans would be spared. The Mississippi River Commission determined that the break would happen in Mississippi, but they warned that if it didn't, New Orleans could be in big trouble. Several of New Orleans' wealthier citizens and business owners tried to persuade the governor to blow up the levee at Caenarvon to guarantee the safety of New Orleans. Finally, he agreed, but only after a fund, guaranteed by Joseph Martine and other bankers, had been created with $150,000 that would be used to compensate victims of the flood in neighboring parishes. The plan ensured that each person who suffered losses would receive twenty dollars.

CHAPTER 37

On April 21, Claude and Abraham had almost finished putting cans into boxes when Peter Pelitire ran into the store. "Claude, you've got to get your family out of here! Soon!" he said, gasping for air.

"Did you run all the way here?" Claude asked, fetching him a cup of water.

"No. I came by boat, but I ran up the levee," Peter said, still trying to catch his breath.

"That explains it," Claude said. "We know we have to leave. We're packing up now."

"You've got to leave as soon as you can. They're going to blow up a levee in St. Bernard Parish."

"Who's going to blow up the levee? How do you know this?" Abraham asked.

"Engineers from New Orleans would be my guess. Yesterday, I went there to help my uncle prepare for the flood, and everyone's talking about it. There are armed men guarding the levees, hundreds of them. I saw them with my own eyes."

"They wouldn't deliberately blow up any levees, I don't think," Claude said. "Even they wouldn't do that."

"Wouldn't they?" Abraham asked. "They force people from their land to build a spillway they think will protect the city. Why wouldn't they blow up a levee or two to protect it? Most people down here believe they did it in the 1922 flood."

Claude thought about that for a moment. "Okay, maybe they would. But where did this information come from?"

"I heard a bunch of the bigwigs in New Orleans had a meeting and decided that's how they would save the city from the flood. Then there was a meeting in lower St. Bernard Parish. Hundreds of people showed up. They were saying that the Corps of Engineers had no right to do this and that they would die fighting them if they showed up to blow the levees. Then some judge read a statement from the National Guard, which basically said that if they found it necessary to breach the levee at Poydras, the whole state militia would be there. And United States soldiers. In other words, if anyone tried to stop them, the militia would take action."

"This is unbelievable," Claude said. "They are going to make sure the river washes us away."

"The people down here have always been expendable," Abraham said. "I'm not a bit surprised."

"When is this supposed to happen?" Claude asked.

"I'm not sure," Peter said, "and I'm not going to wait around to find out."

"I sure appreciate you bringing this news," Abraham said. "We'll spread the word. We've got to get everyone out."

"They said they were going to send trucks to get people out, but I'll believe that when I see it," Peter said.

"We'd better get busy," Claude said to Abraham.

"We've already put everything up high that we could at our house and at my daddy's. Hester is helping Anna-Marie now, so we should probably finish here, and then go help the girls. When we're done, I have to go let Sanon know what is happening. And we should check on Miss Penny," Abraham said.

"Miss Penny is leaving tomorrow," Peter said. "I stopped by her place on my way here. She's going to her sister's house in Texas."

"Good. She's one less person we have to worry about then," Claude said.

"I must be on my way," Peter said. "There's a few more people I need to warn. I wish you both well."

Claude and Abraham wished him well and then went to find Anna-Marie and Hester to tell them the news.

"They wouldn't dare do that!" Anna-Marie said, after Claude explained the situation.

"I believe they would," Hester said. "Look what they just did to us, and no one knows for sure if they blew up the levees during the last flood."

"That is true," Anna-Marie said. "But still, it's not right."

"No, it's not," Claude said, "but since we don't know when this is going to happen, we'd better finish moving everything as quickly as possible."

"The river isn't supposed to crest for another week," Abraham said, "but who knows when they'll blow the levees? We'd better get back to work. I think we should go ahead and try to leave tomorrow. I'm going to go find Sanon now. I want to make sure he gets out okay."

"How are we going to fit everyone and all of our things in the trucks?" Anna-Marie asked.

"We'll manage. It will be a miserable ride, but we'll figure it out," Claude said. "The important thing is to get as much done as possible before we go. Pack only two changes of clothes for the children, and the barest of necessities. We'll have to make do with that while we're gone. Pack the same for all of us."

"Claude Couvillion, you know I can't survive with just two dresses," Anna-Marie said, frowning.

"I'm sorry, but that's all we have room for," Claude responded, but when he saw Anna-Marie's face, he added, "You've been itching to go shopping. I'll buy you some new dresses when we get there."

Anna-Marie perked up and kissed Claude on the cheek. "Sometimes I really love you," she said.

Claude laughed. "Especially when you get to go shopping."

By the time evening fell, everything had been moved as high up as possible, and the packing had been completed. Abraham had returned from the Mulatto camp, satisfied that Sanon and his camp were heading for safer ground. "Prepare yourself and your family," Sanon had warned Abraham. "I see water flowing fast. More water than I've ever seen that will destroy everything in its path."

Abraham didn't mention that when he got back to Homeplace. He couldn't.

A few minutes later, he and Claude were loading the trucks when Captain Richard walked up.

"This is probably my last trip on the river for a while," the captain said after greeting them. "It's getting higher, and the current is running strong. I see you folks are leaving. I'm glad. Some folks are talking about staying."

"We're leaving first thing in the morning. I'm sure you've heard they're going to blow the levee in St. Bernard," Claude said.

"Everyone has by now, I'm sure. I can't figure why anyone would want to stay," the captain said.

"They're supposed to send trucks for them, but the Good Lord only knows if they will," Abraham said.

"Where are you going?" Claude asked.

"The wife and I are going to stay in New Orleans. We figure after they blow the levee, it'll be the safest spot around."

"How is Miss Alice?" Claude asked.

"Oh, she's fine. Thinks she's going on vacation. She loves to go anywhere. Sometimes she rides upriver with me for days or weeks at a time. She loves my job more than I do. We packed up last night and are heading out in the morning, too. I'm worried about what we'll find when we get back."

"We are too," Abraham said. "There probably won't be anything left."

"So much for the new houses everyone just built," the captain said.

"I know," Claude said. "It's downright disheartening, but maybe we'll get lucky."

"Son, I've been on the river most of my life, and I've never seen it like this," Captain Richard said. "Captain Henry and I have been talking about it all week. He's already gone. Tied up his boat in Grand Bayou and headed to Texas. I don't think we're going to get lucky, especially if they blow that levee. If I were you, I'd take anything you treasure with you."

"We don't have enough room. We've got two trucks and five adults and five children. We're trying to figure out how we're going to do this as it is."

"Bring whatever you can't fit down to the boat. It'll be safe there," the captain offered.

Claude shook his hand. "Much obliged. Come up to the house, and we'll see what the girls want to take."

An hour later, Claude and Abraham carried four boxes—two filled with Anna-Marie's treasures and important papers and two filled with Hester's—to the captain's boat for safekeeping.

"We really appreciate this," Abraham said. "You've made the girls very happy tonight."

Captain Richard tipped his hat. "I do what I can. Good evening and good luck to you all."

The next morning, April 22nd, Claude, Anna-Marie, and Madeleine got into the front seat of their truck while the other children rode in the bed. Abraham and Hester got into their truck and Emmanuel and Isaac climbed into the back.

Before they left, Claude sat there for a moment, staring at his home, his store, everything he owned, knowing that when they came back nothing would be the same. Then he silently drove away.

Abraham, too, stared at his home for a moment. As he started the engine, he suddenly felt tired, more exhausted than he had ever felt before. For the first time, he thought that maybe he should take his family and move up north, where so many other black families had moved. It was colder, yes, but he had heard that things were different there. Politicians didn't force you to move off your land. Blacks were treated with dignity. No one deliberately flooded your home because you didn't matter as much as other people did. There, Abraham thought, we might matter. He thought about it all the way to Mississippi. He decided he would wait to see what happened, and then he would speak to Hester about it.

It took almost five hours to get to Biloxi on sometimes muddy, sometimes gravel roads, with numerous stops along the way when nature called to the children.

Collette hurried outside when she saw them pull up.

"It's so good to see you," she said, hugging Claude and then Anna-Marie. "Oh, my goodness, look how these children have grown. Why, Claude Jr., you're almost as tall as I am. Well, don't just stand around. Let's go inside. I've got your rooms ready, and the cabin back there is ready for your family, Abraham. We are pleased that you came to visit, even under such awful circumstances. Is what we heard true? Are they really going to flood y'all on purpose? That's just terrible. It's awful. It's the worst thing I've ever heard. May the Good Lord have mercy on their souls, but as I live and breathe, I just can't believe it. Come in. Your father's in the parlor waiting."

"Hi, Aunt Collette," Claude laughed while he pulled their bags from the back of the truck. "I see you haven't changed a bit since the move."

"Now, why would I? And whatever do you mean?"

"I mean that it's good to see you. It's been what, about a year? That's too long. We'll have to come visit more often," Claude said. "We've just been so busy trying to get everyone settled."

"That would be lovely. I've missed watching the children grow. I can't imagine how hard it's been for everyone who had to rebuild. I'll never get over what they did to us. Come here, Madeleine, you poor dear. Let me look at you." Collette held out her arms, and Madeleine ran to her. "Come along," she said to the other children. "Come see your grandpére. Abraham, you can put your things in the cabin. Bring your family to see it. The key is under the flowerpot by the door."

"Yes ma'am," Abraham said. "We're much obliged to you for lending us your cabin."

"Of course. It's the Christian thing to do. Now run along so Claude can visit with his papa."

Claude was shocked when he saw Charles. In only a year, his hair had turned white, and his hands trembled noticeably. His eyes seemed sunken into his head.

"Papa, are you well?" Claude asked, concerned.

"Of course, I am. What has Collette told you? That woman could never keep her lip buttoned," Charles said, his voice sounding weak and tired.

"She didn't say anything, but I think maybe she should have long before now," Claude said.

"He's fine," Collette said. "He just has a little trouble walking, and there's much he can't remember."

"Oh, stop all the fussing, and let me see my grandchildren. Come here and let me look at you," Charles said. The children gathered around him. He pulled some change out of his pocket and handed each child a quarter. Tears sprang to Claude's eyes as he listened to his father ask each child their name. He looked at Collette, and she put a finger to her lips, warning Claude not to say anything.

"We'll talk later," she whispered.

That evening after dinner had been served and everyone had eaten, Claude asked Collette to meet him on the porch.

"Why didn't you write to tell me that my father's thoughts are muddled?" he demanded.

"He told me not to," Collette said, "and don't you take that tone with me, young man. I'll send you to find a switch like I used to. Don't think I won't."

"How long has he been like this?" Claude asked, ignoring her threats.

"It started after we moved, little things he couldn't remember. It's gotten worse over the last few months. He has good days and bad. Today's a bad today. Tomorrow, he might remember all of the children. It's always worse as evening draws near."

"When we leave, I'm taking him home with me," Claude said. "We'll take care of him."

"Taking him home to what?" Collette asked. "There might be nothing left. No, you leave him here with me. I've been taking care of him all your life, and he's comfortable here. You're not taking him anywhere."

Claude tried to reason with her, but Collette was having none of it. Finally, he gave in. He had never won an argument with Collette in his life, but he wasn't happy.

"You will keep me updated about his condition?" Claude asked. "You will write?"

"Yes, I will most certainly do that. Now, let's get back inside before he starts thinking we're out here gossiping about him. He's very grouchy these days."

For the next few days, Claude and Anna-Marie and Abraham and Hester settled in and began to explore their surroundings. They took the children to see the Gulf of Mexico, and they were amazed by how big it was. They played on the sandy beach while the grown-ups talked, mostly about what might be happening down the river. In the evenings, Claude sat with Charles, telling him stories about the homes they had built and what the East Bank looked like now.

"Of course, everything could be different by the time we get home," Claude said.

"Things are often different," Charles said. "Tell your mother to fetch me some tea, would you?"

"What did you say?" Claude asked, not certain he had heard his father correctly.

"Oh, never mind." Charles reached for his cane.

Before he could get up, Claude asked, "Why don't you come back with me? You could watch your grandchildren grow up."

Charles closed his eyes for a moment and thought about it. Then he shook his head. "I can't do that, son. I couldn't leave Collette. She needs me to take care of her. There's no telling what kind of foolishness she'd get into if I wasn't here."

"Of course, she does," Claude said. "It's okay, Papa. You stay right here."

Later, after Claude and Anna-Marie retired for the evening, Claude told her about his conversation with his father. "He doesn't seem to know front from back anymore. I don't know what to do."

"You let him do as he wants," Anna-Marie said. "He's used to living with Collette. He feels comfortable with her. A move down the river might not be the best thing for him, especially when we don't even know what we're going to face when we get back."

"That's true," Claude said. "I wonder how bad it's going to be."

"Pretty bad, I'd guess, if those folks in New Orleans have anything to say about it."

They lay together staring at the ceiling, each lost in their own thoughts, worrying about what they were going to find when they got back home.

The next morning, Claude and Abraham were outside pruning branches of the trees in the yard when Anna-Marie hurried toward them.

"I got a telegram from Papa. He said a tanker rammed into the levee near Junior Plantation. A big tanker, carrying molasses. Just rammed into the levee, causing a breach," she said, her words coming out in a rush. "At least a hundred feet wide. Water is pouring through."

"Oh, Good Lord," Claude said. "That's only about twelve miles from Homeplace."

"It happened two days ago. Papa said he thinks those bankers in New Orleans paid the captain to do it."

"I'd believe that," Abraham said. "They'd do anything to save themselves."

"I'm just relieved we got out when we did. Try not to fret, Anna-Marie. We already know what's going to happen. Whether it's a tanker or a blown levee, we're going to flood either way."

"It's already started," Anna-Marie said, "hasn't it?"

"Yes, *ma chérie*. I would imagine that it has," Claude said.

Later, they would learn that the 5,000-ton tanker had been tossed about in the raging waters of the river until it slammed into the levee. Although the captain and his men tried to hold the bow in place to keep the water from flowing through, the stern had whipped around and widened the gap. Fortunately, mostly marshland got inundated, although many truck farms were destroyed. The Junior Crevasse, as it would come to be known, turned the land around it into a small bay.

Almost no one in Plaquemines Parish believed that story. According to a witness, the ship that rammed the levee at Junior Plantation, hit it three times in the same spot until it broke. Residents were thoroughly convinced that the breach had been created on purpose.

CHAPTER 38

Leonus was furious. He could not believe that the governor would sign off on a plan to blow up the levee in St. Bernard. He knew exactly what that would do to his parish right below it. Everything would be wiped away. Together with Judge August Robicheaux from St. Bernard Parish, he pleaded with the governor not to enact such a plan. "It's foolhardy," he said. "Half the engineers are saying that New Orleans will not go under. How can you deliberately flood my parish?"

"New Orleans is the most important city in this state," the governor countered. "It must be protected at all costs. I don't like this any more than you do, but I'm getting pressure from all around. It must be done. There isn't another choice."

Realizing he would get nowhere with the governor, Leonus tried to persuade the bankers, also to no avail. He was able, at least, to get them to pledge two million dollars in relief money for those who may be displaced, but that did little to soothe his anger.

"This could turn into an all-out war," Judge Robicheaux warned Leonus.

"I know. They're bringing in the National Guard."

"The people in my parish aren't going to stand for this. They are already guarding the levees armed to the teeth," Judge Robicheaux said.

"Somebody better tell them to go home," Leonus advised. "That's a fight they won't win."

"I'll send somebody they like to talk to them. They won't listen to me. I've put too many of them in jail."

"Me either. Not after the Trapper Wars."

"That was a fight you couldn't win," Judge Robicheaux said, referring to Leonus trying to remove some muskrat trappers from land on which they were homesteading. A deputy had been killed in that fight.

"I say we get our people out. That's all we can do at this point. Those bankers are powerful. They're trying to dissuade the newspapers from publishing any flood bulletins from what I hear," Leonus said.

"I'll take care of my parish. You go take care of yours," Judge Robicheaux said. "We'll talk again once this is over and the damage is assessed."

The next evening, on the 26th, roughly twenty men traveled from St. Bernard Parish to New Orleans. They went to the homes of several of the most prominent bankers in the city to threaten them, armed with shotguns they were prepared to use. The bankers promised that they would be compensated for any losses they experienced if the levee was blown up. Somewhat appeased but still angry, the men returned to their parish without causing any bloodshed.

The next day, there was no doubt left that the levee would be blown. President Calvin Coolidge charged Herbert Hoover, chairman of the relief effort, with examining the Poydras Levee in St. Bernard Parish. The fact that the president of the United States sent someone to look at the Poydras Levee could mean nothing else. Hoover arrived on the 28th on a boat and was walking toward the levee when a man sitting atop the levee opened fire. The bullets came much too close for comfort. Again, dire warnings were issued, and finally those guarding the levees went home to pack what they could carry on their backs or pull in their wagons.

The people in Plaquemines Parish left, as well, leaving most of their possessions behind. They headed north to New Orleans because they knew that there they would be safe. A caravan formed somewhere along the way with people of multiple nationalities, who could not speak each other's languages, hurrying away from their homes in a mass exodus.

All of these people from both affected parishes were scared, defeated, sad, but above all else, they were angry. No one understood why this had to happen.

The National Guard sent soldiers to evacuate the parishes with orders to get the people out, whether they wanted to leave or not. They drove them in large trucks to a warehouse in New Orleans, where Caucasians and Blacks were placed on different floors to wait out the coming flood. The East Bank of Plaquemines Parish down to Pointe á la Hache was now empty, desolate, ghostly.

Official passes were issued for reporters from all over the country, politicians, and a few elite persons who wanted to witness the fireworks, but no passes were issued for local reporters.

On April 29, 1927, at 2:17 in the afternoon, the Corps of Engineers set off the first explosion on the levee at Caenarvon, thirteen miles below New Orleans at the St. Bernard Parish line, and the spot that Hoover had chosen. Spectators watched as the earthen levee expanded and contracted, and a small trench formed, about six feet wide. Another explosion was set off and then another. Still, the levee held, the blue river clay that had formed it proved stronger than they thought. It took ten days and thirty-nine tons of dynamite to force the Mississippi through the 3,213-foot crevasse they had created, but finally the river rushed through at approximately 250,000 cubic feet per second.

In cities and towns all across the South, people who had escaped listened to their radios, their faces mirroring their disbelief. They all knew they had just lost everything.

Anna-Marie and Hester cried. Claude and Abraham walked around outside, looking for something to do, anything that would stop their minds from wandering to Homeplace. Neither man could bear to see the looks of despair on the faces of their wives. The waiting and not knowing what had happened to their homes was excruciating for all of them.

A week later, they received a letter from Antoine. Anna-Marie hurried outside to read it to Hester and the men. When they were gathered around her on the porch, she read it silently. They all watched as her face turned red. Then, with tears in her eyes, she told them what her papa had said.

"They didn't have to do it," she said. "They didn't have to make us flood. Papa says that the day after the first explosion, before the levee broke, the Glasscock Levee farther north broke. He said that eased the pressure on the levees at New Orleans."

Claude couldn't believe it. "You mean to tell me they did this for nothing?"

"Wait. There's more. Then the levees along the Ouachita and Black Rivers broke, and all that water that they said was coming downriver to New Orleans went out to the Gulf through the Atchafalaya Basin just like the water from the Glasscock Levee. New Orleans would not have flooded, and we wouldn't have flooded either."

Anna-Marie had never heard Claude curse, but she heard him curse that day, right before he stormed off. She had never seen him so mad.

Abraham stood there silently, staring off at the horizon, and then he began to pace up and down in front of the house and then to the back until he suddenly dropped to his knees, his fists clenched, and screamed like a wounded animal.

"One more day," Anna-Marie cried to Hester. "If only they had waited just one more day."

Hester hurried to comfort Abraham, but he walked away. "I'm sorry, Hester, but I need to be alone," he said, his voice ragged and broken.

"They need time," Anna-Marie said when Hester came back. "We all need time."

Anna-Marie didn't know it then, but they had plenty of time to digest this news. The waters of the Mississippi raged through the land for another month, and it would be August before the land absorbed all of the water. Little by little, they learned about the devastation.

By the time the waters receded, approximately 27,000 square miles running through seven states had gone underwater. Ten thousand of those square miles were in Louisiana. Damages were estimated to be $400 million.

Throughout the South, 154 refugee camps had been established. Most of these were filled with African Americans, who did not own land, tenant farmers who had nowhere to go. Conditions in the camps were dismal, simply because the American Red Cross was overwhelmed by the massive numbers of people who needed its help.

Two hundred forty-six people perished in the flood, according to the Red Cross, but the National Weather Service reported 313. No one really knew. Some estimates put the death toll at more than 1,000.

In Plaquemines Parish, hunters returned on boats to rescue the muskrats upon which they depended for survival. Their reports were dismal. The East Bank had been decimated, and the West Bank fared only a little better. One hunter reported that he had a difficult time finding landmarks, whereas before he knew every nook and cranny, because the marsh had become the river.

By June, many residents still could not return home. Roads were washed away, marshes were overflowing, and the Mississippi had not yet settled back into its normal boundaries.

At the height of the flood, the Bohemia Spillway diverted 310,000 cubic feet per second. Although officials claimed that the spillway had lowered the river by more than two feet at New Orleans, everyone knew that the breaks in the levees upriver accounted for the lowered river stage, not the Bohemia Spillway.

Herbert Hoover, who oversaw the relief effort, became a hero and set the stage for his presidential bid the following year.

The 1927 flood had affected a large portion of the country and fostered the realization that something needed to be done to contain the Mississippi River. In May of the following year, Congress passed the Flood Control Act of 1928, which gave the U.S. Army Corps of Engineers the authorization to design and build flood control projects for that specific purpose, as well as the Mississippi's tributaries. Immediately, the Corps, realizing that the Bohemia Spillway could not protect New Orleans, began surveying the area around the city to find the best place to build a spillway that would allow the Mississippi River to empty into Lake Pontchartrain when flooding was imminent.

Jefferson Davenport spent the next few months defending his decision to blow up the levee.

Governor Simpson lost his re-election campaign, some thought due to his decision to deliberately flood part of his state, and Huey Long became governor.

By the time many residents could return home, they had decided against it, either because there was nothing left to return to except devastation or because they decided to head north to escape living conditions in the South. Thousands of people migrated from Louisiana after the flood, unable or unwilling to continue fighting the harshness of the elements and the politics.

Anna-Marie and Claude decided to go home and rebuild, no matter what they might find when they got there.

Abraham and Hester decided to go with them, although Abraham still had doubts about the wisdom of returning.

Sanon, too, decided to return to the river, but most of the people who had lived in the Mulatto camp did not return.

CHAPTER 39

In-mid July, Claude said his good-byes to his father. He had fought a good fight to get him to move with them back to Plaquemines Parish, but Charles was equally adamant that he was happy where he was. Claude thanked Collette for her hospitality and for allowing Abraham and his family to stay in the cabin.

"Happy to have y'all. Come back anytime," Collette said. "I'll keep you apprised of your father's condition. I promise."

"I will hold you to that." Claude kissed her good-bye, and then packed everyone into the trucks and headed for New Orleans, where they planned to board Captain Henry's packet boat for the journey home.

Everyone was nervous about what they would find, but Captain Henry assured them that their homes were still standing. "It's a right fine mess down there, especially on the East Bank all the way down to Pointe á la Hache. The West Bank isn't as bad, but Happy Jack and everything north of it flooded something fierce. Everything from Potash down didn't flood. Homeplace is fine. I checked last week when I was down there. *The Pearl* looks a little worse for wear," he told Abraham. "You should have docked it farther south. You'll have to spend some time repairing her. Looks like she was tossed about a bit."

"She was tossed about more than a bit, I'd bet," Abraham said. "I'll have her fixed up in no time. My daddy built her. She's strong as an ox."

"Seems to be," Captain Henry said. "Be prepared, though. Nothing looks much the same until you get to Homeplace."

"How bad is it?" Claude asked.

"Like I said. It's a right fine mess."

Although the captain's words helped soothe their worries, as they got farther down the river their hearts began to sink.

Uprooted trees lined the levees and riverbank. Those that stood were gray, lifeless, stripped bare from the force of the water. At each new village or town, they spotted boats, some flipped over, some smashed to bits, others merely bruised. Some floated aimlessly through the marshland. Some had come to rest atop levees. A strange stench permeated the air. Later, they would recognize it as the smell of mold, which had infiltrated every standing and partially standing structure.

There were no ricebirds, no rice. No cotton fields or corn fields. No fruit decorating the trees.

Everything was quiet, forlorn, and sticky hot.

Every now and then they caught a glimpse of a few people or a boat heading upriver, but the normal hustle and bustle of the river was starkly absent. Plaquemines Parish was a virtual ghost town that spread for miles and miles. As they neared the Bohemia area, they noticed that some of the remaining homes had been pushed from their foundations or spread haphazardly across the landscape. Some houses had been completely ripped apart. Like the boats, they, too, floated aimlessly through the marsh.

"Are you sure our house and store are still there?" Anna-Marie asked Captain Henry.

"I'm sure. Saw them with my own eyes. Abraham's too," Captain Henry said. "Like I said, Homeplace was spared."

Feeling somewhat appeased, Anna walked to the side of the boat and watched as they passed settlements and townships she had known all of her life. Nothing looked the same. Almost everything was destroyed or washed away.

Hester walked over to stand beside her friend. "It looks worse than the last flood. A lot worse," she commented.

Anna-Marie mustered a reassuring smile. "We'll help our friends rebuild. We've done it before. We can do it again."

"Aren't you tired?" Hester asked.

"Yes, I'm tired," Anna-Marie admitted. "And I'm mad as a wet hen. I don't understand how they could do this—and for nothing. It's like we're on our own down here, not governed by the same rules as the rest of the country. Nobody cares if we live or die, if we have or have not. They want our resources, but we will always be expendable. It hurts my heart."

"That's what Abraham always says, that we're expendable," Hester said. "It does hurt. Just looking at Bohemia hurts."

Anna-Marie held onto the railing as Captain Henry swerved to avoid a log. "Poopdeck will be able to pull more logs from the river," Anna-Marie said, as she watched the log until it was out of sight. "We've got to be strong for those who have lost everything. We've got to be strong, or those politicians that did this win."

Hester nodded. "Yes, we will be strong. We have no other choice."

A few moments later, they docked near Homeplace. Each carrying a box or a bag, they set off for home, walking single file like ducks in a row, with Captain Henry leading the way. Finally, they crossed the levee, and got their first glimpse of their homes.

"I can't believe it," Anna-Marie said, heaving a sigh of relief.

"I told you," Captain Henry said.

"I guess we had to see it for ourselves," Claude said, surveying their homes and the store, all still intact, unscathed by the devastation that had occurred farther upriver.

"God has been merciful to us," Hester said, squeezing Abraham's hand.

"Merciful to us, yes," Abraham said. "But what about our friends? They've lost everything again—Sanon and Miss Penny. The Pelitires. What are they going to do?"

"We'll help them," Claude said. "Sanon can stay with you because he'll be more comfortable near Hester, and Miss Penny can stay with us. We can let the Pelitires stay in the room in the store that Anna-Marie uses for teaching. It's the only place big enough for all those children. We'll fix them right up."

"That's a wonderful idea," Anna-Marie said.

"I'll get word to them and bring them back next time I come downriver," Captain Henry said.

Abraham had stood silently while the plans were being made. Sensing that something was wrong, Hester looked up at him. "Are you okay with all of this?" she asked.

"It's just that nothing seems right no more," Abraham said, his eyes filling with tears and his voice cracking. "I'm tired of it. The worst part is there's nothing we can do. We just have to take it any time those politicians feel like stripping us of what we've built. We were fortunate this time, but our friends weren't. It's just not right."

"Hopefully, those politicians learned something this time. Folks are downright mad because everyone knows this didn't have to happen. Hopefully, we'll fix everything, and life will go back to normal," Claude said. "Maybe they'll leave us alone now."

"Maybe," Abraham said. "Or maybe we should move like all those other folks, somewhere where we're treated like human beings that matter."

"Where might that be? Up north? I'm sure those folks have their own problems. Besides, you make your living off the water. You wouldn't be happy away from it. You love it."

"That's true," Abraham agreed. "I don't know any other way."

"Neither do I. None of us do. That's why we'll stay here."

The two men walked the rest of the way in silence, each preparing themselves for the work they knew would keep them busy for months. They both knew they were on a timetable. They had to be finished with everyone's homes by winter, and it was already mid-July.

As promised, a few weeks later, Captain Henry brought Sanon and Miss Penny and the Pelitires to Homeplace. Abraham and Claude had cleaned out the storeroom to make it habitable for the Pelitires. They had brought in two cedar armoires for the family's clothes that Antoine had given them. Anna-Marie and Hester had retrieved a bunch of old blankets from the attic in the store and made eight makeshift beds on the floor. Hester had stuffed cotton into colorful fabrics she found in her cedar chest and stitched nine pillows for the family. Anna-Marie and Hester had hung pictures on the walls while Abraham and Claude had built a small makeshift room for privacy while dressing. When they were finished, they admired their handiwork.

"Not bad," Claude said. "Not bad at all."

Peter Pelitire could barely speak when he saw what his friends had done. Christina, tears streaming down her face, hugged everyone. "We've been so worried," she said. "We didn't know what we were going to do."

"No more need for worrying," Abraham said, gruffly.

"He's right," Claude said. "Y'all can stay here until we get your home fixed."

Abraham, Claude, Sanon, and Peter Pelitire worked side by side for months, each day leading into another in a flurry of activity. They placed ruined furnishings in burn piles and set them on fire. They reset foundations that had been moved by the rushing water and nailed back broken boards. They cleaned out the mold and muck. They replastered walls and painted them. They built bunk beds for the Pelitire children. They rebuilt the porch on Miss Penny's home. At Sanon's insistence, they saved his house for last, but finally they finished that, as well. By October, the men were worn out, but happy.

Anna-Marie and Hester had been just as busy. They worked in the store from morning to night. They called upon their neighbors who had been spared from the flood to donate furniture for those who had been affected. Sofas, tables, chairs, and beds soon filled the barn, waiting to be brought to their new homes.

By late-October, everything was almost completed, and those who had returned to the West Bank were safely ensconced in their homes. But many people simply did not return. Most of the money promised by the bankers did not materialize, and those who did get money received a mere pittance. The application process for aid from the government was difficult for most and impossible for those who could not read or write.

Claude and Anna-Marie once again went into the business of extending credit, but most folks couldn't pay on time if at all, and neither Anna-Marie nor Claude had the heart to push the issue. By the end of that winter, they knew they were in trouble. It had been the worst winter they had ever experienced. Anna-Marie finally broached the subject with Claude.

"We can't go on like this," she said. "We're losing more money than we're making."

"I know," Claude said, "but I'm not sure what we can do. Slowly, people are coming back, and they need us. We're the only store open for miles."

"I have a solution, but you're not going to like it," Anna-Marie said, looking up at him. "I spoke with Papa, and he said he would lend us some money to get through the spring and summer. I agreed that we would take it. I know you don't want to do that, but we don't have a choice. It's either take the money or close the store."

Claude's face turned red, but he didn't say a word. He walked from behind the counter and went outside. When he didn't come back by nightfall, Anna-Marie ran to the house next door to find Abraham.

"Have you seen Claude?" Anna-Marie asked. "He went off earlier, and I haven't seen him since. He's angry with me."

Abraham noticed how overwrought she was and hurried to ease her mind. "He's out in the marsh trapping muskrats would be my guess. Don't worry. You know he does that when he's got something on his mind. He'll be back."

Anna-Marie went home, fed the children and got them settled, and then she went outside and sat on the porch. She waited there for hours until finally she heard Claude's footsteps.

"I'm sorry," she cried when he walked onto the porch. "I just didn't know what else to do."

Claude pulled her up from her chair and hugged her tightly. "It's okay. It's what needs to be done. I just had to go wrestle with my pride for a while. Tomorrow, I'll ask Spit to watch the store, and we'll go visit your Papa. I will ask him for a loan, and we'll keep the store going."

"Thank you! I know how hard this is for you," Anna-Marie said, "but I feel like we have a responsibility to keep the store open."

"I feel that same responsibility," Claude said. "It won't be easy, but it is necessary."

The next morning, Anna-Marie and Claude hopped aboard a packet boat and went to visit Antoine. Understanding what they had been through, Antoine was unusually gracious when Claude, red-faced and head bowed, asked him for the loan.

"Raise your head," Antoine said. "You are the man my daughter chose, for richer or poorer, and what happened down there is not your fault. However, you've got to start thinking like a businessman. No matter how much you feel sorry for folks, you are running a business, and you are in business to make money. Stop extending so much credit, and collect what you are owed. That is my advice to you."

"Thank you, Papa," Anna-Marie said when Antoine handed Claude a bag filled with money.

"Yes sir. Thank you," Claude said. "We will repay this debt."

Antoine brushed that off. "I'm not worried about being repaid. I want my daughter to have a good life."

"I'll do everything I can to make that happen," Claude promised.

"You already have," Anna-Marie said. "And so have you, Papa."

When they returned to Homeplace, Anna-Marie and Claude began restocking the shelves. They tried hard to be more careful than they had been before, but they still couldn't turn anyone down who asked for credit. So many folks needed their help. They found a solution of sorts when they hired Peter Pelitire to work for them. Every month, Peter would go door to door collecting the monthly payments. Peter was a big man, strong, but not at all intimidating. His friendly smile had ladies reaching into their pocketbooks and coming up with at least partial payments, which more than paid his daily wage.

Eventually, the population of the West Bank grew to the point that Anna-Marie and Claude could sustain their business. Abraham fixed *The Pearl* and returned to the bayous to try to find oysters, and Hester, who had become a voracious reader, helped Anna-Marie teach the children. While life on the West Bank would never again be what it had once been, they slowly began to adapt.

But the flood, the spillway, the losses experienced by their friends and customers, lingered in their thoughts.

Always simmering just beneath the surface.

CHAPTER 40

Summer 1928

Huey P. Long was elected governor of Louisiana, thanks in no small part to the efforts of the judge, who campaigned for him in the months prior to the election. He took office on May 21, 1928.

Jefferson was concerned about the growing relationship between the governor and Leonus, and in late July 1928, he telephoned Sal and Pierre and invited them to a meeting at his office.

"Governor Long is gunning for us," he began. "The judge has become his henchman, and you both know how the judge feels about me. The lease agreement with Humble Oil is being negotiated, and we are now positioned to make some real money, but I'm worried, gentlemen. As you know, the day after Long took office, he fired all those folks at the New Orleans Dock Board. Since then, he has been targeting other state-run agencies—the Board of Health, the Conservation Commission, the Hospital Board, the Highway Commission, to name a few. I fear the Board of Commissioners is on his list, at least if the judge is whispering in his ear. You know he doesn't like us. The governor has replaced all those folks with people loyal to him. It's a brilliant strategy actually, but one that does not bode well for us. I want you to keep your ears to the ground and let me know if you hear anything, anything at all that suggests something detrimental to us is afoot."

"Our terms are set in stone by the legislature. What could he possibly do?" Pierre asked.

"I'm not sure, but I don't trust the governor or the judge as far as I can throw them," Jefferson said.

"You've got another two years. I don't see that there's anything he could do about that," Sal said.

"He's a schemer, and he's slick. The rules mean nothing to him. Between him and the judge, I fear they will come up with something to interfere with my plan to become the next president of the board."

"You worry too much," Sal said. "Everyone knows you deserve it, especially now. We should be celebrating, not worrying. We're going to be rich. I say we have a drink."

Jefferson opened his desk drawer and retrieved a bottle of bootlegged Kentucky bourbon. He poured three glasses and then proposed a toast. "To a job well done," he said, raising his glass.

"Exactly how are we going to make money off this lease?" Pierre asked, swirling the liquid in his glass.

"I haven't worked out all the details, but there are a variety of avenues we can take. A little here and a little there will go a long way. Look how much we make off of construction contracts. According to the negotiations so far, Humble would have to start drilling within six months. That gives us plenty of time to figure it out. I'll open a corporation through which to funnel the money. Once they hit oil, and I have no doubt they will, we'll be ready."

"I hope so. We've been working on this for years. We're this close," Sal said, holding up two fingers to demonstrate.

"And keep your eye on Abraham Shushan," Jefferson cautioned. "He and the governor are close allies. I don't put anything past him."

"Shushan's all right," Pierre said. "We've had drinks together a few times over the years. He backed us up on the spillway, if you recall."

"I do recall, but heed my words. He can't be trusted. Watch what you say around him. Don't let him get wind of anything. He's ambitious and greedy. Most importantly, the governor considers him to be a friend. That's dangerous for all of us," Jefferson said.

Jefferson was right to be concerned. Huey Long was indeed gunning for the Board of Commissioners of the Orleans Levee District.

On August 8, 1928, less than two weeks later, the governor convinced the Louisiana Legislature to dissolve the nine-member board of the Orleans Levee District. A five-member board took its place, stacked with the governor's loyal supporters, including Abraham Shushan. The new board, that did not include Jefferson, Sal, or Pierre, voted for Joseph Haspel to be its president.

Jefferson was in his office when his secretary handed him a memo that informed him he was no longer a member of the board and ordered him to vacate the premises. Jefferson called Sal and Pierre, who related that the same thing had just happened to them. Jefferson threw his glass across the room, shattering it to pieces.

Abraham Shushan, who happened to be walking nearby, heard the glass hit the wall. He grinned. He'd have to call the governor to share this tidbit.

Jefferson threw his personal belongings, along with some files and notebooks containing nefarious dealings, into a box and stormed out of his office.

Nobody was in sight, but that didn't matter. As he walked down the hallway, he yelled, "None of you cowards can face me, can you? Come out. Somebody. Anybody. Face me like a man and tell me I've been removed. Come on."

Nobody stirred. Jefferson waited a moment and then walked down the stairs, out the front door, and onto the street. For a moment, he forgot where he had parked, but then he remembered—on the side of the building. He walked to his car, put the box in his trunk, and got behind the wheel. He sat there for a moment, and then he began hitting the steering wheel and shouting obscenities, oblivious to the curious stares he was receiving from passersby.

He had spent years carefully planning his next move—the mineral rights associated with the land around the spillway always dangling in front of him like a carrot. He had accomplished his goals. The lease with Humble would be signed soon, and just when he was within reach of his dream, he was ousted from the board without as much as a warning or a thank you for what he had accomplished.

The next day, Jefferson read about it in *The Times-Picayune*. He tore the newspaper to shreds.

When Leonus heard the news, he chuckled heartily, imagining the look on Jefferson's face when he learned he was no longer a member of the board.

Two months later, on November 8, 1928, the Orleans Levee District signed an agreement to lease roughly 3,500 acres of land in the Bohemia Spillway area to Humble Oil & Refining Company. According to the agreement, the Orleans Levee District would be paid $27,336.83 for a ten-year lease. The levee district received $13,053.75 that day, and it was agreed that $14,283.08 would be placed in escrow at the New Orleans

Bank & Trust Company. The Orleans Levee District granted this land "for the purpose of investigating, exploring, prospecting, drilling and mining for, and producing oil, gas, and all other minerals, laying pipe lines, building tanks, power stations, telephone lines, and other structures thereon to produce, save, take care of, treat, transport, own said products, and housing its employees," according to the lease.

The royalties agreed upon included:

For oil: *One-eighth of that produced and saved from said land, the same to be delivered at the wells or to the credit of Lessor in the pipe line to which the wells may be connected.*

For gas: *Including casinghead gas and other vaporous or gaseous substances, produced from said land, as follows: In case Lessee shall itself use gas in the manufacture of gasoline or other products therefrom one-eighth of twenty-five percent of the market value at the plant of the gasoline or other product manufactured therefrom, quantity of product to be ascertained in a manner recognized in the industry; in case Lessee shall sell gas at the wells, one-eighth of the amount realized from such sales; and in all other cases when sold or used off the premises, the market price at the well of one-eighth of the gas so sold or used.*

For all other minerals mined or marketed: *One-eighth either in kind or value at the well or mine at Lessee's election, except that on sulphur the royalty shall be fifty cents per long ton.*

Humble Oil agreed that if it did not commence drilling within six months the lease could be terminated unless $18,224.55 was deposited in the New Orleans Bank & Trust Company prior to the six-month mark. This would pay for a year-long deferment and could be paid annually for the ten-year lease period.

It was also agreed that, if Humble Oil drilled a "dry hole," the lease would not terminate and the company could continue drilling in other areas as long as there was no cessation in drilling for more than thirty days.

The agreement then extrapolated upon the terms and conditions, with one in particular of note: "It is understood and agreed that this lease is made subject to the prior rights of Lessor to use the lands leased for Spillway purposes, to conduct the overflow waters of the Mississippi River to the sea, and the Lessee agrees to expend its best efforts not to use the leased premises in a manner that will cause any unreasonable interference with trapping or grazing thereon."

The Orleans Levee District had already begun leasing the land to trappers, some of whom had previously lived in the Bohemia Spillway area, essentially leasing their own land back to them for hunting purposes.

Joseph Haspel, president of the Board of Commissioners, and E. Holman of Humble Oil & Refining Company signed the lease.

Jefferson read about the signed lease in the newspaper a few days later. For the first time in his life, he bowed his head and cried. He would spend the next few years waiting to see if Humble Oil & Refining would discover oil in Bohemia. He read *The Times-Picayune* every morning, searching for information about any progress that was made and reading about new projects in store for the Orleans Levee District. He became bitter, hard, vengeful, but there was absolutely nothing he could do.

His best-laid plan had gone awry, and he would never see a dime of the millions that would eventually pour into the levee district's accounts, money that really belonged to the people who had been forced, through his scheming, to sell their land.

Down the river, Leonus Lozano was watching the progress, as well. Earlier that year, he had lobbied the Louisiana Legislature and had succeeded in getting Act 246 passed, which stated that all state-owned lands "beginning at the lower side of the Cuselich Canal at Ostrica and extending to the upper side line of Cupid's Gap" in Plaquemines Parish would be donated and title conveyed to the Grand Prairie Levee District. The fact that he was not a member of the levee district was of little consequence to him. Leonus knew that when all was said and done, he could control the levee district like he had begun to control everything else in his parish. It was just a matter of time. He was the levee district's attorney. Any profits made from this land would be spent as he wished. He had a plan.

He had already taken first steps by opening his own company—River Parishes Real Estate Corporation—and ensuring the passage of Act 246. He planned to lease some of that oil rich land from the Grand Prairie Levee District, positioning himself to be able to, in turn, lease the mineral rights to oil companies. He knew he would have to split some of the profits with the levee district, but he didn't mind.

There would be more than enough money to go around.

CHAPTER 41

"Thank you, Nikolas," Anna-Marie said, when the mail carrier handed her a letter from her father.

Nikolas reached into his sack and pulled out a stack of coupons. "You're welcome. Please give these to Miss Hester."

"Of course. I'll make sure she gets them." Anna-Marie said, opening the letter from her father. She waited until Nikolas left, and then she sat down to read it.

Claude walked up behind her and planted a kiss on the top of her head. "Who is the letter from?"

"Papa," Anna-Marie said. "It's worrisome. He's coming to visit on Sunday at two. He wants us to gather our friends, Abraham and Hester, Sanon, the Pelitires, Miss Penny, Captain Richard, everyone around here who moved from across the river. He says he has news."

"What kind of news?" Claude asked.

"He didn't say. Sunday is Armistice Day, so maybe it has something to do with that." Anna-Marie said, handing Claude the letter. "See for yourself."

Claude sat down next to her and read the letter. "It doesn't say he has bad news, so that's good, right?"

"I don't know. It's so mysterious and not like Papa at all. Usually, when he has news, he just shows up and delivers it. This is different. I wonder why he wants everyone here. I'll be on pins and needles until I know what it is."

"It does seem strange," Claude agreed, laughing. He knew that his wife would fret about this until Sunday arrived. Anna-Marie glared at him until he stopped laughing. "I'm sure if it was bad, he wouldn't have sent a letter. He would already be here."

"I hope you're right." Anna-Marie took the letter from him and read it again. "I'll send Spit to let everyone know, and I'll ask Hester to help me make some hors d'oeuvres. She can bring her special seasonings. We have to feed everyone, of course. They'll be missing Sunday dinner if they're here at two."

"That's a good idea. I hope it won't be too cold. If it's not, maybe Abraham and I will boil up some crabs. He said he was going to check his traps this weekend, and he always gets quite a few even this late in the year."

"Yes, and I'll ask Hester to make thistle salad to go with them. This could be fun. Spit can run the store while we visit with Papa. Oh, I hope it's good news. We could all use some of that."

"Yes, we could," Claude said.

When Sunday came, the weather was perfect—in the high sixties. Anna-Marie decided not to go to church with Claude so that she and Hester could prepare for their guests to arrive. They set up tables in front of the store and covered them with old newspapers. Hester made thistle salad while Anna-Marie arranged trays of fruit, preserves, and baked cookies.

"We haven't had time to do something like this in so long," Anna-Marie said. "I can't wait until everyone gets here. We'll have a lot of food. I cooked a big pot of teal and even put some gizzards in. I know how much the men love those gizzards. I dropped some turnips in, too, and cooked up a pot of rice."

"We'll have plenty enough for everyone, and we'll have the crabs, too. It has been a while," Hester said, sprinkling a little bit of this and a little bit of that on her salad. "Not since we lived across the river."

Anna-Marie thought about that for a moment. "You're right. It's been more than two years. So much has happened during that time."

"Yes, too much. But we survived, and now things are getting a little better every day," Hester said. "The orange grove is planted, along with pear and peach trees. Everyone is settled again. We have much to be thankful for."

"We sure do," Anna-Marie said. "Now if we can just get our husbands to boiling, everything will be perfect."

Claude and Abraham had put a huge pot of water on to boil and then left to pick up Miss Penny.

"They'll be back soon," Hester said. "Look, here come the Pelitires."

Anna-Marie turned to see Peter, carrying a large basket, followed by Christina, Rocco, Victor, Annabelle, CeCe, Daisy, June, and little Petie.

"My, those children get bigger every time I see them," Anna-Marie said, motioning for Peter to put the basket on a table. "What do we have here?"

"I fried up some trout Peter caught yesterday," Christina said, hugging Anna-Marie. "What's a Sunday without fried fish?"

"It wouldn't be Sunday at all," Anna-Marie said. "Claude and Abraham will be back in a few minutes. They went to get Miss Penny, and then they're boiling the crabs."

"I'd better go season the water before they get back," Hester said. "I'll add potatoes, onions, garlic, and carrots, too. Abraham always lurks around when I'm doing it, trying to find out what herbs I use, but that's my secret."

"I'm not sure anyone wants to know what you put in the pot, but whatever it is, it's mighty tasty," Peter said. "Victor, stop digging in that garden. Rocco, go get your brother."

"Do you know what your Papa wants to tell us?" Christina asked Anna-Marie.

"I don't have a clue. It's all so mysterious. Oh, here comes Sanon," Anna-Marie said, watching Sanon ride up on his horse. "And there's Captain Richard walking down the levee. Claude had better get back soon. I'm sure everyone is hungry."

Anna-Marie greeted Sanon and Captain Richard and invited them to have a seat. "If you're hungry now, there's a big pot of teal and some rice on the stove," she said.

"Do you know why your Papa wants to meet with us?" Captain Richard asked.

"No, I don't. I wish I did."

Sanon sat quietly, observing a dark gray cloud that was slowly moving across the sky toward them. Captain Richard followed his gaze. "I hope that's not rain coming," he said.

"It's not," Sanon said. "At least not the kind that's wet."

Hester walked up just in time to overhear their conversation. She turned to look at the cloud, and then she looked at Sanon. He put his finger to his lips, motioning for her to be silent. After Captain Richard walked away, he whispered. "Best to let everyone enjoy as much of this day as possible."

Finally, Abraham and Claude arrived with Miss Penny,

A few minutes later, Antoine arrived. Anna-Marie rushed over to greet him.

"How are you, Papa? Are you well? It's been months since I've seen you," she said, standing on her tiptoes to kiss him on the cheek.

"It's been too long. I am well," Antoine said. "I'm happy to see that you are looking well. And I see everyone is here."

"What do you want to tell us, Papa? It's been driving me mad."

"All in good time, my dear. We can get to that after everyone eats. I see you have quite a spread."

"It's Sunday. I couldn't let everyone miss Sunday dinner. Come over and say hi. Everyone has been waiting for you to get here."

Antoine followed her to the back where everyone was gathered around the boiling pot. "Good day," he said, shaking hands with the men and tipping his hat to the ladies.

"What is this news?" Captain Richard asked.

"Let's eat first, and then we'll get to that," Antoine said.

"Food's ready," Claude announced after he had let the crabs soak for a while. He and Abraham poured them across the tables in the front. The children sat at two tables, the adults at the other. Blacks seated at one end of the table. Whites at the other.

Antoine said grace and then made a toast. "As you know, it's Armistice Day, and I'd like to recognize our veterans who served in the war," he said, addressing Claude and Abraham.

Everyone raised their glasses of lemonade or sweet iced tea. "Here. Here."

Anna-Marie positively beamed. She couldn't believe her father had recognized Claude and Abraham. He has come a long way, she thought, and she squeezed his hand to show her appreciation.

"Here's to next year," Captain Richard added. "Hopefully it will be full of prosperity for all of us."

Everyone raised their glasses again. "Here. Here."

While they picked the crabs, everyone chatted and laughed like old times. Anna-Marie got tears in her eyes as she watched her friends enjoying their meal and each other's company for the first time in several years. For so long, whenever they had been together, it had been to take a house apart, move, or rebuild something. "If there are any leftover crabs, y'all go ahead and pick them, and I'll make some eggplant stuffed with crabmeat," she said. "I'll let y'all know when I make it, and you can come by and get some. No use wasting that good meat."

As everyone ate, customers stopped by to say hello. Anna-Marie could tell they were shocked to see her black friends sharing a meal with her white friends, but no one dared say a word. Theirs was the only store for miles around, and the Couvillions offered credit.

When the meal was over, the men scooped up the newspapers filled with crab shells, and the ladies cleared the rest of the food. Hester wiped down the tables before they all sat down again.

"Children, go and play in the back but stay out of the marsh. You older children watch the younger ones. The grown-ups have to talk without little ears around," Claude said. The children hurried to do his bidding.

"I know you're all wondering why I called you here today," Antoine, seated at the head of the table, began. "I'm afraid what I have to tell you is quite disturbing."

Anna-Marie felt her heart plummet. It must be really bad if her father called everyone together to hear it.

Hester looked at Sanon, who was seating next to her. He reached for her hand. Abraham, seated on the other side, realized that Sanon was silently giving her strength. He reached for her other hand.

"What is it, Papa?" Anna-Marie asked, her fear echoing in her tone.

"Remember how we always knew there had to be another reason why that levee board wanted to take our land to build a useless spillway?"

Everyone nodded. Claude sat up straighter. Abraham leaned forward so that he could better hear what Antoine was saying. Miss Penny shifted in her seat. Sanon squeezed Hester's hand. Peter clenched his fist. Captain Richard bowed his head. Hester didn't move a muscle. She didn't know what was coming, but that cloud directly overhead had already told her enough.

"I've been hearing whispers for weeks, but I didn't want to say anything until I had all the facts," Antoine said. "I have it on good authority that just this week, Thursday, to be exact, the Orleans Levee District signed an agreement with Humble Oil to lease the mineral rights to our land across the river to the oil company."

"What does this mean, Papa?" Anna-Marie cried.

"It means that the levee board and the oil company believe there is oil to be had on our land."

For a long moment, no one said a word, each digesting the information as best they could.

Antoine continued. "Apparently, they've been finding oil in West Louisiana and Texas around salt domes. There's that salt dome over in Nestor."

Claude turned to Anna-Marie. "Remember when those men came, those city slickers? When was that? Not too long after the war, I think. Asking about that salt dome. It was so unusual that you went and discussed it with your papa."

"I remember. And then the judge came in that same day looking for those men."

"I remember," Abraham said. "That judge didn't like me at all."

"I remembered that, as well," Antoine said. "No one will ever convince me that this isn't the reason we had to give up our businesses and move. They must have got wind that they were finding oil around salt domes and that's why they decided to build that spillway down here."

Captain Richard's face slowly turned bright red. He stood up abruptly, knocking his chair backward. "Excuse me, folks, I have to walk away for a moment. What I have to say about this isn't fitting for the ladies." With that, the captain hurried down the road. A few minutes later, his curses traveled back to them on the breeze.

All of the color drained from Claude's face, but he said nothing. He couldn't. He was afraid of what would come out of his mouth.

Miss Penny dabbed at her eyes with a handkerchief. She, too, could not respond.

Hester ran off in the direction of her home, crying loudly.

Abraham ran after her.

Sanon leaned back in his chair and stared at the cloud.

Peter Pelitire said nothing for a moment, and then he banged his fist on the table. Realizing what he had done, he stood up and walked away. Christina followed him.

Anna-Marie could feel an anger like she had never felt before welling up in her chest. "Those bastards!" she yelled. "They took everything from us. They took our way of life, our farms and businesses, our land, our friends. Almost everyone we knew is gone, scattered like the wind. And then they flooded us and made us rebuild again. Those bastards!"

No one left at the table even thought to chastise her for cursing. They all felt exactly the same way.

Finally, Claude, who had been sitting with his hands clenched on the table, put his hand over his wife's. "Do you mean to tell us that all of this was because of oil? They have leased our land to an oil company? Do you know the terms of the lease?" he asked Antoine.

"To my understanding, the levee district will receive a one-eighth percent royalty on any oil they find," Antoine responded.

"And you have this on good authority?"

"I do."

"So all of this, everything we've been through, was so that one day they could put oil money in their pockets?"

"Yes, according to my reasoning, it could be a fortune," Antoine said. "And the worst part is, if there is oil to be had, that money should rightfully be ours."

"What can we do?" Anna-Marie asked.

"Nothing, I'm afraid. Nothing at all, *ma chérie*. I've already spoken with an attorney. The levee board owns the land now. They are within their rights to lease it to whomever they see fit."

"And there's nothing we can do?" Anna-Marie pressed. "You're positive?"

"Yes, I'm positive." Antoine said.

"This is unbelievable," Anna-Marie said. "My apologies Miss Penny, Sanon, Papa, but I must take my leave. Claude, please see that Miss Penny gets home."

Before Claude could say anything, Anna-Marie got up and ran toward the house.

"Give her some time," Antoine said when Claude stood up. "She needs to be alone with her thoughts for a while."

Claude sat down and stared at the levee.

Finally, Antoine stood up. "Miss Penny, can I give you a lift?"

Still dabbing her eyes, Miss Penny nodded her head. Antoine helped her up.

"Say my good-byes to everyone, will you?" he asked Claude. "My apologies for bringing such news, but I thought it might be better coming from me."

Claude stood up and shook his hand, then absently watched as they walked toward Antoine's car.

When they were gone, he turned to Sanon. "A long time ago, you told us that the land had value we could not see. Did you know what the value was?"

"No, I can only see things in glimpses. I never see the full picture," Sanon said. "These things come to me in dreams. It's hard to explain. Bits and pieces of this and that jumbled together with a feeling of foreboding. Some things I see more clearly than others, but I did not know it was oil. I only knew the land held value."

"I remember you said there would be a fight we would win," Claude said.

"Yes, I, too, remember. I believe I said there would be a great fight, one that would be won and lost at the same time."

"What does that mean? How can there be a win and a loss at the same time?"

"I don't know the answer to your question," Sanon said. "I do know that for now, nothing can be done. Soon the river and land will be filled with machinery and wells if they find oil in that dome. Remember, I said everything would change. I'm afraid we will all bear witness to that change. Dark times are coming, Claude. We must gather our strength to face the future. Especially you. You will have to be strong for everyone. These things can dim spirits, but you cannot let that happen—not to your family, not to Hester or Abraham. Keep in mind, there will be good times ahead, as well. For now, I must go, and you must tend to your wife."

After Sanon left, Claude sat by himself at the table listening to the children play. He could hear their shouts and laughter, and for a moment he longed for the time when he had laughed like that—joyfully, innocently, playfully. He could feel despair rising within him, but he pushed it back. Instead, he reached for the anger, letting it wash over him. By the time

Peter and Christina returned, he was pacing up and down, becoming madder by the second.

Peter saw his own anger reflected in Claude's face. "This is hard to swallow, isn't it?" he said.

Claude nodded. "I just can't believe it. Wait. That's not true. After what they've done these past few years, I can believe anything."

"Oil. It all makes sense now. We all knew that spillway would never do much for New Orleans. But who would have thought about oil? And right there in Nestor. It's the darnedest thing I've ever heard," Peter said.

"Yes, not only did they force us to sell at such a low price, but now they're going to steal what could have made all of us wealthy," Claude said. "I'm so mad I could literally hurt someone."

"We all feel that way," Christina said. "Where's Anna-Marie?"

"She cursed and then took off into the house a little while ago. As feisty as she is, I have never heard her utter a curse word."

"You'd better go check on her. We'll collect the children and head back home," Christina said, calling out to the children.

Peter hugged Claude. "Maybe we'll figure something out. Maybe there's a way to get our land back."

"Maybe," Claude said, but he didn't believe that.

After they left, he checked on the children and asked Claude Jr. to keep them outside for a little while longer. He went inside to find Anna-Marie lying in their bed, eyes swollen and tears still running down her face, staring at the ceiling. He didn't say a word. He lay down next to her and wrapped his arms around her, letting her cry.

In the house next door, Abraham was doing his best to comfort Hester, but, like Anna-Marie, she could not stop crying.

CHAPTER 42

By 1929, the Roaring Twenties, during which people across the country had experienced more wealth than ever before in American history, were coming to an end. As the year progressed, Antoine began warning Anna-Marie to save as much money as she could.

"The market is inflated," he told her when she went to New Orleans for a visit in September. "That's not a good sign. There's a recession coming, and I want you to be prepared."

"Thank you, Papa. Business is much better at the store, so I've been able to put a little extra away. Claude was so happy when we were able to pay you back that money you loaned us. He's very proud, you know."

"I could tell," Antoine said. "He's not as bad as we thought he was. I wish your *maman* would come around. If she ever got off her high horse, I believe she would come to respect him. He's a good man."

"You can't know how much that means to me, Papa, just to hear you say that. I don't think *Maman* will ever come around, though."

"She is set in her ways," Antoine said.

"Where is she? Did you tell her I was coming for a visit?"

"I did, but she had a prior engagement, if you can call it that. She went to see her physician."

"Is something wrong?"

"Nothing to worry about. Some kind of female problems I know nothing about. I'll let you know if the report isn't good, so don't fret about it."

"Okay, but please let me know if there's anything I can do."

"I will. Now tell me what's going on down the river. You know, I'd much prefer to be sitting on my porch back in Nestor. Living with your *maman* has never been easy. Part-time was much better, but don't you tell her I said that. I'll deny it," Antoine said, winking at his daughter. "The worst part is being away from you and the children."

"I miss you, too, Papa. You simply must come visit more often."

"Claude sent me a letter and told me you've been having doldrums since my last visit. I do apologize for the outcome of that visit, but I thought it best to let everyone know. Are you feeling better?"

Anna-Marie nodded. "That was a hard pill to swallow, and I'll admit I didn't handle it well. Claude finally shook me out of my doldrums by reminding me that my family needed me and that he couldn't bear to see me so miserable. It was time for me to pull myself together. I was madder than a wet hen, and even sadder than that."

"I know. If they strike oil, all of that money belongs to the people they forced to move. Instead, the politicians will profit from it, while the people down the river keep on working for minimal wages. Now pay heed to what I'm telling you. Save everything you can because I have a feeling things are going to turn sour all over the country soon."

"Yes, Papa. I will let Claude and Abraham know. It's best to be prepared."

"Have y'all heard about the new spillway they're planning?" Antoine asked.

"We did hear something, but we didn't get any details."

"They're planning to build it some twenty-five miles upriver from New Orleans. Supposedly, it will allow the river to flow into Lake Pontchartrain when it gets too high. I guess the powers that be finally figured out that the one in Bohemia would never work. It makes a lot more sense to build a spillway upriver. It's going to be made with a concrete weir that runs along the river. I don't really understand how it will work, but when it's opened, it's supposed to divert the overflow from the river into the lake, which will take it all the way to the Gulf. This way, the water will have somewhere to go. They're going to name it the Bonnet Carré Spillway."

"Are they going to give us our land back now that they won't need our spillway?" Anna-Marie asked.

"I'd bet not in a million years," Antoine said.

"So they are just going to leave our spillway as it is?"

"No, Bohemia Spillway will be much different if they find oil down there. I'm sure that much more time will be spent drilling for oil than diverting the water from the river," Antoine said.

When Anna-Marie returned to Homeplace, she shared what her papa had said with Claude and Abraham.

"Of course, we're not getting our land back," Claude said. "It doesn't matter if they build a spillway on every corner in New Orleans, we'll never get that land back. Not as long as they think there's oil there. And your papa's right. I've heard talk about a recession lately, but no one really knows much. It's just talk right now," Claude said.

"Thanks for the warning," Abraham said to Anna-Marie. "I'll be sure to tell Hester to sock a little more away. Unfortunately, the oyster crop this year has been one of the worst I've seen. That flood really disrupted the reefs, but I've been able to harvest some here and there. Claude, you should come out cooning with me when you get a chance. You haven't been out in a while."

"That's my fault," Anna-Marie admitted. "He's been so worried about me that he didn't want to leave my side. I'm better now, so you should go," she said to Claude. "You would enjoy that, and besides, you've been working every day. You need a break."

"Maybe you could talk to Hester, if you wouldn't mind," Abraham said to Anna-Marie. "She's still in her mood. Hardly smiles these days. It worries me to no end."

"I'd be happy to. We've all been unhappy for too long. It's time for things to get better. Tell her to come help me in the store while y'all are out in the bayou. I'll take care of it."

"Thank you," Abraham said.

The next morning after Claude and Abraham had gone, Anna-Marie waited impatiently for Hester to arrive. When her friend finally walked into the store with Isaac, Anna-Marie was shocked by her appearance. Hester always took special care to braid her hair and then wrap it neatly into a bun. Her hair was loose, flowing, unkempt. There was a look in her eyes that Anna-Marie recognized well—despair. Anna-Marie had seen that look more than a few times over the past months when she peered into her own mirror. She knew she had to do something.

"Isaac, go play with the children. They're in the back picking satsumas. Hester, you sit right here by me. We should talk."

"What do you want to talk about?" Hester asked.

"That look I see in your eyes. Where's your light gone? Where's your pretty smile?"

Hester's eyes filled with tears, and she looked down at the floor. "I'm just not myself right now," she said.

"I know how you feel. I've been that way for months. Claude finally gave me what for and got me out of it, and now I'm going to do the same for you. Remember when we came here? I told you that you and I would have to be strong. Ever since my papa told us why we lost the land, well, for me that was the final straw. I had no strength left to give. I felt angry and betrayed. I was tired. Exhausted. Tired of keeping my spirits up through trial after trial."

Hester's gaze traveled to her friend's face. Anna-Marie had her full attention. That's exactly how she felt.

"Hester, it's time to pull yourself together. Like my family needs me, your family needs you. Emmanuel's health is waning, and he will soon need you to care for him more than you already do. Abraham is unhappy because you are unhappy. Isaac can feel the unhappiness that surrounds him. Is that what you wish for your family?"

"No," Hester said. "I want my family to be happy."

"Then it's up to you to make that happen. Pull yourself together. Braid your hair. Look outside at the pretty flowers we planted. Watch your vegetable gardens grow. Listen to the birds, to the chattering of the squirrels. Watch the ships go by from the levee. Look for things to make you happy, and if you look hard enough you will find them."

Hester sat there quietly for a moment, thinking about what her friend had said. Finally, she stood up. "I must go fix my hair," she said.

Anna-Marie hugged her. "That's what I wanted to hear. We will be okay. We have our families and each other. That's all that is important, really."

"You're right. I'll get Isaac and go home and pull myself together."

"Leave Isaac here. Let him play with the children. Take some time for yourself. Think happy thoughts. Visit Sanon. See if he can help you. Maybe he has some herbs that could be beneficial. Then come back tomorrow and let me know that you're going to be okay."

"I will do that," Hester said. "I'll try my best."

"That's all I ask," Anna-Marie said. "If we let them beat us down, they win. That's what Claude told me. Remember that."

While Anna-Marie and Hester were recovering from the blow they had been dealt, over in New Orleans, Jefferson Davenport was trying to accomplish the same thing. His removal from the Board of Commissioners had thrown him for a loop. At first, he was furious, more furious than he had ever been. Then the realization set in that he would never see one dime of any oil money. He called every political ally he once had, but their doors were suddenly closed to him. He called his friends. They didn't answer. Even Pierre and Sal had turned their backs on him.

As that year wore on, Jefferson waffled back and forth between anger, abject misery, and hope that he could get another government job that would give him enough power so that he could somehow manipulate things over at the levee district. That was a pipe dream. Before the year was up, Abraham Shushan became the president of the Orleans Levee District. Any hope that Jefferson would ever regain his seat was dashed. Jefferson had made too many enemies—Leonus Lozano, Huey Long, and Abraham Shushan, the three men who controlled most of Louisiana.

With dwindling funds and little hope of ever realizing the rewards of all of his planning, Jefferson began to spend most of his time in the speakeasies in the French Quarter. Inevitably, he would get into a brawl, and the manager would ask him to leave. He would show up again the next evening for a repeat performance, not even remembering what had happened the night before.

Jefferson's hopes were revived when, just a year after Huey Long was elected, impeachment proceedings began against him. On April 6, 1929, the governor was impeached by the Louisiana House of Representatives on eight of the nineteen charges he faced—from bribing lawmakers to carousing with strippers and carrying a concealed weapon to his alleged attempt to arrange the murder of a state representative. The atmosphere at the Louisiana State Capitol was so intense that fistfights broke out on the House floor. The governor was not convicted in the Senate, and he would serve out his term, thanks in no small part to the efforts of Leonus Lozano, who represented him throughout his impeachment ordeal.

Then on Monday, October 28, 1929, the Dow Jones lost thirteen percent of its value. The following day, Black Tuesday, as it came to be known, sent the stock market spiraling downward another twelve percent and set into motion a Great Depression that soon spread around the world. People panicked and began selling off everything they could. By the middle of November, the market was down almost fifty percent. Whereas before there had been plenty of work to go around, suddenly factories around the country closed, laying off workers, who were forced to learn how to survive with nothing.

In the early 1930s, in city after city across America, bread lines formed, and people lost their homes because they had no income. Down the river, life went on as usual. Most of these people were so poor they barely noticed that a Great Depression was debilitating the rest of the country. They had always survived off the land and the river. They would never go hungry because of the natural bounty that surrounded them—seafood, livestock, and crops, as well as the rabbits, ducks, and squirrels that were plentiful. The river also provided valuable wood that came downriver every spring when the water rose. Building homes and businesses was simply a matter of utilizing that which the river provided.

The job market, too, did not suffer as much in lower Plaquemines Parish, because of the constant demand for the food the parish produced. Folks said that the soil was so rich in the Delta they could plant tenpenny nails, and three-foot crowbars would grow. That wasn't far from the truth. While some in the rest of the country went hungry, the folks in Plaquemines Parish survived off the land and the bays and bayous as they always had.

Soon the Potash Salt Dome in Nestor on the East Bank was abuzz with activity. Humble Oil & Refining drilled thirty-nine wells in the area, but found only minimal amounts of crude.

As they watched the progress, folks who had moved to the West Bank became more and more determined to try to get their land back. The Orleans Levee District was equally determined that wouldn't happen. Through a letter read into the minutes of a Board of Levee Commissioners meeting in November 1929, General Counsel James Wilkinson and Assistant General Counsel George Piazza make the levee board's position perfectly clear:

The Orleans Levee Board is entitled to great credit in zealously pushing forward this pioneer project [Bohemia Spillway] which led directly to the creation of the Bonnet Carré Spillway above New Orleans, insuring safety to that city from overflow and so largely aiding the State itself.

In doing this work and in saving two levee boards from serious financial conditions, it has been forced to spend over a million dollars.

In payments of this to property owners alone for private property in that area it has spent $406,000. It has had to take down many miles of front levee and to build an upper side levee from the river towards the sea. It has not received a dollar in taxes from this spillway.

It's chances for a discovery of oil in paying quantities on its lands is, as yet, a matter of hope, but it would take 10 million barrels of oil from wells on lands leased by it to make it whole.

We have been advised that there has been a movement by former property owners in this spillway to contest the right of the levee board to royalties on any oil that may be found on the area bought and paid for by the Levee Board.

The scripture says:

"The love of money is the root of all evil."

Our opinion is that there is no chance of these beneficiaries getting more of the "root" than they have already gotten.

It may however interest them to have to tender some $406,000 back to the board for property bought by the Levee Board in fee simple before asserting any such rights, as they could not expect to sell their cake and keep on eating it.

Not long after this letter was written, Humble Oil drilled deeper and hit pay dirt. More and more wells were drilled, and more and more oil produced. Those folks who had moved from the East Bank to the West Bank watched the activity with heavy hearts. The land they loved was transforming before their eyes, and the Orleans Levee District would soon be laughing all the way to the bank. Then, in 1930, oil was discovered at Lake Washington on the West Bank. Suddenly, wells were being drilled even closer to their homes, and Abraham and Claude worried that they could once again be forced from their land.

Jefferson, too, kept a close eye on was happening in Bohemia. Things were moving faster than even he had anticipated. Over time, his anger turned to bitterness and then evolved into depression and obsession. Sometimes he would take the train to Bohemia and then walk to Nestor. He'd sip from a flask as he observed the progress, becoming angrier and more morose each day. Then he'd return to New Orleans for another night of drinking and brawling.

In the winter of 1931, Jefferson's body was found in an alleyway in the French Quarter after he was stabbed in a fight. He had wandered out of a speakeasy and into the alley, holding his side as blood gushed through his fingers before he dropped to the ground.

No one called the police.

No one shed a tear.

No one came to say a prayer for his soul when he was buried in a pauper's grave outside of the city.

By the end of 1931, the Bonnet Carré Spillway was complete, negating any need for the Bohemia Spillway, which had outlived its usefulness in only five years; however, there was no way the Orleans Levee District would consider returning the land to its rightful owners or the valuable mineral rights that land possessed.

CHAPTER 43

April 1932

"Why did we pick Homeplace?" Abraham asked Claude. The men were heading to a new reef in Grand Bayou Abraham had leased the week before. "The oysters are coming back," he had told Claude. "You've got to come with me. I haven't seen them like this in years."

Claude, happy to get away for even a day, turned to make sure it was okay with Anna-Marie, who was already nodding her head. "Go. Hester and I will take care of the store. Take Poopdeck and Spit with you. They need a day with the men."

The next morning, the four men set out early, eager to spend a day on the water.

"I don't know," Claude said. "Because it was so close to home? But how could we have known that our lives would one day be filled with the sounds of machinery testing for oil? Already, the river doesn't look or sound the same."

"No, it doesn't. It's a crying shame," Abraham said.

"I wonder what it's going to look like when they're done," Poopdeck said.

"I don't think they'll ever be done. Not as long as there's oil to be had. Who would have thought that automobiles would have created this mess?" Abraham said.

"Not me," Claude said. "I remember I was so happy when I got my first jalopy. If I had known what was going to happen, I'd have stuck with my horse."

"Me, too." Abraham agreed, pointing to the east. "We'd still live over there in our peaceful community. Now the Takos are gone from the East Bank, but some of them bought camps on this side of the river. Most of them live in New Orleans, but they'll spend weeks at a time at their camps working oysters and fishing. The Italians have moved to New Orleans, too. Most of the Mulattos are gone up north. Everything has changed, and I don't like it."

"And now, they're building that sulfur mine over near Ronquillo Settlement. I heard tell that they're building a whole new town. Going to call it Grandeport. They're dredging the river to create enough land for the terminal and the town site. It's crazy," Claude said.

"I read all those reports in the newspaper about the country being in a depression, and look around. I've never seen so much work going on. Not as long as I've lived on the river," Abraham said.

"It's worrisome, for certain," Claude responded. "I fear this whole area is going to hell in a hand basket."

"That's what my mama used to say," Spit said. "She didn't live long enough to see all this, but she knew right where everything was headed."

"Your mama was a wise woman," Abraham said. "I heard you and Albert here applied for a job building that town in the marsh."

Spit hung his head. "We were going to tell y'all, but we haven't worked ourselves up to it yet."

"Now's a good time as any," Claude said.

Poopdeck leaned on the railing of the boat. "Spit and I were talking, and they need strong men who can build. Lord knows we can do that. It's time we started building something for ourselves. Spit's got his eye on Miss Betsy from Nairn, and I've been having a hankering for that young lady over in Happy Jack for years. We decided that we want to make an honest living and maybe settle down."

"If these ladies will have us," Spit added.

"Well, I can't argue with that," Claude said. "If those bigwigs are gonna come down here and build, you boys may as well profit from it. You have my blessing. Invite your young ladies to the store and let Anna-Marie and Hester give them a once over just to make sure they will do."

"They'll do," Spit said. "No doubt about that. I even quit drinking so I can ask for her hand proper-like. Me and Poopdeck have been finding a lot of wood on the batture every time the river goes down, so we have a good start on building our homes."

"Glad to hear that," Abraham said, pulling the boat into a landing. "Now get your minds off the ladies, and let's fill these sacks with oysters."

"Yes sir," Poopdeck said, saluting before he put on his gloves.

The men spent the rest of the day pulling oysters from the bottom of the bayou. When they were done, they headed in, exhilarated because the deck was almost full.

"I haven't had a haul like this is a long while," Abraham said.

"That'll fetch a pretty penny at the cannery," Claude said. "Pay Spit and Poopdeck, but don't worry about me. I should be paying you for taking me with you today. This was mighty enjoyable."

Abraham agreed. It had been months since Claude had been on the bayou with him. "Oyster season is almost over, so I'm glad you came out today."

"So now you'll go after shrimp?"

"I'd like to do a little deep sea fishing out in the Gulf," Abraham said, "but I need to check on what the markets in the city are paying. With the Depression and all, they may not be paying like they used to. I know they're not paying as much for oysters."

"Look at that," Spit said, pointing in the direction of the river.

Abraham and Claude turned to see oil shooting up high into the air. "Looks like they hit another vein. Just more oil to run into the river. They're going to kill all the oysters. Mark my word. One day, there won't be hardly any left," Abraham said.

"You may be right," Claude agreed.

Later that evening after the children were asleep, Anna-Marie asked Claude to sit with her on the porch. As they sat there watching the stars flicker over the Delta, Anna-Marie listened as Claude told her about what he had witnessed that day. Anna-Marie didn't respond like she normally did. She just sat there in her chair, rocking back and forth, staring at the sky.

"Is something on your mind?" Claude asked.

"Yes, I have something to discuss, but I don't want it to come out the wrong way. I don't know how to say it."

Claude sat up straighter. This didn't sound good. Anna-Marie never had a problem speaking her mind.

"What is it?" Claude asked. "Just say whatever it is."

"As you are aware, my *maman* has been pushing for Madeleine and Jeanne to go to finishing school in Paris. My Papa says that's all she talks about. I've been against it, as you know, for many reasons. I'm afraid to send Madeleine to a new environment where people are unaccustomed to her lack of an arm. Here, everyone is used to it. No one even looks twice at her anymore. She is at an impressionable age where cutting remarks can wound a young girl."

"I don't want to send them, either," Claude interrupted.

"Now, I'm not so sure," Anna-Marie said. "I think maybe we should send them away for a while."

"I don't understand." Claude shifted in his seat. He did not want to have an argument with his wife about this, especially after having such a good day. "What has made you doubt your decision?"

Anna-Marie was quiet for a moment, and then she said, "Isaac."

"What does Isaac have to do with it?" Claude said, keeping his voice low. Abraham and Hester could be outside and walk up unexpectedly.

"Have you noticed the way Isaac looks at Madeleine? Ever since the day she lost her arm, he has protected her fiercely. They have always been very close."

"I don't understand. What's the problem?"

"I was watching them today, and I saw Madeleine looking at Isaac in the same way he looks at her. They're getting older now. Isaac is already fifteen, and Madeleine is not too far behind. I think they are falling in love."

Claude leaned back in his chair and thought about that for a few minutes. Finally, he reached for Anna-Marie's hand and closed his fingers around it. "That won't do," he said. "That won't do at all."

"I know. It's been bothering me all day. I love Isaac with all my heart, and you know I do. He's a fine young man and will make some young lady a wonderful husband one day, but that young lady cannot be Madeleine."

"Madeleine would be shunned. Ostracized," Claude said.

"Yes, and Madeleine is already different because of her arm. Remember that time she came home from Papa's crying because a neighborhood boy had made fun of her."

"Yes, he called her terrible names."

"Exactly. I've never forgotten that or any of the other instances when someone made her cry. I can't help but think what it would be like for her if she falls in love with Isaac. We can't allow it, Claude. We just can't. I love Hester, and I know you love Abraham. They're like family to us, but we simply cannot allow this attraction to mature. We've got to nip it in the bud."

"I agree," Claude said. "Completely. You're right. This cannot be allowed to happen." Even as he said it, Claude felt a tinge of guilt. Abraham was his best friend. They had been to war together. They had weathered storms and floods and being forced from their lands. He had helped Abraham bury his mother. He and Anna-Marie had crossed so many lines because of this unusual friendship, but this was one line he could not cross, even at the risk of his friendship.

"I'm glad we are in agreement, but I'm worried," Anna-Marie said. "Hester knows I don't want to send the girls away. I've complained about my *maman* trying to make me. She will be suspicious if I suddenly change my mind. I know she suspects a romance is growing between our children. Just last week she mentioned how close they are. I don't want to lose her over this."

"I was just thinking the same thing about Abraham. I don't want to lose either of them, but what else can we do? I will not have our daughter treated poorly because she is too young to understand the world and the way it works."

"I will send word to Papa that he can tell *Maman* to make the arrangements. Jeanne is a little young for finishing school, but I won't send Madeleine off by herself. They will need to look out for one another."

"Yes, send him a letter tomorrow," Claude said.

The next morning, Anna-Marie wrote a letter to her father. She explained that she had changed her mind and that she would like both girls to go as soon as possible. "Ask *Maman* to make the arrangements, and tell her that Claude and I insist upon paying the fees."

When Nikolas came to deliver the mail, Anna-Marie handed him the letter. "Please don't lose this one. It's very important," she said.

"I will handle it carefully," Nikolas said. "Is Miss Hester around?"

"No, she's next door," Anna-Marie said. "Maybe next time she'll be here."

Nikolas' face brightened. "Maybe so. Well, give her these," he said, handing her coupons he had cut from the Sunday newspaper.

"I'll make sure she gets them."

"And this." Nikolas pulled a piece of apple pie from his sack.

Anna-Marie started laughing. "True love never dies, does it?"

Nikolas beamed at her. "No, it never does," he said.

Later, when Anna-Marie gave Hester her coupons and her pie, she could barely look her in the eye. She hated that she had to do this. She loved Hester, and she felt like she was betraying her, like she was acting the way Mildred had acted. She was convinced, though, that she was doing the best thing she could do for Madeleine. She took a deep breath and then asked Claude to watch the store.

"Let's take a walk," she said to Hester. "It's a beautiful day."

Together, they walked up the levee and scattered the chickens when they got to the top. "What's on your mind?" Hester said.

"Oh nothing. Just tired of being in the store on such a pretty day," Anna-Marie said, smiling brightly at her.

"That's the second time you've said it was a pretty day, so now I know something's off. What is it?" Hester stopped walking to stare at her friend.

"It's my *Maman*," Anna-Marie said. "She has been pressuring me to send the girls to finishing school in Paris. I've been resisting, but now I don't think I can. I've told Papa they can go."

"But you were dead set against it just the other day."

"I know, but Papa thinks it might be a good idea." Even as she said the words, Anna-Marie had to turn away. She couldn't lie while looking at her friend. She just couldn't.

"You've bucked your parents at every turn," Hester said. "Why is this any different?"

"I guess because I went, and it was good for me. Taught me to see things differently than other folks."

"If that's your reasoning, then let them go. But if you're just bowing to pressure, then don't do it. These are your children. They don't have any say."

"You're right, of course. It's just a hard decision, and now that I've made it, I'm experiencing some regret," Anna-Marie said, turning to walk back in the direction of the store.

Hester stayed where she was for a moment. When she caught up to her friend, she put her hand on Anna-Marie's arm. "This doesn't have anything to do with me telling you how close Isaac and Madeleine are becoming, does it?"

Anna-Marie looked away. "Of course not," she said.

Hester could see the color rising in her friend's cheeks. She watched her for a moment.

Anna-Marie stood there, trying to appear normal, but she grew increasingly uncomfortable under Hester's gaze. "We'd better get back," Anna-Marie said.

"Yes, we should," Hester agreed. Nothing in her voice suggested that she didn't believe her friend. Nothing in her manner as they walked along revealed the hurt that was welling up inside her.

When they got back to the store, Hester said that she had to get supper ready, and she said her good-byes.

Anna-Marie anxiously watched her walk away, hoping that she had not upset her friend.

"How did it go?" Claude asked.

"I think she knows," Anna-Marie said. "I tried to hide the truth from her, but she knows me too well."

"What did she say?"

"Nothing. She said absolutely nothing, and then she said she had to go home to cook supper."

"Well, if she didn't say anything, maybe she didn't suspect anything."

"I'm afraid she did. She asked me if this was because Isaac and Madeleine were getting too close. I said, "of course not,' but she knew I was lying. She knew, Claude. She knew."

Later that evening, Hester told Abraham about the conversation. "They don't want Madeleine to fall in love with Isaac. That's why they are sending her away. I'm sure of it. Anna-Marie never could tell a lie. Not to anyone. You should have seen her when I asked her if that was the reason. She said it wasn't, but she couldn't even look at me when she said it."

Abraham was quiet for a long while. He sat in his favorite chair, staring at the bricked floor around the wood-burning stove, thinking. Finally, he looked at Hester. "If it is the reason, what does it matter?"

"They are our friends. They have always treated us as equals. Now, after everything we've been through? Now they change the rules?"

"They are our friends, Hester. They have always treated us with respect. With more respect than any white person we've ever known. Because of them, we still have our home. Because of them we have this land. Because of them, Isaac has lived a different life than other children like him. Because of them, we have the friendship of the captains, the Pelitires, Claude's father, and his aunt who took us in during the flood. How can you say they are not our friends?"

"I didn't say that. I said that they are changing the rules now," Hester said.

"If they need to change the rules, then so be it. They've broken all the rules of proper white society for us. If they don't want Madeleine involved with Isaac romantically, can you blame them? You know better than anyone what that could do to the girl. Look what you've been through because you married me. You've been rejected by your own people. You, better than anyone, should understand this."

"Well, I don't," Hester said, stamping her foot. "I don't understand it at all."

With that, she hurried outside and walked along the levee until she had almost reached Nairn. When she returned, she didn't speak to Abraham. She didn't want to speak to anyone.

The next morning, Abraham went over to discuss the matter with Claude.

While Anna-Marie watched the store, Abraham and Claude sat on the front porch.

"Anna-Marie told me Hester might be upset," Claude said.

"She is," Abraham said. "She's very upset."

"I can understand why." Claude stood up and went inside the store. He came back with two glasses of blackberry wine.

"A little early, isn't it?" Abraham asked.

"I have a feeling we'll need these," Claude said with a grimace.

"You may be right."

They sipped on their wine for a moment. "Look, Claude. I want you to know I understand. I do. I've watched what Hester has been through because she married me. I know you don't want that for Madeleine, especially considering what else she has had to deal with. I just wanted to let you know that I do understand. I think you are making the right decision for your family."

"But where does that leave us?" Claude asked.

"It leaves us right where we've always been. I owe you and Anna-Marie so much, and I will always love you both no matter what life brings. The fact of the matter is that we are different. We live in a world that doesn't really accept our friendship. They deal with it, but they don't accept it. That world would certainly not accept Madeleine and Isaac, and I do not want to put them through that either."

"What about Hester?"

Abraham took another sip of his drink. "That's not going to be so easy. She is hurt. I don't know how long it will take her to get over it. I will do my best to talk to her, but she's a stubborn woman."

"They both are," Claude said.

"One of the many reasons we love them. It'll work itself out in time. You just do what you feel you must, and let me worry about Hester."

"Anna-Marie is in the store fretting about it right now. She was so upset last night."

"Oh, so was Hester. They're emotional. Let Hester get used to the idea, and everything will right itself. I'd better go check on her. She wasn't speaking to me last night." Abraham stood up, shook Claude's hand, and walked back home. He hoped Hester had come to her senses. He couldn't imagine what their life would be like without the Couvillions.

Hester did not come around for a long while. Years, in fact.

Anna-Marie tried everything she could to make it up to her friend, but Hester was having none of it. She felt betrayed. She felt like Anna-Marie didn't think Isaac was good enough for her daughter.

At night, Anna-Marie and Claude would sit on their front porch, and Abraham and Hester would sit on theirs next door. Claude would wave to Abraham, and Abraham would wave back. There was no more discussing everything that was going on around them. There was no more joking and laughing. Sometimes Anna-Marie would catch Claude staring at their neighbor's front porch wistfully, and she felt horrible. Claude missed his friend.

Abraham did everything he could to convince Hester that Anna-Marie and Claude had made the right decision, but his comments fell on deaf ears. When Hester sat on the porch, she didn't even look to her left. There were times, though, when she couldn't help but notice that Abraham sometimes sat in his rocking chair and stared over there.

Madeleine and Jeanne stayed in Paris for three years, coming home for holidays and summer vacations. By the time they returned for good, Isaac was already gone. When he turned eighteen, he moved to Baton Rouge to attend Southern University. He had dreams that one day he would become an attorney and help his parents get their land back.

Two years later, right before his junior year began, Isaac married a girl—Sarah Washington—whom he met at the university.

Anna-Marie and Claude heaved a sigh of relief. Perhaps now, things could get back to normal.

Getting back to normal took a little more time, but a few months after the wedding, Hester approached Anna-Marie one afternoon as she was digging in her garden.

"You were right," Hester said. "I'm sorry for the way I've acted. Isaac is very happy, and I'm happy for him. A romance between our children would not have been good for either of them."

Anna-Marie looked at her and grinned. "Did Abraham send you over here?"

"He's been trying to get me over here for a long time."

"I know. He's been grumpy every time I've seen him. I think he's been most upset by our tiff."

"Yes, I know. Whenever we would sit on the porch, I'd catch him looking over here. I'm sorry I reacted so poorly."

"I understood," Anna-Marie said. "If the situation were reversed, I'd have probably acted the same way, except I'd have given you what for. You know me."

Yes, I do," Hester said, laughing.

"I'm sorry I didn't just tell you the truth. I couldn't. I didn't want to hurt you, but I hurt you anyway. I'm so sorry,"

"Me, too," Hester said.

Anna-Marie stood up and hugged her friend.

They both started laughing when they heard Abraham shouting from his front porch, "Thank you, Lord Jesus. Thank you."

CHAPTER 44

1934-1942

"Y'all will have to come see it for yourself," Antoine said to his daughter. "It's pretty incredible." Antoine had come to visit Anna-Marie for a few days, mostly to get away from his wife, although he told Anna-Marie it was because he missed her. They were enjoying some lemon cakes Hester had made when Antoine began to tell her about the new airport in New Orleans.

"Claude will want to hear about this," Anna-Marie said, opening the front door and calling to her husband. "Before you come out, call Abraham and tell him to come over. Tell him to bring Hester with him."

A few minutes later, everyone was gathered on the porch. "Go on, Papa. Tell them."

"I was telling Anna-Marie about that new airport on the lakefront in New Orleans."

"I heard something about that," Claude said. "It's supposed to be real fancy."

"It's state-of-the-art, for sure," Antoine said. "But the thing is, they built it right in the lake, or where the lake used to be."

"How is that even possible?" Abraham asked.

"I don't know. They built some kind of retaining wall around part of the lakefront and then poured hydraulic fill in until they had made land. That wall is around 10,000 feet long. I really have no idea how all of that works, but they did it. The airfield is around 3,000 feet long, and I think that both land and seaplanes can use it."

"I've never heard of such a thing," Anna-Marie said. "They built an airport in the lake?"

"Part of it, yes. And it gets better. The actual facility is supposed to be some kind of modern architectural wonder."

"I wonder how much all that cost," Claude said.

"Around $4.5 million from what I hear," Antoine said.

"Paid for by the taxpayers, I'm sure," Hester said.

Antoine cleared his throat. "Most of the money to fund it came from the levee board." He looked at Anna-Marie and then Claude, Abraham, and Hester, watching the look on their faces as what he had just said registered.

Anna-Marie stood up. "You mean to tell me that they have so much money they can build an airport in the middle of Lake Pontchartrain?" She stomped her foot for emphasis.

"Yes, *ma chérie*. I'm afraid so. I've heard they're making millions upon millions every year. Living high on the hog, they are. And it gets worse. They named it Shushan Airport after Abe Shushan, president of the levee board."

"Ooh! I'm so mad I could scream," Anna-Marie said.

"This sure doesn't seem right," Abraham agreed.

"You know, after that Jefferson Davenport died like a dog in an alley, I thought maybe the politicians on that levee board might come to their senses," Hester said.

"I'm afraid not. We'll never get that land back, not with all that money they're making," Antoine said. "Y'all should come see the airport. It's quite something."

"No, thank you," Claude said. "As long as I live, I'll never go to see that airport. You can mark my words on that."

"I agree," Abraham said. "I'd drive to Mississippi and catch a plane there if I needed to go somewhere before I'd fly out of that airport."

"We won't be flying anywhere," Hester said. "We can't afford it because they took our money to build an airport."

That wasn't all the Orleans Levee District was able to do with their money. New levees were built, old levees were shored up, and the city's drainage issues were addressed. Eventually, the name of the airport would be changed to the New Orleans Lakefront Airport after Abraham Shushan was arrested for fraud.

Shushan wasn't the only one dabbling where he should not have been.

Leonus had finagled a way to profit from state-owned lands in his parish through his River Parishes Real Estate Corporation. With the help of his friend Huey Long, who was now a U.S. senator, they leased state lands to themselves and then sub-leased the land to oil companies, funneling the profits into their businesses.

Through his representation of the Grand Prairie Levee District as its attorney, Leonus was able to influence board members to withhold recognition of the Orleans Levee District's claim to some of the land in lower Bohemia. The Grand Prairie Levee District leased approximately 10,000 acres to River Parishes Land Development Corp. The cost of the lease—three cents per acre. Leonus, in turn, subleased the land to Humble's competitor, Gulf Refining Company. After Gulf struck oil, Leonus began collecting the royalties that would make him a millionaire.

His friend, Huey, was also building his fortune and earning a reputation for being a bit off his rocker. No one could ever be sure what he would do next, but no one underestimated his ability to get what he wanted by whatever means necessary. Everyone knew he had his sights set on the presidency.

On September 8, 1935, those dreams were dashed. Dr. Carl Weiss, former president of the Louisiana Medical Society, shot the governor at point blank range inside the Louisiana State Capitol as Huey was walking back to his office after a late meeting. Huey's bodyguards shot and killed Weiss, who felt that the governor had dishonored his family. Huey was rushed to a Baton Rouge hospital, but his life could not be saved. The governor passed away two days later, his manner of death ensuring that he would become a legend in the state and guaranteeing that conspiracy theorists would have plenty to keep them busy for decades.

Everyone on the river was shocked when they heard the news.

"How can a U.S. Senator get shot right there in the State Capitol?" Hester asked. "It doesn't make any sense."

"Doesn't he have bodyguards?" Anna-Marie asked.

"Yes," Abraham said. "His bodyguards shot the guy."

"What is this world coming to?" Claude asked. "This is disheartening. I know we all think he was crazy, and God forgive me for speaking ill of the dead, but he was. With that said, even he didn't deserve that. Can you imagine?"

"No, I can't," Abraham said. "That guy that shot him was pretty brazen."

"You think he had cause?" Anna-Marie asked. "Like maybe the senator was having a clandestine affair with his wife?"

"Anna-Marie, shush!" Claude said. "We don't know that, but if you repeat that, it will spread down the river faster than a lightening bolt."

"I think it's sad," Hester said. "And you all know how much I hate politicians."

"Yes, we know," Abraham said, laughing.

"He was a bit crazy, but he did do some good things for the state. I have to admit that," Claude said. "We've got roads now that weren't there before and new bridges everywhere. They just finished that bridge they named after him, and now we can drive across the river."

"And children now have free textbooks because of him," Anna-Marie said.

"He did some good things for the poor with his Share the Wealth Program, too, if I recall correctly," Abraham said.

"What good things?" asked Hester. "We're poor. What did he do for us?"

"Okay, he didn't specifically do anything for us, but at least he tried," Abraham said.

"Well, I think it's a shame that he got shot like he did," Claude said. "A real shame."

"I wonder where they'll have the funeral," Anna-Marie said.

"I'm sure wherever it is, it will be a sight to see," Hester said.

And it was. Huey's funeral was a spectacle befitting his life, held on the Capitol grounds and attended by more than 100,000 people who waited in long lines to pay their respect to the former governor who had told them "Every man is a king." Friends and foes alike stood with heads bowed over his copper-lined casket draped in an American flag and surrounded with white roses, orchids, and daisies. The Reverend Gerald L. K. Smith gave the eulogy, noting that "His was the unfinished symphony." Huey was buried on the front lawn of the tallest state capitol building in the country, his own brainchild, and when viewed from a distance, a statue of him erected in his honor almost appeared to be his headstone.

Huey's untimely demise was a blow to Leonus, but he didn't allow that to slow him down. He spent the rest of the decade firmly establishing himself as "King of the Delta," and he ruled his parish with an iron fist. A hardcore segregationist, Leonus did everything he could to ensure that blacks and whites did not commingle in schools, restaurants, and churches in his parish. "Separate but equal" meant nothing to him, and he dedicated his life to ensuring that blacks were not treated equally. Before he came to power, there had not been many issues between the races along the river, but Leonus set out to change that and would spend much of his career fighting against civil rights for African Americans.

"Something needs to be done about that judge," Abraham said to Claude after Claude told him that Leonus had come into the general store to check on things.

"He likes to nose around now and then," Claude said.

"I'm glad Isaac doesn't live down here anymore. He'd be in big trouble with that judge with that mouth of his," Abraham said.

Claude nodded his agreement. "You may be right. That judge is trying to change the way people think down here, trying to force his opinions on us."

"Well, I won't stand for it," Anna-Marie said. "He'd better not come in the store when I'm there. I'll give him what for and maybe even box his ears."

Claude and Abraham started laughing, but then they stopped as fast as they started. "No, Anna-Marie. Lord knows what would happen if you did that. In one day, our business would go away, just like that. I'm serious. Remember who he is. Think about everything he's done. He'll stop at nothing to get what he wants."

"He's right," Abraham said. "I sure watch my step around him, and I've warned Hester to do the same."

"I'm not afraid of him," Anna-Marie said.

"You should be," Claude said. "He's not one to cross."

"We should all just stay out of his way," Abraham agreed. "He doesn't act like other folks around here."

He was right. Leonus did everything he could to further his own agendas—making money and keeping blacks in their places. Throughout his tenure as "King of the Delta," he was constantly scheming or fighting with the Orleans Levee District, which was involved in numerous disputes in their pursuit of the same revenue Leonus was after.

Many lawsuits ensued through the years. The Orleans Levee District sued the Grand Prairie Levee District over the leases, but by the time the courts clarified the levee board's claim to the land, Leonus was already a wealthy man.

While Leonus was busy trying to make his fortune by whatever means necessary, Antoine set about trying to recoup the losses his family and friends had experienced at the hands of the Orleans Levee District. He gathered influential friends who had once owned businesses on the East Bank—the Tabonys, the Edgecombs, the owners of Poydras Realty, the owners of Gulf Coast Oyster Co., the owners of Whitney Bank and Trust, priests, the Haspels, with the exception of Joseph Haspel—and he began a campaign to win back the mineral rights that had been stolen from them.

"We can do this," Antoine said, standing behind a podium at Bertaut & Biggs while addressing the crowd of people who had shown up to discuss the matter. "We must keep putting pressure on our friends in Baton Rouge who create the laws. If we withhold our contributions, if we take our plight public, if we whisper in their ears loud enough, eventually they will listen."

Antoine was right. In 1938, the Louisiana Legislature crafted legislation that addressed the issue of mineral rights in the state, making certain mineral rights with regard to properties acquired by the state imprescriptible, meaning not transferable.

An ecstatic Antoine called a meeting and made the announcement. "This means," he told the group, "that we have cleared the first hurdle toward getting back what is rightfully ours. Now we must fight even harder."

In another room across the city, the Orleans Levee District had called a meeting of its own.

"There's no way in hell we will ever give those people that land back or those mineral rights," Louis LeBlanc, the new president of the levee board, said, pounding his gavel for emphasis. "We paid for it. I don't care what we have to do. It doesn't matter if that spillway has outlived its usefulness. It's ours. We own it lock, stock, and barrel, and it'll be over my dead body when we give up any mineral rights associated with it. Prepare yourselves, gentlemen. We have a war on our hands."

Everyone voiced their agreement. Those mineral rights had already turned into a goldmine, and no one was willing to give one cent back to the rightful owners of that land.

In 1940, that act was repealed, and a new law was created, which allowed property owners to retain certain mineral rights for ten years after the sale of the property.

"That won't do us a lick of good," Antoine told Anna-Marie when he learned about the new law. "Common sense should tell all those lawmakers in Baton Rouge what is happening here, but they're all the same. Those New Orleans politicians have all the money they need to line pockets that need to be lined, and they're doing it with our money, damn it. It ain't right. The Bonnet Carré keeps New Orleans safe, but greed keeps us from getting back what is rightfully ours."

"The worst part is that nobody cares about right or wrong," Anna-Marie said. "Nobody."

"You're right about that," Antoine agreed, "but that won't stop me. I'll fight them until my dying day. One day, they're going to give us that land back and the mineral rights that go with it."

Although Antoine and others fought for years, filing lawsuit after lawsuit, motion after motion, the Orleans Levee District would not budge. Its attorneys argued that the law was not retroactive, and they continued to benefit from the oil revenues while people like Claude, Abraham, Peter Pelitire, and Sanon continued to work their fingers to the bone to eek out a living across the river from the oil boon.

While the lawsuits played out in Louisiana courtrooms, there were also numerous efforts made by interested parties to close the spillway. Once the Bonnet Carré Spillway opened, many in state government recognized that although the Bohemia Spillway did divert some water when the river got high, it was nowhere near as effective as the Bonnet Carré Spillway. By 1935, maintenance of remaining levees in Bohemia had been virtually abandoned. Robert S. Maestri, who worked with the Louisiana Conservation Department at the time, shared his concerns in a letter, which stated that the Bohemia Spillway should be closed because the silt deposited when the river flowed through the spillway was destroying the oysters. The spillway "appears to no longer be of necessity," he wrote. The Corps of Engineers disagreed. Major John H. Curruth stated in response to Maestri's letter, "The relief outlet functions, as planned by state officials, in lowering flood stages at New Orleans and below."

On May 11, 1942, the legislature reaffirmed the boundaries that had been established in 1924 and revised by Act 246 in 1928, through Louisiana Act 311, which extended the boundaries beyond Cuselich Canal to Cubitt's Gap fifteen miles downriver and from the river to the sea, making it impossible for Leonus to sublease the land below the spillway. The Act confirmed that the Orleans Levee District's ownership of all of the land began when the spillway was built, even though the boundaries were later revised.

The Orleans Levee District also sued the federal government for its holdings in the spillway area, but the federal government, aware of the possible revenue that land could provide in terms of mineral rights, refused to surrender its land.

These debates would continue for decades. Meanwhile, the effect the spillway and oil production was having on the seafood industry was disheartening for those who depended on it for their livelihood—fisherman, shrimpers, and oystermen like Abraham—who would find themselves struggling even harder to earn a decent living from the river and bayous that had once held such bounty.

CHAPTER 45

As the years went by, Hester and Abraham and Claude and Anna-Marie sat on their porches each evening and watched as everything around them changed. Ronquillo Settlement was no longer a small quiet settlement, due to the influx of people required for mining at the Grand Ecaille sulphur mine. The name of the settlement had been changed to Port Sulphur in 1932 by Freeport Sulphur Company, a company that would become the second largest sulfur producer in the world. More and more people moved to the West Bank to work at the mine.

Bohemia, too, had become a hub of activity with oil wells springing up everywhere. The popularity of automobiles and electricity was beginning to create high demand for oil, and oil companies were drilling wells all over south Louisiana and in the Gulf of Mexico.

"It's too much, isn't it?" Anna-Marie said to Hester on a cool evening in early September 1939. They were sitting on Anna-Marie's porch—lit with a single light bulb overhead—reading the newspaper. The flickering light of oil lanterns and candles had been recently replaced with light bulbs that now illuminated their homes. "So much going on around here and in the rest of the world. I'm praying that we don't get involved in that war over in Germany."

"Me, too." Hester said.

"I've been reading about that Hitler feller," Claude said. "He's invading Poland right now. It's worrisome. And now France and Britain have declared war on Germany. That's how we ended up in World War I. Some country over there declaring war on another. You remember, Abraham?"

"That's not something a man forgets," Abraham said.

"What if they have a draft like they did last time?" Anna-Marie asked.

"Mercy, don't even think that," Heather said.

"It's possible if the United States gets involved," Claude said. "We need to pay close attention to what's happening over there."

"I can't bear the thought of our boys going off to war," Anna-Marie said. "It was bad enough when you and Abraham were overseas. I don't know what I'll do if they get drafted."

"I know," Hester said. "Isaac and Sarah just had the baby. Did I tell you they named him Jacob Abraham after my father and Abraham? They're calling him Little Jake. I thought that was so nice. If Isaac has to go to war, that would be heartbreaking."

"That's exactly what happened to us," Abraham reminded Hester. "And to you, too," he said to Claude and Anna-Marie.

"Look, here comes Sanon," Claude said. "We can ask him what's going to happen."

"I'll fetch him some orange wine," Anna-Marie said.

"We didn't know you were coming," Hester said to Sanon after everyone greeted him. "We would have made refreshments."

"I was on my way back from Nairn, and I thought I would stop by to say hello," Sanon said. "Is everyone well?"

"We were just talking about all of that nonsense brewing overseas," Claude said. "What are your thoughts on the matter?"

Sanon rolled his eyes. "I have never understood why men cannot solve disputes in a civilized manner," he said. "That German leader—he is of the devil, which makes him very dangerous. I fear that soon everyone will become involved, including us."

"I was afraid you were going to say that," Abraham said. "We're worried about our boys."

"With good reason," Sanon said.

"So you think we'll end up in the war?" Anna-Marie asked nervously, handing him the wine.

"I do," Sanon said. "The next few years may be very dark indeed. I have seen the signs."

"Will our boys be all right?" Hester asked.

"That, I can't tell you," Sanon said. "I can't say who will return from war and who will not. It is for God to decide."

"We wouldn't want to know that anyhow," Anna-Marie said. "Can you imagine knowing before they left that they wouldn't come back? That would be terrible."

"Yes, it would. Perhaps we should think about something else," Claude said, changing the subject. "I heard that the Freeport Company is bringing telephones to Plaquemines Parish."

"I don't understand how those things work. How can you talk to somebody who's not standing in front of you?" Abraham said.

"Some kind of wire that stretches from you to them, I hear. Apparently, the rest of the country already has them," Claude said.

"I find it hard to believe that I'll be able to talk to Papa in New Orleans from here," Anna-Marie said.

"The world is changing quickly," Sanon said. "We can get places quicker because of cars and now we don't have to visit to talk."

"I'm not sure I'm going to like that," Hester said. "What is life without visiting with folks?"

"It has a good side," Claude said. "Think about it. If something happens and we need Sanon, we can call him instead of going to get him. He'll get here faster."

"That is true," Sanon said. "It will be helpful in emergencies."

"And since I don't get to see Papa much, at least I can talk to him," Anna-Marie said.

"Be careful what you say," Abraham cautioned. "I heard that people all along that wire can hear what you say. I don't like other folks listening to my conversations."

"That's a good point," Claude said. "It's called a party line, although why they call it that is beyond me."

"I wonder what they'll think up next," Hester said.

"Who knows? It seems like every day they're coming up with a new gadget for this or that or a new way to do things. I don't know who has time in a day to spend thinking this stuff up," Abraham said.

"At this rate, they'll have us visiting the moon one day," Anna-Marie said.

"You may not be wrong," Sanon said. "If we came back one hundred years from now, we probably wouldn't recognize our own world. I see so much change in my visions. Change I don't understand."

"Well, if you can't understand, then there's not a shot we will," Abraham said.

"I don't understand why people don't just let things be," Anna-Marie said. "All this talk about progress, and what is it doing but mucking everything up?"

"That's true," Hester said. "Look what the oil companies and the spillway are doing to our oysters. Abraham was saying just the other day that the oysters are looking bad this year."

"I did say that," Abraham said. "They're smaller, and they don't look healthy. If things keep going like they are, I'll be out of a job."

"Don't worry, Abraham. We'll hire you," Anna-Marie said. "As long as we have the store, you'll never have to worry about a job."

"What if some newfangled invention replaces your store?" Abraham asked.

"Well, we survived Fremin's Grocery opening in Port Sulphur, so I think we'll be okay," Anna-Marie said, laughing. "Claude was worried we'd go out of business. And George Lincoln down in Nairn is still going strong, although he extends as much credit as we do from what I hear. He has to raise oranges to supplement his income and keep his store going. Personally, I think he just keeps that store open to help feed his friends."

"The same could be said about you and Claude," Hester said.

"You folks worry too much," Sanon said. "We've weathered so many storms together that I'm sure we'll be able to handle whatever comes to us in the future. Now I must go."

After everyone left, Anna-Marie and Claude stayed outside talking for a while longer.

"Time passes so quickly," Anna-Marie said. "It seems like just yesterday you and Abraham were going off to war, and now we might face that with our children."

"If it happens, I'll be able to give them guidance," Claude said.

"Oh, really?" Anna-Marie said. "I think I'll send them to Abraham for that talk. Didn't you get wounded in the war?"

"You're funny," Claude said, laughing as he reached out and gently pulled her hair.

"I like to think so," she said. "But seriously, what are we going to do if they go off to war?"

"We're going to pray. That's all we can do," Claude said.

In 1940, Claude Jr., Charlie, and Isaac voluntarily enlisted in the Army, each of them wanting to serve their country despite their mother's objections. When Pearl Harbor was bombed on December 7, 1941, Anna-Marie and Hester cried all day. They knew exactly what that meant. Their boys were going off to war and might never come home. Hester and Anna-Marie spent the next few years worrying every minute of every day.

When Germany surrendered on May 8, 1945 and then Japan on September 2, 1945 after atomic bombs eviscerated Hiroshima and Nagasaki, Anna-Marie and Hester shed tears of joy. Their sons had lived through a war that had cost approximately 60 million people their lives, including 407,000 American military casualties and 12,000 civilian casualties. When the war was over, all three boys returned physically unharmed, but the war had affected each of them differently. Isaac was quieter, more withdrawn. Claude Jr. had difficulty sleeping. Charlie joked about anything and everything, thinking if he laughed enough he would forget the horrors he had witnessed. Before long, Abraham and Claude began taking them out in the pirogue at night to whack muskrats.

World War II changed the world's dynamic, and the United States emerged as the leader of the free world. Cities across the country grew larger and became more populated.

Life on the river moved a little slower.

Abraham's father, Emmanuel, passed away in 1946, after suffering from a long illness and a broken heart. He had never been the same since Florence died. Hester often told Abraham that it seemed like he lived each day just to get through it. Abraham and Claude brought his body to Bohemia and buried him there, next to Florence. "What if somebody sees us?" Hester asked.

"I dare anyone to try to stop me," was Abraham's response.

No one did.

Claude's father, Charles, passed away the following year. By the time he died, he no longer recognized his son or his grandchildren, and it broke Claude's heart every time he saw him. Charles was buried in New Orleans next to his wife.

In 1948, progress made its way to the West Bank as the road that led from Belle Chasse to Homeplace was finally paved.

Miss Penny passed away in the summer of 1949. She had married Captain Henry two years after the 1927 flood, and they had spent twenty happy years together. When he took ill in the winter of 1951, it was Sanon who tended to him, and it was Sanon who found him dead in his bed holding a photograph of Miss Penny next to his heart.

Antoine Bertaut suffered a heart attack and passed away in 1954. He was buried in St. Louis Cemetery No. 2, located on Claiborne Avenue in New Orleans. A brass band accompanied him to his final resting place. Claude comforted Anna-Marie for the whole year it took for her to adjust to her life without her papa. After Antoine's death, Grace, aware of the effect her husband's death was having on her daughter, went out of her way to be nicer. She visited Anna-Marie once each month and resisted the urge to make disparaging remarks about Claude.

Madeleine and Jeanne had both married and moved to Slidell, Louisiana, on the North Shore of New Orleans. They married cousins, so both of their last names became Chastain. Madeleine gave Anna-Marie and Claude four grandchildren, and Jeanne gave them three. Claude Jr. married a nurse he met at Touro Infirmary in New Orleans where he served his residency. The couple had two children—a son named Claude Couvillion III and a daughter named Marie. Charlie, who now sold real estate in New Orleans, married a young lady from Plaquemines Parish whom he had met in high school. They, too, had two children. Grace spent much more time with her grandchildren than she had ever spent with her daughter. Anna-Marie appreciated the time Grace spent with them, and she and her *maman* became closer than they had ever been. They remained close until Grace's death in 1956.

Before she died, Grace gave Anna-Marie a gold and diamond watch that had been handed down from her mother. "Wear this always," she said, "and think of me kindly."

In 1956, Claude and Anna-Marie bought their first television. Although reception was sometimes poor, they soon learned that if they adjusted the antenna, the picture would more often than not come into focus. Abraham couldn't believe that someone could watch other people in their living room. Now instead of gathering on the porch each afternoon, sometimes when Hester and Abraham would visit Anna-Marie and Claude, they would watch television together. Abraham and Hester began saving and bought one for their home in 1957.

The 1950s brought more change to Plaquemines Parish in the form of rising racial tensions. African Americans were tiring of the inequities with which they contended on a daily basis. Leaders, such as Martin Luther King, Jr., began a Civil Rights Movement that would one day change the order of things in America. Isaac listened carefully to King's teachings and realized that he wanted to play a part in effecting this change. He had witnessed what his parents had gone through over the years, and he was angry about the unfairness of it. He decided that he would attend the newly opened law school at Southern University, and in 1957 at the age of forty, he earned his law degree. Hester and Abraham could not have been more proud.

"Who would have thought?" Hester told Abraham. "Our son. A bona fide lawyer. I would have never believed it if I didn't watch him graduate and see his degree for myself."

"That was the proudest moment of my life," Abraham said. "When he graduated from college before the war, I was proud, too. Remember, Hester? We couldn't read or write until we were grown, and now our son is a lawyer. Things are changing again, but this time in a good manner."

"They won't change that much around here," Hester said. "Not if that Leonus has anything to say about it. He's squashing any talk about us having equal rights, even throwing people who speak up in jail. You should warn Isaac that he needs to be careful."

"Isaac's smart. He knows how to handle himself."

"I'm telling you it don't matter how smart he is. If the judge gets wind of Isaac raising a stink around here, he'll find himself at Fort St. Phillip in no time."

"Well, he's a lawyer now, so he'll know how to get out," Abraham said, smiling at his wife. Hester just glared at him.

At the house next door, a similar conversation was taking place.

"I'm so proud of Isaac," Anna-Marie said to Claude. "He really wants to change things, and I pray he's successful."

"He is certainly determined," Claude said. "I'm proud of him, too."

Isaac would spend the next decade immersed in the fight to create equality between blacks and whites. He orchestrated peaceful demonstrations and clandestinely spoke at small gatherings of people in Plaquemines Parish when he was in town. Leonus Lozano was equally fervent in his opposition to civil rights for African Americans. His antics during this time were so outrageous that, in 1962, he was excommunicated from the Catholic Church.

Meanwhile, the Orleans Levee District continued to invent new and better ways to protect New Orleans from floods. By 1954, the district had made so much money from oil revenues that the Senate passed a bill reducing taxes the Orleans Levee District collected from five mills to three and-a-half mills. In 1962, the millage was again reduced to two-and-a-half mills. By 1962, reports concluded that the board had collected approximately $15 million in royalties, which would equal roughly $147 million in 2023. Whenever reports on the oil revenues would appear in the newspaper or on television, the former residents of Bohemia would become angry all over again. That feeling of being robbed never went away. Everyone knew things should have been different for them, and each time they witnessed the poverty in their parish or struggled to pay a bill, those old feelings resurfaced.

In 1965, devastation visited once again in the form of Hurricane Betsy on September 10. Betsy made landfall at Grand Isle as a Category 4 hurricane packing 140-mile-per-hour winds. The storm breached levees in New Orleans, and parts of the lower Ninth Ward were inundated. Almost every town below Empire—Buras, Triumph, Fort Jackson, Boothville, Venice, and Tidewater—was decimated. Coffins were dislodged from their underground homes and floated on the water. The roads, paved only years before, peeled up like tar paper. Months later, when the folks in Plaquemines Parish were allowed to return, they did what they always did after a major hurricane. They rolled ups their sleeves, cleaned the mold from their homes, repaired the damage, and rebuilt their lives. Once again, Homeplace was spared from major damage, but some oil companies and other industries moved out of Plaquemines Parish, deciding it was too risky to do business there.

At times during the sixties, Anna-Marie and Claude and Hester and Abraham had difficulty adjusting to their changing world— the Civil Rights protests, President John F. Kennedy's assassination, the Beatles invasion in 1964, the beginning of the Vietnam War, the hippie revolution, drug usage by America's children, and the assassination of Martin Luther King Jr. in 1968. They watched it all on their televisions and then discussed it on their front porches with the Pelitires, Captain Richard, and Sanon.

Captain Richard passed away in early March of 1969. He had pushed barges up and down the river well into his later years. After he retired, he spent the rest of his life traveling with his wife, Alice. Together, they explored the country and even traveled to Europe a few times, but he always enjoyed coming back to the river he loved. As his family and friends watched from the shore, the wind scattered Captain Richard's ashes down the river.

On March 19, 1969, Leonus Lozano passed away, his death marking the end of an era for the residents of Plaquemines Parish, who would never again be subjected to such an uncompromising leader. Abraham and Claude agreed that his passing was not a great cause for sorrow, and they did not attend his funeral.

Four months later, on July 20, Hester and Abraham, Anna-Marie and Claude, and Sanon sat in front of the television at Claude's house and watched something they never dreamed would happen, something Anna-Marie had jokingly predicted years before—Neil Armstrong took man's first step on the moon, describing it as "magnificent desolation." They watched in awe, along with about a half-billion people around the world, as Armstrong stepped down from the lunar module and made a statement that still resonates. "That's one small step for man, one giant leap for mankind."

Sanon was mesmerized by the video of the moon's surface. "It's not so mysterious after all, now is it?" he commented.

"Sure it is," Hester said. "Remember, we can only see the surface. No one knows what's going on beneath it."

Somehow the moon landing signified to each of them that even in the darkest of times, mankind could accomplish incredible feats.

In August of that year, Hurricane Camille, the second-strongest hurricane to ever make landfall in the United States, slammed into Buras in Plaquemines Parish and then into the Gulf Coast near Waveland, Mississippi, with winds of 160 miles per hour. From Venice to Port Sulphur homes were washed away or damaged to the point that reconstruction would be impossible. New Orleans experienced more flooding than ever before. All along the rivers and bayous in South Louisiana, boats and ships were sunk or sitting askew on land far from their original location. Abraham was devastated when, weeks later, he found *The Pearl* in the marsh in Bohemia, her bow broken in two. He carefully salvaged her intact wood and recreated her on a much smaller scale. After the storm, again Plaquemines Parish was closed to outsiders for months while utilities and roads were repaired.

Camille seemed like a fitting end to the 1960s. "Perhaps she blew away all the bad mojo that seems to hang over this place," Sanon said to Abraham as they surveyed the damage.

"I sure hope so. I'm tired," Abraham said.

"We're all tired, but what can we do? This is our home," Sanon responded.

"True," Claude said. "But we're getting a little old for all this physical work. Not a lot I can do nowadays. Good thing we have sons."

"I've already called Isaac," Abraham said. "He said he'd pick up Charlie and Claude Jr. on his way. They'll be here tomorrow."

"I hope they're planning to stay a while," Sanon said.

"I'm sure they'll be here as much as they can," Claude said.

The seventies wrought even more political upheaval in the form of Watergate and the Vietnam War. Amid Richard Nixon's resignation and demonstrations against Vietnam, the country's prestige suffered. In Plaquemines Parish, that decade created a change in the demographic as Vietnamese refugees began to arrive in the United States, and like so many before them, the Vietnamese scattered down the river. The government did everything it could to provide resources for the refugees, who brought with them a strong work ethic and even stronger family values. They adapted well to life in Plaquemines Parish and soon became successful shrimpers and commercial fishermen, introducing new ways to catch and cook seafood.

In 1980, Anna-Marie and Claude made the difficult decision to sell the general store. Claude had suffered a stroke in 1974 and was now confined to a wheelchair. It simply became too hard to try to manage it, even with the help of cashiers they hired.

"I feel like I'm giving up on my father's legacy," Claude said the day before they signed the act of sale.

"That's nonsense," Anna-Marie said. "You've served his legacy well. He was very proud of you."

"I wish at least one of our children would have stayed here to take over for us."

"They have their own lives, and that's as it should be. They're all happy. We really couldn't ask for more," Anna-Marie said. "Besides, people are driving to New Orleans to shop at Schwegmann's now. We're doing the right thing, Claude. It's too much for us at our age. We can retire, and we won't have to worry about finances now."

"I'm sure you're right, but this still hurts."

"I know, but just think about all the things we'll be able to do now."

Claude, sitting in his wheelchair, laughed out loud. "We can barely get around, woman. What are we going to do?"

"We're going to sit on our porch with Abraham and Hester and watch the ships go by. That's what we're going to do. And we're going to enjoy every minute of it."

For the next four years, that's exactly what they did.

By 1984, most of the folks who had once lived in Bohemia were long gone, but some of their children, Isaac included, had not forgotten what had had happened to their parents sixty years before.

CHAPTER 46

July 1984

Anna-Marie, satisfied that her gumbo was perfect, walked out onto the porch to greet Isaac. She couldn't wait to hear his news.

"Your mama says you're being very mysterious," she said.

Isaac grinned and gave her a hug. "Not mysterious, Miss Anna-Marie. I just have news that I'd like to share with everyone at once."

"Well, I can't wait to hear what it is," Claude said. "Anna-Marie has been talking about nothing else."

"That's not true," Anna-Marie said, swatting at him with her cane.

"It's true," Claude whispered to Isaac.

A few minutes later, Abraham and Hester walked over. Anna-Marie and Claude gave them a few minutes to visit with their son until Hester came inside and said that Sanon had arrived. Anna-Marie placed glasses of iced tea onto a tray, and Hester helped her carry it outside. Claude followed in his wheelchair.

"It sure is getting harder to walk up these stairs," Sanon said, his cane wobbling as he slowly navigated each one.

"Abraham, give him a hand," Hester said, worried that he would fall.

Abraham looked at her like she was crazy. "What am I gonna do? I can picture both of us splattered on the ground after we make each other fall."

Claude struggled to get up from his wheelchair. "I'll help him," he said.

Abraham burst out laughing. "What are you gonna do?"

"I'm going to help him get up here. That's what I'm gonna do," Claude said.

"Mr. Claude, I'll help him," Isaac said, jumping up from his chair and hurrying to the stairs.

"Thank you, son," Claude said, sitting back down and rolling to his

329

usual spot on the porch where he and his best friends had been visiting, gossiping, and solving their problems for so many years. Over the decades, he and Anna-Marie had made many changes to their antebellum-style home, expanding it little by little after each flood or hurricane. Now, with the children gone, it was much too big for them, but Anna-Marie did her best to keep it up. The front porch, though, had never changed. They left it as it had always been because their memories lived and breathed on that porch. From there, they had watched the world go by with their friends.

"Yes, thank you," Sanon said, once he was safely seated. "Why did you want to meet with us, Isaac?"

"I have news," Isaac said.

"Good news, I hope," Anna-Marie said.

"Yes, don't you be calling us together to bring us bad news," Hester said. "We've had enough of that."

"It's very good news, Mama," Isaac said.

"Well, go on, son. Tell us. It's almost time for my nap," Abraham said. Claude and Sanon nodded their heads in agreement.

"I'll get right to it then," Isaac said, standing up. "This morning, the Louisiana Legislature passed a new act. The governor hasn't signed off yet, but he will soon."

Claude interrupted him. "They're always coming up with new acts and laws, always butting into our business. So what have they done now?"

"They've ordered that the land in Bohemia be returned to its rightful owners," Isaac announced. "As you know, they've been debating the issue for years, but they never saw fit to do anything about it. This morning that changed."

For a few moments, no one said a word. They just stared at Isaac, who was grinning from ear to ear.

Then they all spoke at once.

"No, they didn't," Hester said.

"Are you serious?" asked Abraham.

"This can't be true," Claude said.

"Repeat what you just said, please," Anna-Marie said.

"I had a feeling the tide had turned," Sanon said.

Isaac repeated his announcement. "You're getting your land back.

It's true, I swear. You know how, since 1981, they've been investigating whether the land was taken legally?"

"Yes," Abraham said. "We are aware, but we didn't expect anything to come of that."

"Well, apparently the Natural Resources Committee took this task seriously, but in the end, they decided that it was illegal for the levee board to take your land. That started a chain of events that has been leading to this moment. Remember two years ago Representative Frank Patti tried again, but it failed again. Then last year, they did that constitutional amendment that said the state had to return land when it no longer served a purpose to the state. Everyone knows the spillway hasn't been used for years. I mean, that's obvious if you take a boat to Bohemia. It's a mess. Well, Representative Patti and Senator Sammy Nunez sponsored a new bill stating that the purpose for the spillway no longer exists."

"We know this," Abraham said. "What happened today that changes any of this?"

"They voted this very morning." He pulled a stack of papers from his briefcase. "Sammy Nunez gave me this and permission to show it to you. The governor hasn't signed off on it yet, but he will soon. I didn't want to tell you about it before in case it didn't pass."

"Read it aloud so everyone can hear," Abraham said. "I want to hear every word."

"I'll skip over some of the mumbo jumbo and get to the pertinent part," Isaac said and then he began reading:

Act No. 233. An act to declare that the public and necessary purpose which may have originally supported the expropriation of certain property in the parish of Plaquemines for the construction of a spillway, known as the Bohemia Spillway, has ceased to exist, to order the return of certain property, including mineral rights, acquired therefor by expropriation or purchased under threat of expropriation, under certain terms, conditions, and procedures, and subject to certain rights, and otherwise to provide with respect thereto.

The Legislature of Louisiana hereby declares that the public and necessary purpose set forth in Act No. 99 of 1924, which may have originally supported the expropriation of property, or any right of ownership thereto, on the east bank of the Mississippi River in the parish of Plaquemines for the construction of a spillway, known as the Bohemia Spillway, has ceased to exist insofar as it ever may have affected the ownership of property, including mineral rights. The Legislature of Louisiana hereby orders the Board of Levee Commissioners of the Orleans Levee District, the board, to return the ownership of said property to the owners or their successors from whom the property was acquired by expropriation or by purchase under threat of expropriation. Neither the provisions of this Act nor any actions pursuant to this Act shall affect the title to land which was the subject of litigation on the effective date of this Act.

"It goes on to establish the rules about returning the land," Isaac said, skipping over Section 2, and then he continued:

Section 3. The Board of Levee Commissioners of the Orleans Levee District shall provide a thorough accounting to the secretary of the Department of Natural Resources, or his designee, concerning all revenues received from the affected property. The information so provided shall be made available to applicants. The board shall comply with the spirit and letter of the rules and regulations adopted and promulgated by the secretary of the Department of Natural Resources.

Section 4. The secretary of the Department of Natural Resources shall begin steps by January 1, 1985, to notify affected persons.

Section 5. The return of property by the board to the owners or their successors shall be subject to all servitudes and rights-of-way, whether acquired by expropriation or otherwise, or surface or mineral leases, or other valid contracts executed by or with the board prior to the effective date of this Act. Any deed whereby any property is returned shall state that such property is subject to such rights.

"There's more, but you get the gist," Isaac said, handing the papers to his father.

"We're really getting our land back?" Hester said, tears streaming down her face.

"Yes, Mama. You're going to get your land back. There's an application process you'll have to go through, but you will get your land back." Isaac leaned over and hugged Hester, his shoulder muffling the sound of her crying.

Anna-Marie hugged Claude. She was crying as hard as Hester.

Then she helped Claude up, and they all hugged each other.

"If I were a little younger, I'd be doing a dance across this porch," Abraham said. "Did I hear you say that the mineral rights are ours, too?"

"Yes, you heard that correctly," Isaac said.

"You mean we're going to be rich?" Hester asked.

"I don't know about that, Mama. There are a few wells over there that are still operational, but most of the oil is coming from the Gulf now."

"We should have been rich for the last fifty years," Sanon said, " but we can't dwell on that anymore. We can go home if we want even if the only way to get there now is by boat."

"I can't wait to tell the kids," Anna-Marie said. "They're not going to believe this. Oh, and we have to tell Peter Pelitire and Christina. I'll go call them and tell them to come over."

"I just can't believe it," Hester repeated. "Did you know this was going to happen?" she asked Sanon.

"I knew something was changing," Sanon said. "There will be three blood moons this year. That's highly unusual. Sometimes, when things come in threes, the natural order of things is restored and bad fortunes are reversed."

"Just having our land back will be good fortune, indeed," Abraham said. "I can't believe it took sixty years."

A half hour later, the Pelitires arrived, and Hester asked Isaac to read the act to them. After listening carefully to every word, Peter had to sit down. Like Hester and Anna-Marie, he couldn't control the river of tears that ran down his face. Christina stroked his hair, struggling to control her own emotions.

"It's like the weight of the world just lifted from my shoulders," he said. "This thing has been lingering for so long. Finally. Finally, I can believe there might be some justice in this world."

"I think Benjamin Franklin said it best," Isaac said. "He said, 'Justice will not be served until those who are unaffected are as outraged as those who are.'"

CHAPTER 47

1985-1987

With the passing of Act 233, everyone who had been affected by the Bohemia Spillway mistakenly assumed that their land would be returned to them immediately, but in Louisiana's political climate, nothing happens quickly or easily. The Orleans Levee District filed suit contending that the act was unconstitutional. Members of the board panicked. They had no idea how they would continue operations without the revenues from oil production in Plaquemines Parish upon which they had depended for decades. Act 233 was eventually declared unconstitutional by a 19th Judicial Court judge in Baton Rouge, but the Louisiana Supreme Court overturned that decision.

In 1985, the Legislature passed Act 819, which directed that the certification of the heirs to the land be completed.

The certification process was laborious and took years to complete. Claimants had to prove that they were indeed heirs of the original owners and the original titles to the land had to be found. In South Louisiana, important papers like titles and birth certificates routinely disappear or are ruined during hurricanes and floods. Sixty years of nature's fury left many heirs without a paper trail. Even the application was difficult for many people, including the educated, to fill out. All questions had to be answered, and many of the answers were unknown. Family trees had to be submitted to the committee overseeing the process.

On December 15, 1988, members of the Tabony family wrote a letter to the committee that exemplified the difficulty people were having with the application process:

Dear Mr. Poret,

*Thank you very much for your letter and enclosures of 28ᵗʰ Nov., for which
I enclose postage. I am unable to enclose the application form in this letter, as
I am not quite sure how to answer questions 4, 6, 7, (Judgement of possession)
and 8 (Certified copies of Plaquemines Parish Clerk of Court records) due to
the following:*

*It appears that in 1925, no one knew of my grandfather's existence (please
see tree.)*

*Joseph H. Tabony and Mathilde Bayhi settled at the Bohemia Plantation
and had two sons, Francois and Anselme.*

*In 1846, Anselme's wife Augusta, expecting a baby, left her son Joseph
Henry with his father whilst she made the journey to England, possibly to see
her ailing parents. During the voyage, Alfred Charles was born. Should you
have time to read them, the enclosed letters are from her.*

The letter was signed Jeanette and Roy Tabony, who were cousins, and
the letter was sent from Kent, England. Included were letters from family
members dating back to 1882. The Tabony family had purchased Bohemia
Plantation in 1925 from Reuther Seed Company in New Orleans and had
owned it for decades. They were so well established on the east bank of the
river that Tabony Road is still there to this day.

By the time all claims were received, there were approximately 50,000
applicants. The sheer volume of people staking claims overwhelmed the
committee charged with processing them, and the waiting continued.

Isaac handled the application process for his parents and for Anna-
Marie and Claude. As one year and then another passed, Isaac reassured
them that their land would eventually be returned to them.

"I don't think we'll ever get to live on our land again," Hester said to
Abraham one evening in March of 1986 as they looked out over the Delta.

"You may be right, but who knows? Isaac said things are progressing."
Abraham responded, reaching for her hand.

"I hope so. I fear we don't have much longer," Hester said.

Abraham let out a deep sigh. "I know. You're right about that."

And she was. Hester passed away a few weeks later. Abraham woke
up one morning in June and reached for her hand. It was cold. Before he

even looked at her, he knew she was gone. He kissed her forehead and then gently caressed her cheek as sobs wracked his body.

When he could bear to leave her side, Abraham called Isaac.

Then he walked over to Claude and Anna-Marie's house. Claude knew the minute he saw Abraham's face what had happened. So did Anna-Marie. She escorted him inside and handed him a stiff glass of whiskey. They all sat there for a while, mostly silent, comforting each other just by being together. Then they all walked back to Abraham's house and said their good-byes.

Isaac buried Hester on her land in Bohemia next to her parents and her brother.

"She's at peace now," Abraham said, helping Isaac shovel dirt over her casket as best he could. "She's finally home."

When he was finished, Abraham placed Hester's rock—the one Sanon had made for her so many years before—on her grave.

Anna-Marie and Claude did everything they could to comfort Abraham, but he was lost without the woman he had rescued from a hurricane and lived with for almost seventy years. Abraham died two months after Hester. Somehow he managed to climb into *The Pearl*, which had sat behind their house for years, and that's where Anna-Marie found him, still holding the tiller.

Isaac reunited his father and mother, burying Abraham beside Hester, while Claude and Anna-Marie stood there watching.

Heartbroken.

After Abraham and Hester passed away, Anna-Marie and Claude lost some of their spark. Their friends had been their family. They had lived side by side for so many decades. They had lost a valuable piece of themselves, and they didn't quite know how to go on without them. Their children and grandchildren visited, which they enjoyed, but on those evenings when they sat on the porch by themselves, the loneliness crept in, and they spent most of their time talking about Hester and Abraham.

"You remember how Abraham saved my life in the war?" Claude would say.

Anna-Marie always nodded. "But tell me again," and Claude would tell her again.

"Remember when Mildred used to come in the store, and she was so ugly about Hester?" Anna-Marie would say, and Claude would always laugh.

"I do. Remember that time I sent her on her way?"

Anna-Marie would laugh. "Those were such good times when we had the store across the river."

Claude always agreed. "I remember when you told me I was going to marry you. I'm so glad you did. You've been the greatest blessing of my life."

"And you of mine," Anna-Marie always said. Then she would lean over to kiss him.

Claude passed away in October of 1987 when the air was beginning to cool and migrating birds from the north were starting to fly into the marsh. Anna-Marie found him slumped over in his wheelchair on their front porch in his usual spot. She sat there with him for a long time, just holding his hand and talking to him like she always had. She thanked him for the love he had shown her for so many years. She told him how much she loved and admired him. She told him how hard it was going to be to face each day without him. Then she called Claude Jr.

At Claude's funeral service, Sanon, from his own wheelchair, spoke about the man he had come to know, the man who had accepted him despite their differences, the man who had helped build his home after they moved across the river.

Peter Pelitire shared stories about how Claude had helped him survive over the years, how he and Abraham had taught him how to build houses and fix things. He spoke about Claude's character and the love he had for his family and friends.

The funeral was attended by mostly family because Claude had outlived most of his friends, but the family that he and Anna-Marie had created was extensive now—four children, eleven grandchildren, and nineteen great-grandchildren.

After the service, Anna-Marie stood by Claude's casket for a long while. She didn't want to leave him. Finally, Madeleine walked up to her. "It's time to go, Mama," she said, placing her arm around her mother's waist.

Anna-Marie leaned over and touched her husband's hand for the last time, and then she walked out of the church with her daughter.

She buried Claude next to where their house had once stood in Bohemia. As she watched his casket being lowered into the land that he loved, she assured him that one day she would join him there.

"And when I do, I'll be holding the deed to this land," she promised.

CHAPTER 48

Because of the massive number of claims submitted, it had become impossible to sort and track them with the limited number of people who had been tasked with the job. Finally, a special master was appointed to oversee the process. Plaquemines Parish donated the office space necessary for him to do his job in a government building in Belle Chasse. The special master reviewed the claims that had merit and investigated them further before he recommended whether they should be approved or denied. The cost to submit an application was $175 per tract of land owned, a sum that was more than some of the owners had been paid for smaller tracts.

By 1988, most of the land had been transferred to the families of the original landowners in Bohemia, but no one had received a dime of oil revenues. While drilling had slowed tremendously in the area, there were still some active oil wells. Some people received titles to land that was no longer in its original location because the property lines had been shifted through the years.

A series of lawsuits were filed against the Orleans Levee District. Some plaintiffs wanted the levee board to pay royalties dating back to the 1930s when the levee board began receiving them. Those lawsuits were quickly thrown out of court.

However, in February of 1988 a class action lawsuit filed by Haspel & Davis Planting and Milling Co. Ltd., Jean Mayer Connell, Joseph Jean Torre, Sr., Bohemia Planting Co. Inc., Leonie Davis Rothschild, and Arthur Q. Davis had merit. They sued for "payment of revenues from the Bohemia Spillway from 1984 until the time their property was transferred to them by the Levee Board."

They did not win their original lawsuit, but the court reversed on appeal and determined that they were entitled to the mineral rights and any royalties that stemmed from those rights from June 29, 1984—the date that Act 233 went into effect—to the present day.

Still, the levee board did not pay the landowners, and the lawsuit would continue to be litigated for twelve long years.

The special master's job would last until 1992 when the last of the verified heirs finally received title to their land. His office collected approximately $240,000 in deposits from applicants and billed another $88,381 to indigent applicants whose claims were successful.

In 1994, H. Baylor Lansden, managing director of the levee board, certified that "the granting of the injunctive order sought by the petitioners would require the expenditure of funds such that a deficit in the financial obligations of the levee board would be created." Simply stated, the levee board did not have the money to pay.

In October of 1996, the 25th Judicial District in Plaquemines Parish held that claimants were to be paid royalties from the date they acquired title to the land after the levee board returned it. The 4th Circuit Court of Appeal overturned this decision. By 1996, the levee board owed the titleholders in Bohemia almost $24 million.

In 1997, the board came up with a new demand in court filings, claiming that the Department of Natural Resources and its own board's transfer of the land back to the original owners or their descendants had not been legally transferred because no one had determined whether the land had been expropriated or if it had been sold under the threat of expropriation. The levee board could no longer spend money the way it had in the past, and board members wanted that land back. The board lost that fight.

Act 1364 of 1997 put an exclamation point on that defeat. The Louisiana Legislature agreed that the landowners should be paid royalties owed plus interest from the date of the passage of Act 233.

In January of 1998, the court dismissed all claims made by the levee board with prejudice, ruling that, "As a matter of law, upon the passage of Act 99 of 1924, any purchase the Levee Board made in the Spillway was made under threat of expropriation."

The levee board appealed that ruling and lost.

By the time a settlement was reached between the claimants and the levee board, a new millennium had begun, and the levee board had spent more than $3 million to hold on to its earnings. The levee board finally agreed to pay the descendants of the landowners $2.3 million dollars, with another payment of $18.7 million dollars to be paid in yearly installments of $2.6 million if the levee board earned that amount in royalties. Included in the settlement was an agreement that if the levee board did not pay the full yearly amounts due, the descendants of the landowners would be immediately entitled to the full amount that had been deferred. The court issued a consent judgment to that effect.

When the initial payments were split between the many landowners and businesses involved in the lawsuit, that $2.3 million didn't go far. Between 2000 and 2006, the claimants received only a small portion of the agreed upon payments, and only a few of the original landowners were alive to receive a dime. It was as Sanon had once predicted—they had won and they had lost at the same time.

In 2006, Haspel & Davis, et al, filed a lawsuit in federal court in an attempt to force the board to pay them, claiming that the levee board had violated the "Takings Clause" and had taken their land in an unconstitutional manner. The landowners won again. The court ruled that the levee board owed them $17.4 million dollars, plus interest and attorney's fees, payable immediately.

What followed was a series of appeals and motions and judgments that went back and forth through the courts, resulting in legislation (Act 1 and Act 23 of 2006) that stripped the levee board of its power and created a new Board of Commissioners for the Southeast Louisiana Flood Protection Authority-East and the Southeast Louisiana Flood Protection Authority-West to oversee flood control and levee building and maintenance. The Acts further stated that the Orleans Levee District's assets that were not flood-control assets would be managed by the state as of January 1, 2007.

In the end, the levee board prevailed. The 2006 decision was reversed, and the levee board did not have to pay the $17.4 million dollars immediately.

By 2023, the levee board had paid $10 million dollars to the rightful heirs of the people of Bohemia of the $220 million the land had generated. Of that, Haspel & Davis, which owned more land than anyone around the salt dome in Nestor, was paid $2.2 million. The rest was split between the petitioners involved in the lawsuit. Haspel & Davis and the Haspel family received the titles to some of their properties, but not all of them.

Those people who could not make it past the application process—some simply because they could not afford the fees associated with the process and others because they could not prove relationships—did not receive anything, and the levee board still holds the titles to those properties.

Bohemia will never become home to the descendants of the people who once created thriving communities there. Today, it is accessible only by boat. And every year when the river gets too high, Bohemia floods.

A few miles below Pointe á la Hache on Highway 15 near where Bohemia Plantation once stood, a cattle gate stretches across the road, preventing landowners or sightseers from driving any further. To the left, an old rusty white sign standing on metal posts reads, "Property of Exxon Company, U.S.A. Possession of alcohol, narcotics, firearms, explosives, weapons, hazardous substances, or articles without proper authorization is not permitted on Exxon premises." The sign contains additional warnings that state that any person entering the premises is subject to be searched, but that part is rusty and much of it unreadable.

The spillway sits abandoned with only a few hunting camps and cemeteries whose tombstones are almost completely buried in silt to remind those who walk along the levee that this was once a bustling area of Plaquemines Parish.

The levees that remain are overgrown and sinking, victims of neglect, floods, and hurricanes.

What remained in Bohemia after everyone moved has been washed way.

The actions of the Orleans Levee District in 1924 killed population and economic growth in one quarter of Plaquemines Parish for the next one hundred years, including losses in the form of oil revenue, hunting, trapping, fishing, and agriculture.

In 2005, Hurricane Katrina devastated Plaquemines Parish on both sides of the river. Bohemia Plantation, the last remaining landmark in the area, suffered catastrophic damage, and it, too, is gone now.

The oyster industry has suffered tremendously over the years, but when British Petroleum's Deepwater Horizon spilled 4.9 million barrels into the Gulf in 2010, the seafood industry shut down completely for several years. Even today, those who fish oysters in the area report that the oyster population is only thirty percent of what it once was.

No one really knows what happened to Sanon. He just disappeared into the marsh one day and was never seen again. Peter Pelitire swore it happened on a blood moon. That's what he told Anna-Marie when he visited her back in 1988 at Madeleine's home. The Mulattos who remain on the West Bank sometimes sit outside at night when the moon is high and listen for his voice to whisper to them on the breeze.

After Claude passed away, Anna-Marie initially refused to leave the home she shared with him. He was in that house—his clothes, his books, his favorite chair—but as time went on, Anna-Marie found that living there alone, without her husband, was unbearable. She tried, but each night as dusk settled in, she would sit on their front porch alone, staring at the stars, and Claude's absence became overwhelming. She would remember the laughter and the talks they had sitting next to each other. She would remember her tears and how he had always been there for her, through thick and thin. Those memories made her laugh and cry, sometimes at the same time.

Finally, after one year when she could take it no more, she called Madeleine and asked her daughter to come get her.

Anna-Marie lived her final year surrounded by her children and her grandchildren who went out of their way to keep her entertained. She laughed a lot during that year, especially at the antics of her great-grandchildren, but she soon began to look forward to the day when she and Claude would be together again. She had not felt whole since his passing.

In October of 1989, two days before the second anniversary of Claude's death, at the age of ninety-three, Anna-Marie went to join her husband. While her family mourned her loss, everyone knew she was right where she wanted to be. Claude Jr. talked at length about that in her eulogy, which depicted the love his parents had shared.

Anna-Marie had been witness to a world that had changed faster than any other time in history. She had lived without electricity and indoor plumbing, without automobiles, televisions, telephones, or refrigerators. She had sent her husband off to fight for their country, and then her sons. She had lived before desegregation in a world she couldn't understand, and she had cheered louder than anyone when her African American friends were accorded the same rights she enjoyed. She had watched man walk on the moon for the first time.

She had been forced to move and rebuild and then rebuild again over and over through the years. Her life had not been easy by any stretch of the imagination, but she had lived it with optimism, strength, and a sense of humor that had always pulled her and everyone around her through any circumstance. Hers had been a life well lived.

Two weeks before Anna-Marie passed away, Isaac came to visit. He sat down beside her wheelchair and placed an envelope in her hand.

"What is this?" she asked, her voice frail and tired, her hand trembling.

"Open it," Isaac said, smiling.

He watched her face as realization dawned, savoring this moment.

Anna-Marie reached for his hand and held it in hers. "Thank you, Isaac. Thank you. I can go home now."

After her funeral, Anna-Marie's family boarded a boat and brought her back to Bohemia.

She lies there still, peacefully nestled in her beloved land next to the man she chose for herself so long ago.

Tucked beneath her folded hands is the document Isaac gave her—the deed she promised Claude she would bring to him.

HISTORICAL NOTE

Charles Ballay, district attorney for Plaquemines Parish, grew up in Homeplace, Louisiana, where he heard stories about the Bohemia Spillway for as long as he can remember. He always knew this was a story that needed to be shared. Even today, when the spillway is mentioned in his parish, older folks still shake their heads. No one who lives along the Mississippi River has forgotten what happened there one hundred years ago. They are living witnesses to the desolation, the destruction, the barren landscape left behind, where once existed a thriving, diverse culture of people who lived off the bayous and the crops they grew. There is much to be learned from these people—strength, tolerance, courage, adaptability, and endurance—despite whatever the New Orleans Levee District or Mother Nature inflicted upon them.

This book is a work of historical fiction, rooted in the actual story of the Bohemia Spillway. Outside of our main characters, the names mentioned with regard to land ownership, the number of arpents each person or business owned, and the amounts for which they optioned their land under threat of expropriation are real and were gleaned from a report the Real Estate Committee gave to the Board of Levee Commissioners for the Orleans Levee District on April 20, 1925.

Some true-to-life characters, such as Huey Long, are portrayed, but the dialog between these characters is fiction.

Charles Ballay (mentioned in Chapter 27) was the great-uncle and Ben and Suzanne Ballay (mentioned in Chapter 34) were the grandparents of the coauthor of this novel. George Lincoln, (mentioned in Chapters 29 and 45) was the grandfather of Plaquemines Parish Historian Roderick Lincoln.

While the main characters represent what life was like in the early 1920s on the East Bank and then the West Bank of the river, they are a work of fiction—a compilation of the stories shared with us by the gracious people who grew up in Plaquemines Parish—many in their eighties—whom we interviewed in the course of writing this book.

With that said, much of this story is true:

- The traditions and day-to-day activities
- The 1915 hurricane and the destruction it wrought
- The 1922 flood
- The creation of the Bohemia Spillway so far south of New Orleans and the expropriation of the land in the spillway area
- The 1927 flood and the dynamiting of the levee at Caernarvon
- The Bonnet Carré Spillway
- Reports on oil leases and how the Board of Commissioners of the Orleans Levee District spent the many millions they made
- Descriptions of how the Orleans Levee District fought to keep the Bohemia Spillway land, the oil leases, and the money it made away from the rightful owners
- The numerous lawsuits surrounding the Bohemia Spillway that were filed by various entities, including the lawsuits that finally gave the people in lower Plaquemines Parish their land back and a long overdue victory even though they have not realized the full scope of the monies they are owed

In November 2023, the East Bank Levee Authority agreed in a memorandum of understanding to give the struggling New Orleans Lakefront Management Authority (LMA) $150,000 and all future oil revenues earned from the remaining land it owns in the Bohemia Spillway area beginning January 1, 2024, unless the LMA experiences a surplus in any given year. In the event of a surplus, the overages would be returned to the East Bank Levee Authority.

ACT NO. 99

Senate Bill No. 226   By: By Mr. P. H. Gilbert, Substitute for Senate Bill No. 180, by AIr. P. H. Gilbert.

AN ACT

To authorize the Board of Levee Commissioners of the Orleans Levee District, in order to reduce flood levels and to better protect from overflow by high water of the Mississippi River the City of New Orleans; to create in the Parish of Plaquemines a spillway or waste wier, or other means to that end: to authorize said board to acquire by expropriation the necessary property for such purpose, and to contract with the Board of Commissioners for the Grand Prairie Levee District and the Board of Commissioners for the Plaquemines Parish East Bank Levee District to pay and retire the bonds and other indebtedness of said levee districts; to remove the levees in the area affected by the work contemplated; to provide the necessary funds therefor, and to repeal all laws in conflict herewith. Notice of the intention to introduce this act has been published in the localities where the matters or things affected are situated, all in the manner required by Section 6 of Article IV of the Constitution of the State, and evidence thereof has been exhibited to the Legislature.

Section 1. Be it enacted by the Legislature of Louisiana, That the Board of Levee Commissioners of the Orleans Levee District be and it is hereby authorized in its discretion in order to reduce the flood levels of the Mississippi River and to better protect the City of New Orleans from danger of overflow by the high waters of the Mississippi River, to construct or cause to be constructed on the east bank of the Mississippi River in the Parish of Plaquemines a spill way or waste wier, or other works, so located and designed according to plans and specifications as shall have been approved by the State Board of Engineers and the Mississippi River Commission.

Section 2. That the Board of Levee Commissioners of Orleans Levee District be and it is hereby authorized to acquire by purchase, donation or expropriation the lands or other property necessary for the construction of such works. It shall also be authorized to receive and expend for said purpose any funds contributed to it by the United States Government or any of the Levee Districts of the State benefitted by said works, which said Levee Districts be and they are hereby authorized to make such appropriations for that purpose as to them seem meet and proper.

Section 3. The Orleans Levee District is hereby required, as a condition precedent to removing any levees or taking possession of private property or any property, to acquire by purchase or expropriation and to pay for all lands and property privately owned within the area covered by the proposed plan from the. upper to the lower limits thereof and from the Mississippi River to the sea.

Section 4. That the State Board of Engineers be and it is of hereby directed to cooperate with the said Board of Levee Commissioners of the Orleans Levee District in the preparation of the necessary plans and the construction of the necessary works. The cost thereof to be paid by the Orleans Levee District.

Section 5. That the Board of Levee Commissioners for the Orleans Levee Districts be and is hereby authorized and directed to arrange with the Board of Commissioners for the Grand Prairie Levee District and the Board of Commissioners for the Plaquemines Parish East Bank Levee District whereby the bonded and other indebtedness of said two levee districts, as to the area to be affected by the proposed works, shall be acquired by sail [sic] Orleans Levee District, be paid for by it, at values as of June 17, 1924, and cancelled: and said two levee districts be and they are hereby authorized, upon the completion of the plans and after their approval by the State Board of Engineers and the Mississippi River Commission, to consent to the removal, at the expense of the Orleans Levee District, of the Levee systems of these two districts in that portion of the levee systems thereof as may be determined by the Orleans Levee District shall be removed.

Section 6. That the Board of Levee Commissioners of the Orleans

Levee District he and it is hereby authorized, for the purpose of raising the funds required under the provisions of this act, to levy annually for such length of time as it may determine, such taxes, within the constitutional limitation, as may be required; and these taxes, and other revenues may be by it funded into bonds or other evidences of indebtedness, bearing not more than six (67) per cent per annum interest, the proceeds thereof created by a sale at not less than par and accrued interest, to be used for the purpose of the acquisition of the property and the construction of the works herein authorized.

Section 7. That all laws or parts of laws in conflict herewith, be and they are hereby repealed. In case any section or sections or part of any section or sections of this act shall be found to be unconstitutional, the remainder of this shall not thereby be invalidated, but shall remain in full force and effect. As this act is designed to meet an emergency, it shall be broadly construed.

Approved by the Governor: July 14, 1924.

ACT NO. 311

Senate Bill No. 66   By: Messrs. Ott, Arras and Lanier

AN ACT

To confirm and quiet the Board of Levee Commissioners of the Orleans Levee District in the ownership and control of all public lands in the Bohemia Spillway when it was constructed by said Levee Board in obedience to Act 99 of the Legislature of 1924.

WHEREAS, there has been exhibited to the Legislature due proof of the publication of notice of intention to apply 1015 Act 311 Act 311 [sic] for the passage of this act in conformity with Section 6 of Article 4 of the Constitution of this State, and

WHEREAS, by Act 99 of 1924, the Board of Levee Commissioners of the Orleans Levee District were authorized and required to locate and construct a spillway in the Parish of Plaquemines, east bank, in the then Grand Prairie and East Bank Levee Districts, and

WHEREAS, with the consent and approval of the Board of State Engineers and the United States authorities, the said Orleans Levee Board did locate said spillway in the Grand Prairie Levee District and in the East Bank (back) Levee District in the entire area from the lower line of the Bohemia Plantation to the upper line of the Cuselich Canal, Embracing all the area in those limits between the Mississippi River and the sea, and

WHEREAS, the Grand Prairie Levee Board at that time had a right of entry of all State or public lands in said area when said Act 99 of 1924 was proposed and passed as well as the right of taxing all lands in said area, both ad valorem and acreage, which latter right was shared in by the East Bank Levee District, and in order to protect the rights of the bondholders

351

and other creditors in said districts, the payment of which debts were dependent on said rights, and

WHEREAS, in order to make Act 99 of 1924 Constitutional, the said Orleans Levee Board, before divesting said two boards of existing rights in said area, was required by Section 5 of said Act to arrange with said two boards as to the payment of such share of their indebtedness as would have become rendered worthless by said divestiture, and

WHEREAS, the said Orleans Levee Board did in obedience to said act agree to pay and has paid to the Grand Prairie Levee Board and to the East Bank Levee Board the entirety of their outstanding indebtedness amounting in all to One Hundred and Eighty-three Thousand Dollars, and was thereby entitled to and invested with all the rights, title and interest of each of said boards in the entire area of said spillway where the property was dedicated for said uses, and

WHEREAS, said former rights of both of said two former levee boards accrued to and became the rights and property of said Orleans Levee Board, save that same were thereafter non-taxable and could not be alienated or sold, as same were intended for and dedicated to the purposes of said spillway and have been so used for the past sixteen years by the Orleans Levee Board, and

WHEREAS, under Act 160 of 1926, the legislature of this state did declare in the preamble of said act, that the Orleans Levee Board did construct said spillway, which has been in existence for 16 years, and

WHEREAS, it being impossible to maintain levees, either front or rear, in a spillway, and in accordance with the fact that with the construction of said spillway both of said former levee boards have been removed and ousted from said spillway, the legislature, by Act 246 of 1928, recreated and reorganized said former Grand Prairie Levee District in the section below said spillway, from Cuselich Canal, above, to Cubitt's Gap, 15 miles below its former lower boundary. Therefore

Section 1. Be it enacted by the Legislature of Louisiana, That the right, title, ownership and possession of the Orleans Levee Board of Levee Commissioners of the Orleans Levee Dis- District trict [sic] to all public lands in the area of the Bohemia Spillway between Bohemia Plantation, above, and Cuselich Canal, below, and from the river to the sea subject to whatever valid leasehold rights as may have been granted by the Grand

Prairie Levee District on lands previously granted and conveyed to it, prior to the passage of this Act, be now confirmed, quieted and acknowledged, it being recognized that said rights, ownership and possession came into existence when said Orleans Levee Board located and constructed said Bohemia Spillway in the year 1925.

Section 2. That all laws and parts of laws in conflict with this act be and the same are hereby repealed.

Note-The foregoing Act having been submitted to his Excellency, Honorable Sam H. Jones, Governor of the State of Louisiana, for his approval or disapproval, and the same not having been acted upon within the time limit prescribed by the Constitution of this State, the same has become a law by limitation.

(Signed) JAS. A. GREMILLION,
Secretary of State.
July 15, 1942.

ACT NO. 233

House Bill No. 1196 By: Messrs. Patti, Benoit, Borne, Damico, D'Gerolamo, Diez, Doucet, Downer, Fernandez, Guidry, D. Hebert, M. Hebert, Jenkins, LeBleu and Ullo and Senators Landry and Nunez.

AN ACT

To declare that the public and necessary purpose which may have originally supported the expropriation of certain property in the parish of Plaquemines for the construction of a spillway, known as the Bohemia Spillway, has ceased to exist, to order the return of certain property, including mineral rights, acquired therefor by expropriation or purchased under threat of expropriation, under certain terms, conditions, and procedures, and subject to certain rights, and otherwise to provide with respect thereto.

Notice of intention to introduce this Act has been published as provided by Article III, Section 13 of the Constitution of Louisiana.

Be it enacted by the Legislature of Louisiana:

Section 1. Pursuant to authority of Louisiana Constitution Article VII, Section 14(B), the Legislature of Louisiana hereby declares that the public and necessary purpose set forth in Act No. 99 of 1924, which may have originally supported the expropriation of property, or any right of ownership thereto, on the east bank of the Mississippi River in the parish of Plaquemines for the construction of a spillway, known Act 233 as the Bohemia Spillway, has ceased to exist insofar as it ever may have affected the ownership of property, including mineral rights. The Legislature of Louisiana hereby orders the Board of Levee Commissioners of the Orleans

Levee District, the board, to return the ownership of said property to the owners or their successors from whom the property was acquired by expropriation or by purchase under threat of expropriation. Neither the provisions of this Act nor any actions pursuant to this Act shall affect the title to land which was the subject of litigation on the effective date of this Act.

Section 2. The secretary of the Department of Natural Resources shall have rule making and procedure making authority consistent with the Administrative Procedure Act, R. S. 49:950, et seq., for the purpose of establishing procedures and guidelines for the receipt and evaluation of applications, notification of applicants, review of denials by hearings, relaxation of technical rules of evidence, settlement and distribution of funds for successful applications, and any other rules and procedures reasonably necessary for the orderly implementation of the return ordered herein. The secretary shall proceed immediately upon the effective date of this Act with steps necessary for the development and adoption of rules and procedures to begin the implementation of the provisions of this Act by January 1, 1985.

Section 3. The Board of Levee Commissioners of the Orleans Levee District shall provide a thorough accounting to the secretary of the Department of Natural Resources, or his designee, concerning all revenues received from the affected property. The information so provided shall be made available to applicants. The board shall comply with the spirit and letter of the rules and regulations adopted and promulgated by the secretary of the Department of Natural Resources.

Section 4. The secretary of the Department of Natural Resources shall begin steps by January 1, 1985, to notify affected persons.

Section 5. The return of property by the board to the owners or their successors shall be subject to all servitudes and rights-of-way, whether acquired by expropriation or otherwise, or surface or mineral leases, or other valid contracts executed by or with the board prior to the effective date of this Act. Any deed whereby any property is returned shall state that such property is subject to such rights. Any party to a contract in effect on the effective date of this Act with the board concerning property affected by this Act shall be entitled to make payments and give all notices required or permitted under such contract to the secretary until the title to the property affected has been transferred. When such contracts provide for renegotiation of rent between any person and the board, or provide that any person may seek approval by the board, such person shall be entitled to Act 233 renegotiate such rent or to seek and obtain such approval from the secretary until the title to the property affected has been transferred. Any sum deposited with the secretary pursuant to this Act which represents rent, royalty or other sum attributable to land being returned, shall be paid by the secretary to the appropriate persons.

Section 6. This Act shall become effective upon signature by the governor or, if not signed by the governor, upon expiration of the time for bills to become law without signature by the governor, as provided in Article III, Section 18 of the Constitution of Louisiana.

Approved by the Governor: June 29, 1984.
Published in the Official Journal of the State: July 31, 1984.

ACKNOWLEDGEMENTS

So many people helped us with the research for this book. We would not have been able to recreate what life was like in Bohemia before 1924 without their knowledge, memories, and documentation. We would like to acknowledge a few of them:

Roderick Lincoln, historian of Plaquemines Parish, shared his time and infinite knowledge about the area with us. He gave us many interesting facts about the culture, landmarks, and people of the area, generously helped us collect photographs, and helped us to ensure that this work was historically accurate.

David Haspel, former president of Haspel & Davis, whose family experienced the events in this book firsthand and who shared invaluable maps and documentation with us.

Wilma Heaton, a former member of the Orleans Levee District, who shared with us her knowledge of its inner workings and provided us with documentation, which allowed us to tell this story more accurately.

Dave Cvitanovich, whose knowledge of lower Plaquemines Parish and the people who once lived there helped us recreate a way of life.

Tammy Fucich, whose family lived in Nestor and who spent many years researching what happened there.

Reverend Theodore Turner, who grew up in Homeplace and offered valuable insights about the people from Plaquemines Parish.

Byron Enclade, an oysterman who grew up in Pointe á la Hache and shared his knowledge of fishing oysters and shrimp and the relationships between African Americans and Caucasians at that time.

Donald and Merle Ansardi, who grew up on the East Bank of Plaquemines Parish and recalled for us their stories of fishermen, trappers, food, and culture.

Paul and Doris LeBeouf, who shared with us their knowledge of boatbuilding and oyster luggers, and their family memories of the area around Ostrica.

Mary Pennison, who grew up in Point Pleasant and remembered fascinating details of what life was like before her family moved to the West Bank.

Hester Henry, who shared her stories about her life in Pointe á la Hache, just a few miles from where Bohemia Plantation once stood.

Rosina Phillips, whose Native American family lived in the Grand Bayou area where they hunted and trapped and fished.

Maurice and Karen Phillips, whose memories about the wildlife and crops were a tremendous help.

Cathy Vogel and Sue Israel for the countless hours they spent editing this work of historical fiction.

The employees at the Louisiana State Archives, the LSU Libraries Special Collections, and Plaquemines Parish Clerk of Court Kim Turlich-Vaughn and her staff, who helped us find court cases, newspaper articles, and old letters.

Lastly, and most importantly, Charles would like to thank his beautiful wife Claire for her patience and support throughout the research and writing of this book. He would also like to acknowledge his sons and daughters-in-law Charles II and Lisa, Brian and Amanda, and Ben and Kelly for their support in the retelling of this important story. Charles would like to thank his parents Herman and Ivalou (now deceased), his sisters Carol and Virginia, and his brother Herman Jr. for walking the levee in Homeplace with him numerous times, looking across the Mississippi River at what was the Bohemia Spillway and imagining with him what it would be like if the towns and the people still existed across the river.

Your assistance is greatly appreciated.

BIBLIOGRAPHY AND RESOURCES

Books and Studies

Barry, John M. "Rising Tide: The Great Mississippi Flood of 1927 and How it Changed America." Simon and Schuster. April 2, 1998.

Buras, Janice P. *Way Down Yonder, Beginnings on the Mississippi Delta*. Down the Road Publishing, Inc., 1993.

Davis, Dave B., and John D. Hartley, and Ruth Wiens Henderson. "An Archaeological and Historic Survey of the Lowermost Mississippi River." 1979.

Jeansonne, Glen. *Leander Perez, Boss of the Delta*. University Press of Mississippi. 2006.

Lopez, John, Ph.D., and Theryn Henkel Ph.D., Ezra Boyd Ph.D., Paul Conner B.S., Megan Milliken B.S., Andrew Baker M.S., Kristian Gustavson M.S. and Luis Martinez M.S. "Bohemia Spillway in Southeastern Louisiana: History, General Description, and 2011 Hydrologic Surveys." Lake Pontchartrain Basin Foundation, 2013.

Meffert, Donald J. and Good, Bill. "Case Study of the Ecosystem Management Development in the Breton Sound Estuary, Louisiana." Louisiana Department of Natural Resources, Coastal Restoration Division.

O'Donnell, E.P. *The Great Big Doorstep*. Houghton Mifflin Southern, 1941.

Stuart, David R. and Jerome A. Greene. "Archeological Survey of the Proposed Bayou Lamoque Revetment." 1983.

Twain, Mark. *Life on the Mississippi*. James R. Osgood & Co. 1883.

Newspapers and Periodicals

Down the Road
"Ostrica, A *Down the Road* Community." October 1991.

The Advocate (New Orleans, La.)
"300 unique New Orleans moments: Leander Perez is appointed judge in 1919." September 28, 2017.

The Daily Beast
"How A Segregationist's Vicious Racism Backfired and Saved Jury Trials." August 9, 2020.

The Daily Review (Morgan City, La.)
"Wants Territory All to be Taken." June 20, 1927
"Nature takes crack at rebuilding La. marsh." July 10, 2012.

The Louisiana Weekly
"Heirs Question Levee Board Efforts—History of the Bohemia Spillway." May 21, 2001.

The Lower Coast Gazette (Plaquemines Parish, La.)
"Another Important Land Transaction." February 6, 1909.
"Railroad right of way to Bohemia." August 27, 1910.
"Spillway Consent Given." November 7, 1925.
"Daisy Crevasse Scare." April 17, 1909.

The New York Herald Tribune
"Friends and Foes Alike Mourn Passing of a 'Colorful Fighter.'" September 11, 1935.

The New York Times
"Hundreds in Louisiana Regaining Family Land." October 24, 1986.
"Leander Perez Jr. is dead at 68." October 6, 1988.

The Orleans Morning Tribune
"Aunt Louisa, Former Slave, Dies here at age of 110." May 6, 1930.

The Plaquemine Gazette. (Plaquemines Parish, La.)
"Council Appropriates Borrow Land Area for Rebuilding, Elevating Plaquemines Levees." October 22, 1965.

"Bohemia Spillway Available for 33,000 Acre Wildlife Project." January 17, 1969.

"End of Bohemia Spillway Class Action Lawsuit Draws Near." August 2, 2002.

"The Bohemia Plantation, History, Charm Reflected in Old Home." Roxanna S. Giordano, Publicity and Landmarks Chairman.

The Plaquemines Protector (Point á la Hache, La.)

"Bohemia and a Sore Felt Need of More Protection." May 25, 1901.

"Charter of the Olga Oyster Shipping Company, Inc." November 14, 1925.

The St. Bernard Voice (Arabi, La.)

"Klorer's Theory Sadly Exploded, L.H. Perez and A.S. Nunez Clearly Show." February 22, 1930.

The Times (Shreveport, La.)

"Legislation will establish dangerous precedent." June 24, 1984.

The Times-Picayune/Nola.com (New Orleans, La.)

"Estate Sale, Riceland Plantation." February 12, 1871.

"Auction Sales, Bohemia Plantation." February 24, 1876.

"The Telephone, Its Use Tendered Free For Levee Purposes—The Lottery's Gift to Plaquemines." March 3, 1890.

"Bohemia Crevasse Bad for the Oyster Industry." March 19, 1903.

"The Storm in Plaquemine, The Worst Wind Experienced in Many Years." September 30, 1906.

"Bohemia Orange Farm, Valuable Tract of Land at Public Auction." July 14, 1912.

"Bohemia Plantation Sold." July 28, 1912.

"Plaquemines Court Convenes." February 4. 1916.

"Wires down—City cut off from outside. The city emerges from worst hurricane experience, barometer lowest on record, wind velocity greatest ever reported." September 30, 1915.

"Transfer of U.S. Holdings Fought by Levee Boards." January 13, 1929.

"As the Council Moves to Back the Legislation." June 16, 1982.

"House OKs returning Bohemia Spillway land." May 31, 1984.

"House: Return Spillway Land, Orleans Levee Board would have to hand over royalties." June 19, 1984.

"Notice of Return of Bohemia Spillway Lands, Plaquemines Parish." February 9, 1987.

"Debunking the Bohemia Spillway myth." May 1, 2001.

"Preserving History in Wake of Katrina." January 19, 2006.

"Lakefront authority to get oil money from Bohemia Spillway." November 17, 2023.

The Town Talk (Alexandria, La.)
"Board: Bohemia Spillway Works." May 25, 1983.

Documents and Reports

"Act 1364 of 1997 Status Report" by the Board of Levee Commissioners of the Orleans Levee District to the House and Senate Committees of Natural Resources. March 1, 2005.

Board of Commissioners of the Orleans Levee District report to the Louisiana Department of Natural Resources certifying landowners. 1992.

Board of Commissioners of the Orleans Levee District. "Mississippi River Levee." October 17, 2005.

Bohemia Spillway Expenditures. June 22, 1982.

Bohemia Spillway from the 1840s to the present.

Department of Natural Resources, Office of the Special Master "List of Bohemia Spillway Tracts." 1992.

Document from Board of Commissioners about how much was spent for land in spillway area.

Grand Prairie Levee District board petition. 1908.

Huling Settlement Levee Leak document. 1893.

Humble Oil Lease with Orleans Levee District. November 21, 1926.

Lands of the Plaquemines Parish Commission Council East of the Mississippi River: Legislative history of the Grand Prairie Levee District and the Lake Borgne Levee District.

Lincoln, Roderick. Emails about Bohemia Plantation and the origins of the Huff family. January 2020.

---. "From Sixty Mile Point (Nairn) to Point Pleasant, A Tour."

---. "Ostrica Quarantine Station, Ostrica Lock."

Memorandum from Jack Pierce Brook to Alicia Reggie re: "Bohemia Spillway Area." May 27, 1987.

Minutes from the meetings of the Board of Commissioners of the Orleans Levee District. 1924-1929.

Ory G. Poret, Inc. "Bohemia Spillway—Plaquemines Parish, Summary of Evaluation of Applications." March 11, 1988.

Petition from Samuel M. Fucich to the Grand Prairie Levee District. Filed 1908.

Pointe á la Hache Relief Outlet. Engineering Report to Accompany Request of Orleans Levee Board to the Mississippi River Commission from the minutes of the Board of Commissioners of the Orleans Levee District.

Report from the Real Estate Committee to the Executive Committee of the Board of Levee Commissioners of the Orleans Levee District. Proposed Plaquemines Outlet. April 20, 1925.

Resolution passed by the Board of Levee Commissioners of the Orleans Levee District at its meeting held on August 9, 1924.

Resolution No. 03-19-15-12, Closing of Escrow Account for Bohemia Spillway Claims. Southeast Louisiana Flood Protection Authority-East. March 19, 2015.

Seemann, G. Frederick. "Final Report, Office of the Special Master, Bohemia Spillway Project." 1992.

Subleasing of land in Bohemia Spillway document. 1925.

Swamp Land Patent transferred to the State of Louisiana by Franklin D. Roosevelt. 1935.

Timeline—A timeline of activities, legislation and environmental events that affected the Orleans Levee District. "Historical Perspective of Bohemia Spillway." 1924-2000.

Letters

1925: Letter to the Board of Commissioners for the Orleans Levee District from the committee appointed for the purpose of appraising lands on the East Bank of the Mississippi River in Plaquemines Parish.

April 7, 1926: Letter from Benjamin Waldo, general counsel for the Board of Commissioners, to Thomas Furlow.

April 8, 1926: Letter from Benjamin Waldo, general counsel for the Board of Commissioners to Peter Muntz.

April 10, 1926: Letter from Benjamin Waldo, general counsel for the Board of Commissioners, to Charles McCabe.

November 1929: Letter from General Counsel James Wilkinson and Assistant General Counsel George Piazza read into the minutes of the Board of Levee Commissioners.

December 15, 1988: Letter from Jeanette and Roy Tabony to Mr. Ponet.

Summaries

Dier, Chris. "When the Levee Blew Up: A Public Execution of a Community." February 16, 2014.

Furness, Amanda. "Heirs question levee board's efforts—History of the Bohemia Spillway." May 2001

"Historical Perspective Bohemia Spillway, 1924-2000." Permanent historical document. Louisiana House Research Library.

"Historical Summary of the Creation—The Bohemia Spillway." May 1983.

Jeansonne, Glen. "Leander Perez." November 4, 2013.

Lane, George. "Katrina Coverage, analyzing the news reports and politics of the New Orleans hurricane—Comment with historical background." December 2005.

Lincoln, Roderick. "Chronological History of Plaquemines Parish." 2021.

Lopez, J.A., McCartney P., Kulp M., and Kemp P. "The Bohemia Spillway in Southeast Louisiana: What little we know and what we should Know." Lake Pontchartrain Basin Foundation, Pontchartrain Institute for Environmental Sciences, and National Audubon Society. 2008.

Accounts of Life in South Louisiana

Buras, Janice P. "At Work in Heaven, Reclaiming Bohemia Spillway Properties was the last wish of Mona Fox Menge." November 1990.

Core, Dublin. "People Bought and Sold at Bohemia Plantation." 1794-1795.

Davis, Ronald L.F., "Racial Etiquette: The Racial Customs and Rules of Racial Behavior in Jim Crow America."

Fucich, Tammy. "Nestor of Bohemia Spillway."

Lincoln, Roderick. "Interview with Lawrence Tabony." June 12, 1986.

Simms, Mary Dannon. "The Life of a Little Confederate Girl." 1863-1943.

Lawsuits

"Bohemia 2009 Table of Authorities Grand Prairie Levee Board Lawsuit." 2009.

Board of Commissioners of Orleans Levee District v. Gomez. 1993.

Emery, et al v. Orleans Levee Board. 1945.

Haspel & Davis Milling & Planting Co. LTD, et al. v. Board of Levee Commissioners of the Orleans Levee District, Court of Appeals of Louisiana Fourth Circuit. 1999.

Haspel Davis Milling Planting Company LTD LLC III v. State of Louisiana, Movant-Appellant. United States Court of Appeals. Fifth Circuit. July 23, 2007.

Plaquemines Parish Government v. Department of Natural Resources, State of Louisiana. 2008.

Richardson & Bass v. Board of Levee Commissioners of the Orleans Levee District. 1955.

Succession of Carter Ursin and Charles Ursin and the Heirs of Joseph C. Eusan through Warren H. Eusan, Michelle Eusan, Ahmed Collins v. Board of Levee Commissioners of the Orleans Levee District of the State of Louisiana. 2012.

Webb Worthington Trust, Madison Land Company, MDT Partnership, Clifford Webb, LLC, Henry Haller, Jr., Margaret Haller Crosby, and Patricia Haller Bunn v. Board of Levee Commissioners of the Orleans Levee District, Board of Commissioners of the Southeast Louisiana Flood Protection Authority—East, and the State of Louisiana through the Division of Administration. February 25, 2008.

Louisiana Legislative Acts

Act 93 of 1890

Act 99 of 1924

Act 246 of 1928

Act 292 of 1928

Act 311 of 1942

Act 233 of 1984

Act 819 of 1985

Act 1364 of 1997

Federal Acts

1928 Federal Flood Control Act

Interviews

Byron Encalade

Dave Cvitanovich

David Haspel

Donald and Merle Ansardi

Hester Henry

Maurice and Karen Phillips

Mary Pennison

Paul and Doris LeBeouf

Roderick Lincoln

Rev. Theodore Turner

Rosina Phillips

Tammy Fucich

Wilma Heaton

Maps

Bohemia. Orleans Levee District. 1925.

Bohemia Spillway map

Gulf of Mexico map

Happy Jack and Dime. 1891.

Map showing ownership and appraisal value of land and Improvements. Lower line of Bohemia Plantation to Nestor Canal. Proposed Plaquemines Outlet to accompany report of the Real Estate Committee to Executive Committee, Board of Levee Commissioners, Orleans Levee District. April 1925.

Plaquemines Parish/ Pointe-á-la-Hache map

Potash Salt Dome map

Resurvey Map. 1935.

Series of maps of Bohemia (1-9)

Socola Canal across from Bohemia map

Spillway map of landowners

ABOUT THE AUTHORS

Susan D. Mustafa is a *New York Times* and *San Francisco Chronicle* bestselling author, as well as an award-winning investigative journalist. Her books have been translated and published in nine languages. She has been prominently featured in several docuseries and numerous television programs that have aired on FX, A&E, Hulu, Discovery, Investigation Discovery, Discovery Canada, Lifetime, Oxygen, and National Geographic. Susan was born in New Orleans and resides in Baton Rouge.

Charles J. Ballay is the district attorney and a native of Plaquemines Parish. He was born in Port Sulphur, Louisiana, and grew up in the adjacent area of Homeplace. He earned a law degree from LSU Law School in 1976 and began practicing law in Belle Chasse that same year. In 1980, he began working as an assistant district attorney, and, in 2008, he was elected as the district attorney of Plaquemines Parish, a position that he continues to hold today. Charles is married to Claire Bonneval, and they are the parents of three sons and grandparents of eleven grandchildren. Charles and Claire reside in Belle Chasse.

Printed in the United States
by Baker & Taylor Publisher Services